THE POISON MACHINE

Also by Robert J. Lloyd
The Bloodless Boy

THE

POISON
MACHINE

ROBERT J. LLOYD

MELVILLE HOUSE PRESS

NEW YORK & LONDON

The Poison Machine by Robert J. Lloyd

First Melville House Printing: August 2022

Melville House Publishing
46 John Street
Brooklyn, NY 11201
and
Melville House UK
Suite 2000
16/18 Woodford Road
London E7 0HA

mhpbooks.com
@melvillehouse

ISBN: 978-1-61219-975-7

ISBN: 978-1-61219-976-4 (eBook)

Library of Congress Control Number: 2022938594

Designed by Richard Oriolo

Printed in the United States of America
1 3 5 7 9 10 8 6 4 2

A catalog record for this book is available from the Library of Congress

The endpapers for this volume are engravings depicting the
Bibliothèque Mazarine and the Bastille, ca. 1650.

TO KATE, WITH LOVE.

CHARACTERS

MR. HARRY HUNT, Observator of the Royal Society of London for the Improving of Natural Knowledge, Investigator for the Board of Ordnance.

MR. ROBERT HOOKE, Curator of Experiments of the Royal Society of London for the Improving of Natural Knowledge, Gresham Professor of Geometry, Architect, and Surveyor for the City of London.

MISS GRACE HOOKE, Robert Hooke's Niece.

MRS. MARY ROBINSON, Robert Hooke's Housekeeper.

COLONEL MICHAEL FIELDS, Anabaptist Preacher, Old Soldier for Parliament.

MRS. ELIZABETH HANNAM, Harry Hunt's Landlady.

SIR JONAS MOORE, Surveyor-General of the Board of Ordnance.

MR. ISAAC NEWTON, Lucasian Professor of Mathematics at Trinity College, Cambridge.

HORTENSE MANCINI, Duchesse de Mazarin, the Most Beautiful Lady in the Kingdom.

MR. MUSTAPHA, Hortense's Manservant.

THOMAS OSBOURNE, The Earl of Danby, Lord High Treasurer.

MR. RICHARD MERRITT, Danby's Man.

M. MICHEL CHASSE, also known as LEFÈVRE, an Assassin.

M. JOSEPH BOILOT, another Assassin.

M. CHARLES VERDIER, a third Assassin.

MRS. PRISCILLA LEACH, a Housekeeper.

MR. JAPHIA BENNETT, an Elderly Sailor.

MARIE-ANNE MANCINI, Duchesse de Bouillon, Hortense's Sister.

M. ETIENNE MERCIER, Marie-Anne's Butler.

M. GABRIEL NICOLAS DE LA REYNIE, Lieutenant Général of the Paris Police.

MR. BARTHOLOMEW SLOUGH, a Capable Man.

CAPITAINE EUGÈNE DE BEAUCHENE, a Sea Captain.

M. JACOB BESNIER, a Flying Man.

M. FRANÇOIS DE LA POTERIE, a Bibliothécaire.

M. HENRI SARAZEN, a Bibliothécaire's Assistant.

MESSRS. THERIOT, GAUTHIER, and DRAGAUD, French Anti-Monarchists.

SR. PERAS, a Spanish Trawler Captain.

QUEEN CATARINA DE BRAGANÇA, Queen Consort of England, Scotland, and Ireland. (More usually, QUEEN CATHERINE.)

CAPTAIN MACWILLIAM, of the King's Foot.

COLONEL SACKVILLE, of the King's Foot.

A SERGEANT, of the King's Foot.

TWO SHIVERING WOMEN, Prostitutes along the Strand.

VARIOUS FELLOWS of the Royal Society, including SIR CHRISTOPHER WREN.

VARIOUS FRENCH INTELLECTUALS, Members of Marie-Anne's Salon.

VARIOUS PRISON GUARDS, of the Grand Châtelet and the Bastille.

VARIOUS SERVANTS AND COOKS, at Somerset House.

VARIOUS CATHOLIC PRISONERS, for Execution.

THE POISON MACHINE

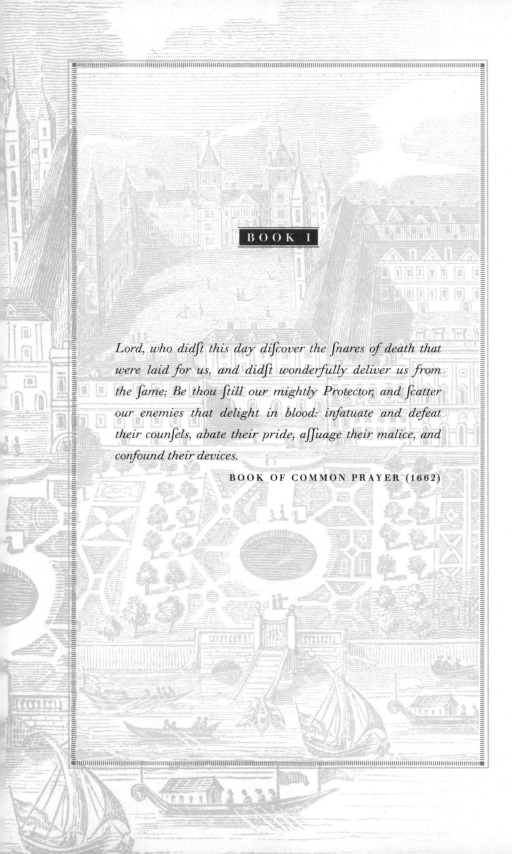

BOOK I

Lord, who didſt this day diſcover the ſnares of death that were laid for us, and didſt wonderfully deliver us from the ſame; Be thou ſtill our mightly Protector, and ſcatter our enemies that delight in blood: infatuate and defeat their counſels, abate their pride, aſſuage their malice, and confound their devices.

BOOK OF COMMON PRAYER (1662)

CHAPTER ONE

THE THREE

ASSASSINS

A SKIFF SLIPPED PAST TWO BRIGANTINES moored close in by the quay. Three men inside it all wore black coats, with collars pulled up to their chins, as much to keep themselves concealed as to keep out the rain.

Cloud shrouded the moon. The night's pressing darkness suited them.

One of the men, as far forwards as he could sit, murmured directions. The man he guided, far larger, pulled sculls with strong hands, his strokes not raising a splash. The third man sat behind.

A rope dragged a second skiff, a twin of the first, behind them. Looking dangerously low, it was weighted down by bundles. Sharp protrusions pushed into the canvas covering them, and coiled tubing escaped from under it. Despite the rower's size and obvious strength, he struggled to make headway against the river's flow.

The wind made the waves dance. The boats swooped and rolled over the water.

The man calling the way was bareheaded, his hair tied back, exposing a high forehead liberally smeared with soot. The man rowing wore a tight seaman's cap and tough-looking gloves.

The third man had a black hat with a wide circular rim, hiding him from view.

Without a lantern, the navigator had to judge all the different blacknesses, one against another. Beyond the brooding shape of the Tower, darkest of all, lurked the mass of the City, stretching away and up from the Thames. Only a few lights on land indicated life: lamps or candles, or a wandering watchman carrying his searchlight. The water dully mirrored these points of brightness.

The hulls of the brigantines curved high over them. No one stirred on their decks. No noise signalled the pacing of a watch. These were East India Company ships, sailed from the Barbadoes. Water slapping lazily against them, they conversed together in creaks and rattles, urging departure as if they yearned for the ocean.

Sneaking by them, each man stopped breathing, anxious not to betray their presence. Coffee roasting inside the nearest ship made their noses twitch.

They relied upon the cold and the rain to stop any anchor watch patrolling the decks. Keep him near a stove's comforting glow.

Next, past the *Erebus*, a Navy second-rate, newly fitted, its planking gleaming smartly. Only a single stern light far above them illuminated its anchorage; the navigator stayed well clear, keeping to the darkness beyond its reach. The smell of tarred surfaces, hemp cloth, oil, and flax wafted over the water. The ship awaited its full complement of men, and those soon to join it—yet aware of the fact or not—were mostly ashore, spread-eagled boozily along Wapping High Street.

To the west, from under London Bridge the clacking throb of the Morice waterwheels, as they pumped water through the City's conduits, grew louder. To the east, the men could see the great Navy sheds of Storehouse

Yard and King Henry's Yard, filled with provisions for sea journeys months long. They passed more water gates, piers, and river stairs, slicked with sewage scumbled against them.

The skiffs moved on, slowly, quietly, their trails scratching white on the water. The Tower's silhouette expanded ominously as they reached almost to its foot.

The navigator turned and pointed to a wharf running along the new quayside wall. Its rickety supports rose drunkenly from the river. The man at the oars slowed his strokes, steering them towards it.

'Hoy!' A voice called out from the quayside above them.

The three men kept perfectly still, their faces turned downwards to the belly of their boat.

The darkness had not served them well enough.

A face peered from over the quayside wall. 'Be you honest men?' The man waved a lantern, its metal frame clanking at the end of a staff.

'*Aussi vite que tu le peux!*' the navigator urged the rower. '*Vas pour cette jetée!*'

The rower no longer cared about any noise he made. His powerful strokes sped them towards a flimsy jetty protruding from the wharf. They would have to run to St. Katherine's Stairs. Gripping onto the rail as the boat rocked wildly, the navigator, Boilot, shouted to the man under the hat. '*Qu'allons-nous faire?*' What shall we do?

'*Nous devons le tuer. Il nous a vu,*' he replied. We must kill him. He saw us.

Behind him, the rower, Verdier, strained at his sculls, hefting them through the water, but Boilot knew anyone running along the quayside could easily keep up with them. The voice had sounded elderly, perhaps belonging to one of London's watchmen employed to keep them from the almshouse.

They covered the distance to the small sufferance wharf, its jetty barely higher than the level of the water. Crashing against its timbers, their skiff skewed sideways. Boilot jumped to the jetty and slipped on the rain-sodden wood. He fell on his back, his feet in the river, the impact winding him. Verdier dropped his sculls to follow, scrabbling his way next to him, and quickly tied their boats. The third man reached for the higher platform of the wharf and climbed up in one swift, easy movement. Boilot rose from his fall, sliding again.

Boilot and Verdier crashed along the length of the jetty and turned onto the wharf, where their companion waited impatiently. They all reached the foot of St. Katherine's Stairs, pitching steeply up to the quay, to where the watchman had called to them.

The man in the hat waved Boilot to go ahead. Breathing hard, Boilot reached the last stair, and found himself on the quayside.

He saw no one. He jogged between two sheds, where the shadows were deepest, keeping his footsteps light. The smell of fat from meat brought in by a Greenland whaler—the boiling performed that day on the quayside—nearly overpowered him.

As his colleagues reached him, Boilot motioned them to silence, pressing his lips together with his fingers. He listened into the blackness surrounding them, his concentration probing it for the sound of a boot or the rattle of a weapon.

All he could hear were the Morice waterwheels and the rain hitting the ground, until a new sound joined their noise. It became the din of cobbles pounded by horseshoes, with the rumble of wheels behind.

Torn between running from the noise of the carriage or looking for the watchman, Boilot chose to stay perfectly still. Ahead of them, at the end of the short lane, the horses slowed, their driver uncertain, and came to a stop. The coach's wood, leather, and iron all made their individual groans and grumbles at halt.

The three men pressed back against the side of the shed.

Holding a lantern, the coach driver jumped down from his seat. He was tall and thin, and wore a purple cloak.

At the moment they had readied themselves to fly at him from the shadows, the man with the hat recognized him. '*C'est Monsieur Merritt! L'homme de Seigneur Danby.*'

He moved into the light and removed his hat, revealing a strange face tapering from a large forehead with a single eyebrow across it to a small mouth and sharp chin.

Richard Merritt held out his hand, to be surprised by the lack of pressure from the Frenchman's grasp.

The watchman called again. 'Hoy!' They could hear his boots approaching.

Boilot moved along the quay, treading softly, stifling a curse as he tripped on a loose cobble. He took a knife from a sheath on his hip and gripped it close to his side.

He reached an upturned wherry raised on blocks for repair. The light from the watchman's lantern skittered across its wet planks, reaching around its curve.

It lit up Boilot's face.

At the sight of a man appearing as if magicked from the darkness, the watchman cried out. Boilot sprang forwards, grabbing at him, but missed, catching hold of his staff instead. He pulled at it, hard.

The watchman fell heavily, landing on his side. 'For the love of Jesus, spare me,' he pleaded. 'And for the love of your fellow man.' He drew his legs into his body, protecting his head with his hands. Not daring to look up at Boilot, instead he pressed his face into the rough, wet cobbles.

He was aged and frail. Just his misfortune to be here, doing his duty at St. Katherine's stairs, at the moment the three Frenchmen arrived in London.

Boilot reached out and stroked the watchman's hair. With his other hand, he slid the knife's point through the man's coat, seeking soft flesh between ribs, angling the blade to pass between the bones.

The knife went in, and searched about, cutting into lung.

Recognising he was not to live, the watchman lifted his eyes to Boilot's. He clasped his hands together. '. . . Maintain . . . defend . . . true reformed Protestant religion . . .' he croaked. He could taste blood in his mouth. He tried to rise, but could not. Boilot helped him, turning him to sit against the wherry so he could look over the river, at the lights of Southwark.

The watchman's eyes moistened. His breathing slowed, then stopped. His head lolled back and came to rest, his jaw sagging to one side.

Verdier arrived next to Boilot. Together, they studied the watchman, as if seeking some enlightenment on the nature of death. Finding only stillness, Verdier moved to pick up the body by the armpits, and Boilot took the feet. They carried him to the edge of the quayside. Verdier found a pair of loose cobbles, which they placed into the dead man's pockets.

Moving smoothly to them, the man with the single eyebrow and sharp chin signalled his assent. Boilot and Verdier heaved him into the water, then threw his staff and lamp in after.

As they watched the dead man disappearing into the Thames, and the last bubbles and ripples settle, the three Frenchmen each made their signs of the cross.

CHAPTER TWO

THE UNWELCOME LETTER

MR. ROBERT HOOKE, CURATOR OF EXPERIMENTS at the Royal Society of London for the Improving of Natural Knowledge, and its Secretary *pro tempore*, made his rapid way up Pig Street. A busy man, he was also Gresham College's Professor of Geometry , and Surveyor to the City of London. He worked as an architect, too: plaster dust from the works at Somerset House powdered his face. Queen Catherine wished them complete by the time of her Consult, and he worried there was not enough time.

With his silver eyes and grey hair, he was a pale and ethereal presence scuttling towards the College.

In his hand, a letter. He held it stiffly before him, as if it led him along.

After last night's rain, the afternoon sun raised a mist from the pavement and warmed his crooked back, but did nothing to improve his mood.

Hooke bristled. Although, he reflected, he had no right to bristle.

He sniffed, his tubes full of sticky goo. Then he tutted.

Why should he bristle? He had no jurisdiction over the letter's addressee, except as a mentor, and, hopefully, as a friend. As someone who took care to protect him from himself—although Hooke had often failed to do so, the young man's nature being headstrong.

Headstrong, but gaining a reputation as an able natural philosopher. Who desired to replace Hooke as Curator—Hooke now acting Secretary after Henry Oldenburg's unfortunate death, and too stretched to be both. It must be ratified by the Council, naturally, and Hooke could show no preference. The Royal Society needed the best man. One or two other possibles, yes: not as skilled, not so diligent, but without the unfortunate streak of obstinacy. Less likely to be . . . *troublesome.*

Hooke passed a shop with its windows smashed. The second he had seen that day. An indignant family stood outside, looking at the damage. Some of their goods, and even their furniture, lay broken on the road.

Catholics, he presumed. He nodded sympathy at them, but received only sullen looks in return.

Discomforted, he scurried on. Broad Street now, his thoughts soon returning to the letter. He had collected it at Garraway's coffeehouse on Exchange Alley, when there for his habitual hot chocolate and a glance at a Muddiman's news sheet. He considered again the curious fact it had been sent there. The wax seal—three cannons and a cannonball for each above them—and the writing, easily recognized, made plain it was from Sir Jonas Moore, Surveyor-General of the Board of Ordnance.

So, Hooke induced: Sir Jonas was out of London, with no way of finding the address he wanted. Didn't send the letter to Gresham College. Which likely meant he hoped Hooke would not see it. No doubt there was some calculation of the risk he *would* see it—which meant the letter was important enough to send anyway. Sending it to Garraway's was a clumsy attempt to bypass him, Hooke thought. Perhaps done from consideration for his feelings—its sender was not normally a careless man.

Sir Jonas was careless, though, Hooke was sure, of the consequences of this letter.

It was a threat: to peace, to continuity, to the well-being of the Royal Society. And to the young man about to open it. Its sending was like plucking at a taut wire, exciting its full length into vibration.

Hooke passed the church of St. Peter-le-Poer, then turned through the archway leading into Gresham, as he had done several thousand times before, to walk through the stable yard. Into the cool shade of the colonnaded walkway surrounding the quadrangle, towards his rooms at the southeast corner of the College.

He looked again, reproachfully, at the name on the letter.

SITTING ON THE window seat of her uncle's dining room, Grace Hooke overlooked the quadrangle. The noise of footsteps had distracted her from the globe she traced with a wistful finger along the journeys she could take. Her only travels were between her mother on the Isle of Wight and her uncle in London.

She turned to the man with her, who was busy at the dining table surrounded by the clutter of philosophical instruments, books, and curiosities.

Frowning at her movement, he lifted his spectacles, beginning to despair of his drawing. As she sat sideways to the window, the daylight spilled over her. It was the light, he told himself, he tried to reproduce. Put aside the teasing way it shone through her dress's fabric, revealing glimpses of her form.

'Uncle returns,' Grace said. 'Looking unhappy.'

They heard Hooke let himself in, then his characteristic climb of the stairs: the shuffle, the lopsidedness. He entered the dining room, combing plaster from his eyebrows with his fingertips.

Hooke stared at them both, hoping to see the immediate past, wanting to know what they had spoken of, or—a worse thought—done. He could not approve of how close Harry and Grace had become, even if their satisfaction with one another was clear. Seeing nothing amiss—although Grace was immodest in her choice of dress—he passed Harry the letter. Affecting a tranquil air, he went to adjust his new long-case night clock, its numerals made luminous by an oil lamp placed behind them, made to his design by Edward East.

Harry studied the seal, with its cannons and cannonballs, and the writing.

> *Mr. Henry Hunt,*
> *At Garraway's in Exchange Alley, by Cornhill, London*

'It's from Sir Jonas Moore,' Harry said.

'Our Vice President,' Hooke answered. 'But not Royal Society business.' He pretended to forget the matter of the letter, and, apparently pleased with the clock, went to hang up his coat.

Grace shot a look at Harry. A letter for him was unusual. A letter from Sir Jonas was momentous. And that it was sent to Garraway's, not to Harry's home at Half Moon Alley nor to Gresham, she thought, was curious.

Harry answered her look with a Punchinello gurn, peeled off the wax, and opened up the letter.

> *15th March 1678/79*
> *Sir.*
>
> *I am in the Fens of Norfolkshire, at the place named Denver, where a dead Man has been found bye the Sluice. I desire your Opinions. I saye no more of it, so your Minde maye remayne cleer of previous Notions.*
>
> *Your Skills and your Charackter suit you well for the Matter. I beseeche you to assist me. I wish you to work with me as an Investigator at the Board of Ordnance. As did I before. I am allowed by the Master-General to give three times the Paye you receive from the Royal Society.*
>
> *Doe not think upon it long. The Body will not keepe.*
> *Your Friend,*
> *Jonas Moore*

Badly concealing his impatience to know the contents of the letter, Hooke opened the manuscript copy of John Wallis's *Treatise of Logick*, which Wallis had asked him to review. The King's cryptographer had worked at it for years; at last, he thought it nearing readiness for publication.

Harry passed the letter for Hooke to read instead, observing the change on the older man's face as he did.

'I'm still against working for the Ordnance,' Harry assured him. 'I wish only to be Curator. Although, in truth, it's a generous offer.'

Hooke's voice was quiet. 'The Royal Society could never pay as much to an Observator.'

'Would it improve the pay of Curator?' Grace asked her uncle.

Hooke pressed the end of his nose. 'I will enquire it of Mr. Colwall, but we have so few subscriptions coming in.'

'The money's no matter, Mr. Hooke,' Harry said, causing Grace to raise her eyes to Heaven. 'I became embroiled with the Board of Ordnance before. I've no wish to become so again.'

He pointed to the clock. 'It's nearly time for the demonstration.'

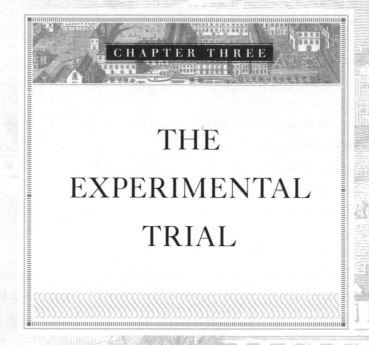

CHAPTER THREE

THE EXPERIMENTAL TRIAL

THE READING HALL, WHERE HOOKE'S DEMONSTRATIONS usually took place, was being repainted, so the Repository had been pressed into use. A long, narrow room, little more than twelve feet wide, it ran the length of Gresham's west gallery. Despite its windows being open, the air inside was torpid. Cloud covered the earlier bright sun; the grey light seemed oppressive. With all the Fellows pressed between the philosophical rarities on shelves along each wall and in chests of drawers and glass-fronted cabinets, there was little room to breathe.

Those who met as Hooke's New Philosophical Club had come to support Harry. All wanted him to replace Hooke as Curator of Experiments, for they knew his talents well. They felt frustrated that other Fellows, less experimental but with more political weight, could block them. After Secretary Oldenburg's death—the coroner's certificate declared from an ague—the politicking had been intense. The President, Viscount Brouncker, was soon ousted, Hooke leading the group wanting to attract more Fellows, and therefore subscriptions, to make the Society viable again. They blamed Oldenburg and Brouncker for its decline.

The Council was divided, the Fellows still split. Friendships had been strained, and even severed.

Hooke's group sat together. His close friend Sir Christopher Wren, mathematician and architect. Sir John Hoskyns, Master in Chancery, and baronet. Thomas Henshaw, alchemist and the King's Undersecretary of the French Tongue. Daniel Colwall, merchant and the Royal Society's Treasurer. Nehemiah Grew, physician and plant anatomist, whose days were currently spent cataloguing the Repository's collection. There was some talk of him becoming an Assistant Secretary to Hooke, when his role was made official. Edmund Wylde, Member of Parliament and Commissioner for the Navy. The always penurious antiquary, John Aubrey.

Also, Denis Papin, whose friendship with Harry had become difficult after Sir Joseph Williamson, the new President, announced he preferred Papin as next Curator. Papin had worked as Robert Boyle's assistant for some five years. The knowledge they were in competition made them both over-polite. Their conversation, once natural, had been reduced to pleasantries and observations on the weather.

Sir Christopher sat next to a boy pickled in vinegar, Aubrey by a case of exanguious fishes. There was a monstrous calf with two heads, a stuffed African parrot, and an alligator's bones needing sorting. Various growths removed from people and animals. Shells, insects, shrubs, and plants. Metals and ores, salts and sulphurs. Fossils: the petrified indications of animals long gone. Gems, including diamonds, rough as they were found.

The Repository also housed instruments. A condensing engine, a weather clock, a reflecting telescope contrived by Isaac Newton, the Lucasian Professor at Cambridge's Trinity College. A terrella, made in the manner of William Gilbert, to replicate the magnetism of the Earth. And Hooke's repaired air-pump, brought up from the Gresham cellars, where once it had stored the bloodless boy.

Sir Joseph nodded at them from by a human skull still covered with skin. His expression looked frantic and his peruke was askew. After he had publicly called Titus Oates's associate, Israel Tonge, a madman, the pair had taken their revenge. Sir Joseph's name duly appeared in the ever-growing Articles, their list of dangers posed by Catholic malfeasance.

All of London was in thrall to Oates and Tonge, as one after another a Jesuit plotter was revealed. Few dared speak against them, for fear of being accused themselves.

●

HIS HANDS FULL of a model bird's wing, its muscles made with springs, Hooke entered the Repository, keeping the door open with his foot. He expected Harry to be behind him, but Grace had held him back. Harry bent to kiss her, but at the last moment she turned away. Laughing, her fingers slid from his arm as she let him go inside to the men.

Harry bowed respectfully to the Fellows, then stepped up on the dais. He carried a stand and a box. He had thought exhaustingly about which experiment to show: It must be new, it must entertain, but also have enough profundity to raise speculation. It could not just be sound and lights; a spectacular. It needed to *intrigue*.

He brought out a jar from his box. Another, and two more. He placed the stand he had built onto the little desk he had chosen: big enough for the demonstration, but small enough to leave room for the Fellows to gather around it. His stand had a threaded bracket with a turn handle, to allow pressure to be brought upon the materials placed beneath it.

From the first jar, Harry took tiny white crystals, spooning them into a shallow dish. His hands were shaking. He was sure the Fellows could see.

'We learn as much from trials that fail,' Hooke tried to reassure him, but his choice of words did not really serve to encourage.

The other jars held crystals of quartz, some cane sugar, and a salt Harry had prepared. Lastly, he produced a length of pig's thighbone he had sawn across, making an irregular cylinder with two flat ends. He motioned to the Fellows to come closer.

'Rochelle salt?' Sir Christopher guessed, looking closely at the white crystals in the dish.

'Prepared in the manner of Monsieur Seignette,' Harry replied.

'Harry, what are we about to see?' Hooke asked.

Harry had deliberately kept quiet for days about his demonstration, hoping to pique their curiosity. 'Let me perform the trial first, so you may all observe without prejudice.'

Placing the bone into the bracket, he tightened the turnscrew enough to grip it, then produced a thin sheet of gold from his box, which he hung vertically from the stand. He placed it so it almost touched the bone.

He turned the screw. The wood squeaked as it worked its way into the thread. He watched the gold sheet intently. The Fellows became just vague shapes clustered around him. Nothing seemed to be happening. He fumbled for the handle, to turn it more.

In his lodgings at Half Moon Alley, and in Gresham's elaboratory the night before, with Grace helping him, it had worked: Both clearly saw the gold sheet deflected by the piece of bone. All the Fellows knew of electricity, since its investigation by William Gilbert and its naming by Thomas Browne. As long ago as Thales, the effects of rubbing fur on amber had been observed. But this idea of *pressing* to make electricity was wholly Harry's own.

It must happen again. It must.

Although the temperature in the Repository was distinctly cool, Harry started to sweat.

Perhaps the gap between bone and gold was too great. Harry adjusted it, bringing them closer, and turned the screw again. The wooden stand groaned.

Still, there was no effect from pressing the bone.

Nothing for them to see.

A few of the Fellows began to mutter.

'Mayhap, the quartz?' Hooke suggested. 'If I knew what you sought, I might be more helpful.' He sounded peevish.

'I shall give the apparatus another turn, Mr. Hooke.' Harry needed the Fellows to see him as his own man, not still as Hooke's assistant.

His moist palm slipped from the turnscrew. He had polished the wood too well, wanting to make a show of his dexterity. A roughened surface would be better. He would remember for his improved version. He twisted it again.

A dreadful cracking sound came from the stand. He had turned the screw too tightly. The bone resisted. Harry's bracket split in two. The stand toppled. Bracket and bone fell from the desk. The turnscrew dropped out of his hand and bounced across the floor.

Choosing that moment to appear, sunlight streamed cruelly over the desk, with Harry's stand prostrate across it, the broken bracket lying on the dais, and the pig's thighbone over by the door, as if fleeing the Repository. There was no sign at all of the turnscrew.

Harry slowly straightened from his trial. The faces before him wore a mixture of expressions. Some seemed horrified, their eyes wide. Edmund Wylde had his hand to his mouth. Sir Christopher winced as if in pain. Some looked sorry for his predicament, which made Harry feel unaccountably angry. John Aubrey supported him, he knew, yet looked as if he stifled sniggers.

And was that a look of complicity the President, Sir Joseph, directed at Denis Papin?

Harry's shoulders slumped. Blotches of red coloured his cheeks.

First to speak was Robert Hooke. 'Harry, your investigation into the pressing of bone may continue, if the bracket in my observatory will suffice. Currently, it holds my selesnoscope. Similar in size and shape, and, I would say, more robust.'

'A stronger one is needed, clearly,' Papin said.

Hooke moved to the door, opened it, and gestured through. 'Go, Harry.

Fetch my bracket. We shall perform another trial, and you may try yours again upon your return. Monsieur Papin, you, too, have a trial for us?'

Harry picked up the broken bracket from the dais, then replaced the stand on the desk.

'Don't bother with that,' said Papin. 'I must remove it for my demonstration, which needs more room than yours.'

Harry turned from the Fellows, all still watching him, and retreated from the Repository.

As he returned to Hooke's lodgings, through the colonnaded walkway, his eyes were stinging. He wiped at them. What best to do? Well, he would try Hooke's bracket. What else could he do? He could not simply sulk, although that was all he wanted to do.

Back in Hooke's dining room, Grace saw his stricken expression and rushed to him.

Unable to bring himself to speak, even to Grace, Harry squeezed her hand, then climbed the steps to the observatory above Hooke's lodgings, a high platform built over the roof of the College. He tried to take Hooke's selesnoscope from its stand, wrestling with the release.

The skyline over Bishopsgate began to spin. He felt sick. A sudden feeling of his chest constricting. With it came the terrifying notion he was doomed to fall from the observatory into the quadrangle below.

For over a year, this dizzying dread had occasionally visited him, since a misadventure at the top of the Fish Street Monument. He could not believe it should afflict him now, when he most needed to impress the Fellows.

He knelt and put his hands flat onto the wooden planks. He willed himself to calm, pleading with his own body. Slowly, his breathing resumed a normal pace. At last, he managed to hoist himself back to his feet and drag Hooke's stand with its bracket back down to the dining room, where Grace awaited him.

'I shall try again,' Harry said.

She kissed him.

HARRY STOOD LISTENING for a while outside the Repository door. The room was silent, which seemed strange. As no one was talking he would not be interrupting, so he opened the door as quietly as he could.

A thump on the wall next to him was followed by the Fellows loudly applauding. Bewildered, Harry ventured in. He could see Denis Papin at the far end of the room, aiming a gun just to the side of the door. Turning, Harry saw a wooden target. It swung from a bullet's impact, but there had been no sound from the gun. Papin held the weapon up for the Fellows to see, then held it towards Harry as he came in.

'My air-gun, Harry.'

Harry turned to the target, a series of holes neatly clustered at its middle.

Sir Joseph stepped forwards to bring Harry further into the room. 'Monsieur Papin has shown the accuracy and silence of his air-gun, and Mr. Hooke has demonstrated his flying wing. Mr. Hunt, are you ready to try again your pressing upon bone?'

Harry held up Hooke's stand to show him, along with the bracket. The sunlight shone through the hole made for the turnscrew in Hooke's bracket. Harry observed the thread cut into the wood. It was quite worn, from the times Hooke had used it in trials here in the Repository, or in the Reading Hall, or in the gallery, or in the elaboratory, his dining room or up on his observatory.

The light picked out each wind of the thread's helix in sharp relief.

He exhaled all the air out of his lungs and pressed his scalp with his fingers. 'I must go back,' he told the Fellows disconsolately. 'I've left behind the turnscrew.'

'Worry not,' Sir Joseph said, not unkindly. 'A shame to forgo your experiment. I must return now to Whitehall, to meet with the King. He disbelieves Titus Oates, and thinks I can be of help against him. We may observe the assuredly curious effects of pressing on bone another day.'

CHAPTER FOUR

THE FELLOWS' TOAST

HARRY SAT ALONE IN ONE OF the booths with his brown leather coat on. Other customers clustered as near to the fire as they could. Icy wind from Fleet Street assaulted them every time the door opened. Outside, one of the chains holding the Bell's sign had broken. They could hear the dull smack each time it hit the wall. None of the staff were willing to brave the weather to fix it.

After a second quart pot of ale, his thoughts had become fuzzy, but still Harry winced each time he thought of his equipment scattered over the floor, or of the moment he realized his forgetting of the turnscrew.

His failure made his cheeks burn.

What had possessed him to think pressing a piece of pig's bone might hold the interest of the Fellows? They had also witnessed a silent gun, and another of Hooke's thirty-several ways of flying. He stared into his drink, observing the way the head collapsed as the bubbles worked their way from the foam.

Another blast of air from the doorway made him look up. It was Robert Hooke, entering with Sir Christopher, who had once been Gresham Professor of Astronomy, but was now Surveyor of the King's Works. He had built the Bell as a place for the workmen rebuilding St. Bride's church, burned in the Great Conflagration.

Sir Christopher spotted him and waved, and steered Hooke towards his booth, tacking a course across the busy tavern.

Watching the approaching Secretary made Harry think of the price Hooke had paid for his experimentalism. As a child, Hooke had been upright, but his back—from so long being bent over machinery or making observations—had warped. If he had not developed his hunch, he would be far taller than Sir Christopher.

'Seeking solace, Harry?' Sir Christopher asked, as the two men reached his table. His face was still youthful, unlined by age. 'Robert, more claret? Or are you eager for the port?' Wren swatted his reddened cheeks. 'Unseasonably cold! It was pleasant this afternoon. This wind!'

'I shall take first, some watered cider,' Hooke replied, after sneezing loudly into his handkerchief. He had already shared two bottles of claret with Sir Christopher in the Devil.

Sir Christopher's face came close to Harry's, sending fumes over him. 'Harry?'

'Some Danzig bread wine,' Harry answered mournfully.

'After beer? As a remedy for your hurt pride, it may prove efficacious, though in moderation only. Else, it shall only exchange one sorrow for another.' Wren looked around at Hooke, and spoke out of the side of his mouth. 'He means to punish himself for the failure of his experiment.' He turned back and placed his hand on Harry's forearm. 'What were you hoping to show? The pressing of a length of bone. Very mysterious. I cannot imagine.'

'I've observed electricity emanate from bone, when pressed with enough force,' Harry replied. 'Also from quartz, and sugar, and Rochelle salts.'

'Merely from the pressing? What can this signify?'

'I wished to raise the debate,' Harry said.

Hooke put his hand on the back of Harry's neck, and squeezed sympathetically. 'You must not allow this to discourage you.'

'I had hopes for the Curatorship. Monsieur Papin will take that place now, I'm sure. The President saw my humiliation.'

'No such decision has yet been taken,' Sir Christopher said firmly. 'Papin is a worthy natural philosopher, certainly, but Sir Joseph has other matters to consider. For he finds himself ensnared in this Popish Plot.' He turned to Hooke. 'Harry does feel sorry for himself, does he not? As you said, Robert. As you said. Let us get sore heads in his honour!'

Hooke raised an imaginary glass. *'Drink brings maturity, and maturity brings drink.'*

'A cask of wine works more miracles than a church full of saints,' Harry offered.

Sir Christopher regarded him doubtfully, unsure if Harry risked blasphemy. Before he could make up his mind, he spotted the landlord, Mr. Danvers. Sir Christopher called him over and explained what they were about.

'Bread wine for Mr. Hunt. Mr. Hooke wishes only for weakened cider. Dutch peach brandy for me.'

'Flavoursome,' Danvers said. 'I also have at last the Greyfriars *aqua vitae*, Sir Christopher, from my man in Perth.'

'We may take a circuitous route to the Greyfriars,' Sir Christopher answered. 'But shall arrive there in the end.'

When Danvers had returned, bringing bottles, tankards, and glasses, Sir Christopher again picked up the reins of conversation. He was aware that Hooke, starting to look as if the earlier claret disagreed with him, did not feel garrulous. Most certainly, neither did Harry.

'We could recover the brain from a temperate's corpse and compare it to that of a sot. A subject suitable for your microscopical enquiries, Mr. Hooke? Or would it make for a better trial to take two lifetime-long abstainers, and infuse strong drink into one only of them, shortly before death? It may be considered unchristian to do so—I speak partly in jest.'

Sir Christopher's philosophical pondering was broken off by the arrival of Daniel Colwall, the Royal Society's Treasurer, who brought with him Thomas Henshaw.

'Harry, you look as miserable as Prometheus upon his rock,' Colwall said. 'I am so very sorry about your experiment.' He had the clean look and the quietly fashionable clothes of a very affluent man.

'He should replace Mr. Hooke as Curator,' Henshaw said. 'Despite his misfortune today. We know he owns the abilities.'

'We are yet to convince Sir Joseph,' Wren said. 'Electricity from the bone may have done so.'

'There are other plans for him.' Hooke's voice broke slightly, and he looked down into his weakened cider. He stood, raised his tankard to the group, then gulped down the remaining cider with a single draught. 'Brandy!'

Sir Christopher quickly poured him some, at the same time looking puzzled by his interjection. Hooke took the glass and tipped the drink straight down.

'I see you mean business,' Colwall said, taking off his coat. 'I shall procure more of the same. Mr. Henshaw, do you wish to join us?'

Henshaw considered a while, rubbing his jowls. 'Some genever, I think.'

Colwall went to the serving table and negotiated a level of credit. 'Just make mention to me when we are spent up, Mr. Danvers.'

The landlord looked amazed. Colwall, as Treasurer, was rarely celebrated for generosity.

Colwall returned carrying a bottle of genever and various bottles of claret.

'Genever, Mr. Henshaw?' Sir Christopher asked, settling into his place. 'A remedy, really, is it not? Invented by Silvius as a diuretic. Does it work upon pride, do you think? For Harry's, here, is hurt.'

'I observed the damage done to it at Gresham,' Henshaw replied, as he produced an Indian pipe. 'It looked an intriguing trial.'

'I shall demonstrate it again,' Harry answered. 'With an improvement to the bracket.'

'Metal, rather than wood,' Hooke said, his face now subtly green. 'Lesh chansh of breaking.'

'And the handle was too smooth,' Harry remembered.

'I notished,' Hooke replied overloudly.

After much clinking and pouring, the five men raised their glasses to one another, and drank to the success of Harry's future experiment.

'To Harry!'

'Harry!'

'To Harry, as Curator of the Royal Society!'

A loud disturbance made them look up from their toast. Edmund Wylde and John Aubrey tried to squeeze through the doorway at the same time, neither willing to give way to the other. It was their laughter that raised itself above the general noise of the tavern. From behind them another man pushed through. Clearing the obstruction like meat from a choking throat, Dr. William Croone surveyed the Bell's interior and all the people in it. They, in turn, stared at this disruption, bemoaning the chill it brought through the still-open door. Croone's legs bent under the weight of the two pints of port he had downed with his dinner. Two more Fellows, Abraham Hill and John Hoskyns, followed through the door: this time sequentially, but each looking as unsteady as Croone.

The newcomers all removed their perukes to cool their heads, the drink-sweat under them too uncomfortable to bear for the sake of fashion. They stood holding them, studying the booths and tables, trying to find other members of the New Philosophical Club. Wylde and Aubrey supported one another, fearing they might ground themselves.

The group was elderly, grizzled, and silver-haired, all except Croone, who owned an impressively bald head. Its fissures, as his scalp bumped over his skull, looked like a river delta drawn on a map.

Wylde was the first to see Hooke, Wren, Colwall, Henshaw, and Harry, and he motioned to his colleagues to follow.

'I must piss!' Wylde announced as the two groups met. 'I shall require relubrication upon my return.'

'Rumbullion!' Aubrey cried. 'You wish for the same?'

'Rumbullion, but twice!' Wylde turned and disappeared through the back of the tavern.

Aubrey held Sir Christopher's shoulders to move across him, to sit between him and Harry. Harry steadied him as he bundled himself over.

'You are already well oiled,' Sir Christopher observed. 'We must draw level with you.'

'The unfortunate influence Wylde has upon me,' Aubrey replied pitifully.

'A more unfortunate influence is drink,' Sir Christopher said.

'The two in combination doubly so. Would you assist me? I'm out of coin.'

'I am buying,' Colwall said, disappearing inside his own pipe smoke. 'Rumbullion, you say?'

'That's kind.' Aubrey looked around him, then at Harry. 'Rebaptising your soul with bread wine, Harry?'

'*Materialis causa* in one glass,' Croone said, as he also climbed across Sir Christopher, who looked testily at him. 'Shitten luck your trial did not work. Be not too downhearted.'

Hill and Hoskyns stayed at the end of the long table, debating if they could complete the same journey. Eventually they moved past Hooke, who rose unsteadily for them, to the other side of the table.

'We were making a toasht to Harry,' Hooke explained when they were all settled. 'To the more happy repetishion of the trial of preshing upon bone.'

'And Rochelle salt,' Sir Christopher said. 'As prepared by Monsieur Seignette.'

'Was there sugar, too?' asked Aubrey.

'And quartz,' Harry added, bitterly.

Croone leaned upon the table and massaged his bald scalp, his eyes tightly closed. 'A toast! An admirable reason to drink!' He was a little behind the conversation. 'There are many reasons to drink, yes. One reason, the enjoyment of a fine wine, certainly. Another, celebration of a friend, always . . . Another reason?' He searched himself, his forehead a mass of lines of concentration, the creases rising upwards onto the pink hemisphere of his head.

'Thirst could be construed as a reason, simply. Not that I need such a reason, for I myself am as full as a tun, but yours, Mr. Hooke, will certainly do.'

By the end of this speech Croone had lost his energy and the use of his lips.

When Wylde returned, with spatters of urine down the front of his breeches, they all completed the toast to Harry, each man adding his own variant on their hopes that his experiment would succeed next time he demonstrated it.

Wylde's toast consisted of '*If I die, let me die drinking in an inn!*'

They drained their glasses. Sir Christopher called over a serving girl to replenish their drinks. As she listened to them fussing over their next choices, Aubrey smiled stupidly at her. She was young and solemn-looking. Her dark eyes regarded them steadily: she had already seen enough, in her short lifetime, of the foolishness of men.

'You stand no chance with her, Mr. Aubrey,' Wylde averred, after she had left them. 'You're old enough to be her grandfather. You have no coin. And, you are full of drink. You could not do what nature designed you to do, even if she did accompany you outside.'

Sir Christopher looked disapproving. 'You discuss the girl as if she were a doxy.'

'I mean no offence to her, Sir Kit! I mean only to reveal to Mr. Aubrey his lack of condition for rantum-scantum.'

'There would be no p-p-point to his endeavour, you mean?' Hill stammered, an impediment which afflicted him after a second bottle of wine.

'Exactly! An endeavour doomed to failure, on any front,' Wylde replied.

'A-A-As Harry's failed today.'

'Ah, poor Harry. I am sorry for your difficulties,' Wylde said, nodding vigorously. 'Your bone slipped out.'

'Fell off, as I recall,' Henshaw said, puffing happily on his pipe.

'It spilled over the floor,' Colwall said with a start, catching on to the game.

'Your equipment failed you,' Croone said, at last opening his eyes.

'From vertical to horizontal in the blink of an eye.' Aubrey looked pleased with his contribution.

'It certainly compared poorly to Monsieur Papin's weapon,' Hoskyns added.

'He did not get his s-s-screw.' Hill swayed, not knowing whether to laugh, or be sick.

The men puffed out their cheeks, and pursed their lips, and looked down at their hands with tears in their eyes. Even Sir Christopher, and—most hurtfully of all—Robert Hooke.

Greatly offended, Harry stood, buttoned up his coat, bowed to each of the men with him, and, staggering from beer and bread wine, pushed his way through the crowd.

Behind him, the Fellows could contain their laughter no longer. It burst from them: loud, raucous, and wounding. Harry slammed the door and marched out into Fleet Street, not even pausing when the Bell's sign smashed to the ground just in front of him, pulled off the wall by the wind. Its metal frame sparked on the paving stones.

He stepped over it, and returned with stiff-legged strides to his lodgings in Half Moon Alley, in Bishopsgate Without.

CHAPTER FIVE

THE DOTING

LOVERS

UNDER THE PALE HAZE FROM A lamp marking the way, Harry passed through one of the medieval breaks in the Roman wall to cut across the grounds of the Bethlehem Hospital. Newly built on the marshy land drained to make the grand park it occupied, the vast building stretched across his vision.

Usually, coming this way, Harry felt lifted by pride. For he had assisted Mr. Hooke to design and build the Hospital, with its light and airy rooms, devoted to the modern and compassionate treatment of London's mad. With the laughter of the Fellows still in his mind, though, and the clanging of the Hospital's nine o'clock bell signalling the end of visiting hours, it became something sinister. Its wings reached out for him.

Clumsy from drink and feeling queasy, still harking on the Fellows' discourtesy—none even addressed him as Mr. Hunt, for to them he was always Harry—he went into the churchyard, crossing the rough open ground where the old hospital had stood. Tree branches shook themselves fricatively in the wind, seeming to warn him away. He only left behind this foreboding mood when he turned into Rose and Crown Court, then Half Moon Alley. These were ordinary and mean houses, untouched by the Conflagration, narrow ways between them, jettied storeys leaning over him across the street. A stranger might find them intimidating, but Harry welcomed their familiarity.

While fumbling at the door of his lodgings, Harry heard a heavy and purposeful stride, followed by an explosive opening of the door.

Colonel Michael Fields, whose bald, liver-spotted head carried an ear whose top was missing, appeared.

Soldier for Parliament in the times of the Civil Wars, Leveller turned Anabaptist preacher, Fields had been spending more and more time there. Although their friendship had become firm, Harry knew it was not him the Colonel came to see. The incentive for his visits was Harry's landlady, Mrs. Elizabeth Hannam.

Although thin, she was undoubtedly attractive. The wonder was her husband holding her affections for so long. Her growing fondness for Fields had accelerated Mr. Hannam's dismissal from her life. His dreary failure to provide, or to keep hold of the little money that came into their household— mostly by her efforts—had finally persuaded her to harden her heart. After his return from a spell inside a debtor's gaol, the last Harry had seen of him was his disbelieving face as she chased him from the house.

'Good to see you, again,' Harry said, coming inside, having to steady himself with a hand on the wall. Barely a pause before the 'again,' but the Colonel caught it.

'It has become a habit.' He looked diffidently at Harry. 'So! I feel I should ask your permission—perhaps as there is no one else to ask.'

'Permission? To see Mrs. Hannam? I have no say in that.'

'Not only to *see* her.' Fields let a smile play over his mouth, which gave way to his extravagant laugh, short and loud. 'I have asked her to become my wife!'

Harry felt a great surge of affection for the old man. 'She agreed?'

'She did. I ventured to enquire, despite my certainty she would turn me down. Some legal business must separate her from her first husband, then I shall be her second.'

'It's sudden, Colonel, but I'm pleased. For both of you.'

Fields held out his arms, and Harry moved into his strong embrace. The smell of Fields's coat, and of his tobacco, made Harry feel safe in a way he rarely did. When released, he found his eyes were moist, which Fields took to be happiness at his announcement.

'For I was an hungred, and she gave me meat. I was thirsty, and she gave me drink. I was a stranger, and she took me in. I am a lucky man, Harry, to find affection at last. I was alone for so long, I thought my remaining days would contain only solitude—ah! My love!'

'Would you line me up with the sheep, Michael?' Mrs. Hannam asked, recognising his misquoting of Matthew. She had appeared from the withdrawing room, and stood with her hand on the door frame, grinning slyly.

'Well, you are no goat.' Fields gave a low chuckle. For a moment—to Harry's great consternation—it looked as though he was moving to pinch her, but the old man stopped himself.

'You've told Harry, I hear,' Mrs. Hannam said, looking bashfully at her lodger. Harry went towards her to embrace her as Fields had embraced him, but his movement was awkward, especially so in the narrow passageway. She slid away from his hold, avoiding the smell of his alcohol-soaked breath, and led Fields back to the withdrawing room.

Harry stayed in the little hallway, struggling to remove his arm from his coat sleeve.

When he joined them, Mrs. Hannam was sitting in her armchair by the fire, and Fields stood with one elbow perched on the mantelshelf, filling his pipe. Harry looked at the little clock on the wall, a brass lantern clock he had converted by adding a pendulum with a spring mechanism, making it more accurate than with its original weights. It was not long past nine, but felt much later. He sat heavily down at the table, which seemed to tip from side to side as if suspended like a swing.

Mrs. Hannam looked sharply at him. She had suffered Mr. Hannam's fondness for the alehouse. Harry felt a sting of shame, replaced by resentment at her too-harsh judgment.

Fields caught the look between them and raised his bushy eyebrows. *'And when they are in their cups, they forget their love both to friends and brethren, and a little after draw out swords.'* He pointed his pipe at Harry. 'A rare thing, Harry, to see you in your cups.'

'A rare day, Colonel. I sought solace in drink. Also, I met with Mr. Hooke and some of the other Fellows. They're difficult men to refuse.'

'Solace? A dangerous course you take. Strong drink soon becomes a necessary companion, turned to for the slightest of reasons.'

'Reasons enough tonight,' Harry replied. 'For I've decided to leave the Royal Society, and take employment with Sir Jonas Moore.'

'Do I hear you rightly? For the Board of Ordnance?' Fields sucked at his pipe. 'You refused its offer before.'

'The Society, I find, doesn't value me nearly so much.'

'Mr. Hooke loves you like a son,' Mrs. Hannam said. 'Tomorrow you'll awaken sober, and more sensible.'

'This afternoon, I lost the chance to be Curator. This evening, I was mocked by the Fellows. By Mr. Hooke, even. It's time to leave. Sir Jonas asks that I travel to the Fens.'

Fields rubbed at his arm, an old injury which still troubled him, especially in the spring. 'The Fens? A dreadful place. I was there, for a time, in the Wars. How the bog dwellers tolerate it, even if they have become senseless to the bites of all the mosquitoes, is mysterious to me.'

Fields glanced at Mrs. Hannam, who shook her head at him.

'Heed what Elizabeth says. Give time for your thoughts to settle. The Royal Society has been your life.' Fields suffered a coughing fit as he mistimed his inhaling from the pipe. 'You would not wish to swap Gresham

College for the Fens,' he said, when he had recovered. 'Whereabouts, in the *Fens*, does Sir Jonas desire you to go?' Fields's distaste for even saying the word was evident.

'The Denver Sluice, part of the works to drain the marshland. A body has been found.'

Mrs. Hannam stood, ready to retire. 'I'll leave you men, since I dislike talk of bodies. Don't decide, Harry, as I say, until the morning. I'll bid you both your good nights.'

'Elizabeth! Wait, my love,' Fields said. 'I shall come with you.' He extinguished his pipe, tapping it out into the fireplace. 'So, think on it, Harry. Always be cautious at times like this, for such choices make the shape of your life.' From time to time, since the Wars, Fields suffered from tremors, and his head gave a brief, convulsive shake now. 'Take my word, won't you, from wisdom gained through years of tumult, and my survival of them. And besides, you are as drunk as a blood.'

He took Mrs. Hannam by the hand, and together they left Harry to his own thoughts.

From upstairs, Harry could hear the low tone of the Colonel's voice, but his words were indistinguishable down in the withdrawing room. He turned sideways in his chair, and brought his knees up, clasping them to his chest with his arms.

The last of the fire glowed, winking orange and red.

As Harry drifted off to sleep, he knew his decision was already made.

CHAPTER SIX

THE UNEXPECTED PASSENGERS

NO SIGN OF THE STAGECOACH YET. Although he was early, Harry was not the first to arrive. About half a dozen others travelling north shivered, too, standing by the Standard pump, their baggage piled beside them.

Already that morning he had visited the Armouries at the Tower of London to accept Sir Jonas Moore's offer of employment. There, a note waited for him, demonstrating Sir Jonas's assurance of Harry's decision. The note was an instruction to advance to Mr. Henry Hunt his first quarter's pay, with travelling costs given extra. He was sent to the Treasury office to collect it, where he was glad of little need for talking, as his head still hurt from the Bell.

The bag of coins clinked pleasingly, weighing down his pocket. As he checked it for the severalth time that morning, he noticed a young man waiting apart from the crowd. Standing for the coach over by the London Stone, he seemed to want to catch Harry's attention. A lank of blond hair escaped from under his tricorne hat. An amused look on his face irritated Harry, as it seemed a superior expression.

Protection, perhaps, arranged by Sir Jonas? Surely not: Sir Jonas, or one of his men at the Armouries, would have warned him of possible danger.

The more Harry looked at him, the more he thought he should know him. Not from the College, though. Not a mechanic, or a junior operator.

Harry jumped, from a heavy hand placed on his shoulder.

'So! Good morrow to you, Harry!'

'Good morrow, Colonel,' Harry replied, forgetting the stranger. He felt the same strong emotion as when they embraced the previous evening. That Fields had come to see him off touched him further than he would have thought possible.

Fields appeared invigorated by the morning's chill. He had on his favourite montero and his old campaign coat, and he had polished his boots. A long scarf warmed him, bright orange to commemorate his Parliament past. His sword protruded from under his coat, the scabbard's tip scraping the wall behind him. A canvas bag hung from his shoulder.

Noticing that Fields looked ready to travel himself, Harry raised an eyebrow.

Fields grinned. 'You have made your choice. I shall not speak against it, for it is yours, and yours alone. I, too, have had time to consider.'

Harry made no mention of falling asleep in his landlady's chair as soon as she and Fields had gone to bed, or that he had given the matter no further thought at all. Sir Jonas's offer was too enticing to refuse. Since waking, his resolve to leave behind Mr. Hooke, Gresham College, and the Royal Society's employ had increased, needing no conscious thought to do so. He felt his choice was the right one; it sat comfortably with him, somewhere between his chest and his stomach.

Hooke would be appalled at such sentiment. At such illogic. But Harry no longer cared about that. When he last saw Hooke at the Bell, as the Fellows mocked him, Hooke had worn a look of callous enjoyment.

Fields produced his pipe, and with the speed of a lifetime's practice soon had tobacco glowing in its bowl. He coughed loudly, and spat, and looked around them, scanning the other travellers. Harry was not sure what he searched for, but his inspection, once complete, seemed to satisfy; Fields gave his pipe a little tap in the air to signal his content.

'I have considered it, too, as I say. As your mind is made up, then I have a suggestion. I could come with you.' Fields took Harry's silence as reticence. 'I have experience, you know, which might prove useful to you.'

'But what of Mrs. Hannam?' Harry managed. 'She'd miss you badly.'

Fields looked apologetic, the same face he had made when discussing it that morning with her. 'I have reassured Elizabeth we shall not be long, as I doubt it not. To leave Mr. Hooke, and the safety of Gresham College, could be the making of you. But I, surely, can be of help to you, who are unversed in such matters. Elizabeth is understanding. I think she wants me to enjoy a last adventure, as if our marriage shall not be adventure enough. What do you think, Harry? Would you take this old man with you?'

'But you described the Fens as dreadful,' Harry said, smiling broadly. 'Are you sure you wish to come?'

'I expect my memories colour them so. Yes, I am sure. If you will have me.'

○

THEY HEARD THE sound of the coach as it lumbered past the Royal Exchange. Looking too heavy for its unfortunate horses, it was big enough for eight people inside, and four more at the rear, at the mercy of the elements, in what was little more than a reed hamper. The coach's paint was scratched and worn. Streaks of mud adorned its sides. There were no springs to soften the jolts from the road, Harry saw. He hoped the cushioning was generous.

The Board of Ordnance had ordered a place inside for him. Harry reached for the letter informing the driver so. Luckily, there was room, too, for Colonel Fields.

Harry felt very grand stepping up into the coach, his bags stowed on top by the driver's boy. Allowing Fields to squeeze by to sit at the window, Harry's

self-satisfaction—his journey about to begin and the Colonel coming with
him—soon disappeared when he felt the seat's hardness through his tailbone.
The journey to Cambridge was usually fifteen hours or so; this early in the
season the roads were muddy, so progress would be slow.

His situation quickly worsened. A stocky man with no neck, smelling
like milk left to curdle, settled next to him, unconcerned about the pressure
he exerted on a fellow traveller's thigh.

Then, another man sat opposite, his boots knocking Harry's. Harry
pulled his foot back and looked sharply at him.

It was the young man in the tricorne he had noticed earlier. Not only
did this man stare impolitely, but he leaned forwards, coming uncomfortably close. Harry pulled himself back in his seat, his fist automatically
clenching at the overfamiliarity.

'Hello, Harry,' said the voice of Grace Hooke.

Fields turned from his window and let out his explosive laugh.

Grace placed her hand on Harry's knee. 'If I had asked, you would have
said no. I did not ask.'

She wore breeches, a quilted waistcoat, and a blue topcoat of expen-
sive-looking cloth.

'You're disguised. As a man.' Harry's amazement made him stupid. It
quickly turned to anger. He had said his goodbyes at Gresham that morning, after telling her of his decision to meet Sir Jonas Moore. She had given
no intimation she might follow.

'Easier,' she replied, annoyingly breezy. 'And, it feels more . . . *adventurous*.'

'You have been outflanked, Harry,' the Colonel said.

Grace passed Harry a letter. 'From Uncle. For Mr. Newton at Trinity
College. He asks that you deliver it.'

'I'm to be his postman? I imagine he'd no notion you'd accompany it on
its way. He'll be furious.'

She looked entirely unconcerned about her uncle's feelings on the
matter.

'It's not safe for you to travel with us,' Harry said, primly.

'Equally, then, it cannot be safe for you to travel with me.'

Outside, there was a discussion between the driver and another coach-man involving the difficulty of the way through Whitechapel. Then the coach moved off, swaying and lurching over the road's rough undulations.

'Too late,' Grace said. 'You shall have to tolerate my company.'

For the first time, Harry smiled at her, forced to admit to himself his pleasure that she was there. 'In truth, I've never had to *tolerate* your company.'

'Colonel Fields, have you ever heard such charming words?'

'He is a charming fellow,' Fields replied, winking at her.

'Any girl would be pleased.'

'You're still a girl, then?' Harry asked her.

'Sir, you risk indelicacy.' Grace placed the back of her hand on her cheek in a caricature of highborn refinement, as if about to faint away.

They left Cornhill, with all its smart houses built to the new regulations instituted after the Conflagration, most standing on plots mapped out by the man they left behind them, Robert Hooke. The coach took them out through Bishopsgate, and on into the suburbs.

When reaching Hackney, Fields pointed out the redoubts' remains, part of the defences thrown up against the Royalists in the Civil Wars.

They headed for the Great North Road—the ancient line of Ermine Street—leaving London behind them.

CHAPTER SEVEN

THE
TRAITOR'S END

HIGH-PITCHED SQUEALING FROM THE CHILDREN. SHRIEKS and curses from their mothers, anxious to keep them from the crush. Menaces from the men protecting their families. The shouts of those selling food, drink, projectiles.

The platform, high on its frame, looked like a ship at anchor with the flow of people around it. Some from the crowd climbed its beams, although what they hoped to see from there was unguessable. Perhaps proximity was all. A need to feel, rather than observe.

The wealthy rented stands for an eye-watering fee. Cheaper were the carts, pulled by horses as wild-eyed as the pedestrians they nodded aside. The watchers forced themselves into impossible spaces. Some climbed onto the carts, to be pushed at or punched by those who had paid. One cart was rocked violently, its driver having caused offence. Its horse reared up, kicking out and breaking faces.

Black-hatted and red-coated, the King's Foot Guards failed to calm them. Knocks from musket butts made people argumentative. Sneaky jabs to a uniformed back. A sly kick at a soldier's ankle. All innocence when the man swung around. All outrage if he retaliated with a swipe.

Too few soldiers to suppress this mob if it became truly rowdy. Those who guarded the edge, furthest from the grim platform, looked nervously towards the Tower for reinforcements.

●

AT LAST, HE appeared. The traitor William Howard, First Viscount Stafford. Bent forwards, head low on his chest. More soldiers led him through the crush.

A growl went through the people. Here it was: the reason they had come, the reason they risked being crushed one against another. The moment of release—of purgation—was due. The thrill of it made them shudder.

His last chance not to dissemble. To speak before God.

And then the death.

Stafford could hardly hear the noise and was barely aware of the bodies around him. Despite the crowd and all the jostling, as he reached the scaffold it was the handrail he noticed. Quickly sawn, the wood was rough to his palm, and he soon let go for fear of splinters. Absurd, he thought, as he mounted the steps. But it was his body's natural reaction.

The sudden jerk of his hand brought him to. Details around him sharpened and magnified, as if seen through a lens. A flag snapping in the wind on the White Tower. A woman leaning from a window in Muscovy House. Latecomers pushing through from Seething Lane. Every sound, too, became amplified. The bells ringing in the new tower of All Hallows Barking. A man screaming obscenities at him. Gulls squawking overhead.

And the platform creaking in the wind.

At his trial, the accusations had dazed him. Two accusers, stepping forwards and backwards as they took their turns, like mechanical toys.

The worst of them, that Titus Oates, was the very Devil, able to recall
every fantastical notion of his scheme. The other, Israel Tonge, was
nonsensical.

At the top of the steps, Stafford stopped. A man was straightening a
block of wood, new and gleaming.

He had another object Stafford recognized, despite its being inside a
bag. Granted by the merciful King.

Pushed by the soldier behind him, Stafford edged onto the platform.
The headsman placed down the block, then covered it over with black baize.
Stafford reached inside his coat to produce two guineas. Both men nodded
their understanding of one another.

Stafford nodded, too, at the recorders, poised with their pens. He handed
them some papers to save them the effort: copies of the words he planned.
The minister scowled at him.

Stafford walked to the rail. How very many people there were, come to
Tower Hill. They fanned out before him, reaching almost down to the moat.

He looked over them, his head turning slowly. As they hushed to hear him,
he leaned forwards and gripped the rail, fearful his voice would fail him.

'By the permission of . . .' Little more than a croak. No chance those at
the front could hear, let alone those behind. He cleared his throat and began
again. 'By the permission . . . of Almighty God . . . I am brought here to
suffer death, as if guilty of high treason . . .'

The wind had him shivering. His knees threatened to give way. Some
jeered his efforts, comparing badly to others they had heard.

He reached for a deeper, louder voice. 'In the presence of eternal and
all-knowing God, I protest I am as innocent as it is possible for any man
to be.'

Now his words were stronger and picking up pace; the crowd started to
settle.

'Had I a thousand lives, I would lose them all, rather than falsely accuse
myself, or any other. For then I should have no hope of Salvation . . .'

He spoke on, until the minister, wanting to cut him short, coughed behind him. Stafford turned and stared at the man, who was sweating in his vestments, then slowly turned back to the crowd.

'I hold murder in abhorrence, and have ever done! If I could free myself, and establish what religion I would, and what government I would, all by the death of these perjurers who have brought me to this place, I would not cause their murder.'

The minister stepped forwards impatiently. 'You disown the Romish Church's indulgencies?'

'I am not ashamed of my religion,' Stafford replied, his voice still loud for the mob. 'It teaches nothing but the right worship of God and obedience to the King. I believe there to be one God, one Saviour, and one Holy Catholic Church, of which, through the mercy of God, I die a member.'

Stafford turned, took off his rings and his watch—it was just past ten o'clock—and the crucifix from his neck. He passed them all to a captain of the Foot Guards, who helped him with his coat. The headsman gave him a silk cap. Having taken off his peruke, and adjusted the cap carefully to cover his hair, Stafford lay down on the black cloth and placed his forehead on the block.

This wood felt smooth, and hard.

He stretched forwards.

The headsman took the sword from the bag and withdrew it from its scabbard. 'What sign will you give?'

'No sign at all,' Stafford replied. 'Take your own time. God's will be done.'

'Forgive me.'

'I do.'

APART FROM SOME skin and windpipe, the single blow took Stafford's head from his body. The executioner cut through the remainder with his knife, then lifted the head to the crowd.

'Brave words, they were,' Richard Merritt, standing at the scaffold's foot, observed. Blood had sprayed the shoulder of his cloak. 'He had some sympathy, at the end.'

He paused, to wonder if Stafford's head still had knowledge of the world, or else his thoughts had been snuffed out in an instant.

Seeing disapproval on his master's face, he attempted to mollify him. 'One more Papist dispatched.'

'One only, at a time, is too slow,' Lord High Treasurer Danby replied.

CHAPTER EIGHT

THE LUCASIAN PROFESSOR

THE COUNTRYSIDE BECAME LESS AND LESS hilly, until it assumed a startling flatness. Even so, night had fallen by the time they reached Cambridge, after a bone-shaking twenty hours on roads often little more than mires.

As they had rolled from Hartfordshire into Cambridgeshire, the seemingly endless plains and the vast sky arching overhead made Harry fearful. Above him, the quantity of air made him feel fragile, as if his being might seep out into the landscape's emptiness. The enclosure offered by London's narrow lanes kept you anchored. There was safety in their embrace. Even the Colonel's proximity, sitting next to him, and Grace opposite—although he found her nearness disquieting—did not lessen his sensation of dissipation. A quieter version of his panic on Robert Hooke's observatory, above Gresham College.

The Colonel had spent most of the journey reading his *Book of Common Prayer*, a present from Elizabeth Hannam. He still mourned the loss of his *Soldiers Bible* he had kept since the Wars, destroyed when his Anabaptist chapel had burned.

Grace stared out at the countryside. Anything Harry wished to say to her was made difficult by the strangers in the carriage, who would listen in, so the time passed largely in silence.

At last, they disembarked from the coach, nodding relieved farewells to the milk-scented man, and found their way to the Eagle and Child, a pleasant-enough inn with two rooms free. Harry and Fields took one, and Grace the other. Harry and Grace shared a look as they went to their separate beds. Grace took a candle with her, declaring herself scared of the dark.

IN THE GREY light of another cold morning, Fields led the way. His manner displayed his ability with direction-finding and his inability to listen when focused on a mission. He would get them to Trinity, he assured them, insisting each town was essentially the same: a river, a bridge going over it, and a church. 'Everything else being only variation and repetition.'

It was easier to follow than argue. Harry and Grace shared a look, a mixture of frustration and amusement, as Fields took them to the marketplace for tobacco, indicating that Harry should pay for it from his Ordnance-filled purse. Then he turned them around to Trumpington Street.

To Harry, as he followed the Colonel's broad back, Cambridge seemed a muted and joyless place, its colours bleached and grimy. Lying low on swampy ground, its highest feature was the ruined castle overlooking the town, which Fields pointed out to them with his ever-present pipe. 'Cambridge was the headquarters of the Eastern Association of counties,' he said. 'The castle was broken up, in forty-seven or so, by order of Oliver Cromwell, to make it useless for the Royalists.'

'You were never here?' Harry asked.

'I do not regret it.'

The town's shabby buildings compared poorly to the Colleges, which looked like palaces. It did not need a disapproving Fields, who had once been a Leveller, to point out the difference in wealth, even with his pipe. Students walking by—whose robes, blacks and blues and purples and scarlets, and hats with all manner of trimmings and tassels, denoting Colleges, degrees, and a bewildering array of ranks and status that took an insider's knowledge to understand—seemed to provoke a hostile indifference from the townspeople.

Past King's College chapel, then left down Trinity Lane, shadowy with high walls on either side. Another chapel stood to their right, and they were confronted by a gatehouse. It had one large gate to allow through carriages and horses, and one smaller gate for pedestrians. A statue of Henry VIII looked down on them, grasping his sceptre as if worrying he might lose it.

Piled with building materials, a line of carts backed up the length of the lane. A gang of strong-looking men waited for admission, rubbing their hands in the cold.

'Trinity?' Fields barked, seeking confirmation from a student in purple exiting the smaller gate. He got a panicked nod in reply.

A talk with a workman revealed the College was undergoing renovations. Harry knew of Sir Christopher's commission to build a new library there. The man he spoke to was engaged in laying its foundations, close to the river. Also, Nevile's Court was being extended, and the Bishop's Hostel was nearing completion.

An old porter opened the large gate to let the builders through. Harry motioned to Fields and Grace for them to go through, too. They were unchallenged, the porter thinking them a part of the work teams—he took a longer look at Grace, dressed in her mannish clothes, but dismissed the sensation he had of oddness.

Trinity's great quadrangle opened before them, surrounded by the halls with their high Tudor facades and towering chimneys. A strange stone structure sat in the middle, which turned out to be a fountain. Trinity was a much larger and grander version of Gresham College, each side being about twice the length of Gresham's galleries. More buildings lay beyond and out of sight, Harry knew from his talk with the builder.

'*The care of this world, and the deceitfulness of riches, choke the Word,*' Fields observed caustically, looking around him.

The workmen walking on, and the porter having disappeared, they approached the nearest person they could see, who busied himself washing clothes at the fountain. Harry asked where they could find Mr. Isaac Newton.

The undergraduate directed them back towards the gate, but just to the left of it, as to the right was the library. 'Up the first steps. Look for a door with two holes in it, down by the ground. One large, one small—like our Great Gate.'

Harry, perplexed by this direction, wondered if the student played a joke on them.

○

AGAIN IT WAS the Colonel who insisted on leading the way, even though Harry had got them in and found out Newton's whereabouts. They recrossed the court, climbed the dark stairway, and found a door on the right. As the student had told them, it owned a much smaller door cut into it, almost semi-circular. Next to it, a second door about half the height of its partner was also cut through. Experimentally, Harry pushed at the smallest door with his foot. It opened at his prod, shutting back on springs when he released it.

'*Aargh!*' The door being opened was unwelcome. They heard footsteps pacing quickly inside. A long-faced man with very white skin was suddenly staring at them, his lips curling angrily.

The man pointed down at the small door, then made a swiping gesture at them. The main door shut as rapidly as it had opened.

Huddled on the landing, Harry, Fields, and Grace looked at each other. Tentatively, Harry knocked at the largest door, the one built to a human scale.

'*Huurrgh!*' Again the footsteps could be heard, slower this time. '*Mwweerrr!*'

The door opened again. The man's red-rimmed eyes looked them over, and he snorted loudly through his nose.

'Mr. Newton?' Harry asked.

The man took a long, deep breath. 'Mmm?'

Harry took this to be agreement. 'I have a letter, from your friend Mr. Robert Hooke, who esteems you highly.'

The man looked at them each in turn again, and sniffed.

'The Royal Society's Curator. And its Secretary,' Harry added, hoping to elicit more from the Lucasian Professor.

'You disturb my work,' Newton replied. 'But a letter from Mr. Hooke? Always welcome.'

'I'm sorry I opened the little door,' Harry said. 'I was curious about its use.'

'Everyone who goes past wants to fiddle with it,' Newton complained.

The Professor was tall, with an equine face. As well as red-rimmed eyes, his lips, generously curved, were red, too, and kept shiny by his habit of running his tongue around them, especially when looking at Grace. He wore no wig. His hair was long, and although he looked to be only in his mid-thirties, Harry guessed, it was almost completely white.

Harry introduced himself, careful not to mention the Board of Ordnance. Then he introduced the Colonel, and Grace as being Robert Hooke's nephew. Newton showed no interest in him or the Colonel, nor any curiosity why a Royal Society Observator would travel accompanied by an old soldier. He was far more solicitous towards Grace, his eyes constantly directing themselves at her.

Newton's rooms reminded Harry of Robert Hooke's, similarly messy with papers and equipment. A wine-coloured gown was thrown carelessly over a chair. Through the window, Harry could see down onto a neatly kept garden with a large wooden shed built against the College wall. The grass by its windows was stained different colours, scarred from where Newton had flung chymical mixtures.

Newton moved next to him, and nodded towards the building. 'My elaboratory. Trinity will not let me conduct my trials inside. There have been one or two . . . accidents.'

'I'd very much like to see it.'

Newton looked uncomfortable, and evasive. 'Perhaps, perhaps. We shall see.'

He offered his visitors some audit ale, and bustled about fetching it. He focused completely on the task, and conducted it silently, preferring to fuss around his unexpected guests rather than speak to them.

When his visitors were settled at the table with their ale, Grace sipping at it with distaste, Newton opened the letter from Hooke. He did not sit, but paced around his room as he read. His cat, a tabby, jumped onto Fields's lap, pushing her face against his hand as he stroked her.

Harry picked up a piece of Iceland crystal from the table, observing its properties of double refraction, but a hard glance from Newton made him hurriedly put it back down.

Finishing the letter, Newton folded it, running his nails along the folds to crease them.

'Mr. Hooke speaks highly of you, in his letter.'

Harry started with surprise. Grace's face, too, showed she had not known Hooke had made an introduction.

'I was his apprentice,' Harry said by way of answer. Then there was a silence, which threatened to become uncomfortable.

'Why two holes in your door, Mr. Newton?' Grace asked, eventually.

Newton looked crossly at her, but seeing her face again, his expression quickly softened. 'The cat, there, sitting upon the Colonel, had kittens.'

Harry hesitated to ask the next question. He risked a glance at Grace, and at Fields, knowing they shared the same thought.

'I shall tell you,' Newton huffed, catching the look. 'As everyone asks.' His movements around his room became rapid. He seemed to be approaching a state of agitation. 'I had suffered from a lack of sleep, which often afflicts me, my mind taken up by the problems of light and its refrangibility—the matter I discuss with Mr. Hooke, here.' He waved the letter at them. 'I sawed the smaller hole in a daze. *Of course* I knew the kittens could utilize the hole I cut for their mother. *Of course* I knew her kittens would outgrow the second hole.'

He made a face, stretching his features, as if to say, *so there.* 'I shall block them up. They are more trouble than they are worth.' His voice was gaining in volume, and the flicking of his tongue increased.

Harry thought he had better steer the conversation away from the holes, and the small doors covering them, as he had the chance to speak with a man much admired at the Royal Society. Newton's refracting telescope had pride of place in the Repository, although Hooke had caused him offense by pointing out its deficiencies.

Having delivered the letter, though, Harry also wanted to get on, to meet Sir Jonas, his true reason for coming to the Fens.

And Newton showed no willingness to discuss natural philosophy with him. Instead, surprisingly, he brought the conversation to the Colonel.

'You were for Parliament?'

'I was,' Fields replied, stroking the tabby, and unperturbed by Newton's sharp tone.

'Edward Montagu purged these Colleges. Half of the heads and Fellows were forced to leave. We were cleansed of all our monuments of *idolatry* and *superstition*.' Newton spat the words out.

'The town, too, no doubt,' Fields said, still looking unruffled. 'Enthusiastic times. You must have been but a boy.'

Newton ignored his observation. 'Oliver Cromwell was a regular visitor to Cambridge.'

'You say that as though it were a crime.' Fields had a subtle smile, as if enjoying himself. 'It can hardly be a surprise, as his family is from near here. For a while, I know, the Eastern Association's committee had its headquarters in the Bear Inn, by Sidney Sussex College, where he was a student. They also used the castle, until it was broken.'

'Did you visit?' Newton demanded. 'In the Wars?'

The cat yawned, and stretched. 'I never did,' Fields replied softly, rubbing the old wound on his arm. 'My soldiering took me elsewhere.'

Harry felt sorry for his friend, who under his alarming exterior was the most affable of men.

Fields had no need for Harry's solicitude. 'Cromwell, you remember, protected these Colleges, and argued for open discussion,' he said. 'He encouraged religious speculation.'

Newton looked indignant. Then he looked at Grace once more, sighed, and simply turned his back on them.

It was time to leave.

BACK OUTSIDE, WALKING away from Trinity, they giggled at Newton's strangeness, and his flagrant admiration of Hooke's fictitious nephew.

'You make a good-looking lad, Grace,' Fields said, chuckling. 'And not yet shaving.'

He led them to find transport for their journey to the Denver Sluice, trying for the river, but this time managed to get them lost. They found themselves back in the town.

'A river, a bridge, a church,' Grace teased him, as they asked their way to the Cam.

Fields did not laugh, but instead became moody, as they walked together towards the Backs. He looked tired from their long journey the day before. Perhaps, also, he was more affected by Newton's animosity than he let on. Harry felt a twinge of guilt at accepting the old man's offer to accompany him, but Fields had seemed pleased to do so.

A last adventure, he had called it at the coach station.

They found a small barge, bound for King's Lynn.

The river was peaceful, snaking through the water meadows. Cows wandered across them, splashing through the damp.

CHAPTER NINE

THE DENVER
SLUICE

AT POPE'S CORNER, SOUTH OF ELY, they crossed the imaginary line where the Cam became the Great Ouse. The bargeman, with one lively eye and one perfectly still, complained of the limitations placed on size and draft by the structure they headed for. After building the Denver Sluice and draining the Fens, the river level had dropped.

Along Ten Mile Bank. To their left, the New Bedford River, an impossibly straight line bisecting the landscape. He could utilize it to judge the Earth's curvature, Harry mused, trying to think of ways to surmount the problem of light's refraction through the air—if using telescopes, say—to accurately gauge the declination of the water's surface.

'Built by prisoners taken after the Battle of Dunbar, mostly,' Colonel Fields informed him, breaking into his thoughts.

Impatient for King's Lynn, the bargeman told them he would steer close to the bank to let them off; they did not warrant stopping. As he slowed, Harry waved his thanks and jumped to the path. He turned to help Grace, but she jumped equally nimbly and just as far. It was Fields who needed to reach for Harry's arm as he made the jump, and then rest, swaying, bent forwards with his hands on his knees.

'Are you sick, Colonel?' Harry asked him.

'I do not travel well upon water. Since the voyage I took to Ireland, in the wartime, its motion has disagreed with me.'

Harry thought of his own fright when confronted by a drop. 'Breathe deeply, Colonel. Renew the air in your lungs.'

Fields pulled himself upright, blowing through his cheeks. He looked ashamed to have shown such weakness.

'Are you recovered?' Harry asked. 'We must find Sir Jonas.'

Fields nodded shakily, and Grace took his hand. Together they walked away from the river, down the bank.

The draining of the Fens had led to a shrinking of the peat, and the dropping of the level of the land. It left the rivers higher than the terrain they flowed through, with embankments to either side. From the steep slope the three friends descended, the marshlands spread out before them like a quilt: a haphazard patchwork of islands, covered with reeds and sedge, with shivering willows, alders, and twisted hawthorns protruding sullenly from the wetland. Some trees formed up to protect each other from the vicious winds that excoriated this flatness. Others were solitary, like deserters in search of a safer place. Harry heard a curious sound, which Fields assured him was the drumming of snipe. A sparrowhawk, seemingly interested in them, swooped low. Across these flat plains, church spires miles away could be seen, and windmills and wind pumps for clearing away the water. The ground bore wounds of dark peat where turf had been cut away. Little settlements rose from the damp, boggy ground, chimneys pushing fingers of dark smoke into the sky, making Harry wonder what kind of lives the people eked out from this land.

They reached the Denver Sluice. Built by the Dutchman Cornelius Vermuyden some thirty years before, Harry had conceived it as far grander than it actually was. Instead, it had only three arches, each just big enough to let the small ships and barges able to use the Ouse and the Cam through, and it was surprisingly low above the water.

A gang of men with their picks, shovels, and wheelbarrows worked to rebuild the embankment where a landslide had pulled it away. Back on level ground stood a group of red-coated soldiers and three tents, all centred around a fitfully smoking fire. The soldiers had built their camp on a little island of peat. Against it rested a small boat, a ship's jolly boat for a landing party, its prow grounded on the peat.

There was no way of getting down there without wading through the water, so they had to submit to getting their feet soaked, splashing their way to the camp.

A horse announced their arrival with its whinnying. By the time they reached the first tent, Sir Jonas waited for them, and two of his soldiers with him.

Greeting them all with a firm grasp of the hand, he beckoned for Harry and Fields to come closer to the boat. 'I was told of your arrival,' he informed them. 'And came to meet you.'

When Grace walked forwards to approach it with them, he held out the flat of his palm.

'You stay there, Miss Hooke,' he said. 'Your uncle would never forgive me.'

●

'THIS STRETCH OF water, the New Bedford River, is also called the Hundred Foot Drain, named after the distance between its banks. Here, its bank was breached.' Despite his many years in London, Sir Jonas's Lancashire accent had never softened. 'The peat dried out, the peat shrank, the bank collapsed, the water flooded out. The torrent brought forth this boat, which before had been submerged.'

'And with it, the body you wrote of,' Harry said.

'Inside it, yes. We dragged it here, so it was out of the water. Look more closely, Harry, into the bottom of the vessel. I shall say no more, as I wish your observations made freshly.'

Harry splashed his way to the boat, which apart from its prow lay in shin-deep water. Enough of the lettering remained to see the name of its ship painted on the stern: *Incassable*. It was only when he looked over the side that Harry saw the body. He also saw Sir Jonas had used subterfuge in his letter to bring him here sooner. The body would have kept perfectly well. Little more than skeletal remains, held together by the clothes it was dressed in, it lay between the planks that served as the jolly boat's seats. Water, lodged in the hull, half covered it.

It was small. Another boy, like the boy discovered at the Fleet last year?

A cannonball, which sat on what had been the stomach, weighed the remains down to the bottom of the boat. It pressed into the tattered clothes, rotten from the water's action. What still clung to the bones gave the appearance of a military uniform. Harry observed a buff coat, the metal clips fastening it severely rusted. The trousers, once black or dark grey, were of thick felted wool. A sash's remnants hung off the body. Impossible to judge what colour it had been. A wide-brimmed leather hat, with a strip of similarly discoloured cloth around it, lay next to him, jammed under the seat.

Why did this child wear a uniform?

The skull, cleaned by its long immersion in the water, had a dull shine, and showed clearly the manner of death: a large round object, about five inches in diameter, had shattered the frontal bone over the left eye.

Fields joined Harry at the jolly, and inspected the body with him. *'If we confess our sins, he is faithful and just to forgive us our sins, and to cleanse us from all unrighteousness.'* He looked at Harry, seeking agreement, but when none was given, he gestured at the rotting clothes. 'Nothing to tie him to a regiment. A man's colours were often chosen from his own preference.'

Harry reached in and pulled at the body's legs, bringing the feet from beneath the seat. 'These boots have spurs attached.'

'Then he appears to have been an officer of Horse.'

'For Parliament, or for the King?'

'No knowing from these remains.' Fields picked up the hat and wiped the mud from the cloth around it. 'Often, you could not tell on the field.' He showed the cloth to Harry.

'Silver thread runs through it,' Harry observed.

'Some—of both sides—liked ostentation. Others preferred plain.' Fields dropped the cloth back into the boat. 'Whoever he was for, another took against him.'

Fields lifted the cannonball from the stomach's remains and placed it into the depression on the body's skull. A perfect fit. 'This ball brought him down, and kept him down.' He handed it to Harry, who grunted, unprepared for the weight. 'I remember them as heavier,' Fields said. 'It is a ball from a culverin. It weighs fifteen pounds.'

Harry jounced the ball in his hands, feeling its weight as if about to throw it. He slid his fingers over the pitted iron, made rougher by the rust that coated it. 'It's poorly cast,' he said.

'Made as circumstances allowed. Cannon expel whatever is before their charge. They do not require round shot. They can fire chainshot, balls chained together. Picture that spinning towards you! And grapeshot, small balls inside a bag, spreading out when fired. Iron bars, too, especially at sea, to take down sails and rigging. Sometimes heated, to set fire to the enemy.'

'A culverin must be large to project such a ball.'

'The length of two men, perhaps? They needed eight horses to pull them.'

'As this body's in a ship's boat, this ball was presumably from its ship. That ship being *The Incassable*, I imagine.'

Sir Jonas listened closely, saying nothing, only nodding his agreement occasionally.

Harry picked some scraps of cloth from the ball, and passed them to Fields, who felt them between his fingers. 'Canvas,' the older man observed. 'The remains of the bag it rested on, after the ball was used to kill him.' Fields lifted his own canvas bag, to show its similarity.

Harry placed the ball on the ground beside him, where it pressed into the sodden earth. 'This boat's too big for the boy to have rowed it alone.'

'It's small, for a jolly boat,' Fields replied. 'Little more than a dinghy. Four men, I would say, would usually row a boat this size.'

'Do you think one large man, a strong man, might manage it? Against the river, if it came here from its ship.'

Fields rubbed again at his arm. 'A strong one, perhaps.'

'The man who killed him, do you think?'

Fields merely shrugged, saying nothing.

Moving closer to the body, Harry inspected the depression made in the skull, putting his finger inside to test the shards surrounding the damage. Bits of bone fell into the cavity. Next, he studied the cranium, running his hand over its fissures and sutures. He looked into the two dark spaces which once held the eyes. He pulled at the teeth.

He turned around to Sir Jonas. 'Was anything else found with this body?'

Sir Jonas produced a small leather bag, its strap broken. 'Only his pocket, taken from his waist. Nothing else was inside the boat. To sink it, it was holed, chopped into by a sword or a knife. When we lifted the body, nothing lay beneath. Then, we put him back as we found him. And waited for you.'

He threw the pocket at Harry across the short distance between them. Harry caught it deftly.

Knowing the Board of Ordnance's Surveyor-General had kept this body for him made Harry flush with pleasure.

He opened the pocket, largely intact despite its years of submersion. It still held some coins, and a small knife in a sheath, more like a letter-opening knife than any real kind of weapon.

The top of the knife's handle, which was capped with silver, had two letters engraved: *J. H.*

The coins were a mixture of English and French, along with some other tokens. None had a date later than 1644. Harry passed them to Fields, who studied them for some time, sorting them, making them into little piles in one hand, while scratching at the stubble on his head with the other.

'So! Another mystery for you, from the time of the Civil Wars,' Fields said. 'Who was this boy?'

'This was no boy, Colonel.'

○

THE THREE MEN removed the body from the boat, Fields and Sir Jonas following Harry's direction, and laid it on a groundsheet on a higher part of the little island, amid the tents. Grace waited there, looking resentful. The soldiers had crowded around her, but their conversation had been rebuffed. Sir Jonas kept her away from perusal of the body.

Harry cut at the uniform with a knife borrowed from the Colonel, to disturb the skeleton as little as possible. Even so, with little sinew or connecting tissue, the bones fell apart from each other. Harry rearranged them on the sheet as closely as possible to their original configuration, paying particular attention to the ribs. Some of the bones were missing, taken away by the action of the water while the boat had been submerged.

'Tell me why this was not a boy,' Sir Jonas demanded, once Harry was satisfied with the arrangement.

Still kneeling by the body, Harry drew their attention to the dome of the skull. 'These separate plates, the frontal bone, the parietal bone, the occipital, the sphenoid bones at each side, gradually come together with age. When we're young they're not fixed to each other, to allow our brains inside to grow.'

'These, conversely, are joined,' Sir Jonas said.

'But not so much as to show old age,' Harry said. 'I've observed many skeletons, helping Mr. Hooke in the rebuilding of churches. Their headstones tell us how long they lived. When cleared from their graves, the differences are apparent.'

He picked up the mandible and held it out to them. 'Look, also, at the teeth. His wisdom teeth are still present. But all his teeth are worn.'

Then he took a rib from the collapsed chest. 'Do you see its end, where once it joined the sternum? In a child, these rib-ends are smooth. This is rough, and jagged.'

Sir Jonas took the rib and inspected it, turning it this way and that. 'So, all together, these signs show us he was a fully grown man.'

'Fully grown! He is not even two feet tall!' Fields exclaimed.

'A dwarf, then,' Sir Jonas said, his face carefully blank.

'Most dwarves own limbs too short for their bodies, or bodies too short for their limbs,' Fields said. 'This man is like you or me, though reduced in size.'

'You concur he was a dwarf, Harry?' Sir Jonas asked.

'He was not a child, I know. My estimation is . . . he was of about thirty years or so.'

Sir Jonas replaced the rib. With an expression of dark amusement mixed with admiration, he considered the young man he had sent for.

'You know who he is,' Harry said.

'Your observations prove my suspicions. At least, to my satisfac—'

Fields broke in angrily. 'Why summon Harry to this inhospitable bog, to identify a dead dwarf, whose name you already know?'

Sir Jonas held up a placatory hand. 'Your knowledge of bones, Harry, shows he was adult. The soldier's uniform, the body's smallness, and the initials on the knife all told me this man was Jeffrey Hudson. As you guessed, Colonel Fields, he was an officer of Horse—a captain—for the King.'

Fields scoffed, making clear his doubts on Hudson ever deserving his rank.

'Do you know of him, Colonel?' Harry asked.

'I *did*,' Fields replied. 'He was the then-Queen's dwarf, presented to her in a pie, at some banquet or another. *Lord Minimus*, she called him.' He wrinkled his nose. 'Henrietta Maria's toy. A human toy. It lacks dignity.'

'He became her great favourite,' Sir Jonas said. 'Rarely leaving her side, even through the Wars.'

'Hence his being dressed up as a soldier, like a doll.'

'You do him injustice,' Sir Jonas said. 'When the Queen took him with her to the Netherlands, and then to France, seeking money for her husband's fight against Parliament, he proved himself a warrior. Hudson was an excellent horseman, and a better shot. In France, he killed a man in a duel. Charles Crofts, the brother of the Queen's Master of Horse. That man underestimated him, as do you, and insulted him. Hudson shot him through his heart.'

Harry stood up, wiping dark mud from his knees. 'I've also heard of Jeffrey Hudson, for I've seen his blue silk suit. A pair of his boots, too. They're part of Mr. Ashmole's knickknackatory at Oxford. I went there with Mr. Hooke. The suit of my memory would fit this man.'

After a long look out at the flatness of the land before them, he looked back at Sir Jonas. 'If you knew this to be Hudson, why should you ask me here? He's lain dead since the Wars. As many others do.'

'Quite right,' Fields agreed. 'The dead from those times constantly reveal themselves. Why the trouble over this one man? Even if he was the Queen's dwarf.'

Sir Jonas eyed the Colonel coolly. 'Duelling being frowned upon by the French, Hudson was sent home in disgrace. This was in the month of October, in forty-four. On his way across the Channel, he was captured by Barbary corsairs—pirates, no more, no less—then forced to serve with them at sea. Or so his story goes. He returned to England some ten years ago, his ransom paid by Government Scheme. He claims a pension from the King.'

Harry ran his fingers through his hair. 'You say Hudson's still alive?'

'Well, at least, a man who calls himself Jeffrey Hudson. He has resided in Hudson's house, at Oakham, in the County of Rutland, since his return.'

'A second dwarf, living as this one?' Fields's voice was full of wonder. 'A candidate for being the real Captain Hudson's murderer, surely.'

'The same thought occurred to me, Colonel.' Sir Jonas shifted uncomfortably. 'Also, there is more. He works for the Board of Ordnance—for me—as an Intelligencer.'

'Bringing you intelligence of what?' Harry asked.

'His knowledge of France is useful. He knows important people. Even men inside the French court. I thought it was from friendships made when there with the Queen. To keep up his pretence of being Hudson, he must have fooled them. As he fooled me.'

'He must have fooled the corsairs, too, if they released him through Government Scheme,' Fields said.

Sir Jonas smiled bleakly. 'That is some comfort to me, at least.'

'He must be questioned,' Harry said, even now not seeing why Sir Jonas had sent for him. 'To see if his story may be unpicked.'

'We are in full agreement, Harry.' Sir Jonas put his arm around Harry's back and pulled him to him. 'That is exactly what I want. Only, he has dis-appeared. I wish you to help me find him.'

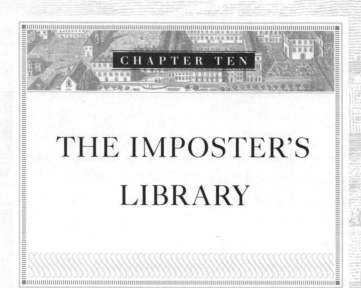

CHAPTER TEN

THE IMPOSTER'S LIBRARY

AFTER A NIGHT IN DENVER, WHERE they bought blankets and hired horses, the next day was spent riding towards Oakham. Near Stamford, as dusk fell, Fields found a place by a stream and under a tree to make camp. Harry, unused to riding, dismounted his horse with an aching back and a tailbone begging for mercy.

'*Blessed is he that shall eat bread in the Kingdom of God,*' Fields announced, sitting close to their fire, before a meal of a loaf and an unlucky rabbit they had found on the road, dropped by a fox at their approach. While they ate, Fields regaled them with his wartime exploits. In the bright moonlight, his eyes and teeth flashed silver as he spoke. After telling of the west country, and Worcester, and his travels to Ireland, he told them of his friend John Lilburne, known as Freeborn John the Leveller, who opposed Charles I, and then Oliver Cromwell.

'I visited him in Dover Castle, when he was imprisoned there,' Fields said, swallowing the last of the rabbit and reaching for his tobacco. 'His resolve was unbending, as he opposed Cromwell not for his own sake, but for the people's.' Fields pointed his pipe at Harry. '*I know nothing that makes a man a magistrate over me but law, and while he walks by the rules of that law which make him a magistrate, I shall own him as a magistrate, but when he tramples it under his feet, and walks by the law of his own will, I for my part cannot own him for a magistrate.*'

'Why do you point your pipe at me?' Harry asked, resentfully.

'Well,' Fields replied, 'you must concede, you jumped quickly to assist Sir Jonas. Do not serve as the stairs by which others reach their honour.'

'I serve in return for payment, as most men do. I worked for the Royal Society until Sir Jonas presented a more generous offer.'

Fields blew a derisive plume of pipe smoke behind him, over his shoulder.

Taunted by the gesture, Harry felt his temper rising. 'You soldiered, so can hardly pretend to have been your own man.'

'By my consent. Willingly given. Certainly not for reward, as often I went without pay.' Fields lowered his pipe. 'We are tired. I am tired. I meant not to cause offence. Let us sleep. We shall be less tetchy in the morning.'

Grace pulled the last of her meat from its bone with her teeth, and it tore away in sticky strands. 'I agree with Michael. You, Harry, are too keen to impress those above you. And too sensitive when they disagree with you. Or, as the Fellows did, when they tease you.'

Harry tightened his jaw. Fields was right: he was tired, and he did not wish to say anything to Grace, or to either of them, which he might later regret. 'You still feel hurt by Sir Jonas refusing to let you see the body. Let us sleep, as the Colonel says, and be less disagreeable when we wake.'

'I am disagreeable?'

'No, I mean we disagree—'

'We do. For I am not hurt, even slightly, by Sir Jonas keeping me away from your dead man. Why should I be? Every day, I am dismissed and condescended to because of the limitations placed upon my sex. I am well accustomed to it, so whyever should I be hurt?'

'Because you're dressed as a man, you expect to be treated as one. But you're a girl.'

She threw down the rabbit's bone. 'Because *you* dress as a man, you expect to be treated as one. But you are a boy.'

Harry had not dared ask the question, but by now he was in the mood to do so. 'Who loans you those clothes you wear?'

It was as he had feared. 'Why, my very good friend Denis Papin,' Grace replied.

●

THE COLD HAD breached his blanket and worked itself into his core. He had hoped to seek warmth from Grace, but when they settled for the night she had been careful to place herself to the other side of the Colonel.

Now, she rode ahead. In the light of morning, in her mannish clothes—Denis Papin's clothes—she looked nothing like the famous Mr. Robert Hooke's niece: expensively educated, and an object of speculation for various gentlemen of London. Some of whom held hopes.

It was hardly his fault Sir Jonas had insisted on keeping her back, Harry thought. He would have welcomed her observations on the dwarf's skeleton.

But she was a distraction, he decided, from his search for the man calling himself Jeffrey Hudson.

They met a snowy-white drove of geese coming towards them, on their way to London, driven by only two men. There must have been at least a thousand birds; the noise of wings and beaks was piercing. The horses became frightened, Grace's made especially twitchy. She had to dismount, walking beside it to calm it, pulling hard on its reins to steady it.

Reaching Oakham—Harry still wondering if he was driver or goose—Fields, whistling cheerfully, led them through the town. Invigorated by his night's sleep and being back on a horse, he turned in his saddle and winked at Harry. 'So! Let us find the home of Jeffrey Hudson.'

They clopped past All Saints' church, which towered over the other buildings of the town.

By the Buttercross, a woman directed them back to the High Street, to a surprisingly large cottage facing directly onto the road. Its thatch looked to be recent, all the paint was clean, and pansies in vases brightened up the windows.

They dismounted and tied their horses to the halter post.

At Harry's knock, the door was opened by an elderly woman, who despite her years stood perfectly vertical and was as neat as the cottage she kept. Her hair was hidden under an old-fashioned coif, severe-looking and tight to her skull. The only sign of dishevelment was the pinkness of her eyes; she looked as if they had disturbed her crying.

Harry showed a letter, signed by Sir Jonas, identifying him as being with the Board of Ordnance. He was vague about the two others with him, hoping she would assume the letter covered them, too.

'You wish to find one of your own,' she said. She led them inside, the front door leading immediately into a plainly furnished dining room.

She told them she was Mrs. Leach, Captain Hudson's housekeeper. 'Your journey here is wasted, for the Captain is gone.'

'Where has he gone?' Fields asked, surprisingly brusque, Harry thought, in his manner towards her. She flinched away from the large bald man with a scar around his head and a wound which had taken half his ear.

'Did he say where he was leaving for?' Harry asked her more mildly, looking warningly at Fields.

'He did not.' As he had brought the Colonel with him, she was frosty, too, with Harry.

'Have you worked for Captain Hudson for long?'

'Ten years, or thereabouts. Since the death of my husband.' Although a housekeeper, she had the manner of speaking belonging to a well-educated gentlewoman. Harry guessed at a widow's reduction of her circumstances, dependent on her marriage.

'Ten years? Just after his release from the Barbary pirates.'

'Soon afterwards,' she agreed.

'Did you know him before?'

She looked at Harry with a measuring eye. This young man did not look typical of the Board. The Captain's visitors had tended to be rougher, more like the Colonel. 'We grew up together, here in Oakham. His small-ness made him famous in our town. Now we are more famous for being where Titus Oates was born.'

'The Saviour of the Nation,' Harry said unguardedly, his tone betraying his distaste.

'You are out of step with the prevailing view,' she stated, not requiring confirmation of his.

This was dangerous ground, which Grace guided them from. 'You knew Jeffrey Hudson as a boy, Mrs. Leach,' she said, brightly.

'I was a little younger, but knew him well, until he left with the Queen.'

'He exchanged one form of servitude for another,' Fields said, looking triumphantly at Harry.

'You equate serving the Queen with being taken by pirates?' Harry said, needled by the sly allusion to the previous night's conversation.

'Did he seem much changed upon his return?' Grace asked gently, feel-ing the need to step between them.

Mrs. Leach's eyes gleamed, seeing in Grace a sympathy towards her lacking from the men. 'Come through, to the library.'

She took them into a long, narrow room. Books lined its walls on both sides. A desk stood at the end furthest from them, its chair facing the door they had come through. The highest shelf was at the height of Harry's chest. There was also a stool, solid enough to stand on.

'The Captain is . . .' Grace paused, seeking the words. '. . . *very* short, isn't he?'

'You soon cease to notice,' Mrs. Leach said, managing a smile. 'He is so interesting a man, with such a pleasant manner, it becomes the least aspect of him.' She looked pointedly at Fields.

'How tall is he?' Grace asked her.

'Well . . .' She went to a shelf, and showed its height. 'I would say, up to here.'

Harry looked at the distance from the floor. 'About three and a half feet tall.' The dead man in the boat had been far shorter, not even two feet tall. Tiny, by comparison. 'I heard he was shorter.'

'The strange thing is, he used to be.' The housekeeper had begun to thaw a little towards Harry. 'He grew when he was away. He said it was from the change of his diet, from rich to plain. Plain eating is a habit he has kept to ever since. When with the corsairs, he almost doubled in height. A fact which greatly pleased him.'

As she spoke, Harry walked the room's length, studying the books, until he reached the desk. Many of the books were French. All of them, he realized, were systematically and laboriously ordered. A library, he had read, had to have order as an army needs order, otherwise it did not deserve the name.

Without order, a palace is merely a heap of bricks and stones.

At this end of the library were Hudson's theological books, bibles and biblical studies, various commentaries from scholastics and historians, then heretics and heresies. Next to all this theology were books devoted to physic, then to jurisprudence, and, on a lower shelf, to mathematics. The next books were devoted to humanity. Here, as all the sections did, the books started with the most universal and then the most ancient. Harry saw classical texts, and histories of ancient times, and moved through time to recent affairs—especially, he noticed, those of France: its religious disputes, its monarchy, and its prominent politicians, including the Cardinals Richelieu and Mazarin.

Philosophy began with Hermes Trismegistus, went through Plato, Aristotle, to Lullius, and finished with Bacon, Gilbert, and Gassendi. There were also books on philology, on languages ancient and new.

Up above all these books were manuscripts, bundled together. Again,

Harry saw, by order of subject rather than author, organized as meticulously as the books, kept higher up to avoid damage.

'The Captain is a bibliophile, as you can see,' Mrs. Leach said.

'Was he always a reader?' Harry asked.

'After his return from captivity, he was a changed man. Who would not be? He had been held by pirates for a quarter of a century. He wanted only a quiet life, one free from trouble and danger. His love of reading was a part of that, I think.'

'So, not a reader as a boy,' Fields said.

'Not bookish at all, as I remember.'

'The books are beautifully kept,' Grace said. 'All dusted, and oiled.'

'I always enjoyed assisting him with his library.'

'Is it you who arranges these books so meticulously?' Harry asked.

'Oh, no,' Mrs. Leach laughed. 'I follow the Captain's instructions, though we have had many an enjoyable talk as to how a book should best be placed.'

Her smile changed rapidly to a frown. She had seen something by the window, which had a cushioned seat across its width. She picked up a book from the seat, and returned it to its place, pushing it back into position.

Fields looked about him, at the library's order and homeliness. 'Did Hudson find here the quiet life he wished for?'

Mrs. Leach paused. 'He did.'

Fields suddenly looked emotional, as if keeping back tears. He missed his new home in Half Moon Alley, and Elizabeth Hannam, Harry realized.

Mrs. Leach, too, looked as if she would cry again. 'Until recently, I should say, he did. Apart from his reading, which he did there'—she pointed to the window seat—'and his walks, which he liked to do about the town, and his letters, which he wrote at his desk, and the eating of his plain meals with me in the kitchen, it was always quiet. We liked routine. We both found some comfort in it.'

She fell silent. There was an obvious closeness between housekeeper and master. Far more than between most employees and their employers, Harry thought.

Grace reached out to stroke Mrs. Leach's hand, which was blotched and lined with blue veins. The skin had lost its stretch, so it moved and sagged under her touch.

Mrs. Leach looked at her sadly. 'Always quiet, until some Frenchmen came to stay. Three of them. A week ago, yesterday.'

'Frenchmen?'

They said their names were Verdier, Boilot, and the third was Chasse. They caused the Captain great disquiet.'

'How so?' Grace asked her.

'They brought with them strange luggage.' Mrs. Leach caught Harry's enquiring look. 'I did not see, as it was all kept in the outhouse, under cover. They would not tell the Captain what it was. They warned him from the subject when he asked. Chasse even took and kept the key to our outhouse. A bully, that man. Whatever the luggage was, it was bulky. And heavy. When they took it away, it left great marks upon the ground.'

'How did these men come to be here?' Harry asked.

'On the Board of Ordnance's instructions, I presumed.' She looked at both men dubiously.

'That may explain why Hudson should tolerate such affront, in his own house,' Fields said.

'I thought that, being from the Board, you would know.' Mrs. Leach suddenly stopped, and pinched the sides of her nose together, until she regained control of herself. 'Their leader, Chasse, was strange-looking.'

They all looked at her quizzically.

'He had one long eyebrow, which stretched across his forehead. He was hairy. As if his skin repelled a razor.'

Harry felt his skin prickling. The description was familiar.

'Oh, another man came, too,' she remembered. 'Tall. Thin. He wore a purple cloak. He was English. I never caught his name. When they were gone, the Captain went soon after, but left no word behind him. He was careful not to. He made a fire in the garden of his letters.'

'Incriminating letters, no doubt,' Fields said.

'You have no notion where he is now?' Grace asked.

'Nor whether he is alive or dead.' The old lady's resolve finally broke. Her shoulders shook, and tears came. She put her head on Grace's shoulder. 'Why do you dress as a man, my dear?' she said. 'You are such a pretty thing.'

Grace smiled at her. 'On the road, it is easier. It keeps away unwanted attention.'

'Really? I knew as soon as I saw you.'

'Would you show us where the Frenchmen kept this luggage?' Harry asked her.

Still sniffling, Mrs. Leach led the way from the library, to take them through the cottage to the outhouse.

As the others followed on—Grace tutting at his insensitivity as she went past him—Harry went to the shelf to see which book the housekeeper had replaced so surreptitiously.

He called after Mrs. Leach. '*Ordo est maxime qui memoriae lumen adfert.*'

'It is order that gives light to memory,' she translated, for the Colonel's benefit, whose expression betrayed he had little Latin. 'You know your Cicero, Mr. Hunt?'

'Some,' Harry replied.

○

HAVING INSPECTED THE scars where the outhouse's cobbles had been gouged by metal—the marks showed several heavy bags or bundles—they said their goodbyes to Mrs. Leach.

'Did you find our visit useful, Harry?' Fields asked, leading his horse along the High Street, looking for somewhere to eat.

Absorbed in remembering the conversation with the housekeeper, and thinking on Captain Hudson's library, the question confused Harry. He took a moment to reply. 'When I saw the books, I recognized the system of their placement. Hudson—or, rather, the man who pretends to be him—orders his library following the method of Gabriel Naudé. Naudé was Cardinal

Richelieu's librarian, and afterwards Cardinal Mazarin's, working to build up his great collection, now kept at the Bibliothèque Mazarine, in Paris.'

'You are knowledgeable upon books, Harry, I give you that,' Fields said, yawning into his horse's neck, and wondering why Harry, usually discreet with the store of information in that retentive brain of his, was telling them about a French librarian. Should he not be more interested in the luggage Mrs. Leach had spoken of, and the Frenchmen who transported it?

'I know of Naudé,' Harry continued, missing Fields's waning interest, 'as I have read his book *Advis pour dresser une bibliothèque*, translated by Mr. Evelyn, a Royal Society Fellow, called by him *Instructions Concerning Erecting of a Library.*' Feeling suddenly exhausted, Harry rubbed his face with his hands. '*Ordo est maxime qui memoriae lumen adfert*, I said, and Mrs. Leach asked if I knew my Cicero. But it was from *Instructions Concerning Erecting of a Library* I knew the phrase. Naudé quotes Cicero, and Mr. Evelyn leaves it in the Latin.'

Both Fields and Grace were looking at Harry, wondering what was to come. Harry gave a wry smile, recognising he had led them an orthogonal way to his point. 'It was *Advis pour dresser une bibliothèque* Mrs. Leach replaced when we were in the library. Sir Jeffrey had been reading it by the window.'

Fields looked less than impressed. 'You think the leaving of that book on the window seat to be significant.'

Grace pulled at her horse, a nervous creature still giving her trouble. 'Would you not read equal significance into any book out of its place?'

'Possibly,' Harry conceded. 'But it follows after a pattern.'

'Perhaps there was no time to replace the book, having to leave quickly,' Grace suggested. 'Or Hudson took something from it, then left the book behind.'

'What would he take from it?' Harry asked her.

Grace frowned. 'A note? A list? A name? Who knows?'

'I had an idea,' Fields announced. 'Both of you are clever in ways I am not, so I take no offence if you dismiss it. We have clung to the notion that the skeleton is Jeffrey Hudson, and the living man the impostor. Perhaps, instead, the man known as Hudson has every right to the name. Perhaps the other was killed *because* he was an impostor.'

'But if Jeffrey Hudson lived in his own house straightforwardly, then why should he run when the dead dwarf was discovered?' Harry asked.

'Well, my thought is, Hudson murdered him. He fears being found out for his crime.'

Grace stopped, her horse stopping with her. Fields and Harry halted, too. 'Mrs. Leach said the Captain had changed,' she said. 'Even that he had grown taller when he was away. She was observant enough to see through my disguise straightaway. She knows full well he is not the same man.'

'You seem taken with the idea,' Harry said.

'I think she prefers the new to the old, is all.'

Fields took out his pipe. 'You do anything for love. You accept anything, too.' He pointed towards an inn. They could smell pork and potatoes being roasted. 'We are left with the question: Where is the Jeffrey Hudson we seek? Whether he be the first Jeffrey Hudson, or no?'

'Who are these Frenchmen?' Harry said. 'What did they carry with them?'

'And who is the tall, thin man, in the purple cloak?' Grace added.

All silently agreed that here was where they should eat, they tied their horses by a hedge of blackberry bramble outside the inn. 'Hudson escaped from France after his duel,' Harry thought aloud as they did so. '*The Incassable*, a French ship, presumably, as it has a French name. The library, containing French books, arranged as a Frenchman, Gabriel Naudé, saw fit. Books about France, and Cardinal Mazarin, the man Naudé worked for in Paris. A copy of *Advis pour dresser une bibliothèque* left upon the window seat. The three Frenchmen with whatever was in their luggage. Sir Jonas told us Captain Hudson traded intelligence on the French. I wonder, therefore, if he has gone to France.'

'This is thin, is it not?' Fields said. 'Mr. Hooke would never consider it proof.'

'I no longer work for Mr. Hooke,' Harry pointed out.

Fields raised his hands as if surrendering. 'So! What next?'

'The nearest port's King's Lynn. If the living Hudson has fled the country, perhaps to go to France, we may find news of him there.'

'The dead one must have come from there to reach the Denver Sluice,' Grace said. 'He came along the river.'

Harry looked at her gratefully. 'We can ask more about the dead Hudson, too.'

'You will not find anything after so many years,' Fields said, rubbing dolefully at the skin where the top of his ear used to be.

The Colonel's pessimism seemed out of character. Harry looked at the old man and sighed, suddenly realising that that was what Fields was: an old man. Although still fit for his age, Fields had a lifetime of experience, much of it harsh. He had been battered by the Wars, which often replayed in his mind.

'You do not have to come,' Harry said. 'You could return to London.'

Fields was silent, deep in thought for a while.

Harry turned to Grace, who was picking at a chestnut on her horse's foreleg, which had become entangled with some bramble. 'Shall you come with me?'

Grace smiled at him. 'Willingly.'

It was like the sun had broken through cloud. Harry felt immediately elated, although sometimes he could not keep up with her, or predict her moods. She had obviously forgiven him for whatever had upset her, or at least she had put it aside. Questioning Mrs. Leach must have cheered her.

'Forgive me,' Fields said, pleased his companions were friendly again. 'I do not mean to be so gloomy. My age, I think, and I am away from Elizabeth. Of course I shall come with you, Harry. And I shall endeavour to be more helpful to you.'

CHAPTER ELEVEN

THE HANSA KONTOR

TWO DAYS LATER, HAVING TAKEN THE old Roman road from Water New-ton along the Fen causeway, with another night's camp near March, they approached King's Lynn. Harry was becoming more used to riding such distances. The aches in his back and his thighs had eased, and the motion of his horse he now found comforting rather than alarming.

It was still unseasonably cold. Frost made the road slippery for their horses. Grace's had gone lame on the second morning. She shared Harry's saddle, sitting in front of him. Harry reacted to their proximity; there was no way of hiding it, but she made no mention of it. From time to time Fields grinned mischievously at them, but did not tease them further.

Even with Grace so close, though, the seemingly endless Fens still un-settled Harry, with their flatness and open skies.

When they passed through its South Gate, they could see King's Lynn was a town of well-maintained streets, medieval merchants' houses, guild-halls, warehouses, and a large market square. The place hummed with trade. Harry felt himself relax. It was a little-London, he thought, more homely than the rough camps, the intimidating skies, or the rural small-ness of Oakham. Or even Cambridge and its Colleges, their high walls and stout gates separating them from the town.

They could ask at the port about *The Incassable*. How long had it been since it plied its trade with the town? Would anyone remember its visit in 1644, bringing the hapless Jeffrey Hudson with it? Harry still thought it was the real Hudson left dead in its jolly boat at the Denver Sluice.

Finding their way to the port was a straightforward mission, not need-ing Colonel Fields to lead them, as ships' masts extended over the rooftops of every building except the church of St. Margaret, whose stone shone a rich yellow in the late-afternoon light. Its three square and castellated tow-ers made it look more like a fortress.

When they got to the quayside, the wind was harsh, unleashed at them from the northeast, stinging as if it peeled off a layer of skin. Puddles of ice waited for the unwary. There was little space in between the goods being unloaded from the merchant ships to find any shelter. Sacks and boxes, bar-rels as tall as a man, and bundles covered with canvas and roped secure were hefted by harassed-looking porters.

Many kinds of ship harboured there. A Dutch *fluyt* disgorged lengths of timber, swinging them out on a crane. An argosy had barrels of wine, its crew changing them with impressive speed for wool. A brig brought coal down the coast from Newcastle. A barque, being loaded with grain grown on the reclaimed Fenland. A graceful *chebec*—so called according to Fields, Harry not knowing the type—had a crew with dark skins and full beards and wearing headcloths. They made Harry think of Hudson being taken by the corsairs of North Africa, before coming back a changed man.

Jostling for space were the smaller ships: lighters and flyboats, and two-masted ketches, and hog boats offloading herring.

Harry wanted an office where he could ask about *The Incassable*. Fields, he knew, always comfortable in his own skin, would have been deep in conversation by now if he had not been letting Harry lead the way. Harry was aware, too, of Grace becoming impatient, so he discourteously broke into a conversation between a dark-suited man—possibly a merchant, whose way of standing thrusted his hips forward as if relieving himself—and a man who must have been the oldest person there on the quayside.

The old man, under a hat as broad as an umbrella, looked at Harry with rheumy eyes, but carried on with his talk.

Fields stood straighter and gave a quiet cough; all it took to silence the man.

'I wonder, do you know of a ship called *The Incassable?*' Fields asked.

Harry wondered if he should be annoyed by Fields's interference, or grateful.

'*Incassable,*' the old man said, a string of spittle at the corner of his mouth. The dark-suited man with him smirked.

'Yes, I think that's how it's said,' Fields replied. 'A French ship.'

'*Incassable.*' The man sucked air through his few remaining teeth. 'Not *The Incassable.* Just, *Incassable.*'

'You know it?'

'Knew it. A pretty while ago.' He scratched his chin. 'Ask at the Kontor. It was an 'Ansa ship.' He pointed back along the quayside, the way they had come, then jabbed his finger to the left.

HARRY AND GRACE fell in behind Fields, striding off towards the lane the old man had shown them. A short distance up was a long, low timber-framed warehouse. In front stood a line of handcarts, loaded with goods either coming or going from the quay.

Once inside, having confirmed it was the Kontor of the Hanseatic League, they were shown to a smoky office, to find a man absorbed by hefty ledgers shelved behind his desk. He would grab a ledger, scribble a few hurried words, consult a very long list, then move back to the shelves for another. If it were not for the pipe he puffed on, he could easily have been mistaken for an automaton.

Harry coughed loudly, emulating Fields. The man put up his hand to make him wait, then changed his mind. He pushed his ledger back into its space.

'Sorry. Once you starts it's difficult to stops.' The clerk was dark-haired and pasty faced. Wrinkled pouches sagged under his eyes.

'We look for *The Inc* . . . we'd like information about a ship named *Incassable.*'

'French. Old,' the man replied, his eyes blinking from the act of recall. 'Not strictly a Hanseatic League ship—is that why you comes here? But these things are . . .' He made an oscillating motion with his hand. 'We hired her. Or parts of her, I should says. To take our cargoes. Funny ship. Odd looking. Two masted. Rigged like a lugger, but her hull like a schooner. Bit ungainly, to my mind. Fast, all the same. Went all over. Sweden. Denmark. Scotland. Ireland. Dutch Republic. Spainish Netherlands. France, obviously. Spainish Kingdoms. Galicia. Portugal. All the way down to the Sharifate of Marrakesh.' He took a great suck from the pipe. 'Tenerife . . .'

'So, when was this?' Harry broke in.

The man closed his eyes. 'From August of twenty-seven . . . and the last time . . .' He tapped his lips with his forefinger. '. . . February of sixty-six.'

'You need not check your ledgers?' Harry was amazed.

The man chuckled at him. 'You's more impressed than you shoulds be. I could leaves you so. No, no, I shan't. I recalls it, because we first used her at the time of the La Rochelle seige. O' course, I wasn't here then. My father dids the job before me. He made me reads the old stuff. We last used her in the wars with the Dutch.'

'What happened to her?'

'The English Navy captured her, mistaking her to be Dutch. Representations was made.' He sniffed. 'By the League, whose cargoes she carried, and by her French owners. She was used as a fireship, as part of Sir Robert Holmes's bonfire, the following August—his raid on the Netherlands. Hundred and forty ships sets aflame. A glorious end to her, I s'poses.'

Harry turned to Grace, who raised her chin at him. Sir Robert Holmes, now the Isle of Wight's Governor, had courted her. Her uncle had tried to broker a marriage, but she had refused them both.

Harry returned his attention to the clerk. 'Do you remember *Incassable* coming to King's Lynn during the Civil Wars?'

'I does. Trade don't stops because of local difficulties.' He saw Harry's look of ignorance. 'At first, King's Lynn was for Parliament, but changed sides. Parliament cames to capture the town. Besieged for three weeks, before it surrendered. Even so, goods was smuggled in.'

'But not for the benefit of the town, nor its people,' Fields spoke up.

The clerk looked uncomfortable. 'Trade must goes on. *Some* was for the town.'

'For those rich enough to afford your prices—which were stiff, no doubt.' Fields looked rattled, and Grace put her hand on his arm to calm him.

'Was the ship here, in King's Lynn, in October of 1644?' Harry asked.

'Now I *wills* have to look.' The man winked, glad of Harry's intervention. He shot back from his desk, and his arm went straight up to a ledger high on the shelving. He brought it down just as rapidly, giving the leather a wipe. 'October forty-four?'

They watched his finger slide down the hundreds of entries, of cargoes received and delivered.

'Yes,' he affirmed abruptly. 'Tobacco. And indigo, it says here. Leaves from Le Havre. Not much else I can tells you. I bet she hads Huguenots, too, but that cargo's not recorded. The captain's name is, though. Capitaine Eugène de Beauchene. Retired now, I believes, and lives in Paris. Not a well man, I hears.'

The clerk shrugged apologetically, feeling he had been helpful enough. 'I needs to get on. There's one man in King's Lynn can helps you. Old Japhia Bennett. His noddle's not what it was, but he served on *Incassable*. Asks about at the quayside.'

As they made their way back from the Kontor, they failed to notice a tall muscular man with black skin peel himself from the wall behind them, and follow.

CHAPTER TWELVE

THE ANCIENT
SAILOR

ALONG THE QUAYSIDE, THEY ASKED FOR the whereabouts of Japhia Bennett. The porters, suspicious of strangers, offered only silence and hard stares. As they were about to give up, an old soldier sitting on a low wall, his wooden leg placed awkwardly before him, indicated a tavern.

Fields pointed to Harry's purse. *'Deliver the poor and needy: rid them out of the hand of the wicked.'*

To the soldier's amazement, Harry gave him a silver sixpence, having nothing smaller.

The Turk's Head stood on the waterfront, its walls badly weathered by salt. Inside, it stank of tobacco, a fug of smoke clinging to the ceiling. The owner behind his serving bench wiped invisible specks from its surface. None of his customers looked away from their conversations, or from their drinks.

'They are wary of being pressed,' Fields said. 'You can understand why we are not welcome.' He stood directly in front of the owner and leaned in towards him until their noses almost touched. The man had no choice but to look up from his wiping.

'We seek Japhia Bennett,' Fields told him. 'Like me, he is too old to serve at sea.'

On seeing the Colonel's age, his battered face, and his reduced ear, the man became braver, and belligerent. 'You're not of King's Lynn.'

Fields growled.

Harry, thinking a less confrontational approach would yield better results, and a more pleasant atmosphere between them all, gently placed his hand on Fields's forearm. 'We need intelligence, nothing more,' he told the owner. 'Bennett may help us with a ship which used to trade here.'

The owner neatly folded his cloth, put it on the bench, and stared dumbly at them. Grace eased aside the two men with her and presented him with another sixpence, which did not immediately disappear; the man was as surprised as Harry and Fields at the bribe's generosity.

'Down to the river, go north beyond St. Nicholas.' The man was suddenly eager to please. 'You'll see all the fishing boats. Look for one called *Rediviva*. It's a dogger, if you know the type. Bluff-bowed, wide-beamed. Two masts. One long, and one short.'

●

SALTING AND SMOKING took place along this stretch of the Ouse's bank. The smell stuck to the inside of Harry's throat. Their passage along the quayside was slowed by having to negotiate nets, either rolled up tightly or spread out for repair. More nets extended from drying sheds, spilling out as if retched, hung high enough so Harry, the Colonel, and Grace could walk beneath them. They had to avoid all the other detritus from the fishing fleet: the barrels and boxes, lines, and traps

Asking for *Rediviva*, they were directed northwards, to the fleet's far periphery.

At last, they found her. Rimed with salt, her paint was chipped and bubbled, clinging despairingly to the wood. There was no one on the deck, but the smell of pine tar and the sound of hammering led them around her, to where an old man worked on her dory. The man caulked her hull, hammering oakum into the timbers to make them tight.

When he saw them, he paused his mallet in midair. It was the ancient rheumy-eyed man who had directed them to the Hanseatic League's Kontor.

Now bareheaded, his vast hat beside him, his hair was a messy frizz of grey. He smiled toothlessly at them. 'You've learned more of *Incassable*?'

Harry nodded at him, suppressing his annoyance at the old man's game. 'We were told you served as one of her crew. We're interested in the wartime, and a man who took passage aboard her.'

Bennett placed his mallet next to his tar pot, and stood up, stretching his old back. He stepped around the boat, and shook Harry's hand, his handshake strong but unsteady. He shook the Colonel's, too, more reluctantly Harry thought, but when he got to Grace, he took her by her wrist and kissed the back of her hand. 'You dress as a man, to escape the accident of your sex. I've known other such women as you, serving at sea, with us men. Many our equal, needing no special consideration.'

Grace reclaimed her hand from his grasp, smiling at his open admiration. The old sailor's expression darkened as he turned back to Harry. 'You bring up matters better left forgotten.'

'This matter returns itself,' Harry said. 'A visitor from the past. Have you heard of Captain Jeffrey Hudson? We think he returned from France on *Incassable*, in October of 1644. From Le Havre.'

Bennett looked blankly at him. ''Udson? I don't recollect . . .'

'A dwarf,' Fields cut in sharply. 'The Queen's creature. Like a witch's familiar.'

Bennett visibly relaxed. 'You hold no affection for that Queen, then? You for Parliament? Our views coincide, then. I thought you a King's man.'

'I served alongside Cromwell himself,' Fields growled. 'Why would you take me to be Royalist?'

'I'm mistaken, as often I am, nowadays. I should've guessed from your scarf.' He picked up some hemp and dropped it into his pan, pushing it around in the thick tar. 'It was a busy time. I saw many people, and've forgotten most. But I do recall a dwarf. I've no idea of 'is name. I remember, 'cause it was curious to see one so small dressed as a soldier.'

'What size was he?' Harry asked.

Bennett looked confused. ''E was a dwarf. Short, as required.'

'How short? Exactly? It might be important.'

'Tiny. But not misshapen, as some are. Just like you or I, but reduced, as if seen from far away. No taller than two feet, I'd say. Per'aps even smaller.' Bennett took the tar-soaked length of hemp and placed it against the clinkered planking of the dory.

'I remember the taking of the jolly boat,' he continued. 'It was the smallest of *Incassable*'s boats, which 'ad three. Even so, its stealing was a grave crime against the crew.'

'Hudson couldn't have taken it on its own,' Harry said. 'It's too big for someone so small to manage.'

'I don't remember others being with 'im, if that's what you ask me.'

'Could one other have rowed it, or must there have been more?'

Bennett looked past them, up towards the quayside. 'One could do it, I reckon, if tall enough and strong enough.'

Harry looked significantly at Fields. 'As we discussed at the Denver Sluice.'

Fields grunted. 'One perhaps, but more likely others with him.'

Bennett picked up his mallet, and pointed with it. 'Who's 'e who watches you? That African upon the quayside?'

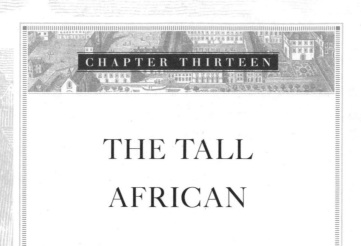

CHAPTER THIRTEEN

THE TALL AFRICAN

THE MAN SEEMED COMPLETELY AT EASE. What threat could they pose to him? Harry was young, and certainly no fighter. Fields, although he had been a soldier, would be no match for him, as he was tall, muscular, and in the prime of life. Grace, spirited as she was, was a young woman.

Harry's assessment made him see how vulnerable they were, travelling about the country with only the Board of Ordnance's authority to protect them. Against any real trouble, they were defenceless.

Mrs. Leach had mentioned a fourth man, tall and thin. This man watching them was tall and thin, but would she not have mentioned his skin? It showed clearly he was African.

At first, Harry thought him a crewmember of the chebec at the quayside, but when viewed more closely he seemed less like a sailor. His clothes were expensive, and seemed to constitute a uniform: a turquoise-coloured waistcoat over a crisp white shirt, turquoise breeches, and black shoes, highly polished. Despite the cold, he wore no coat or hat. He kept his hair close-cropped to his skull. He had fine features, and his skin was a shiny purplish brown, darker than any other African Harry had seen in London.

The man made no move, antagonistic or otherwise. Even so, walking towards him, and away from Bennett, Harry instinctively went ahead of Grace. Fields, his breath steaming, could not keep up on the slippery shale. There was a high step, timber overgrown with grass, from the beach to the level of the road. Harry pulled himself up using a mooring post. He turned to help Grace, then turned quickly back when he heard the man move forwards.

The African grinned at his panicked reaction. He extended his arm for Grace, who accepted it. Together, they waited, and helped Fields climb the same step.

'I am Mustapha,' the man said. 'My mistress wishes to meet with you.'

Harry shook Mustapha's offered hand. The skin was soft. Not a labouring man. Certainly not a sailor. 'Your mistress?'

'The Duchesse de Mazarin.'

Harry gazed at him inanely, astonished. The King had introduced him to the Duchesse at Whitehall Palace, when Harry searched for the murderer who drained boys of their blood. 'I'm busy, here in King's Lynn, for the Board of Ordnance,' he said, after recovering himself.

'She already knows this.' Seeing Harry's continued confusion, Mustapha explained further. 'The King told her.'

Sir Jonas must have informed the King. The finding of Hudson's body, and his impersonator's disappearance, must be important enough to do so.

'It might be some time before I return to London,' Harry said.

Mustapha grinned again. 'That is why she is here, in King's Lynn, to meet with you.'

CHAPTER FOURTEEN

THE BEAUTIFUL

DUCHESSE

AT THE GLOBE, BACK IN KING'S Lynn's market square, they waited in the parlour of the suite of rooms occupied by Hortense Mancini, the Duchesse de Mazarin. Outside, icicles hung down from the eaves, their ends dripping meltwater. Between their shafts the busy market could be seen, distorted and splintered through the frosted windowpanes. Inside, sea coal crackled in the fire basket, flames popping smuts over the hearth.

Mustapha tended the fire, flicking more coals on with his fingers, and prodding them languidly with an iron.

The Duchesse entered from what Harry could see was a bedroom. She left the door open wide, revealing bedclothes left tangled as she had kicked them back. Clothes, tried on, then discarded, were dumped carelessly around the room. A table had playing cards splayed over it, and little piles of money, and empty bottles and wineglasses not yet cleared away.

The clothes she had eventually chosen were simple and mannish. Trousers, a waistcoat, a demure blouse buttoned high on her throat. All elegantly cut to fit a lean and athletic body. Grace, wearing Denis Papin's clothes, appeared lumpish by comparison.

She was as Harry remembered from when he last saw her: spectacular. She had a flawless complexion, high cheekbones, eyes with pupils almost completely black, and a wide, shapely mouth. Men had fought duels just to own one of her portraits: she had been painted as Cleopatra, as Aphrodite, as Diana, and was displayed in palaces, castles, and great houses throughout Europe.

Harry coughed to clear his throat, which he found was dry and scratchy. Grace narrowed her eyes at him.

'Harry!' The Duchesse's voice was deep. Also, it was playful and confident. As if they were just her toys, and could be made to do her bidding. Her Italian accent savoured the vowel and rolled the double R, making the commonplace exotic. *Haarrry.*

'Your Grace,' Harry said, his gaze involuntarily going down to the floor as he spoke.

'Hortense, if you please. To call me otherwise places a distance between us, which need never be there.'

To Harry's amazement, she went towards him and without preamble kissed him on both cheeks. She turned and kissed Fields, too. 'Colonel Fields.' Her saying his name stretched it to an extraordinary length: *Feeeyalds.* 'You have the King's respect, even though you fought against his father.'

The Colonel muttered an incomprehensible greeting. Harry smiled at him, amused by the old man's uncertainty, mirroring his own.

'And who is this?' Hortense inspected Grace. 'Gorgeous, whoever you are, though you do your best to hide it. I have seen you before, when walking in St. James's Park.' She stroked Grace's cheek with the back of her fingers, then led her to the sofa facing the fire. '*Veerrry* beautiful. We all remarked upon it.'

'I am Grace Hooke.' Grace sounded haughty, trying hard not to be flattered by the Duchesse's attentions. Sitting as elegantly as deportment lessons had taught her, she did not ask who had done the remarking.

'Ah! The niece.' Hortense removed Grace's hat to study the way she had tied her hair. Once satisfied, she sat herself far more elegantly on the same sofa, then raised her feet as if on a swing. She motioned to Harry and Fields to sit, too.

'Would you like wine? And we have some candied cherries.'

She had the habit of twitching her lips, as if resisting laughter.

●

HARRY AND FIELDS had moved two chairs closer to the sofa, and each held a glass of Burgundy. Standing nonchalantly by the window, Mustapha drank wine, too, having poured himself a full glass. Harry wondered who had played cards in the bedroom with the Duchesse.

·'You wish to know why I am here,' Hortense said imperiously, as if there could be no other possibility. 'In King's Lynn.'

Harry made to respond, but she cut across him. 'You saw the dwarf. I shall tell you why he interests me. You searched his body?'

'We did,' Harry answered. 'Though Sir Jonas Moore had already done so.'

'You found nothing of worth?'

Harry looked at Fields, whose face was impassive, and shook his head. 'A soldier's tools. A few coins from the time of our Civil Wars. Some were French. We know, from the boat he lay in, he had been aboard a French ship, *Incassable*.'

'*Incassable*? It means *Unbreakable*.' Hortense ran her tongue over her teeth, playing over them lingeringly. An effect Harry thought calculated, but successful all the same.

'You expected something valuable upon the body.'

'I asked clumsily, didn't I? This is why I lose at Manille. I thought Captain Hudson had something very valuable. Very precious. Something of mine. Something of my family's, more correctly, for it was my uncle's. Cardinal Giulio Raimondo Mazzarino.' She patted the sofa's plush seat. 'Called Mazarin, in France. Sit here. Next to me.'

A little hesitantly, Harry moved from his chair and did her bidding, to the other side of her from Grace.

Hortense pressed her hands together as if praying, resting the tips of her fingers under her chin. Harry was conscious of the heat emanating from her.

'Catholics cannot abide Protestants,' she pronounced. 'Protestants cannot abide Catholics.'

'In truth, I respect any way of worshipping,' Harry protested.

She gestured for silence with her hand. 'I speak generally, of course, which you can allow, for we are friends. Toleration makes you vulnerable. With the tales being put about by Titus Oates, Catholics, like me, are doubly so. You stay within your faith, which is Protestant. Not to invites suspicion. You would be a recusant. You, Colonel Fields, I know, are more free thinking. An Anabaptist.'

'We should come to religion freely, is my view,' Fields replied. 'It is why I dislike the baptizing of children.'

'Your belief makes you detested by Catholics and Protestants alike. That is one thing that binds the two religions: their hatred of others. Religion is by nature disputatious. You know all this, for you are not children. The reason I bother to say it, is that all this dispute has led to centuries of wars, one religion fighting another. All this fighting has cost the lives of many. It has also—and this is my point—cost money.' She emptied her glass, then refilled it herself; Mustapha made no move to do so, and she made no sign she expected him to. 'Money must be paid to wage war. Often, it must be borrowed. There are people of business who lend the money for others to go to war. The madness is, the money paid back by one side often goes straight to their enemy. And everyone knows it! In times of war, though, cash, credit, investments, property, become undependable. Unstable. But there is one currency people continue to trust, even in wartime, and so they lust after it.'

'You mean gemstones,' Fields said. 'Especially, diamonds.'

'Yes! Diamonds! People will pay unimaginable sums for them, beyond any sensible reckoning of their worth. Also, they can be pawned. The pawning of diamonds has funded the wars of Europe.' She smiled at them in turn, but bestowed her most spectacular smile upon Harry. 'There is one diamond, in particular, I am interested in.'

'Which diamond is that?' Harry asked, his voice gone husky.

'The Sancy diamond. Have you heard of it?'

'It is the largest diamond in Europe,' Grace obliged, looking just as stonily at Harry across the Duchesse. 'Indian cut. It was among the English Crown Jewels, before it was sold to the French.'

Hortense wrinkled her nose in appreciation. 'As clear as water, if slightly yellow. It came from a place called Golconda, in the southern part of India. Mountainous country. After it rains, the people there search the mountain streams for diamonds waiting in the water to be taken.

'From Golconda, it was smuggled to Venice, long ago, in the fourteenth century. The Duke of Milan gave it as part of his daughter's dowry when he married her to the Duke of Orleans. Men being men, the Duke of Burgundy had her husband murdered. On her deathbed, she made her children swear they would avenge their father's death.

'Her son used her jewels to fund an army, but it was defeated. Burgundy took all of them, including the Sancy. It passed to his son, Philip the Good, but *his* son, Charles the Bold, lost it when fighting the Swiss at Grandson. Soldiers took most of the Burgundy booty. The Sancy disappeared.

'How he came to have it, I do not know, but years later, the Bishop of Basel sold it. To the Pope's banker, a man named Fugger. Fugger had it cut in two, each piece still bigger than any other known diamond. It is the larger one we follow. Fugger traded it to the King of Portugal for a monopoly on the import of Indian pepper.

'Even after the Battle of Alcácar Quibir, when the Portuguese nobility were enslaved, the Sancy stayed in Portugal. Portugal had to raise the money for their ransom—but from where? Of course, their jewels—but still not the Sancy. Even then, Portugal kept a hold of it.

'The Portuguese King, Don Antonio, escaped to France. The French

King had no money to assist him, but Nicolas Harlay de Sancy, his ambassador, did. He paid Don Antonio's debts, and took the diamond.

'After Henry of Navarre became King, he, too, of course, was poor, from so many years of fighting the French religious wars. He had sold all his jewels to the English Queen, Elizabeth. With all his money, de Sancy continued to influence him. De Sancy used the diamond's value to raise an army against the Swiss. When delivering the diamond to the pawnbroker, his servant was murdered by thieves. De Sancy had him cut open. It was found in the man's throat.

'De Sancy fell out of Royal favour. The King owed him money, which seldom endears one man to another. De Sancy tried to sell the diamond, but no one would pay his price, seeing it as still belonging to Burgundy.

'The Queen of England, Elizabeth, was the only person who would have paid its true value, but she died. Finally, de Sancy managed to sell it to the new King, James I. Who had it put into his hat.'

She refilled her glass again, making an elaborate mime of surprise that it was empty. She also refilled Harry's, but Fields and Grace refused her.

'When England's Civil Wars began, Queen Henrietta Maria took the Crown Jewels to Holland, needing money to help her husband fight Parliament. Captain Hudson, the man now found dead in a boat, went with her. But the Prince of Orange, being Protestant, was cold to her, and Amsterdam's merchants would not touch the Crown Jewels, believing them not hers to pawn.'

'It was her personal jewellery she used, to buy cannons and powder to supply her husband's army,' Fields said. He brushed his coat fastidiously with the edge of his hand, as if cleaning the past from it. 'At the same time, he raised his standard, at Nottingham. When she tried to rejoin him, at Bridlington, Parliament's Navy shot at her from the sea.'

'She escaped, dressed only for the night, and barefoot,' Hortense said, admiringly.

'She styled herself *She-Majesty Generalissima*.' Fields almost spat the words. 'Parliament declared her a traitor.'

'Henrietta Maria was fiercely loyal to her husband. She re-joined him at Oxford. But Oxford being sick with typhoid, she returned again to France.'

'Still with the Sancy?' Harry asked.

Hortense nodded, and placed her hand on his leg, high on his thigh. Despite seeing Grace's expression, she did not move it. 'And with Hudson, too. They escaped through Cornwall. A storm battered their ship, but they managed to reach Brittany, climbing the rocks to get ashore. Little Louis was only four years old, so France was controlled by his mother. And Cardinal Mazarin, the richest man in France. My uncle.' She said it with a twist of her lip.

Hortense caught Harry's puzzlement. 'I had little fondness for him. A cruel, vain, greedy man. I was happy when he croaked. Anyways, he refused to help Henrietta Maria, not wanting to make an enemy of the English Parliament. She settled in Nevers, where other refugees from England joined her, including her Master of Horse, William Crofts, and his brother, Charles.'

'It was Charles who insulted Hudson and fought him in a duel,' Harry recalled from Sir Jonas Moore's information at the Denver Sluice.

'The dwarf had been with the Queen through all her adventures,' Fields said. 'Perhaps he resented these more recent arrivals.'

'Her courtiers thought the duel a tremendous joke,' Hortense said. 'The only serious one was Hudson. They charged each other on horseback.'

'Hudson shot Crofts,' Harry said.

'Through the head,' Hortense replied happily. 'My uncle had prohibited such duels, so to avoid his disfavour the Queen banished Hudson.'

'For his own protection, I shouldn't wonder,' Fields said. He gave one of his shudders and smacked his lips, as if getting rid of a bad taste.

'In standing up for himself, he lost everything. His place by the Queen, his living, and his rank.'

Harry saw his glass was empty. His thoughts were becoming fuzzy, not helped by the feeling of Hortense's hand. 'But the duel didn't cost him everything. You believe he had the Sancy.'

Hortense gave his thigh a little squeeze. 'Henrietta Maria had agreed to its sale to my uncle. He did not share the scruples of the Amsterdam merchants, as her price had come down. Documents were drawn up. She passed its ownership to him. He had paid, but not yet taken delivery. He was never to have it, for the diamond disappeared when Hudson disappeared.'

'There was no sign of it when we searched his body,' Harry told her.

'You did not look for it, did you? So, it would have been easy to miss.'

'Difficult to miss the largest known diamond.'

'He would have hidden it.'

'And now, you, too, lust after the Sancy,' Grace said.

Hortense laughed, delighted by her observation. 'Well, not so much the diamond itself, but its value. I would sell it. You see, marrying my husband brought our fortunes together but made my property his. He suffers from jealousy, which makes him distrustful. He sent me to a convent, so disguising myself as a man—as do you, Grace—I escaped to England. My friend Charles offered me shelter, for the sake of our friendship—I nearly married him once, before his restoration. But my uncle refused him. Penniless and powerless, Charles was then but a meagre prospect. When made King again, my uncle quickly changed his mind. Old Mazarin offered him five million livres to take me. I was to be traded like a piece of meat.'

'An expensive cut,' Fields said drily.

'Not expensive enough.' Hortense raised her glass to the memory. 'Charles turned him down. He could not forgive the humiliation of my uncle's original refusal. But, in his kindness, he lets me stay in London and grants me a small pension. Legally, the Sancy is mine, or at least partly, for my uncle left it to me and my three sisters. An easy thing, to bequeath a diamond you do not have. A quarter of its worth would keep me rich until the end of my days. If you help me, I would pay you. Will you go to the Denver Sluice again, to see if Hudson had the diamond?'

'He was murdered,' Harry said. 'We may presume to take the diamond from him.'

'But who would have known of him having it?' Hortense asked. 'Henrietta Maria only told my uncle of its disappearance days after. He ordered an investigation, sending agents after him. They never found Hudson, or the diamond.'

'Nothing was known of his voyage on *Incassable*?' Harry asked her.

'Nothing at all was heard of him.'

'Until the story surfaced of his being taken by corsairs, and serving with them at sea.'

She nodded. 'I knew nothing of that until the King told me of Sir Jonas's discovery. I never knew Hudson had returned—or, at least, a man claiming to be him.'

'He's lived quietly in Oakham,' Fields said. 'Deliberately so, it would seem.'

Hortense rose from the sofa. Harry's thigh still sensed the warmth of her hand.

'You could undertake your own search for me?' She ran her tongue over her teeth again. 'To find the diamond?'

Harry looked across the space she had left at Grace, who turned away from him, and then at Fields sitting in the chair opposite, who stared at him intently, awaiting his answer. 'The man who impersonates Hudson has not benefitted from it. His home is too poor. Apart from his books, he has little of worth.'

'I did not say it would be easy,' Hortense said. 'Search for the diamond at the Denver Sluice. If you do not find it there, would you undertake your own investigation into its whereabouts?'

'I'm tasked to find Hudson's replacement, by the Board of Ordnance. I think him gone to France. I wanted to ask at the port here, to find out if anyone saw him.'

'*Wanted*. Now, I can tell, you want instead to find my diamond. If you think him in France, I would pay for you to go there. My sister, Marie-Anne, lives in Paris. She, too, I know, would be anxious to help you.'

'You will never find the diamond, Harry, after all these years,' Fields said. 'And you cannot forget your duty to Sir Jonas.'

'Why not continue with that?' Hortense asked. 'Only, look for the diamond, too. The dwarf knows of it, I'm sure.' She raised her chin as if defying them to disagree, and as if saying it made it so. 'Would you do it, Harry, for, say, five hundred pounds?'

The colour draining from his cheeks, Harry looked at Fields, and then at Grace. Both looked as shocked as he was. His salary as the Royal Society's Observator had been forty pounds a year. He had hoped to become Curator to boost this to more. The Board of Ordnance now paid him 120 pounds.

'If he does not find the diamond, can you afford such a sum?' Fields asked Hortense.

She looked confused. 'Of course,' she said, her notion of poverty markedly different to theirs. 'And if you do find it, I shall pay four times as much.'

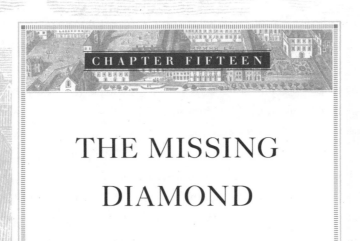

CHAPTER FIFTEEN

THE MISSING DIAMOND

THE MIRROR REFLECTED LAZULINE SKY AND fine wisps of cirrus. Sunlight sparked from the ripples blown across it by the breeze. The swaying reeds brushed each other, and a bittern made its eerie call, booming from within them.

The jolly boat still lay half submerged, its prow grounded, its stern gently swaying. As far as they could tell, it was untouched since Sir Jonas and his men had cleared their camp away and left, taking Hudson's remains with them.

Harry reached through the mirror, breaking the surface of the water inside the boat. Its coldness numbed his hand. He searched along the planks, slick with algae, for anything large enough to contain the Sancy diamond. Or even to feel the hard surface of the diamond itself. Silt roiled the water, making it opaque. Apart from the hole chopped to sink the boat, all he found were more remains of Hudson's bag. Sir Jonas had not thought the shreds of old canvas worth taking.

Colonel Fields stood at the jolly's stern, by the painted word *Incassable*, the lettering worn and faded. He squinted in the sunshine, scanning over the landscape as if the diamond might simply appear in one of the reed beds, or in a branch of a stunted, twisted tree, glinting at him in this bright light. In the cold and clear air, every detail of the flat landscape was sharp, as if wanting to impress itself on the eye like Mr. Newton's needle.

The work gang had completed filling in the breach of the bank, and were not to be seen. It was quiet; only two vessels upon the river. The water's level was equal on either side of the sluice, allowing them to navigate freely. One headed upstream towards Cambridge, the other towards King's Lynn, from where Harry, Fields, and Grace had ridden that morning.

Grace stood apart from the two men and away from the boat, but this time through her own volition. Unable to sleep, for much of the night she had brooded over the conversation with the Duchesse. Harry had been like a little dog, so eager to please her, to have her close attention. For a long while, Hortense even had her hand upon his thigh, and he had made no attempt to remove it. As they said their goodbyes, even the Duchesse's suggestion—no hint she expected refusal, so it was really more a command—that she and Grace should ride together back in London had not blunted Grace's resentment. Grace had no desire to be her friend, nor her plaything. The parallels between them—their choice to dress as men if occasion suited them, and their respective uncles' bargaining to find the most advantageous matches for them—were insignificant compared to their differences. Grace had heard the rumours of the Duchesse's scandalous relationship with the King's daughter, Anne, Countess of Sussex. Who had not? For they were all about London.

Oblivious of Grace's thoughts, Harry continued his search of the jolly's interior, which revealed nothing. There was nothing under the seats, or inside the boxing in the stern.

He stood, shivered, shook the water from his numbed arm, and rolled down his sleeve.

'What best to do, Colonel?'

'We will never find it,' Fields told him bleakly. 'Look how far this boat was washed from the Drain. The diamond could have fallen through at any point on this line.' The Colonel indicated the portion of bank which had collapsed, where the boat had been disgorged from the New Bedford River. 'Assuming it was ever with the dwarf.'

Harry looked along the line of Fields's extended arm. The old man was right, of course. But the sum of money the Duchesse offered would change his fortunes. By way of answer, he squatted behind the boat and groped in the reeds, feeling for anything hard, pointed, Indian cut.

Fields rolled his eyes to Heaven, and the muscles of his jaw flexed impressively, but he, too, stooped down to the wet ground, and began to search under the boat. Then they both lifted it, standing at either end, grunting with the exertion, and moved it aside. The old wood sagged, the jolly boat close to falling apart. They searched the depression it had made, but found nothing of worth. They only disturbed an adder, which whipped away from their approach at the last moment before Harry's hand settled upon it.

Grace watched them for a while, as they continued what must be a fruitless search, but then decided she could not just stand by. She walked beyond Colonel Fields, a distance away from Harry, and swept the ground under the water. Her fingers bumped only twigs and stones.

All three of them searched around the boat. Occasionally, one of them would bring something up, and clean it off in the water, flicking the wetness off with a shake. They found nothing. No further belongings: no coins, no equipment, and certainly not the Sancy diamond. Harry even picked up the old cannonball used to murder Hudson, although he knew the diamond could not be beneath it, for he had placed it down himself.

They tracked their way from the boat to the bank, in case the slide to its resting place had dislodged the diamond. A matter of yards took them nearly two hours. When they had searched high up the newly repaired bank, they looked into the river, at the dark water flowing past them.

'Even you, Harry, must give up now,' Colonel Fields said, wincing from his labour, trying to press life back into his knees. His face was pale, and his eyes were streaming. 'Just the wind,' he said, answering Grace's look of concern.

'Harry, we have searched enough,' Grace said, looking at her fingers, wrinkled and senseless, rather than at him. 'You would need an army to have a chance of finding it, even if it lay here. It is the Duchesse's conjecture only that Captain Hudson had it. Give up now, or you will go mad with the searching.'

Harry made no answer, instead looking around them, curling his toes in his sodden boots. He had lost all feeling in his hands.

'So, Harry, what next?' Fields asked, still bent forwards, grasping his knees.

A dark feeling rose up from Harry's stomach, a black biliousness, and with it a certainty that whichever choice he made, it would be the wrong one.

Two thousand pounds.

'Let's return to London,' he said.

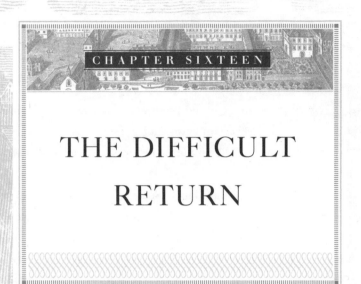

CHAPTER SIXTEEN

THE DIFFICULT
RETURN

THESE WERE THE LEAST COMFORTABLE SEATS he had ever sat on.

Harry had considered the matter for some miles, as they bounced over uneven road. The cushions had no give in them at all. Their stuffing had formed tight irregular balls that dug spitefully into his buttocks. Every time the coach's wheels hit a hole, or a rut, or a rock, the impact crunched through him. His pelvis ached, and the base of his spine tingled with each jolt. When the horses slowed, then started again, the lurch on the shafts threw him forwards, and then backwards. Everyone inside the coach squirmed constantly, seeking respite from their discomfort. Every so often, one or other of them groaned as the air came out of them. The harder the bump, the more of them groaned, groaning together, looking at each other with a shared sympathy.

Any conversation had run dry long ago. Opposite him, Grace had been silent for the entire journey, choosing to stare at a point on the coach's interior where its fabric lining was coming apart. Her hands rested on her lap, fingers clasped tightly together.

Harry observed the shape of her wrist as it disappeared enticingly into her sleeve, and the fine tracery of veins under her pale, smooth skin.

She sensed his look, and lifted her head slightly, a movement enough to show her displeasure.

Harry blew out his cheeks. He took off his spectacles, rubbing the bridge of his nose where they rested. He could not believe the way Grace was behaving, from merely the Duchesse's flirtation. It was just Hortense's way—she would be the same with anybody. Surely Grace could see that?

Next to him, deep in his *Book of Common Prayer*, sat Colonel Fields, grey-faced, breathless, tired out from all the travelling. Searching the water-logged ground for the diamond had taken the last reserves of his energy. Even though Fields had insisted on travelling with him, Harry still felt guilty that he exposed the old man to such hardship, instead of leaving him in the warm with Mrs. Hannam at Half Moon Alley.

Harry held aside the curtain flapping over the window. It was useless as far as keeping the cold out, so no one complained. He watched the country-side go by. Little villages, fields, and farmsteads revealed themselves, to disappear again. After a while, Harry experienced the illusion that the places were moving towards them and the coach stood still.

Nearer London, the land lost its flatness. He let the curtain drop, block-ing the view of the prosperous village of Tottenham, its grand houses, mills, and the pleasant meadows it lay in.

They had not found the Sancy diamond. This did not contradict the Duchesse's notion that Captain Hudson had had it with him, for they could easily have missed it. Or else, Hudson may have sent it on, or kept it else-where. But Tottenham turning French was as likely as finding it.

It was a distraction, Harry decided. An impossible distraction, and must be put aside. The Sancy could be anywhere. He now worked for the

Board of Ordnance. He must follow Sir Jonas Moore's instructions, not Hortense Mancini's.

He became aware of Fields smiling at him.

'You did not hear me, being deep in your thoughts.'

'Sorry, Colonel.'

'I could guess what those thoughts might be. I wager I would be near the mark.'

'I remind myself of what we've so far found, ready to report to Sir Jonas.'

'You think, rather, of the diamond, do you not?'

Harry grimaced. 'I can't afford to. I must find the man who pretends to be Captain Hudson. That's Sir Jonas's wish. I need to question the captain of *Incassable*, Eugène de Beauchene. He may have intelligence of the original Hudson. He lives in Paris, or so we were told at the Kontor. I wonder if Sir Jonas would pay for me to go to Paris.'

'Would he not rather send a letter? I notice you say you yourself, alone. If Sir Jonas does instruct you to go, would you wish me to accompany you?'

'I see how tired you are from coming with me to the Fens.'

'I must, it seems, now make allowances for my age. A depressing prospect I wish not to dwell upon. I can still help you, I believe, if you want me with you.'

'If only as company, I'd wish you with me. I'm sure you'd prove more than that.'

Fields looked sorrowfully at Harry. His expression did not brighten, and neither did his voice. 'The dwarf and the diamond. Finding the one might lead to the other.'

'You seem saddened by the thought.'

'I wish not to discourage you. A presentiment, perhaps. You expose yourself to danger. I take no joy from that.' Fields pulled on his front teeth, a dead man's transplanted after the battle at Alton. 'The Duchesse knows this, I think. That is why she promises such a considerable reward.'

'I'd share it with you, of course, if we happened to find the Sancy.'

Grace made an elaborate show of resettling herself on the coach's seat, and for the first time in their long journey she spoke up. Her voice was tight. 'You are generous, are you not? I notice neither of you makes mention of *me* continuing with you.'

Harry was wide-eyed, as if she had slapped him. 'It's fanciful to think I could take you to France. It's too dangerous. You came by subterfuge on this journey. Uninvited.'

'Uninvited?' Grace's face was flushed. 'I see.'

There was a long silence, apart from the coach wheels rattling and the laboured breathing of two angry passengers. The others crowded with them inside the coach were quiet, listening in to this spat.

'No great matter,' Grace said eventually, returning her gaze to the rip in the coach's fabric. 'I have other admirers. Perhaps they will take me where I wish to go.'

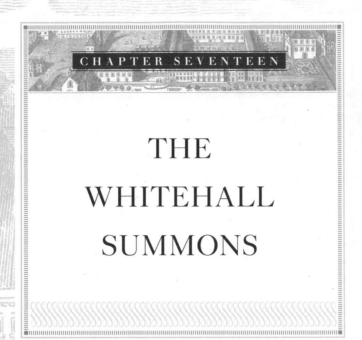

CHAPTER SEVENTEEN

THE
WHITEHALL
SUMMONS

AS WELL AS ITS CONSTRICTION, HARRY welcomed the City's noise. The silence of the Fens was uncanny, and had kept him awake at night. Even in Cambridge and King's Lynn, busy towns both, the relative lack of din unsettled him. He found the smells of London comforting, too, experiencing them anew on his return. The smell of blood and raw meat from Leadenhall Market was strongest, but the herb market added its garnish.

The coach inched along Cornhill and pulled up at the station. Mrs. Hannam waited there, her face shining from the cold. On spotting Harry at the coach's window, she waved her arms frantically at him. He stood aside to let Fields dismount first, being careful not to brush against Grace, who still looked vexed with him.

Fields, pleased to have his feet on solid ground, jogged to Mrs. Hannam.

She let herself be engulfed by his hug, sinking into his battered soldier's coat, pushing back his montero to look more closely at his face, and kiss him joyfully.

'I had the strangest feeling,' she said. 'I knew you would be on this one! I came especially to see.'

Mrs. Hannam was always superstitious. Harry wondered if she had, in fact, come to Cornhill hoping for the Colonel's return on every day they had been away, rather than having any mystical connection with him.

Harry let Grace alight before him. She almost ran down the steps put out by the driver, not once looking back. The last Harry saw of her was a glimpse of Denis Papin's borrowed tricorne hat, bobbing past the garishly painted facade of East India House.

Harry pushed his hand through his hair despondently. He waited for their luggage to be untied and handed down from the coach roof, rather than be too near the Colonel's and Mrs. Hannam's ardency. They still pawed one another and looked deeply into one another's eyes, as if checking each was exactly as they had left the other. The display of their affection embarrassed him. It occurred to him it was time to find new lodgings.

At last, the couple let one another go. Mrs. Hannam wanting to go to Princes Street for a cabbage, they walked together the length of Cornhill. Harry led the way, carrying his and Grace's luggage. Mrs. Hannam and Fields talked excitedly behind him, speaking over one another, finishing each other's sentences, like lovers half their age. Fields spoke of the Fens, of Cambridge and King's Lynn, and how he had not suffered unduly *at all* from his exertions. Indeed, he told her, he felt invigorated by his travels, and rejuvenated by his time on horseback, reminding him of the man he used to be—this last, laughing, after she pinched him playfully, leaving him to know his exertions were not yet over.

Harry knew he should be more pleased for them. But he felt only reprehensible jealousy. A shameful mean-spiritedness, but there it was, bubbling up like water from the Turnmill Brook.

When past the Royal Exchange, a man in a purple cloak, who had been waiting on the corner of Pope's Head Alley, crossed the road towards them.

A tall, thin man with hollow cheeks. His sword belt was around his hips, French-fashion rather than over one shoulder.

Harry, sensing this man had business with him, began to slow. The man's self-assurance went against him being a traveller asking the way.

'You are Mr. Henry Hunt.' A statement rather than a question, and a monotonous way of speaking.

'I am,' Harry replied unthinkingly, not suspecting it would have been better for him to say no. Perhaps it made no difference, for the man could easily have found him another time. At home in Half Moon Alley, or at Gresham College. Or nowadays, he reflected, at the Armouries building in the Tower, the headquarters of the Board of Ordnance.

'You are to come with me, then, please. To Whitehall. The Lord High Treasurer Danby wishes to question you.'

'Question him? Why?' Fields demanded, stepping in front of Harry. Mrs. Hannam stayed behind, her hand to her open mouth.

'Is this any business of yours?' the flat voice asked.

'Is he being arrested?'

'No, no,' the man said. 'Not an arrest. A request.'

Fields brought his face menacingly close. 'With Danby, there is no difference.'

'You said that, sir, not I. Who are you?' The man did not step back an inch.

'I know not this man,' Harry said to the stranger, pulling Fields back. 'I thank you for you intervention, sir, but I shall go with him.'

'No, no, Harry, do not deny me. I shall come with you. I insist upon it.'

Fields turned to give the worried looking Mrs. Hannam a brief hug.

Lord Danby's man, Richard Merritt, shrugged. He did not care either way.

CHAPTER EIGHTEEN

THE
JUDDERING
CLOCK

FROM CORNHILL TO THE PALACE WAS just over two miles. Merritt's coach brought them to the wide-open expanse of Whitehall, more square than street. They went past the Banqueting House, where the platform was built for Charles I's execution, then through the Holbein Gate.

They alighted from the coach, to walk the rest of the way.

There was something insect-like about Merritt's movements: the swinging of his long, thin legs, and the way his knees snapped into place as he walked. Harry and Fields followed him, exchanging anxious glances. Had Mrs. Leach not described a tall, thin man in a purple cloak?

A hotchpotch of buildings made up the Palace. Walking by the tennis court between high, oppressive walls, the passageway seemed to funnel them towards the Lord High Treasurer.

Merritt indicated a solid black front door belonging to a modest building of red London brick. New, as yet undamaged by the London air, it was a
simple four-storey house replacing the ruined Cockpit theatre. It displayed
little of the power of the man who lived inside.

Inside, its brightly painted hall was furnished simply: no clutter, nothing on the walls, no embellishment of any kind. Nothing of Danby's character could be gleaned from these surroundings. Perhaps, Harry surmised,
this plainness described him well enough.

A young man, younger even than Harry, smiled at them diffidently,
seeming to change his mind midway through the expression. 'Mr. Henry
Hunt?' he asked at a startlingly deep pitch, this youth's voice having broken
and carried on breaking. At Harry's nod, he went over and tapped gently on
high, glossy double doors with oversized brass handles, and disappeared
through them.

Harry expected the youth to return, but he did not. Merritt left them,
too, going into a smaller-doored office. Harry and Fields paced around the
hall, both uneasily silent. A chair was positioned against the wall; Harry
wondered if sitting on it would be disapproved of. Thinking of Grace's
words—that he took too much notice of what others thought of him, especially those superior to him—he wondered whether to sit down,
nevertheless.

Before he had settled on doing so, the young man reemerged and beckoned Harry, alone, to go in. When he got to the doors Harry looked back
nervously at Fields, who gave him a half salute.

He entered Lord Danby's office.

Behind the desk, much of the wall was taken up by an enormous clock,
more suited to a church's exterior. It showed—very clearly—the time as ten
past seven. Its minute hand sprang into place with a judder along its length,
as if from a sensual delight at time's passing. It reminded Harry of Merritt's
style of walking.

Beneath the clock sat Thomas Osborne, the Earl of Danby.

There being no chair, Harry had to stand before him, which made him
feel exposed—an effect undoubtedly planned for. Danby was lean and long-

faced, with a moustache which he tugged at as he inspected Harry. Responsible for finding money for the King, as well as controlling its spending, Danby had more power than anyone else in government. Including, most agreed, the King. To buttress his position further, he was known to employ a network of spies, protecting the King's safety as well as his own. At court, he was a vastly unpopular figure, said to have not a single friend. Sitting under his clock, he seemed quite comfortable with that.

'You met with Sir Jonas Moore. At the Denver Sluice.'

Harry could do nothing but agree with the abrupt conversational opening.

Danby gave a sharp little sniff, as if smelling salts. 'You risked one of the agues that brings a man down, there among the reeds. Many have died in that inhospitable place.' He spoke quickly, with little pause between his sentences. 'It was one such unfortunate you saw, was it not, at Sir Jonas Moore's invite? Although, I hear, it was not by nature this man met his end, but by the cruel hand of man.'

Having no wish to do his new employer harm, Harry did not know how much he should divulge of Sir Jonas's business. Even the Board of Ordnance feared Danby's power. 'My Lord, it's as you say. A man was found dead there.'

His answer's economy seemed to please Danby, for his thin-lipped mouth stretched across his face. But there was no warmth in his eyes, which regarded Harry with a detached sort of interest, as he might watch the struggles of a beetle on its back.

'Captain Jeffrey Hudson was found there, Mr. Hunt. Who was once Queen Henrietta Maria's dwarf.' He pulled at his moustache. 'You assist Robert Hooke, do you not? As a Greshamite.'

'No longer, my Lord. Now I work for the Board of Ordnance.'

'After your experimental trial, which ended badly.'

Had Sir Joseph Williamson, the Royal Society's President, told Danby about his attempt to induce electricity from pressing a bone? It could have been any of the Fellows, Harry reflected. 'My leaving wasn't due to that.'

Danby raised a doubtful eyebrow.

'Sir Jonas's terms were generous.'

'He had not yet heard of your failure. You took advantage of his ignorance. Good. You were right to do so.'

'I believe he would have employed me even had he known, my Lord,' Harry replied stiffly.

Danby shot Harry a sly look. 'I tease you, Mr. Hunt. Mr. Hooke, I know, is the opposite of generous.'

'But, my Lord, it wasn't only—'

Danby's raised palm stopped Harry's protest. 'The Royal Society communicates the work of the *virtuosi* to the curious, the tradesmen, the artificers. Practical men, such as yourself.' He smiled his thin smile. 'The King esteems you for your practicality. After last year's business of the bloodless boy. Especially so, with what happened at Shaftesbury's Popish Procession. That your services should be expensive, I am in full agreement with Sir Jonas.'

Although Danby used the word expensive, Harry knew the King paid his Lord High Treasurer a hundred times as much as a Royal Society Observator. Let alone the money Danby made by selling favours. Even with his raised salary from the Board of Ordnance, the difference was vast.

Lord Danby continued. 'As is His Majesty, I am anxious for your future. I have brought you here to offer you one. According to Titus Oates, whose testimony has gripped the nation, Hudson—this second Hudson, I should say, since now we know him an imposter—is a French spy. Sir Jonas thinks him working for the Board of Ordnance, spying for him.'

'Do you believe Oates, my Lord?'

'It matters not if I believe him or no. I must be seen to do everything possible to uncover these perfidious Catholics. Otherwise, I risk being accused of not doing enough. Oates gives up names as easily as he breaks wind. He has eighty-one Articles of Jesuit plotting.'

'Eighty-one, my Lord? Were there not originally, forty-three?'

'As the plot grows, supposedly, then so does his evidence. Of plans against our King, and the safety of our nation.'

'He calls himself the Saviour of the Nation.'

'He does. The people do, too. He has such a hold on their imagination, I
fear we will all fall before this has run its course.' Danby looked anything
but fearful. He smiled again, this time showing his teeth. His eyes, though,
were as expressionless as those of a fish. 'Oates says the dwarf is a Catholic
sympathizer, and plots against the King's life. A dangerous man, then, for
one so little. And just as Oates's evidence appears, the body of the man he
names appears. And just as the body appears, the man who uses Hudson's
name disappears. Now listen, for this is why I have had you brought here.
This impostor, my intelligence tells me, was seen escaping to France. He
left from Clacton. Much smuggling goes on there, so it would have been
easy to find a captain willing to take him. He landed at Dunkirk three days
ago. Although we sold the port to the French, we still have agents there. An
English dwarf's arrival was notable. Then he took a coach to Paris. I wish
you to find him there.'

'I've not yet seen Sir Jonas, so haven't reported to him, nor had instructions from him.'

'Sir Jonas let this dwarf trick him. He relies on you to rescue his reputation. He has not yet informed the King of the man's betrayal, but his embarrassment may only be kept from His Majesty for so long. You continue to
help him, anyways, so long as you help me. I, too, desire you to find the man
going by the name Jeffrey Hudson. Though he has no right to it, other than
a shared smallness.'

Danby rose from behind his desk. Standing, he was far taller than
Harry. 'You will need an introduction to the Head of the Paris police. His
name is Monsieur Nicolas Gabriel de La Reynie. A fearsome man. A learned
man, too. Fond of his Aristotle. You shall appreciate one another, I am sure.
Will you take the old Colonel with you, as you took him to the Fens?'

'I doubt he would come with me to France, my Lord.' Harry could not
ask Fields to go to Paris. He should stay safe at home with Mrs. Hannam.

'Ask Sir Jonas for a letter to cover you both, if the Colonel agrees to
accompany you. You will need passports, too. Do you have the name? La
Reynie.'

Harry nodded that he did.

'One more thing. If Miss Hooke wishes to accompany you, do not allow it. She should not be involved in this business.'

Danby seemed to know everything. His intelligencers, whoever they were, were effective.

'No, my Lord. My Lord?'

Danby looked his blank-eyed look.

'I see you're careful not to write the letter yourself.'

'You are observant, Mr. Hunt, just as His Majesty tells me.'

'You were careful, also, to keep others from this room.'

'My faith in you is confirmed. You work for Sir Jonas, not for me. Although, never forget, you work for me.'

'What do you think will happen, that you distance yourself so?'

For the first time, Danby looked displeased. 'If any shit is about, I prefer to be out of the farmyard.' He called through to the hallway. 'Assistance!'

Merritt entered the room. 'Mr. Hunt is to go to Paris,' Danby told him. 'He will need French money. Pistoles.'

Merritt left again, going off to the strong room.

'Bring the dwarf back to London,' Danby told Harry. 'I shall make your life difficult if you do not.'

The clock's minute hand juddered into place.

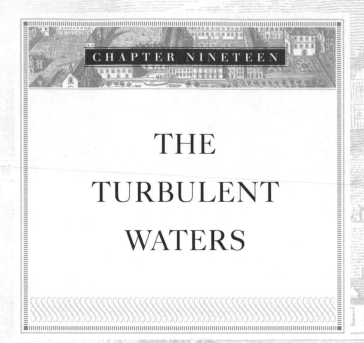

CHAPTER NINETEEN

THE
TURBULENT
WATERS

HARRY ALREADY KNEW OF LA REYNIE. His fame had reached London through the news-sheets. Monsieur de Paris, he was known as. La Reynie's streetlights had made Paris far safer than London, villains being unwilling to work in over-bright spaces.

Here, on the other hand, all was dark. Colonel Fields walked silently next to him as they returned to Half Moon Alley. Along the Strand, going past Somerset House, Fields finally spoke.

'During the wars, I met with General Fairfax there.' He pointed at the huge building beside them. 'He was Commander-in-Chief of Parliament's army. It is also where, later, the dead Lord Protector Cromwell lay in state. In its Great Room.'

The Colonel's hesitancy suggested he spoke to lead to something else. Sure enough, still looking up at Somerset House, which had scaffolding across its facade—Robert Hooke directed the works to improve it—Fields came to a stop altogether.

'Danby wishes you to go to France, to do his bidding?'

'He does,' Harry replied.

'There is no possible way to refuse him.'

'He's too powerful a man to resist.' Harry looked askance at his friend. 'Besides, we thought Hudson had gone to France.'

'You thought it. You still wish to find the diamond.'

'My wishes are neither here nor there, and matter not a jot. The Lord High Treasurer instructs me to find the man who passes as Captain Hudson. As does Sir Jonas.'

'But you will do it for the Duchesse de Mazarin.'

Harry kicked petulantly at a loose stone in the road. 'What chance have I of finding the Sancy? It's been lost since Hudson took it.'

'Did you tell Danby of it?'

'I told him nothing of Hortense's interests.'

'Hortense's, you say?' The Colonel smiled grimly. 'Not the Duchesse's? Have a care, Harry. These are turbulent waters you sail into.'

'I hoped you would sail them with me. And Danby seems to wish it so.'

'Does he now?' Fields looked pained. 'Come, let us return to Bishopsgate Without, and Elizabeth. I have missed her sorely, you know, during our trip to the Fens. I must make it up to her.'

Although there was no salaciousness in the Colonel's voice, Harry found himself blushing.

'And you must build a bridge across the gap to Grace,' Fields told him. '*He that covereth a transgression seeketh love; but he that repeateth a matter separateth very friends.*'

'I still have her luggage. I shall go to Gresham first thing.'

'And I will find us transport to France,' Fields replied.

Harry felt his eyes tickle, as tears threatened. 'Thank you, Colonel.

Your friendship means the world to me.' He clasped the old man to him. 'I can't yet go home with you, though. I must go to St. James's, to see Hortense—the Duchesse, I mean. We need another letter of introduction, for her sister in Paris.'

●

WHEN COLONEL FIELDS reached Half Moon Alley, Mrs. Hannam could not speak, she had been so worried about them being taken to be questioned. In her relief, she clasped him to her, as tightly as Harry had done.

'The things we do for love,' Fields said, kissing her tears away.

CHAPTER TWENTY

THE
INDIGNANT
HOUSEKEEPER

THE FOLLOWING MORNING, AT GRESHAM, THE door to Robert Hooke's lodgings stayed firmly shut.

Harry repeated his knock. Grace was ignoring him. Mr. Hooke was usually out by this early hour, but never her. She liked to sleep in—she and her uncle had had disagreements about it, on many occasions—although she had left her bed readily enough on the morning they went to Cambridge.

He had been a fool. For years he had wanted to be with Grace Hooke. Yet when she had gone to Cambridge, to Denver, to Oakham, and then King's Lynn with him and the Colonel, he had treated her with disrespect. Especially when meeting the Duchesse de Mazarin. It raised a prickle of sweat on his back when he recalled how thoughtless he had been. Grace had shown great fortitude, enduring days in coach and on horseback, even sleeping rough on the roadside. Also, she had proved an able questioner. She had elicited from Isaac Newton why he made his cat doors. Mrs. Leach had told them much, for Grace had shown a sympathy to her lacking in the men. In King's Lynn, she had seen a simple way of getting the Turk's Head's owner to speak to them, even if it meant spending the Board of Ordnance's money. If it were not for the accident of her sex, as Japhia Bennett, the old sailor, had put it—and he, too, had responded favourably to her—she would make an effective investigator into matters such as these.

She was right to be angry with him. His apology must be deep. It would certainly be sincere.

He turned at the sound of footsteps coming across the College quadrangle. It was Mary Robinson, Robert Hooke's housekeeper, carrying a basket of vegetables and a chine of beef.

She did not welcome him after his trip away. Instead, she looked warily at him.

'Mary! Is no one home?' He held up Grace's luggage she had left on the coach.

'Mr. Hooke's left already, for the works at Somerset House.' She took her key from her purse, then lowered her voice. 'You've offended Grace horribly. I know, for her tears have soaked my shoulder. Mr. Hooke, too, is vexed with you. He blames you for her upset.'

Harry took Mary's answer to mean that Grace was inside. 'I've come to explain myself to her, and say sorry. I leave for Paris this morning.'

'Paris?' Mary looked unimpressed, intent on what she had to say. 'You'll need more than a sorry! You took her away, then left her! What you did with her, she will not say.'

'I didn't take her. She went with me. And I didn't leave her. She left me, and her luggage, at the Cornhill coach station.'

'Men! She expected you to follow.'

Harry looked helplessly at her. 'I couldn't have followed. I was summoned by Lord High Treasurer Danby.'

Mary looked doubtfully at him. Harry chose not to add he had walked with Fields and Mrs. Hannam in the opposite direction, Danby's man not intercepting them until they were near the Royal Exchange.

'You assume something because she says nothing, but there's nothing. Nothing happened between us that would be cause for shame—if that's what you assume.'

Mary did not look mollified at all. 'Mr. Hooke's furious with you. You left the Royal Society, despite his designs for you, and all his care for you. For reasons he sees as mercenary. Then you took his niece to the Fens, and exposed her to hardship and danger.'

'But Mary, she—'

'You've broken her heart. I thought you more worthy of her.' With that, Mary took Grace's bags from him, and unlocked the door, positioning her wide frame so there was no room for Harry to slip past.

The door closed behind her. The knocker bounced against it.

Dejected, Harry went to knock again, but Mary's heavy footsteps making their way up the stairs were implacable.

Instead, he turned and walked slowly across the quadrangle. He went into the College library, to choose a book for the journey to France.

When he reemerged, he saw a familiar figure at Hooke's door.

Denis Papin waved. A half smile, which Harry took to be a guilty expression.

The door was opened for him.

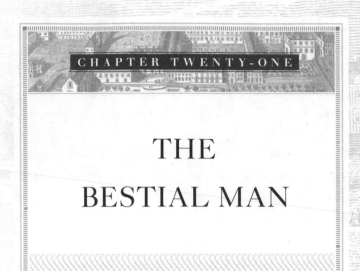

CHAPTER TWENTY-ONE

THE
BESTIAL MAN

SWOOPING FROM THE MIST, A GULL startled him with its shriek.

Harry waited for Colonel Fields on Hooke's new quayside. His battered leather coat did little to protect him from the wind. The morning was chilly. It felt chillier still after his trip to Gresham.

Dark clouds turned everything a brooding grey. The air's moisture fogged the panes of his spectacles.

Grace had refused to see him, and Papin had been there. Harry could think of little else, even when he went to the Board of Ordnance at the Tower. Sir Jonas, back from Denver, quickly provided the necessary letters of introduction and passports.

Harry had got himself to Billingsgate in a dream state.

The quayside was hectic. Far busier, noisier, and more crowded than

King's Lynn. He was surrounded by boxes, barrels, crates, and sacks, and the men who hefted them. Stevedores paced up and down the gangplanks, carrying impossible-seeming loads, balancing them on their heads. Their talk was rough and loud, with the arrogance given by their strength and their number.

As Fields had advised him, Harry travelled lightly. He had bought himself a copy of the Colonel's canvas bag. He felt for the purse of money Richard Merritt had given him. It made him think every glance a knowing one, and made him certain his face would betray that he carried, along with the money from the Board of Ordnance, at least a year's pay for most of these men working here. They could divorce him from it as easily as they rolled a barrel.

He also carried his modified pistol, which once belonged to the Royal Society's dead Secretary, Henry Oldenburg, and a small knife the Colonel had presented last night, before disappearing with a giggling Mrs. Hannam.

His cheeks were numb, and his lips were stiff and chapped. He watched the water slapping against the quay, observing the way it ran in between the piles holding up the wooden gangways, the jetties and wharfs that extended crazily from the waterfront, the connections to each of the ships that berthed here for the business of loading and unloading. The water was choppy, flecks of white spitting from the river, sometimes splashing his face.

Soon, the Thames would take him out to the open sea. It was a journey he had never done. He had never been further along the river than Tilbury, going with Hooke to see the improvements to the fortifications there.

Fields was late, presumably still seeking a captain to take them. Their arrangement was to meet at eleven. It was now gone a quarter past. Waiting gave Harry time to think of his fears. Of Danby. Of travelling to France. Of Paris, an unknown city. And of Monsieur de Paris, La Reynie, who sounded formidable. Of losing Grace. Of hurting Robert Hooke—he could have moved into Sir Jonas Moore's employ less callously to him. Hooke, he knew, was even more stubborn than his niece. He would see Harry's work for the

Board of Ordnance as a betrayal, but to misuse his niece—as he saw it— would not easily be forgiven.

At last, Fields appeared, wearing his usual coat and his bright orange scarf. His sword bounced on his thigh as he strode towards him. He waved when he saw Harry, and increased his pace.

'So! There is a ship, called *The Seraph*.' He stopped short, wiping sweat from his forehead. He turned on his heel, gesturing back the way he had come. 'They have just made a last call for passengers.'

Harry followed him. Reaching the ship, they saw its gangplank was still in place. A family struggled up it with their luggage. A stevedore had stepped up to help them.

As they waited, Harry saw three men pacing towards them. Latecomers, like the Colonel.

The family having moved off it, Harry and Fields stepped onto the gangplank. Fields started up it easily, showing no fear of a ducking in the Thames. Harry was more nervous. It was difficult to balance himself with his awkward bag, and no help that the latecomers behind him had stepped heavily onto the gangplank. A crewman called down impatiently. The wood bounced, and the end resting on the quayside scraped across the stone. Irritated by their selfishness, Harry turned.

The first of the trio was a man whose forehead was strangely shaped: a flat plane of bone across the top of his nose, the shape of his skull spacing his eyes wide apart.

A face he recognized. But it was impossible he should see it again. For it belonged to a man he knew to be dead: He had watched him die, killed at Aldgate by the London mob.

An assassin. A man he had since learned was called Pierre Lefèvre.

'Run, Colonel!'

Fields, near the gangplank's head, did not, but turned to look behind him.

'Run!' Harry shouted again.

Instead, Fields stood fast, and produced his sword. Harry drew level, to stand precariously beside him.

Lefèvre, and the two others behind him, stopped. Lefèvre held his hands open, to show he had no weapon. Harry knew this meant little, for he had seen him in action, and knew his movements were not those of normal men. Lefèvre could close the gap between them in an instant.

'Trouble?' the crewman called.

'Robbers,' Fields replied.

Harry walked backwards, feeling his way with his feet up the steep gangplank, watching Lefèvre. He felt the blood draining from his face. The same dizziness which had afflicted him in Robert Hooke's observatory overtook him again. If he did not get off this hazardous plank, and to the safety of the ship, he would fall.

Seeing his weakness, Lefèvre advanced.

Fields steadied Harry, pulling him with him up the gangplank. Above them, two more sailors had joined their mate, looking over the rail. One had a long boat hook, and he directed it at the three men.

Lefèvre and his men stopped, then retreated slowly back down the gangway. Fields held Harry, manhandling him upwards. A sailor grasped him, too. His movement caused Fields to lose his grip on his sword. It fell in the Thames with a splash.

'Blood and wounds!' Fields swore loudly, something Harry had never heard him do.

The sailor deposited Harry unceremoniously onto the deck.

Pulling the plank up, the crewman gave the signal. The last ropes holding the ship to the shore were released by the stevedores, who kept clear of the three strangers. Especially the odd, bestial-looking one. What the trouble was, they did not know. Some dispute or other, probably over money.

As *The Seraph* drew away, Harry and Fields stared over the side. There were four men together now, for another had joined them. All looked directly up at them: Lefèvre, the two others with him, and the Lord High Treasurer Danby's man, Richard Merritt.

On Lefèvre's face was an expression disconcertingly like hatred.

BOOK II

… la relieure n'est rien qu'un accident & maniere de paroistre, sans laquelle, au moins si belle & somptueuse, les livres ne laissent pas d'estre utiles, commodes & recherchez: n'estant jamais arrivé qu'à des ignorans de faire cas d'un livre à cause de sa couverture, parce qu'il n'est pas des volumes comme des hommes, qui ne sont cognus & respectez que par leur robe & vestement …

GABRIEL NAUDÉ, ADVIS POUR DRESSER UNE
BIBLIOTHÈQUE (PARIS, 1627)

Translated by JOHN EVELYN in his
INSTRUCTIONS CONCERNING ERECTING
OF A LIBRARY (LONDON, 1661) as:

The binding is nothing but an accident & form of appearing, without which (at least so splendid and sumptuous) Books become altogether as useful, commode & rare; it becoming the ignorant onely to esteem a Book for its cover; seeing it is not with Books, as it is with men, who are onely known and respected for their robes and their clothes.

CHAPTER TWENTY-TWO

THE STUBBORN
PRIEST

'WE ARE INNOCENT. WE LOSE OUR lives wrongfully. We pray God to forgive them that are the causes of it.'

'Still stubborn,' the executioner muttered to the captain of Foot with
him. The soldier said nothing. He took no pleasure in these proceedings.

The butcher's block waited in front of the scaffold. The priest, William
Ireland, and the layman, John Grove, faced it. Having been drawn on a
sledge to Tyburn, they already bled, the crowd hurling stones on their way.

The men to do the work held their tools. One had a cleaver. One had a
saw. The basket, of sturdy wicker, was pushed into place at the block's head
by an apprentice. The boy looked queasy. His first time at Tyburn.

Ireland and Grove were guilty of plotting against the King. They had
planned to shoot him at Newmarket. Titus Oates had overheard them in

Grove's home in York Street, and at another house in Wild Street, near Covent Garden. Luckily, Oates told the Sessions, the flint failed at the last moment. Other witnesses, who gave evidence William Ireland had been in Wales when the meetings took place, were not believed. Oates bribed a maid to corroborate his story.

The disbelieving King had postponed the executions, but from fear of popular anger now let them go ahead.

Ireland had made a partial confession, though: he admitted to being a Jesuit, and seeking to convert as many to his faith as he could.

Crime enough.

The executioner gave the signal. A short drop. Ireland, dressed in his Jesuit cassock, kicked the most. Grove seemed more accepting of his fate.

The executioner watched them closely. The two men were to be cut down with no life still in them, as special clemency from the King. When satisfied, he directed the ladder to be placed, and one of his men climbed it to cut the bodies down.

Grove was lowered first, to have his heart cut out. The man with the cleaver stepped forwards, to break open his chest.

The apprentice looked away. But he could not avoid the sound.

CHAPTER TWENTY-THREE

THE TEDIOUS
JOURNEY

PAST A PIRATE HUNG AT WAPPING, then by the Blackwall Dock, and a
Navy ship almost complete. The dockyards of Deptford and Woolwich. Tilbury, with its jagged fortifications.

Fields still brooded on losing his sword, but seemed just as upset by his
own profanity. '*Swear not, neither by heaven, neither by the earth, neither by
any other oath: but let your yea be yea; and your nay, nay; lest ye fall into con-
demnation,*' he said to Harry, by way of apology.

The water was lively with the breeze. Out from the Thames, and into
the open sea.

As *The Seraph* made the turn towards France, the wind dropped and
the sails went slack. Soon after, a fog descended, making it difficult to see
even their own rigging, shrouded by the dense swirls of haze. They headed
for the port of Étaples, on the same coast the Romans loaded up their fleets

to take Britain. The crew had hoped the voyage would last a day. Becalmed by the lack of wind, it took a tedious three.

For the first time in his life, Harry stood on foreign soil. The women here wore bonnets and fish-bloody aprons. The men wore smocks. Few paid him or Fields any attention. If anyone did speculate on the odd-looking pair, the Colonel's bearing, the scars around his head, and the grim set to his face, discouraged them from wondering further.

Each day travelling and each night resting. All became a blur of unplaceable images as the countryside rolled by. The days brought interminable fields, identical homesteads and farms, and crops being scythed by unremarkable peasants with placid, incurious expressions, their faces browned by the silvery light. The air seemed clearer, more transparent, as if thinner than English air—even than under the Fenland skies. Harry preferred the smut-filled London air, reassuringly thick, which pressed insistently to the skin. The nights were spent at indistinguishable stops—poor inns, for the most part, despite Harry's purse being generously filled. Fields insisted that to stay more expensively might draw unwelcome attention.

As they travelled, pressed against other passengers in a succession of claustrophobic coaches, and stayed in their various inns, Harry and Fields grew tired of each other. Every evening, their conversation was the same. In Abbeville, in Amiens, and in Beauvais, Harry still worried away at Lefèvre being at Billingsgate. He had seen the man die.

What should have been an easy choice—for Danby's command to find the man who styled himself Captain Jeffrey Hudson merely repeated Sir Jonas's instruction, and the Duchesse de Mazarin offered generous reward for finding the Sancy—was thrown into doubt by Lefèvre's reappearance. Also, the assassin's standing on the quayside with Danby's man, Merritt.

Either Danby knew of Merritt's meeting with Lefèvre, or he didn't. If Danby knew, then he had allowed it, or he hadn't. If he did not, his man kept it from him.

The lack of certainty made him nervous. Fields warned him he was losing weight. Harry needed to be strong, he said, to face the challenge ahead.

Harry also worried constantly at his separation from Grace, and at Robert Hooke's anger after his decision to leave the Royal Society, as Mary had reported. Fields grew impatient with him: The decision to leave had been entirely Harry's own, and he must stand by it. He had behaved poorly towards Grace, and not tried hard enough to make things right with her. He had taken Sir Jonas's offer of employment too readily, and been too swayed by the beautiful duchesse, Hortense Mancini. He did, however, acknowledge that Danby could not be refused.

Harry took the Colonel's condemnations with a dark resentment, even as he recognized their truth.

For his part, Fields spoke of little else other than Elizabeth Hannam, or complained of the loss of his sword, an old and trusty companion. Harry felt he should be talking more of how they should behave in Paris. There, they would attempt to find a man amid, he had heard, half a million souls.

As they passed yet another monastery, with neat and bountiful gardens tended by tonsured monks, Harry observed out loud that France appeared as England had, before Henry VIII. Before its monasteries were deliberately ruined, their stone robbed long ago. This legacy of Protestantism scarred the English countryside. Harry imagined himself back in England at the time of the Catholics, before the split from Rome. Fields curtly dismissed his fancy, thinking instead of the welcome at Half Moon Alley.

When they reached Île-de-France and the wooded country north of Paris, the coachmen grew more wary. They brought up their weapons in readiness, fearful of attack by bandits. Harry, at a stop by the roadside, rechecked his pistol and loaded it.

L'Isle-Adam was not as paradisiacal as its name suggested, although the Oise, meandering towards its assignation with the Seine, looked cool and inviting from the heat and sweat of the coach.

●

FINALLY, GROWING FROM a blur in the distance—the towers and buttresses of Notre-Dame cathedral first, then the Louvre's expanse, and the Bastille's squat mass—Paris laid itself out before them. The Seine flowed leisurely around the Île de la Cité. Dominating the river, the island looked like a barge, with the smaller Île Saint-Louis in tow. The Île Louvier was green and lush. From these islands, the bridges and streets of Paris radiated out like a great wheel, its circumference the grand tree-lined boulevards, built over the recently pulled down fortifications. Louis XIV no longer considered his city endangered. Beyond these boulevards, though, the city stopped abruptly, with few buildings outside the wheel's rim. Parisians, it seemed, did not share their King's confidence.

Through Montmartre, past the church of Saint-Pierre. As dusk began to settle, the light reddened the stone of the church and the buildings around it, and glanced off its windowpanes.

On down, their coach now running on smooth roadway. The houses were more widely spaced than London's crowded streets, like in Robert Hooke's ideal city—the one he dreamed of building after the Conflagration. It had never happened; Londoners insisted on their original plots.

By the time the coach deposited them outside the Louvre, it was almost dark.

'*For what shall it profit a man, if he shall gain the whole world, and lose his own soul?*' Fields quoted, looking sourly at the building's extravagance.

The blood still sluggish in their legs, they walked past the Palais des Tuileries, its gardens a geometry lesson. Men with ladders were busy lighting the lamps hanging from the walls, or from ledges, making Paris far brighter than London.

The smells of a city and its population made the air comfortingly heavy again. Harry breathed it in, feeling less a stranger.

For once, Fields let Harry take the lead. 'This city owns too many bridges,' he said.

Hortense Mancini had given Harry directions to the Hôtel de Bouillon, the home of her sister. Crossing the Pont Rouge, its old wooden arches twisted and precarious, from the Île de la Cité to the Seine's south bank, they saw skiffs and galiotes, and barges filled with barrels. Looking along the river instead of where he walked, Harry collided with a man unwilling to move aside, making him stagger sideways on the narrow bridge and into the rail. When he looked threateningly at Harry, Fields checked the man, by shaking his head at him to stand down.

The man moved on, no word or glance back at them.

'A warning, perhaps, of how Paris can be,' Fields said. Harry adjusted his coat and checked his pockets. The weight of his moneybag pulled his waistcoat down, where he had sewn it into the lining. His pistol and letters of introduction were still in his canvas bag.

Taking the turn onto the Quai Malaquais, they soon arrived at the Hôtel de Bouillon. Two wings projected from each side of the house's main body, reaching almost to the street, their arched windows looking at them haughtily. Through imposing wrought-iron gates, by the light spilling from inside the house, they could see shaped bushes and trees, and the cour d'honneur, fastidiously swept. Trying the handles, Harry found one of the gates was unlocked. They ventured in, passing a couple of servants without challenge.

The house's facade filled their view: high, wide, and ornately decorated. Built for Macé Bertrand de La Bazinière, once Treasurer to the King, it became home to Henrietta Maria, Louis XIV's aunt. After her death, it was bought by the Duc de Bouillon.

In the large, light-filled vestibule, chessboard-tiled and reaching the house's full height, they were welcomed by another servant. From his superior manner, and his uniform being distinct from others of the household, he appeared to be a butler.

Before they opened their mouths, he greeted them in very correct, although heavily accented, English. Seeing Harry's surprise, the man pointed at them both. 'Your clothing. You can be nothing but English.'

He had a way of tilting his head sideways with a half smile, as if to convey his service was far beneath him, and he only did it as play.

Harry searched the pocket containing his money and his letters of introduction, and presented the letter from Hortense Mancini. Leaving them to stand in the vestibule, the butler took it and went to his mistress.

Fields looked at Harry and arched an eyebrow. He pulled the end of his sleeve with the heel of his hand, to wipe some grime from Harry's cheek.

'So! You must be presentable,' he said. 'For a duchesse.'

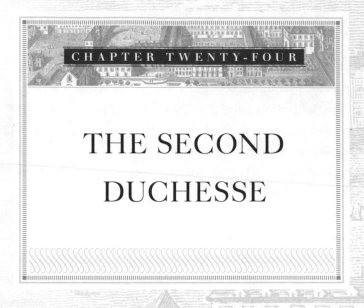

CHAPTER TWENTY-FOUR

THE SECOND DUCHESSE

TO THEIR SURPRISE, IT WAS NOT the butler who summoned them into a reception room, but the Duchesse de Bouillon herself. She came out to greet them. Unmistakably a Mancini, she was a copy of her sister: slightly wider, a little heavier in the face, but with the same colouring and the same dark eyes. But where Hortense was all poise and languorous calm, Marie-Anne was nervous, fidgety, and seemed harassed. She wore no wig, and had the habit of carelessly running her hands through her hair, one after the other: the first to mess it up, the second to smooth it down. Despite this air of distraction, she welcomed them with a dazzling smile, the equal of Hortense's.

She read her sister's letter as she walked across the vestibule. By the time she reached Harry and Fields, she had decided both were her lifelong friends.

She told the butler to fetch drinks and food, addressing him as Mercier. Mercier seemed piqued by this instruction, looking sideways at them as he went.

'Come through, come through.' Her voice was breathier than Hortensc's, and higher pitched. She took them into a room with the largest carpet Harry had ever walked on. Paintings, dimly seen in the candle-light—some lascivious, to his mind—covered the walls. A harpsichord, its case patterned in chinoiserie, took up the room's centre. Its lid was open, the inside showing a scandalous hunting scene, painted contrastingly in the Dutch style.

Marie-Anne settled herself into a méridienne, but quickly became uncomfortable. She shifted fretfully, and toyed with her hair, trying to place a wisp being difficult back behind her ear. Her feet brought themselves up automatically until she lay sideways. She blew air up at her fringe by protruding her bottom lip, then smiled at them again.

'It is hard to be formal, here in my own house.' She motioned them both to sit, and they lowered themselves onto the chaise longue opposite her. The Colonel, in particular, looked out of place on the fine French furniture.

'My salon meets here. Often there are men from the Académie des Sciences. Last month Joseph-Guichard Duverney was my guest.'

'The famous anatomist,' Harry replied.

She beamed at him, pleased by his recognition of the name. 'In fact, we are due to meet tomorrow evening. My sister writes of your work for the Royal Society, Monsieur Hunt. You must attend. In our immodesty, we have discussed the New Philosophy.' She wriggled her way to a more comfortable position, then pointed to a stone bust watching them blindly from its pedestal next to the fireplace. 'He would not have approved of a mere woman being interested in such things.'

'Your uncle, the Cardinal Mazarin?' Harry asked.

'Yes, Jules Mazarin. Born Giulio Raimondo Mazzarino. I want to move him. I feel him watching me, sometimes.' She smiled, for herself rather than for them. 'He made all of this possible. My wealth, and therefore my marriage. I take some pride in him. But also, I know, he was a ruthless man. Of course, for he was Chief Minister of France.'

'He used his rank to gain his wealth.' Fields stated it bluntly.

Marie-Anne did not take offence. 'He replaced his mentor, Cardinal Richelieu. Who, also, used his rank to gain his wealth. Which man was worse, I cannot decide.' She fussed again, and decided to move to her other side, transferring herself across the méridienne. 'I have not seen my sister in a long while,' she said brightly. 'How is she?'

'We met with her in King's Lynn, nearly two weeks ago,' Harry replied. 'She seemed well, did she not, Colonel?'

'*Very* well,' Fields concurred, with an emphasis that Marie-Anne caught the meaning of.

'Hortense captures a man's heart easily, does she not? But never gives her own. This is her appeal, I think.'

'Harry's heart belongs to another,' Fields told her.

'A little less than before, perhaps?'

'I only replied the Duchesse was well,' Harry said primly. It was as if he were a child interrupting a conversation between adults.

'Good!' Marie-Anne displayed her perfect teeth to the Colonel. She waved Hortense's letter at them. 'And you will help us find the Sancy.' She stated it as fact.

'We're in Paris on another undertaking, which must take precedence,' Harry replied. 'To find Captain Jeffrey Hudson.'

'Or, at least, the man who poses as him,' Fields said.

Through the windows, looking across the cour d'honneur and through the gates, Harry could see the lights of Paris, and the Quai Malaquais still busy. How would he ever find the missing Hudson in a city strange to him, with people who spoke another language? Let alone a diamond lost for a quarter century or more.

'The Queen's dwarf.' Marie-Anne looked thoughtful. 'I remember stories of him. He met with my uncle.'

'Did he?' Harry asked. 'When he was with the Queen?'

'Definitely. Here in Paris. My uncle spoke of him. A memorable thing, to meet a man so small.'

'Did the Cardinal suspect him of taking the diamond?' Fields asked.

'He was sure of it. Queen Henrietta Maria told him so. After Hudson killed a man, she dismissed him from her retinue.'

'The Cardinal had already paid for it,' Harry said, remembering Hortense's story.

'It was not the money he missed, for he had plenty more. He desired the diamond only for itself. It obsessed him. After its disappearance, more so.'

'I wonder if the Queen made mischief,' Harry ventured. 'Having the money from the sale, perhaps she sent Hudson back to England with the diamond.'

'My uncle had the same thought.'

Fields rubbed at the old wound in his arm, which ached after the day's journey. 'Her desperation for money, to keep her husband's army equipped, made her dishonest, perhaps.'

Marie-Anne abruptly swung her legs around, and stood. 'Come. The air is too close in here.' She took them through the large double doors leading to the garden at the rear of the house.

Lamps had been lit, illuminating the lawns. Hedges sheltered them from the city's noise. With no wind, the trees were silent, too, and seemed to watch over them. Marie-Anne led them down a flight of stone steps to grass clipped as smooth as carpet, interspersed by statues on pedestals. She looked at the statues distrustfully, as if they watched them, too.

Harry and Fields to either side of her, they walked together over the lawn.

She gave them each a tired smile. 'London is made frantic with conspiracies against your King, is it not? Catholics shall sweep away all those who oppose them, in a terror of popish vengeance.'

'The rumours are greater than the threat,' Harry replied. 'A man named Titus Oates claims to have overheard the plans. Those who don't believe him go unheeded by those who do.'

'We, too, in Paris, are gripped by fear. Here, we all busy ourselves in poisoning one another. Or else, we accuse one another of it. I am said to plot against my husband.' Marie-Anne shook her head. 'I dislike the man, but I would never murder him. In London, you have Oates. In Paris, we have Catherine Montvoisin. *La Voisin,* as she is called—it means The Neighbour—claims to have helped half the court to kill off their husbands, or their fathers, or anyone else inconvenient. The poisons she uses, she calls "inheritance powders." I, myself, have been questioned, in the Grand Arsenal, by the Lieutenant Général of the Paris Police.'

'La Reynie?' Harry asked.

'You know of him?'

'Harry has a letter from the Board of Ordnance,' Fields told her. 'Introducing us to him.'

'For Gabriel Nicolas de La Reynie?' Marie-Anne put her hands together under her chin as if in prayer, just as her sister did in King's Lynn. 'You will be known to him already. La Reynie's *mouches*—his flies—buzz all around Paris. He will wish to know why you come to me. You must see him, soon, otherwise he will wonder why you do not announce yourself. You must go to the Grand Châtelet. In the morning.' She wrapped her shawl around herself more tightly. 'La Reynie leads the *Chambre Ardente.*'

'Ardont?'

She smiled at Harry's accent. '*Ardente.* Burning, but like a passion, yes? The Room of Fire. An old name. It is a court. It sent hundreds of Calvinists to their deaths. La Reynie has reconvened it for these poisonings. La Voisin keeps herself alive by incriminating others.'

She stopped suddenly, a thought striking her. 'Did you tell the Board of Ordnance of the Sancy?'

'I said nothing of it,' Harry reassured her. 'I'm instructed to find the missing Hudson. There was no need to speak of the diamond.'

'That is something,' she said, seeming to cheer a little. 'It is important you find it.'

'We cannot help you,' Colonel Fields told her. 'We are strangers. How will we find the dwarf, even if he is in Paris, leave alone a diamond missing for so long?'

Harry wished Fields were not so blunt, even though he voiced his own thoughts exactly.

At the point furthest away from the house, by the garden's far wall, they turned back, following a neatly raked path.

'Let me bargain with you,' Marie-Anne said, placing her hands on their elbows and drawing them closer in. 'You are strangers, as you say, Colonel Fields. You do not speak the language.' She looked them each in the eye for a protracted moment. 'But *I* might find a dwarf in Paris.' She smiled, showing off her spectacular Mancini teeth. 'I have my own *mouches*. Interesting people, with interesting friends. I have influence, still, and Hudson is conspicuous. A person that small stands out, does he not?'

'In return for your help, you wish us to try to find the diamond,' Harry said.

'No,' she answered, as they approached the house. 'I wish you to find it. If you find the dwarf, you will find the diamond. He knows of it, and where it is.' She gave a firm nod, as if doing so made it true.

Just like her sister, Harry thought. 'I'd be grateful for your help,' he replied slowly, not quite concealing he was humouring her. 'Firstly, I wish to question the captain of *Incassable*. I know he lives here in Paris. *Incassable* was the ship Hudson took from France.'

'Visit him tomorrow,' Marie-Anne replied. 'But see La Reynie first. Do you have protection? Paris, with all its lights, has many shadows.'

'I do,' Harry replied. 'The Colonel, though, has lost his sword.'

'Take one of my husband's, Colonel. He has a fine collection of weapons. Choose any from the armoury.'

They reentered the house. The butler waited in the large room with the harpsichord, having brought food, water, and wine.

Marie-Anne yawned, covering her mouth with her hand. 'Mercier will show you to your rooms. And tomorrow, he will go with you to the Châtelet, to interpret.'

'Goodnight, Harry. Goodnight, Colonel.' She kissed each man on both cheeks, which made them blush, and left the room.

Mercier, her butler, let slip a deliberately loud sigh.

CHAPTER TWENTY-FIVE

THE LATE CONVERSATION

THE FIRE, BUILT AND LIT BY the diffident butler, was far too small for the room. Harry, sitting on his bed, and Colonel Fields, sitting in a chair, both kept their coats on. Mercier had given each man a candle, which burned together on the mantelshelf.

'She will be a useful ally,' Fields murmured.

'She offers the help of her butler.'

'If he is trustworthy.'

'Don't you trust him?'

'I do not know him.'

'He's in her service, and does her bidding.'

'Then, do you trust her?' The Colonel leaned forwards in his chair, resting his elbows on his knees. 'She is nervous, like a cat in a thunderstorm.'

'From these accusations of poisoning, no doubt.'

'This man La Reynie sounds daunting. You must take a care, Harry.'

'You say *you*, Colonel. I'm fortunate that it's *we*, and that you're here to help me.' Harry pulled off his boots.

'It is to you these people come,' Fields replied, screwing up his nose at the smell from Harry's feet. He quickly pulled out his pipe. 'Sir Jonas. Lord Danby. The Mancini sisters, Hortense and Marie-Anne. Your brains they value, not mine.' He searched for tobacco in his bag.

'My brains are sorely tested. I've given them little, so far. It's difficult to think clearly after seeing Lefèvre again.'

'I have seen many men die. I never saw one come alive again. Your mind plays tricks, surely.' Fields filled his pipe as he spoke. 'You wish to warn the King of this Lazarus being in London, I know, for you spoke of it on our journey. But if you were to send a letter, you risk Danby seeing it—it was his man we saw at the Billingsgate quayside with Lefèvre. Even diplomatic post is not immune from Danby's spies, so I would not even send one through the King's envoy. Returning to London must follow finding the dwarf, which we are here together to do.'

Harry rubbed at his feet and glanced at his friend. Fields seemed to have aged even since leaving London. His eyes grew ever paler, more watery, the skin around them ever more sagging. His hands trembled, signalled by the shaking of his pipe. A glow of fondness rose in Harry's chest. He regretted that on their journey they had become terse with one another.

Fields caught Harry's grateful expression. 'Although I am slow, constantly left behind by your quickness, I may see things from another vantage.' He nodded encouragement at Harry. 'So! Let me hear your thinking.'

Harry gathered himself to order the facts of his investigation. 'Well, then. Firstly, the body of Captain Hudson. Found in a ship's boat. Killed by a cannonball, used to break his head. Presumably murdered by another man with him, who rowed the jolly boat.'

Fields nodded again, puffing smoke. 'Or others. There was room for more.'

'Secondly, the servant, Mrs. Leach, who knew Hudson and accepted his replacement. She showed us the outhouse, where we observed the marks of heavy equipment, gouged into the floor. One of the Frenchmen, she said, was peculiar-looking. Did she mean Lefèvre? He looks more beast than man. She said he had two men with him, as there were at the dock.'

'I cannot say who she saw,' Fields said. 'There were three men at the dock, who met with Danby's man. Who knows if they are French?'

'We stand out as English, to one who notices such things. Mercier, the butler, saw it straightaway.'

'Like mustard in a coal scuttle,' Fields agreed.

Harry slid under his bed covers, keeping his breeches on. 'Sir Jonas told us Hudson worked for the Board of Ordnance, to bring intelligence of French affairs. Mrs. Leach told us the same thing.' He removed his spectacles and covered a yawn with his hand. 'Thirdly, then. Hortense Mancini, and her desire to find the Sancy.'

'Her desire for *you* to find it. It is a commission. You would be a wealthy man.'

Harry sighed. 'She may as well ask that we bring her down the moon. Did Hudson take it, after being banished from France after his duel?'

'We would have found it in our searching of his body and the ground around his boat.'

'We could easily have missed it, in that water. Or, it was taken from him.'

'True enough,' Fields agreed, inhaling deeply from his pipe. 'Anyone might have taken it. Think what it could have bought, such a diamond, for the King's side.'

'Or for the side of Parliament.'

'Parliament never benefitted from the money,' Fields said sharply. 'Cromwell would have sold it, undoubtedly, as he sold off the King's paintings and the rest of his treasures. Is there a fourthly, Harry? For I feel my bed beckons.'

'The clerk at the Kontor, at King's Lynn. From him we found the name of its captain. Eugène de Beauchene. We must question him on his memory of a dwarf aboard his ship, and if he knew Hudson had the diamond with him.'

'Hopefully his memory shall be more complete than Japhia Bennett's. He could give us little.' Fields yawned extravagantly. 'It is hard to keep a secret on a ship. I speak from experience. Think of the men's proximity. Hudson found his head staved in by a cannonball at the end of his voyage. Perhaps the diamond being upon him led to his murder by a sailor.'

'Perhaps.' Harry lay back in bed. The mattress was the deepest, the most comfortable, he had ever rested on. 'De Beauchene would recall if crewmen took his jolly boat.'

'Fifthly?' Fields's eyes were now closed. He had rested his head against the back of his chair and his breathing had slowed. His pipe was in danger of dropping from his hand.

Watching the orange light sent across the ceiling by the glow of the fire, Harry did not notice. 'Lord Danby insisted I come to Paris. His intelligencers tell him the imposter's here. I wonder if he knows more than he lets on.'

Fields opened one eye. 'If he knew more, would he not simply send us to the dwarf?'

Harry shrugged pensively. 'We must be mindful of reporting to the Lieutenant Général. We're to go to him tomorrow.'

'In the morning, as the Duchesse advised. It will bring suspicion upon us if we avoid him, if his *mouches* see as much as she says.' Fields coughed, and sat forwards. 'As well as this man you take to be Lefèvre, the dead assassin alive again, another thing makes you desire to return to London.'

'Grace Hooke. As well you know.'

'As well I know. And now, I must go to bed, for all this talking tires me, and my missing Elizabeth does not improve my mood.' Fields sat silently for a while, before realising Harry was snoring. It had been a long day, another of many long days. 'I had but one love in my long life,' he said quietly to himself. 'Now, in my old age, I have found another. It seems a miracle to me.' He stood up slowly, stretching his back, then straightened Harry's bedclothes and placed his coat and bag on the floor, all the while looking at him tenderly. 'Good night to you, Harry.'

Fields took his candle from the mantelshelf and left, shutting the door behind him.

The noise woke Harry from his brief sleep. Remembering the money from Sir Jonas and Lord Danby, and more from Hortense Mancini, he groggily got back out of bed and went to lock the door, but there was no key. The chair Fields had sat in was too low to wedge its back under the handle. Hearing the Colonel's own door shutting softly further down the corridor, he felt inexplicably timid.

He was perfectly safe inside the Hôtel de Bouillon, he told himself.

The danger, if any, started tomorrow.

He searched through his bag and produced the book he had taken from Gresham's library. Getting back into bed, he started to read by the light from the solitary candle.

It was John Evelyn's *Instructions Concerning Erecting of a Library*, the translation of *Advis pour dresser une bibliothèque*, written by Gabriel Naudé. He would read it until sleep came again.

Now well-used, its cover battered from his reading it on their journey, Harry did not yet know how it might help him find the man impersonating Captain Jeffrey Hudson.

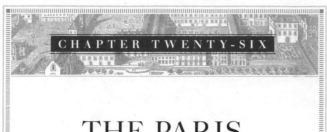

CHAPTER TWENTY-SIX

THE PARIS
POLICEMAN

FROM THE HÔTEL DE BOUILLON TO see Gabriel Nicolas de La Reynie, Lieutenant Général of the Paris police, meant a ride by brouette along the Quai Malaquais. The three men were squeezed into their rickety vehicle: Colonel Fields and Harry wedged together, and facing them, Marie-Anne's butler. Visible through a small hatch, the man pulling them threaded swiftly through the traffic.

Harry could not help but dislike Mercier, whose expression was a finely judged meeting point of amusement and insolence. His hair was combed strangely to one side, something shiny holding it flat, to suppress, Harry suspected, a natural curl. Harry had seen no one else with this hairstyle in Paris. Another example of Mercier's independence of mind.

The sunshine was bright, although the air had not yet warmed up for the day. Ramps to their left dropped steeply to the Seine, hectic with men carrying goods to and from the ships moored at the quayside.

As they swerved to avoid another brouette, Harry hoped again for the crackle of paper inside his coat. But, as he knew full well, there was none.

He had lost the letter of introduction from the Board of Ordnance.

Their passports, also, were gone.

Harry and Fields had searched for nearly half an hour in their bed-rooms, and in the grand parlour where they had sat with Marie-Anne the previous evening. Then, they had searched in her garden.

Harry flexed his hands, trying to relax them.

Fields saw the motion. 'I have said. They dropped from your pocket. Perhaps when you collided with the man on the bridge.'

Harry was sure he had checked for its presence, and felt it in its usual place, with their passports, the previous evening. *After* they had crossed the Pont Rouge.

They rattled east, and past the enormous Collège des Quatre-Nations, founded by Cardinal Mazarin. Mercier told them of the Bibliothèque Maza-rine housed inside: the Cardinal's vast collection of books left to the nation. He sounded proud, as if he himself had donated it.

'I plan to visit,' Harry told him, to meet with the butler's sudden indifference.

In front of the Collège, a zealous-looking man, his eyes gleaming with industry, busied himself scraping off the various posters advertising cures and concerts, plays and places to eat, that were pasted along its front wall. One, wrinkled from its hasty sticking to the stone, proclaimed *L'Exhibition de Monstruosités* taking place over the next few evenings.

'A display,' Mercier told him when Harry questioned him. 'Of—I don't know the English. *Lusus naturæ.*'

'The malformations of nature,' Harry suggested. 'I saw a boneless Dutch woman once, at the Bartholomew Fair.'

'A low entertainment,' Fields growled. 'The afflicted shown as spectacle.'

From the Quai de Conti, they went across the Pont Neuf. A barge piled high with timbers, its crew sitting precariously on its load, slid beneath them.

Paris's widest bridge was also the busiest. The man pulling their brouette sweated and grunted with the strain of steering them over. Bumping his little vehicle up onto the pavement to dodge other carts and carriages, he forced people to step back smartly into the bridge's bastions.

'Quicker to walk,' Fields observed, as they lurched by the statue of Henri IV on his horse. 'And a man would not be yoked for our transport.'

'He exchanges his labour for payment. If he did not think it worth his while, he would choose another profession.'

Fields looked at Harry pityingly, and seemed about to say more on the matter; instead he pursed his lips tightly. The tendons of his neck were rigid, like stretched cords. Harry looked away, avoiding the Colonel's habitual morning gruffness, made all the worse by their fruitless searching.

They turned onto the Quai de la Ferraille, with all its hardware shops. This part of Paris was far poorer than where their journey began. The buildings were dull, their walls crumbling, woodwork neglected. The smell of blood was unmistakable from a nearby slaughterhouse. Together with the stink from the beaches of sticky mud beside the Seine, Harry had to put his hand to his nose.

He looked up at the Grand Châtelet prison's impassive face, its complexion pocked by weather and Parisian smoke. It looked back at him blankly, staring down as it had on thousands of unfortunates before.

○

A ROBUST GATE studded with nails led into the Châtelet's grounds. The place was crowded: a market set up with circular stalls, their roofs made of canvas held up by a central pole.

They nodded their thanks to the driver, who had unharnessed himself and stood rolling his shoulders. Mercier refused Harry's offer to pay, as he had instructions to from the Duchesse.

They passed from daylight to gloom, walking through an archway into the Châtelet itself. Mercier asked a soldier where they could find the Lieutenant Général.

The man had a strand of tobacco stuck to his lip, waving like an insect's leg. He examined the three men before him: the small, slight, bespectacled Harry, dismissed with a curl of his lip; then Mercier, who provoked a flicker of recognition; then Colonel Fields, whose relaxed air and military bearing he seemed to appreciate.

It was the Colonel he addressed. *'Il a des affaires avec vous?'* He has business with you?

Fields turned to Mercier questioningly. The guard's eyes narrowed

'Il aura.' He will have. Mercier had none of his usual sidelong slyness.

'Étrangers?' Foreigners? The man advanced, and looked more closely at them.

'Anglais,' Mercier replied. *'De Londres.'* English. From London. *'Monsieur Henry Hunt et Colonel Michael Fields.'*

'Attendez!' The man turned away and went into a passage, disappearing into darkness.

Mercier nodded, then shrugged at Fields and Harry. 'We must wait. As you would expect, for the Lieutenant Général is a busy man.'

'Of course,' Fields said. 'He is important, we know that.'

Harry looked at his friend anxiously. 'We don't have the letter—'

'He will see us,' Fields reassured him.

●

AFTER A QUARTER of an hour or more, spent mostly in silence except for their feet scraping on the stone floor, another man returned. An officer. He was tall and imposing, and wore a bright blond wig, generously curled.

'Vous souhaitez voir le Lieutenant Général? Vous êtes anglais?' He paused, then tried again in English. 'You wish to see the Lieutenant Général?'

'We are English, yes,' Fields said, looking relieved. 'We must speak with him.'

The officer looked Fields up and down, the old man in his ancient soldier's coat, then smiled politely. 'You have your papers?'

'We are sent by the Board of Ordnance,' Harry said, swallowing nervously.

The man stopped smiling. 'You have your papers?' he repeated. 'Documents?'

'We do not,' Harry admitted. 'We had a letter of introduction, but it is misplaced. Written on the authority of Sir Jonas Moore of the Board of Ordnance, addressed to the Lieutenant Général.'

'We must meet with Monsieur de Paris,' Fields said.

The man pressed his lips together, then sighed. 'You have heard this name. *Monsieur de Paris* . . . Imagine the responsibility! How it must press upon him. Well, we must all do our duty. I cannot let you in if I do not know who you are. We are careful with the personage of the Lieutenant Général.' The man stood a little more upright when he said the rank.

'The Lieutenant Général expects us, I'm sure,' Harry added, thinking of the *mouches*.

'Expected or no, I cannot let you see him if you refuse to prove who you are. You have *les passeports?*' The officer held out his hand.

The Colonel and Harry looked at one another. Mercier looked, in his sideways way, at them.

'We—I mean I—have lost our passports, too,' Harry said.

'They were taken from us, on one of the bridges,' Fields told him.

The officer looked troubled for them. 'Without your letter of introduction, you lose the chance to see the Lieutenant Général. Without your *passeports*, you lose your liberty. You are in difficulties. Difficulties!' He shook his head theatrically, the wig jouncing, then played his fingers over his upper lip as if hatching a plan. 'Let us see if we can help you.' He pointed along the gloomy corridor, towards a guttering lamp's flame floating in the blackness beyond.

As they started off towards it, he made an impatient 'ah' noise, seemingly at his own stupidity. 'You must give up your sword, Colonel. Do you, Monsieur Hunt, also have a weapon? I cannot let you near the Lieutenant Général if you are armed.'

Harry had left behind his modified pistol, not wanting to risk having to give it up to La Reynie. Fields unbuckled his borrowed sword and presented it to the blond-wigged man, who then nodded them into the corridor.

They followed him, Harry stumbling on a raised flagstone unseen in the darkness. They emerged into a large courtyard busy with men—no women here, Harry noticed—who all walked with great purpose, and whose sighting of the officer taking them to La Reynie made them all more intent on their work. He led them up a stairway winding its way up a tower. Occasional arrow slits let in bright shafts of light, flickering as each man passed through.

They went across an old oak floor, furrowed from years of footsteps, through an imposing doorway, and into a brightly lit office.

Its walls were filled with shelves of books. A large pendulum clock ticked loudly, its mechanism rattling its wooden cabinet. The fire crackled from burning unseasoned wood.

On the desk, a stuffed owl in a glass case glared at them, as if blaming them for its plight.

'You wish to speak with Monsieur de Paris,' the man stated, his voice full of regret. 'But you cannot show who you are.' He placed the Colonel's sword on the desk and dropped into his chair.

Harry stepped forwards, and bowed. 'You are Lieutenant Général La Reynie.'

'Whatever would make you say so?'

'Your books. I know of your interest in ancient philosophy. Many have nothing on their spines to reveal what they are, but I do see Aristotle, Plutarch, Ovid, Cicero . . .'

The officer smiled broadly. 'And Virgil, Seneca, Horace, Livy, Tacitus. You take an interest in such things?'

'I assisted Mr. Robert Hooke, at the Royal Society of London. I became its Observator. During my apprenticeship, I read all of these men.'

'I like to know more recent thinking, too. I have Galileo, Descartes, your Francis Bacon, and Thomas Hobbes. You have met with Monsieur Hobbes?'

'I've read his *Lux Mathematica* and his *Leviathan*,' Harry replied. Mr. Hooke met him on several occasions. He's recently dead, sadly.'

'I did not know. Sad news. Scandalous stuff, heh, his *Leviathan*? No hell? No purgatory? Now he will know if he was right, I suppose. In his State of Nature, nothing can be thought right or wrong. And so we combine, by compromise and subterfuge, in our own self-interest. Even to bow the knee to an absolute ruler—it is, after all else, in our best interests to do so. A thin view, is it not? All of us like little machines.'

The officer pushed a large pile of papers to one side, took a blank sheet, and placed it on the space he had made. Although the room was lit by daylight through a large window, a candle on his desk was burning, reminding Harry of the Chambre Ardente. 'Books are not enough to show I am Nicolas Gabriel de La Reynie. Others in the Châtelet have such offices, and such interests. An unexpectedly cultured place, this prison.'

'I knew also by the reaction to you of those who work here, as we walked by them.'

La Reynie nodded, looking happy to be found out. 'My *robins*? They make a good show of competence, do they not? That is unfair, perhaps. Most are good enough. Honest, on the whole.' He turned to Fields. 'You were right. I already knew of you. The English Envoy to Paris, Sir Henry Savile, advised me of your visit. Perhaps it is too great a coincidence an English pair of travellers is here, but let me satisfy myself who you are. I know a little of Monsieur Hooke. I have his *Micrographia*.' He pointed at his copy bound in black Morocco leather, in its place on a shelf behind them. 'He writes of flying, and claims to have done so. How has he achieved this remarkable feat?'

'I myself have flown in a machine designed by Mr. Hooke, across the quadrangle at Gresham College.'

La Reynie gave a silent whistle. 'How did you provide strength enough to the wings? He tells of artificial muscles, but gives us no detail.'

'Mr. Hooke knows more than any man in the world about springs. He employs them, working with and against each other.'

Using the Lieutenant Général's paper, his quill and ink, Harry drew a diagram of the flying machine he had built to Hooke's direction. He made no mention of his broken ankle when it made its unsatisfactory landing.

La Reynie studied the drawing. 'You have a way with a line. This drawing is proficiently done.' He whistled, this time with some volume. 'So, this is how!'

This man was nothing like Marie-Anne's portrayal, Harry thought. He was welcoming. Jovial, and philosophical.

'You, Colonel Fields, were a soldier for Parliament, yes? A just cause, I would say, fighting against a despot.' La Reynie quickly reconsidered, and tapped his head as if to clear it of such thoughts. 'Our King, Louis Quatorze, is a much wiser man. And gracious. Very gracious.' He took back his pen. 'An interesting pair to have before me, no? A man of science, and a man of war.' He seemed to have forgotten the other man, Mercier, who stood with them.

'We met upon another matter,' Harry told him. 'Colonel Fields assisted me then, and we have since become friends.'

'Another matter?' La Reynie looked at him with a piercing gaze, disconcertingly like the owl to the side of him.

'A young child, a boy. I helped investigate his death.'

'Perhaps you are better suited to be a *policier*.' He leaned his elbow on his desk, resting his chin on his fist. 'Sir Henry Saville tells me why you are here in Paris. Let me hear it from you, to see if you agree.'

Had Danby informed the Envoy, or had the Board of Ordnance? Harry knew the Lord High Treasurer wanted to stay as clear as possible from the search for Hudson. He decided it was safer to only mention the Board of Ordnance, as the letters and passports had been written there. 'Sir Jonas Moore employs me as an Investigator. I am required to find a man. Captain Jeffrey Hudson. Or rather, the man who pretends to be him. For the real Hudson's body was found, dead since the Civil Wars.'

'You think him here, in Paris?' La Reynie did not sound surprised, which Harry took as a good sign. Hopefully, it meant Sir Henry Saville had told him of it.

'The man's housekeeper made me think so, when we went to his home.

I wish also to speak with the captain of the ship which transported Hudson from France. He lives here in Paris, we're told.'

'Which ship?'

'It was named *Incassable*.'

'Who said this to you?'

'A sailor who crewed aboard *Incassable*, and who remembered Hudson aboard it.'

'Jeffrey Hudson was famous in his time. A man so small he was hidden in a pie. It would take a similarly small man to impersonate him.'

'The impostor's taller, being a little above three feet high.'

'Yet he passed in England for Hudson?' As he asked, La Reynie began to write.

'He explained his growth on a change of food, after his capture by Barbary pirates.'

'It sounds unlikely. Can such growth occur in a dwarf, late in life?'

Harry shrugged. 'That's by the by. The first Hudson was killed.'

La Reynie scratched his chin. 'And to find the imposter, you come here with the Duc de Bouillon's servant.'

Mercier started, and cleared his throat, but La Reynie shushed him. 'The Duc is away, as often he is. The Duchesse is not.'

La Reynie stood up suddenly and reached for his wax, melted it with the candle on his desk, and impressed his seal ring into it.

'I am happy you are who you say you are.' He held up the papers he had written on. 'Here are your documents while you stay in Paris. If you find your letter from the Board of Ordnance, then bring it to me. You enjoy my protection while you look for this dwarf. I will help you, if I can—if he is, as you believe, in Paris. But in return—as part of our "commonwealth," as Hobbes would say—I expect you to help me. What do you know of poisons?'

'In my medical and chymical work, I've often employed substances which, if used carelessly, are injurious.' Harry's reply was hesitant, halting, as he was worried where the admission might take him.

'Injurious? Your hostess, Marie-Anne de Bouillon, plans to use poisons against her husband.' La Reynie paused, as if expecting Harry to say something. Harry did not. 'At least, La Voisin has told us so. The Duchesse consulted her, she says. Have you seen anything at the Hôtel de Bouillon to confirm her testimony?'

Harry glanced across at Fields. 'We've stayed there for one night. I've seen no poison and I've seen no husband, so my answer must be no. Besides, possessing poisons doesn't mean they'll be used against anyone, to cause them harm.'

'She is not a physician, nor is she a chymist. She is a duchesse. I wish you to tell me everything of her business. Then I will decide if her keeping poisons is suspicious, or no.'

La Reynie picked up the sword loaned to Fields by Marie-Anne, and walked towards the office door, to indicate their meeting came to an end. As they made to leave, he extended his hand to stop them.

'The capitaine of *Incassable* is known to me. He lives in the Place Royale.' He looked at Mercier, and the butler indicated he would guide them there. La Reynie passed Harry his letter, and a second sheet with de Beauchene's address. 'You keep things from me, I know, but I too keep things from you. That the Lord High Treasurer Danby asked you to come to Paris, I notice, you were careful to keep quiet upon.' He offered up the sword back to Fields. 'While you are here, you will report to me here, every morning, first thing. Do not forget, I wish to know everything about the Duchesse de Bouillon.'

CHAPTER TWENTY-SEVEN

THE SUFFERING CAPITAINE

MERCIER GAVE THEM A HISTORY AS they walked. '*Marais*,' he explained, 'means swamp. The marshes were drained by the Templars. After Charles V built his Hôtel Saint-Pol, the aristocracy gathered here. Far enough away from the bad smells of the city.'

As the Rue de la Verrerie broadened, the houses became ever grander, until each was a great mansion, or hôtel, boasting more magnificent façades, more ornate gateways, and more detail on their stonework than the last. Passersby were either the rich, dressed splendidly, or those who served them. Each household vied to better its neighbours, so the servants were dressed splendidly, too. Only their speed of movement marked them out as employees.

The road opened up even further, becoming a wide boulevard where it met the Rue Saint-Antoine. The Bastille's squat towers rose in front of them—Mercier's voice quietened as he told them the prison's name. He hurriedly steered them into the Rue Royale, leading to the Place Royale, where the sea captain lived in retirement.

Elegant arcades of white stone held up the houses. The higher storeys were of red brick, striped with more gleaming stone. Their roof slates were blue, almost purple in the morning sunshine.

The wide-open square, kept free of trees, had paths crossing from corner to corner, and from middle to middle, leaving eight triangles of trimmed lawn. In the centre, these paths all leading to it, stood a bronze statue of Louis XIII astride his horse. The metal reflected the sun. Harry covered his eyes against its glare.

For a merchant ship's captain, the house showed some success in his way of business. They presented their letter from La Reynie to a doorman, detailing who they were, and that they enjoyed the Lieutenant Général's protection. De Beauchene passed instruction: they were to be brought straight to him. They followed his servant up the impressive staircase and were shown to where he waited, a large reception room on the first floor.

De Beauchene sat by the open window, wearing a shirt open at the neck. Sweat showed darkly on the cotton and stuck it to his skin. As he turned towards them, he revealed an abscess under his jaw, which spread up his face to his right ear. His cheeks were pink, and his skin was shredding; he scratched at it, to then glumly regard it under his fingernails. Despite his discomfort, de Beauchene welcomed them warmly, his smile showing gapped and pointed teeth. He beckoned them to sit on the chairs around the room. He showed no inclination to move from his window, so they brought the chairs to him.

De Beauchene kept his eyes almost completely shut. Even looking away from the window, he winced from sensitivity to the light. Harry guessed his ailments to be syphilis and the effects of its treatment; he showed the signs of being poisoned by mercury.

'*Messieurs*,' de Beauchene said, waving the letter from the Lieutenant

Général at them. 'Sirs, I must say.' Strongly accented, his voice came out with effortless volume, filling his sitting room as it had once filled the decks of *Incassable*. He nodded to Harry and Mercier, and stared at Colonel Fields for some time, for so long it became uncomfortable for them all.

'Captain,' Fields said, wondering at the state of the man. 'Are you well enough to speak?'

'*Pardonnez-moi*. I met once with you, Colonel, I think. In a place called L'Île de Ré, the port of Saint-Martin-de-Ré, in fact.'

'No, sir, you did not,' Fields replied.

'A small distance by La Rochelle,' de Beauchene persisted.

'I never came to France, until accompanying Mr. Hunt, here,' Fields assured him, sending Harry an exasperated look.

'*Excusez* . . . long time ago. My . . .' He looked at Mercier for assistance. '*Cerveau? Mémoire?*'

'Memory,' supplied Mercier.

'My memory was to be good, but now it break.'

Such poor recall could be the syphilis, or the mercury, Harry considered, his hopes for their meeting subsiding. Could they trust the man's answers on Hudson? 'We met a member of your crew, who gave us your name. Japhia Bennett.'

'Japhia? *Toujours vivant?*' De Beauchene looked pleased.

'Alive, and residing in the port of King's Lynn,' Fields answered.

'I remember Japhia.'

'I hope you can remember this,' Harry said. 'We saw the jolly boat from *Incassable*. With a dead man inside it. Murdered. His name was Captain Jeffrey Hudson.'

De Beauchene eased himself away from his window. As he came closer, Harry could smell him, and wished he had not left his perch.

'*Le nain!* The little man! A *passager* aboard my ship, *une fois*.' He scowled fiercely at them. 'After, I find he run from Mazarin. If I know, I do not take him. But, he pays me much.'

'Where did you take him to, Capitaine?' Harry asked.

'Where you meet Japhia. To King's Lynn. He have happiness to go there. Happiness enough. Have no choice. It is where I go. Go with wine. *Revenir avec de la laine.*'

'Return with wool, the Capitaine says,' Mercier supplied.

'You recollect this clearly?' Fields asked doubtfully.

'He steal our boat! Who could forget so big *un crime contre l'Incassable?*'

'Do you bring to mind anything more of him?' Harry asked.

De Beauchene blew out his cheeks. 'I do not.' He frowned with concentration, looking at Colonel Fields. 'I see you before, I know it. You had *cheveux*. The hair.'

Fields chuckled, a sound Harry had not often heard. 'In that case, a long time ago. I assure you, I have never been to France before.'

'Not in France, then . . . but somewhere. *Quelque part.*'

'Perhaps, for I have travelled. I do not remember your face. A French sea captain would have stuck in my mind, I am sure.'

De Beauchene waved his hands apologetically.

'Did Hudson keep a bag upon him?' Harry asked. 'His body was found with one—like the bag Colonel Fields has with him, I imagine, although not much was left of it. It had a strap over one shoulder.'

'Too long ago,' he replied, once Mercier translated, for de Beauchene had lost the meaning. In my memory, I see him with bag, and not with bag. I do not know what *image* is the true *image*.'

'He was killed with a cannonball. His skull broken. A fifteen pounder, from a culverin. You would not have noticed such a ball go missing.'

'There, you are wrong,' de Beauchene said, his grin showing the points of his teeth. '*J'aurais certainement remarqué.*'

'He would definitely have noticed,' Mercier said.

They looked at him expectantly.

'The largest cannon I had was *couleuvrine moyenne*. Fire a ball weighs just *dix livres*—ten pound, you say. If a ball for a culverin disappeared, it would first have to appear. That, then, would be *mémorable.*'

'In England, we call them demi-culverins.' Fields sounded incredulous.

'Though the French *livre* is a little heavier than our pound, I know.'

'*L'Incassable* not big enough *pour des couleuvrines*.'

'So the ball that killed him was not from *Incassable*,' Harry said slowly. 'I didn't think to quiz Japhia Bennett about your ship's size of cannon.'

De Beauchene winced again, and clutched his stomach.

Harry moved forwards to assist as de Beauchene pitched forwards, almost falling to the floor. His breaths came in short gasps, and sweat poured from his face.

'You take mercury?' Harry asked him.

He nodded. 'It is not mercury that ruin my stomach. *Pardonnez-moi*.'

'There's nothing to pardon,' Harry assured him. 'What ails you, if not mercury?'

'I, too, once enjoy the Lieutenant Général's protection. He invest in trade. Wool, *surtout*. We friends.' His face darkened. 'Until I was named by La Voisin, who say I go to her for the arsenic poison. I never meet her!' He looked indignantly at them. 'The next I know, I in the Châtelet. La Reynie has a way of the questions . . .'

'A way?' Harry prompted.

'He gives you a glass filled with the water.' De Beauchene smiled grimly. 'A good host, yes? You finish it. He says, have you another. *Bien entendu*, you say no. "Have another," he say again, in way *aimable* he is. "I insist." You have another. For this is Monsieur de Paris. When he tells you, have a three, you know you have the trouble. "I have tell you everything," you say. "We shall see," he say, the smile on his face. "Monsieur La Reynie, there nothing more to tell." "While you are be questioned, you address me as Lieutenant Général!" he shout. You have another glass, *encore*, two his men hold you down, pour the water in you. You see where my story go?'

Colonel Fields fiddled with his injured ear. 'Such rough questioning only brings forth one thing. The story that best ends the torment of those being asked. As a way of finding the truth, it is imperfect.'

'I not lie, even for Lieutenant Général La Reynie,' de Beauchene declared. 'There is a questioner more *effroyable* even than him.' He looked upwards, towards Heaven.

'Fearsome,' Mercier said, visibly shuddering. '*Effroyable* means fearsome.'

'*Finalement*, La Reynie is satisfy I tell him truth. Another, *un homme inférieur*, a lesser man, would have continue with the "rough questioning," as you say it, Colonel.'

He paused, tired by his memory and his telling of the story.

'I not blame him. He do only his work as Lieutenant Général.'

CHAPTER TWENTY-EIGHT

THE CARDINAL'S LIBRARY

THEY RECROSSED THE PONT NEUF, WALKING this time. On making the turn onto the Quai de Conti, Harry told the others he wished to see the Bibliothèque Mazarine. Colonel Fields, breathless and yawning loudly, preferred to return to the Hôtel de Bouillon; he needed rest, and would retire for the afternoon. Mercier was sure the Duchesse must require him by now, so they left Harry by the Collège des Quatre-Nations.

Harry looked for the notice for L'Exhibition de Monstruosités pasted onto the brickwork. Most of the advertisements had now been scraped off by the zealous-looking man; he watched Harry warily, a sharp tool for removal dangling menacingly from his hand, wondering if he planned to paste more placards to the wall.

The notice had survived. Ignoring the man's stare, Harry noted the place: The Butte des Copeaux.

Newly built, the Collège des Quatre-Nations was not yet open to students. Harry, though, had a letter from Marie-Anne to introduce him to the librarian.

Without Fields's competence, or Mercier to interpret, Harry felt alone, yet curiously unencumbered. It was as if their presence had been a weight pressing upon him. He did not analyse this feeling, only felt it, as he reached the stone stairs from the vast atrium up to the reading room.

The Bibliothèque Mazarine was an enormous L-shaped space. To every side, books towered over him, on shelves looking like strata along a cliffside. Unwieldy-looking ladders leaned between great columns supporting balconies. The late afternoon sun sent a golden light through the windows and over the parquet floor.

Marble busts stood mutely around the library: heads on pedestals like trophies taken from defeated foes. Their milk-pale eyes watched him as he walked to the elbow of the L. Once there, Harry turned around slowly, observing the huge space above him, and the thousands of books surrounding him. Tinted by the air, the books on the furthest wall looked blue. More books awaited their final places, still piled up on the floor.

There was no one who might be a librarian, but a desk covered with papers and piles of books, and a pair of spectacles left on it, showed where one usually worked. Harry walked between the rows of tables, each table big enough to seat ten readers, and each with its own chandelier hanging low from the ceiling. These swung gently, from the motion of the air or some vibration through the building's fabric, reminding him of Viviani's visit to Gresham, when he showed the Earth's rotation using pendula.

Just two other men, perhaps with letters of authority like himself, sat at the tables with books open before them. One sent him a complicit look, sharing that his own reaction was much the same when he had first entered this library.

Harry recognized one of the busts, as it was identical to the one in Marie-Anne's house. Cardinal Mazarin was positioned to watch as much of the room as possible, scrutinizing it even after his death. The Cardinal's collection of books was a monument to his acquisitive obsession. Even though the room it was housed in was enormous, Harry found the space contradictorily claustrophobic. Mazarin's greed had made it overwhelming. All the books lining its walls seemed to lean in towards him.

Gabriel Naudé's *Advis pour dresser une bibliothèque* in Hudson's library was a connection to this library. And, therefore, to Mazarin. Harry had brought the book with him, *Instructions Concerning Erecting of a Library*. What made the book so memorable was its being the one book out of place, while all the others sat on their shelves. It could have been left there merely through oversight. Harry felt it was pertinent but did not yet see how. Did he give too much weight to its being left on Hudson's window seat, as Grace had suggested at Oakham?

He thought again of the Latin quotation from Cicero, '*Ordo est maxime qui memoriae lumen adfert.*'

Order is the best aid to clarity of memory.

It was from a passage of *De Oratore*. Cicero tells the story of Simonides, who luckily escaped a roof's collapse, which killed the guests at a banquet. Crushed so completely, the people inside proved impossible to recognize. Able to remember where each guest was sitting, Simonides identified them all.

Harry had not apprehended that someone stood next to him, waiting politely, unwilling to interrupt another man's thoughts.

'*Bonsoir, monsieur. Je crains de devoir vous demander de partir. Je suis sur le point de fermer la bibliothèque.*' The man's voice was calm, and slow. Good evening sir. I'm afraid I have to ask you to leave. I'm about to close the library.

Harry felt himself colour, as though looking at books in a library was disgraceful. He spread his hands at the man, who was less than a middling height, shorter than Harry, and whose wig was the colour of old linen. His face was pallid, and the skin beneath his eyes was mauve. It was difficult to judge his age, but his movements were stiff, as if each had to be considered before its making. He had the look of an indoors creature. Harry guessed he spent most of his life in this library.

'*Je suis anglais. Partir?* I must leave?'

The man looked at him gravely. '*Oui, monsieur.* It means you really must go.'

Harry noticed the reading tables were empty. He had been so self-involved he had not registered the other men leaving.

'*Vous êtes le* . . . *biblio* . . . librarian?'

'*Bibliothécaire.*' The man gestured around the space they were in, as if the responsibility weighed heavily upon him.

Harry produced the letter from Marie-Anne. The librarian went to his little desk and put on his spectacles to read it. He cupped his chin, rubbing it slowly. Harry could hear the day's growth of hair scratching against the man's palm.

'*La Société Royale?*' he said, refolding and returning the letter. 'I can give you a little time. Do you come for a book, or to see the Cardinal's collection?' His English was precise, and apart from a softness to his Rs almost indistinguishable from an educated Englishman's.

Marie-Anne had anticipated the Royal Society's name would be more welcome at the Bibliothèque Mazarine than that of the Board of Ordnance.

'I wanted to see the place all these books are housed in,' Harry answered. 'I'm interested in the collection, too, and the way it's organized. I have a book, an English translation of Gabriel Naudé's, which shows his system.'

The librarian's eyes widened, and his attitude immediately warmed. 'He was the Cardinal's own bibliothécaire.' He walked across the reading room, expecting Harry to follow. 'Mazarin appointed me as Naudé's successor.' He took Harry past three great columns and stopped at a shelf. 'I am François de La Poterie.' He gave a little bow. 'It has been my duty to bring all these books from the Cardinal's home in the Rue de Richelieu. He bequeathed them to the Collège.'

He moved a ladder aside. 'We have the original manuscript of *Advis pour dresser une bibliothèque*, with further notes that Naudé made, and also two copies of the first edition.' La Poterie's voice had quickened; a bibliophile invigorated. He reached up to a shelf as high as he could stretch, then withdrew his arm.

He turned back to Harry, his face contorted. Harry thought him about to burst into tears.

'What's wrong, monsieur?' Harry asked, looking up at the shelf.

The librarian took a deep breath, before gathering himself. 'It is most upsetting. We had two first editions, as I said. Now, it seems, we have only one.'

Harry saw where there was a space between the books. 'It's been borrowed?'

'No, no. As we work to fill the library, bringing books from the Palais Mazarin, no one is allowed to remove them except me and my assistants. No book leaves this building. We had two. I am certain of it. I myself placed them there.'

La Poterie passed Harry the remaining edition, a slim tome bound in red leather. He felt its weight, moving his hand beneath it as if weighing fruit. The librarian, still looking distraught, sniffed at his handling of it.

Harry looked at the gap between the books, then at the ladder La Poterie had moved. 'Where, exactly, was this?'

The librarian moved it into the position he had found it, backwards and forwards until it felt right. 'Here, I think.'

'A little to the left of the book that's missing?'

They both looked up the ladder's length. 'I did not need the ladder to reach the book,' said the bibliothécaire. 'I am not a tall man.'

'So the man who used this ladder is shorter still than you.'

●

THE AFTERNOON MADE way for evening, the sky tinged with pink, the sunlight glancing across the Paris rooftops. The gulls, too, looked pink, and seemed to resent it, making the same harsh noise as London gulls.

Walking along the Quai de Conti, Harry was too absorbed in his thoughts to notice them.

The man posing as Captain Hudson would need a ladder to reach the editions of *Advis pour dresser une bibliothèque*. La Poterie had placed them on a shelf as high as an average man could reach. Necessary, but not sufficient, Mr. Hooke would say, to prove the imposter had been there, for any other short man would need a ladder.

But Harry could not help but think it was the first glimpse of the man he sought.

Harry passed the placard advertising *L'Exhibition de Monstruosités*.

The Exhibition might be worth visiting. An English dwarf in Paris might find such a fair an ideal place to hide. Harry could wait for days in Mazarin's library hoping for his return—a hope based only on a ladder's placement and a book being missing. There had to be other ways of finding him, which could well be more productive.

Behind him, as he walked back to the Hôtel de Bouillon, the bibliothècaire stood at the entrance to the Collège des Quatre-Nations. He checked that Harry looked in the opposite direction, then hurried down the steps, to cross over the Pont Neuf.

CHAPTER TWENTY-NINE

THE DUCHESSE'S SALON

AS MARIE-ANNE HAD PROMISED, GUESTS TO her salon were due to arrive that evening. Wearing a wig, she was unable to play with her hair, so she fiddled with her dress and all the furniture instead.

Harry, too, was nervous. He worried on their lack of clothes to suit the occasion, but she dismissed his protests with a laugh, saying they had not yet met Racine.

Harry and Fields had spruced themselves up as well as they could, but even with newly washed shirts and their shoes freshly polished, days on the road left their marks. Harry felt very shabby sitting in the fine parlour, next to the scandalous harpsichord, whose lid had been closed for the gathering. Fields did not look perturbed at all by not matching the splendour of his surroundings, although he stowed his pipe away when Marie-Anne looked disapprovingly at him.

The first attendee announced by Mercier—the butler stood at the door flourishing the visitor's card, and reading loudly from it as if they attended a society ball—was a large pear-shaped man, bringing with him an air of sadness. It was Jean Racine himself; the man Marie-Anne had mentioned. Harry gathered from her whispered aside that he was a famous playwright who no longer wrote plays, drama being irreconcilable with his newfound zeal for Christianity. This sentiment came to him at the same time as his new wife, she told him, flashing the Mancini teeth. Racine had instead accepted the post of Louis Quatorze's Historiographer-Royal. Despite the enormous salary that came with that job, he was, as Marie-Anne had said, remarkably unkempt.

Racine dipped his head at them and settled himself down on a méridienne, then stared mournfully at his scuffed shoes. Although the Duchesse did her best to encourage conversation, he responded only monosyllabically, as if he would far prefer to be elsewhere. When a maid poured him tea, he became absorbed by the shape of his saucer, hardly looking away.

It transpired he had heard his rival Charles Perrault was due. Marie-Anne, anxious to keep the conversation's flow, told Harry and Fields of the men's dispute, which only made Racine sink into the méridienne further. Racine championed the ancients, contending one could do no better than to imitate them: their ideas, their rhythms, their structures. He grumbled about the current obsession with the new, especially after Marie-Anne used the term 'New Philosophy' to Harry. Perrault, of course, championed the modern.

Harry tried to be neutral and politic, but Fields surprised him by jumping into the discussion, talking of arms and gunpowder, and the invention of the printing press. The printing press, he said, relying on Marie-Anne to translate, had allowed the Levellers to flourish. Without it, he would never have had his eyes opened to the egalitarianism of men such as Overton, Lilburne, and Walwyn.

The Colonel's enthusiasm for the concept of popular sovereignty sent Racine into even deeper silence. To draw him out, Marie-Anne asked him to explain his conception of the three unities: of action—a play should have no subplots; of time—a play should show no more than a day and a night of action; and of place—a play should exist only in a single location, the stage representing one physical space. Racine looked mortified at her, then pleadingly at her butler, who grinned his sideways grin, enjoying the playwright's distress.

The next person to arrive was a large and forceful woman, announced by Mercier as the poet Antoinette Deshoulières. The butler's news depressed Racine all the more. She, it turned out, also disagreed with him, seeing Racine's concept of drama as unnecessarily constricting. Appearing quickly after, the third guest was the anticipated Charles Perrault, a flamboyant writer of fairy tales, who commandeered the conversation with volume and persistence.

At last, Racine became animated, rattling his cup in its saucer to underline his points. As he grew louder, resisting Perrault's egotistical centring of himself in the proceedings, so did Perrault. 'Any character should be portrayed not as they ought to be, but as they actually are!' Racine almost shouted. Fields joined in this discussion too with great gusto. Marie-Anne and Mercier took it in turns to translate, trying to keep up with his animation. Soon the old soldier had become the hit of the evening, the guests able to score points from each other by telling something to him, which he then commented on with his bluff common sense, to everyone's shared delight.

By the time of the arrival of Ninon de Lenclos, an old spinster who took no time to announce she was atheist through and through and convinced she had no soul, the salon was wonderfully lively. With the addition of Jean de La Fontaine, even more scruffy than Racine, Marie-Anne regarded her gathering with great satisfaction.

'It is dangerous to have this many writers in a room,' a voice next to Harry said.

Harry had not noticed a new guest being ushered in by Mercier, his announcement drowned out by Madame Deshoulières proclaiming that self-preservation governs actions one might usually think of as being taken through one's own free will.

'Will there be actual fighting?' Harry asked him, smiling. The new-comer was the same height as Harry, but thinner and lighter. He had an impressively long nose, and blond hair curling profusely behind him.

'I have not been before, to this house. I have not met these people. I know them all only by reputation. I would say . . .' He grinned back at Harry. '. . . Yes.' His English was good, as was his accent. Harry felt ashamed his French was so poor. It was something he resolved to rectify.

'I'm sorry, monsieur. I missed your introduction.'

'Jacob Besnier.' The man put out his hand. 'The Duchesse invited me here, to speak with Mr. Henry Hunt. You are he, are you not?'

'I am. You're not a writer, I take it?'

'Do you? Why should I not be?' The man's look was challenging, but also amused.

'You don't have the callus on either of your hands, between thumb and forefinger, which shows the habitual use of a pen.'

'You are observant. Would you care to guess, then, at what I do?'

'I would say, you're like me. You work with your hands. But not with wood, for that stains the skin with its dust. With metal, then. Your skin's marked with oil, and there are fine particles of metal under its surface. You cut, and file, metal.' Harry looked at him apologetically. 'I can get no nearer than that.'

'Not bad.' Besnier slapped him on the back. 'I am a *serrurier.*' He made a twisting motion with his hand, miming a key turning in a lock.

'I know a little of locks.'

'It is how I make my living. It is not my passion. It is not for my locks that the Duchesse asked me here. She tells me you have flown with the fa-mous Robert Hooke.' He stood taller, puffing out his chest proudly. 'I, too, have made experiments with flight.'

'I've never flown with Mr. Hooke,' Harry said.

Besnier's face fell. 'Oh, monsieur, that is what she said.'

'Mr. Hooke stayed safely on the ground. He designed the glider. I helped him build it. I was the one who flew.'

Besnier's face lifted again. 'Come. I have something to show you. And you may help me.'

Harry followed him through the hall and outside to the courtyard, where a simple cart with a single horse was parked. Besnier threw back the canvas covering the cart, and started to hand out long wooden struts to Harry, with brackets connecting rods and straps, and cords, and panels covered with taffeta, which he had oiled to make completely airproof. It was far smaller than Hooke's glider, and that had been precarious enough.

Besnier beckoned him back inside. 'The Duchesse wishes me to demonstrate.'

'Then you mustn't disappoint her,' Harry said, following him inside. Both men's arms were full.

In Marie-Anne's parlour, Besnier, once he was strapped into his flying apparatus, drew gasps of admiration from the modernists. Even Racine looked impressed as Besnier demonstrated the flying position, holding the two long struts to which he had tied himself at the ankles, and buckled himself into at the shoulders and wrists. The struts, longer than Besnier was tall, had two hinged panels of taffeta, stretched between slender frames, at each end. The panels opened and closed depending on a pull upwards or downwards, and, Besnier assured them, his eyes alive with passion, they could be controlled for manoeuvrability. Lying on a table, on his front, he demonstrated how he moved his limbs, like walking in the air, to keep the maximum area of sail to the wind, and how he could shift direction by using the air to turn. Harry wondered just how much steering was possible, or if Besnier was far more likely to be wholly at the mercy of the wind. A strong gust would surely have him spinning, then plummeting to the ground.

'You have flown in this machine?' Perrault asked, his voice squeak-high in amazement.

'I have, monsieur,' Besnier confirmed.

'You are brave,' Racine growled, as if it hurt him to say.

'I built up my courage,' Besnier replied modestly. 'First I dropped from a stool. Then from a table. Then, a window, and finally, from a rooftop. I flew over the houses in my neighbourhood.'

'You were able to control your landing?' Harry asked him.

'I am alive!' Besnier cried, making old Madame de Lenclos cackle with a show of yellow teeth.

Fields waved to get everyone's attention. 'Harry, you too have something which shall impress these people.'

'What's that, Colonel?' Harry asked carelessly, his mind more on the facts of the flying contraption and Besnier's undoubted bravery.

'Why, your pistol. You have modified it to fire repeatedly, four shots in a row.'

Charles Perrault clapped his hands in joy. He looked gratefully at Marie-Anne, who had surpassed herself tonight. A flying man, and a pistol which shot recurrently. What a world was this, and that he had lived to see it!

Harry, with all the eyes of Marie-Anne and her guests, and Mercier's guileful look, could not refuse. He went up to his room, treading up the stairs unwillingly, and returned with Oldenburg's pistol. He showed all the guests its four barrels, and how they rotated to allow the next bullet's firing.

Besnier still had his flying suit on, and clanked and rattled as he walked about Marie-Anne's withdrawing room.

'Would we be able to show you all more freely in the garden, Madame la Duchesse?' he asked.

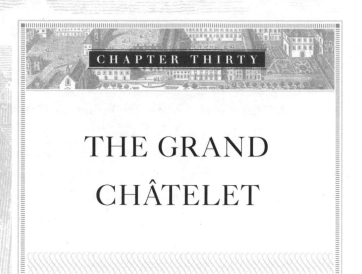

CHAPTER THIRTY

THE GRAND CHÂTELET

THE NEXT MORNING, BEFORE NINE O'CLOCK, Harry and Fields were
back at the Châtelet.

Marie-Anne's salon kept the hours of writers, and Harry was bleary-
eyed from lack of sleep. There had been too many toasts to the success of
Besnier's flying equipment, and to the pistol's loud and repeated firing. Both
had been demonstrated across the length of the Duchesse's garden. Besnier
had flown from an attic window. Harry had fretted for his diminishing
stock of ammunition.

Fields, on the other hand, looked fresher than since their trip to France
began. He had enjoyed himself tremendously, he said, and hoped they
would do it again.

Being led by the same tobacco-chewing adjudant through the long low passageway towards Lieutenant Général La Reynie's office, Harry felt a nerve in his thigh twitching. He thought of Capitaine Eugène de Beauchene's rough questioning.

The owl still glared, not having warmed to them since their last visit. The Lieutenant Général's clock ticked ominously.

'I've not yet found the letter of introduction,' Harry told him, in answer to La Reynie's greeting.

La Reynie, sitting behind his desk, nodded, his impressive peruke swaying, as if this information was exactly as he had expected. His attitude became apologetic, and regretful.

'I require, then, that you give up your weapons.'

Fields stepped forwards and unbuckled the sword borrowed from the Duc de Bouillon, and put it on the desk. Having laid it flat, he tapped it twice smartly.

'It shall be kept safely, Colonel, until its return,' La Reynie reassured him. Fields nodded sombrely, their contract with one another confirmed to his satisfaction.

'I have no weapon,' Harry said, being spare with the truth. He had deliberately left his pistol in his room at the Hôtel de Bouillon.

'Only the Colonel, it seems,' La Reynie replied, ambiguously.

'I can't explain the letter's disappearance,' Harry told him. 'I clearly recall it being in my pocket as we first entered the Duchesse de Bouillon's home.'

'I wondered when you came before. I have thought upon it since. Your letter of introduction, you say, is from Sir Jonas Moore and addressed to me, so why should you check your pocket then? What is your connection with the Duchesse de Bouillon, that you could stay at her house?'

Harry had been careful to keep back Hortense Mancini's commission to find the Sancy diamond. To tell the Lieutenant Général now was to reveal he had deceived him before, even if only by omission. But not to was to risk a greater wrath.

'In truth, I searched for another letter,' Harry answered. 'One from the

Duchesse de Mazarin, Hortense, introducing us to her sister, Marie-Anne. She suggested that we stayed at the Hôtel de Bouillon.'

La Reynie lifted the sword from his desk, as if he thought of drawing it from its scabbard. Instead, he twisted in his chair and leaned it measuredly against the bookcase behind him.

'The Cardinal's fabulous nieces. As beautiful as each other, each in her own way. Which sister does it suit the more, heh, to have you here in Paris?' La Reynie pulled the wing of his long peruke from behind his shoulder, where it had lodged after his turn. 'Your connection, then, is rather with the sister.'

'I met her at Whitehall Palace, the home of the King of England.'

'I know where the King of England lives, Monsieur Hunt.' La Reynie's tone had hardened.

Harry began to feel clammy on his back. 'The King has his own elaboratory, where I've visited with Mr. Hooke. It was the King who introduced me to the Duchesse de Mazarin.'

The owl's eyes seemed to widen at the implausibility of Harry's story.

'I do not doubt you,' La Reynie said airily. 'You worked for the Royal Society. The King's own Society—I would expect you to have met him. Unlike our King. A far more difficult man to see. Some wait at the Louvre, or at Versailles, for days before they get to speak with him. England boasts an approachable monarch. Even with your current fears of Catholic insurrection, he likes to be in among his people. I do not doubt your story he introduced you to the Duchesse, for I have no reason to doubt it. More mysterious to me, though—more worthy of wonder—is why Hortense Mancini should write you a letter of introduction to her sister. You have come to Paris on a matter surely unrelated to her. Your investigation into Captain Hudson's murder.'

'It was a friendly act. She had learned of my visit to Paris.'

'I mean no disrespect, but you are a mechanist. An operator. Skilled, I am sure. Knowledgeable of natural philosophy. But she . . . she is *the Duchesse de Mazarin*. No, no, it is for some other purpose that she wrote your introduction.' La Reynie stood, making Harry step back, although the Lieutenant Général was no closer to him. 'Perhaps she keeps her purpose from you. Perhaps not. But there is a reason for her "friendly act," I am certain.' He moved from behind his desk. 'I shall write to Lord Danby, and explain to him your predicament. I know he wanted you in Paris, too. I will ask him to confirm your credentials. Until I have *his* word of your character, you are to do no more looking into the missing dwarf's whereabouts. You are not to question anyone. If Danby replies swiftly, you should only have to wait a few days.' He stared at both of them. 'Do I have your word you will meet my request? We are all gentlemen together, are we not?'

They nodded their assent. 'We may move freely though?' Fields asked him.

'Of course. You are visitors to Paris. I will not confine you to the Hôtel de Bouillon. See the Louvre. And Notre-Dame. Admire the King's new palace at Versailles. Go to Yvelines, where they begin construction of the Machine de Marly. When finished, it will be the largest machine in Europe, pumping water for the palace's fountains. Philosophical, yes? It is only a half-day's ride away. Or else, you could go to the Bibliothèque Mazarine again, to indulge Monsieur Hunt's interest in books.'

La Reynie smiled at Harry's expression.

'My *mouches* are everywhere. If I hear you have broken your word, you are no longer welcome in Paris. I forbid you to carry weapons of any kind. You shall need to take care without them, in some parts of the city, but I will not have you injuring anyone here.'

CHAPTER THIRTY-ONE

L'EXHIBITION DE MONSTRUOSITÉS

WHEN THEY RETURNED TO THE HÔTEL de Bouillon, Fields asked Harry what he intended to do, now La Reynie had prohibited them from inquiring into Captain Hudson's murder.

'I'd thought of going to the Jardin Royal des Plantes Médicinales this evening,' he answered. Then he then went to his room to nap, closing the door loudly behind him.

Fields, wondering why Harry would wish to see a garden in an evening, spent the rest of the morning in Marie-Anne's, sprawling on one of the benches, letting the sunlight warm his face, alternately dozing and reading his *Book of Common Prayer*.

Marie-Anne herself was absent, having gone to visit a friend in Villennes-sur-Seine. After Harry emerged from his rest, Mercier organized luncheon, which they ate in the petit salon. Despite its name, the room could, Harry imagined, accommodate the whole of Mrs. Hannam's house within it.

There was hardly any conversation with their meal, apart from Harry speculating that the cannonball used to kill the first Hudson must have been carried by his murderer, as it was not from *Incassable*. Perhaps his murderer was never in the jolly boat at all. And that the second Hudson used Naudé's *Advis pour dresser une bibliothèque* as a means of communication. But with whom? Fields seemed uninterested in any of it. Harry kept to himself his worries about Danby's reply to La Reynie, and why the news of Harry's connection with Hortense had so rapidly changed La Reynie's attitude towards his investigation.

In the afternoon, both men repeated their morning's activities, until Harry, dressed warmly with his coat already on, knocked upon the Colonel's door.

Despite La Reynie's command, inside Harry's coat, hanging from his belt, was his pistol. *Paris, with all its lights, has many shadows*, Marie-Anne had said, and knowing Fields was without his sword made him timid. He had brooded over whether to carry it, but felt safer with it than without. La Reynie would only know about it if Harry had to use it.

To get to the Jardin Royal des Plantes Médicinales, more often known as the Jardin du Roy, was a simple walk beside the Seine. If they found themselves at the Bièvre river's mouth, Mercier told them, they had gone too far.

Fields readjusted his Parliament-orange scarf against the cold. 'Why this evening sortie?'

Harry only smiled mysteriously in reply.

The onset of dusk had turned Paris into a golden place, the Seine reflecting the low sun and scattering its colour back into the air. Windows glinted, and walls and rooftops were alive with light. The clouds were stained by lines of crimson, like swabs pressed into wounds.

Into the Faubourg Saint-Victor, past the old abbey and its grand wall of arches. Turning away from the river, they aimed towards a small hill with a windmill perched on its top, which must be, Harry reasoned, the Butte des Copeaux. Earthed over in the fourteenth century, like the many other buttes surrounding the city it was formed by rubbish dumped outside the walls. This butte had grown from wood discarded from the shipyards next to the Port Saint-Bernard.

Walking beside the Jardin's wall, they merged into a noisy crowd converging around the butte. Without Mercier, the speed of conversation around them made it difficult to grasp what was said. Only a few words separated themselves from the hubbub.

Mercier had warned them of the place's nature: so licentious he could not bring himself to give them details. Harry moved closer to the Colonel, whose soothing bulkiness was reassuring.

A showman's high-pitched voice came to them, shouted over the crowd's volume. *'Admirez les possibilités de la nature. Méditez la frontière entre l'humanité et la bête. Le caprice de naissance, qui pourrait produire de créatures singulières.'* Admire the possibilities of nature. Ponder the line between humanity and beast. The whim of birth, which could produce such strange creatures.

Surrounding the hill, stages had been set up in a circle: simple affairs of painted canvas stretched between two poles, with raised wooden stages in front. Some of the canvas backdrops had archways cut through, the cutaway material becoming flaps, fastened across by ties.

'Rendez grâce à Dieu que ces afflictions ne vous aient pas visités!' Thank God these afflictions have not been visited on you!

The shows would move clockwise around the circle. Most of the crowd waited for the next, at a stage with a large banner with a painting of two girls in garish dresses. As the sun set, shadows growing thick and menacing, it was not until Harry looked more closely that he saw the girls were conjoined. Each girl's face was turned away, as if shy of the artist's attention. Faded lettering proclaimed them to be *Les plus belles sœurs fusionnées, Ysabeau et Pernelle.* The most beautiful conjoined sisters, Ysabeau and Pernelle.

How could these girls bear to live with such intimacy? It was all they knew, imprisoned forever in the other's embrace. Harry wondered if there were long silences between them, and bitterness.

Mistakes of nature had been used to deny God's omnipotence. Or else, to show He desired such malformations; they remind us of our blessing, being created in His image. Monstrous births had been blamed on mothers, whose sins, even if only committed in their imaginations, must have corrupted the embryo. They were also interpreted as omens of future misfortune.

Harry was pushed from behind. The canvas flap was opening. The showman stepped up onto the makeshift platform, arms outstretched, welcoming them all. He wore a long robe, like a Druid's. His bald head reflected the lanterns lit around the stage.

He went into a long tale of the twins. Harry managed to comprehend the gist of it. Born in Wallachia, into a poor family. Parents forced from their village by superstitious fear. Father killed, protecting his daughters. Mother escaped, carried them through Bohemia, then Prussia. Then, as good fortune would have it, she happened across L'Exhibition de Monstruosités, when it had arrived in the city of Braunschweig. Wishing to protect them from intolerance, and to celebrate their special beauty, the showman had taken them under his protection.

Harry did not believe half of it. He knew from Bartholomew Fair how exhibits were introduced. Every last one boasted an amazing escape, or had suffered hardship, or shown incredible courage. Always, the fair was their salvation. The notion of the fair as a place of sanctuary lessened the observers' unsavoury guilt. Each member of this crowd, Harry surmised, justified to themselves why they should come to stare.

His reason was simple: he looked for the dwarf pretending to be Hudson. Yet, craning his head forwards, he found himself wanting to see if the twins were as beautiful as the banner claimed.

The showman finished his story, and rapidly walked to the stage's left, gesturing to the door in the canvas.

'*Montrez-vous, mes dames, aux curieux!*' Show yourselves, ladies, to the curious!

A shape stepped tentatively over the canvas sill under the doorway. It turned to face them.

It was not the twins. It was a woman, about forty years of age, already bent and shuffling. Her journey from Wallachia obviously still affected her. She reminded Harry of an old bear he once saw at the Tower's menagerie; it had stared the same way over those watching him, as if to ignore them was to hold on to its dignity.

'*Voici, la mère des filles merveilleuses!*' Here is the mother of the wonderful girls!

There was little interest in the mother. The crowd groaned and muttered, looking past her at the canvas, waiting for it to open again and reveal the twins.

Were they as beautiful as the man insisted? The mother gave no clue, for she had aged badly. Missing teeth, her concave cheeks made her face all chin and cheekbones.

The man on stage smiled at her, and then at the crowd, knowing just what the people wanted, acknowledging he had played a trick on them.

'*Maintenant, vous pouvez voir les belles jumelles.*' Now you may view the beautiful twins.

The flap opened again. At last, the girls appeared, walking onto the stage with their faces angled downwards, so no one could see them. They moved awkwardly, as they were almost back-to-back, joined at the base of their spines, and sharing a hip. They wore a single loose dress, which despite the painting was sober, a dark olive. Bonnets the same colour covered their hair. It was as if they went to church.

One sister had equally matched legs, but the other's leg trailed uselessly, thin and twisted, dragging behind her like a dead branch.

Still the girls had not looked up. Were they identical? Or were they, as some in the crowd began to suspect, not twins, not sisters at all, but merely two girls tied together under a voluminous dress?

The showman had performed this routine a hundred times before. He went to the girls and waited, knowing exactly the moment to reveal their faces to the audience. He waited for the muttering to stop, until he had perfect silence.

Harry could hardly breathe, the crowd's behaviour pressing itself upon him. Bodies pressed against him, too. Fields, squashed beside him, also seemed focused on the little stage and the four people on it, although his expression was one of distaste.

The bald showman held each girl gently by her chin. Slowly, he lifted their faces, to reveal them to the crowd.

They looked around sixteen or seventeen years of age. Their eyes were the same deep green colour, deepened by the lantern light. They slowly removed their bonnets, teasingly, to show their hair was identical, too. Dark, nearly black. They matched each other perfectly.

Slowly, they turned, rotating around the point where they joined, displaying themselves to the watchers. Neither girl turned her head as they spun, so their faces turned as their bodies turned.

Oohs and aahs rose from the crowd.

At the end of their rotation, both girls smiled the same smile at exactly the same time. Their teeth shone in the stage lights. They turned again, the other way, their heads this time moving independently of each other's, each looking at different parts of the crowd. They performed the move smoothly, through repetition.

Some clapping began, but a gruff male voice called out. *'Elles sont jumelles, c'est évident! Mais comment savons-nous qu'elles sont fusionnées?'* They're twins, obviously! But how do we know they're attached?

Harry wondered if this was part of the show, the caller the Druidical showman's accomplice. Whether or not, the man on stage nodded seriously, appearing to carefully consider the question.

'Pour préserver la dignité des filles, nous ne vous le montrons pas ici, sur cette plate-forme. Vous pouvez les voir en privé. Cela vous coûtera plus cher.' To preserve the girls' dignity, we do not show you on this platform. You may see them in private. It will cost you more.

The girls reversed back towards the flap in the canvas, as if time re-wound itself. Still going backwards, they stepped through the hole, and dis-appeared into the darkness behind them, inside the circle made by the stages of the Exhibition.

The showman gestured towards a smaller tent to the right of the stage. Those who needed to see more, desiring evidence of the girls' connection, moved across, huddling at its entrance. All, Harry observed, were men.

Most of the crowd moved off, feeling cheated, to the next stage.

Harry pulled at Fields's arm, to go with them.

'You do not wish to see, as these other men do?' Fields spoke contemptu-ously, pointing to the huddle being organized into a queue by two brawny fair workers.

Harry smarted at his tone. 'I wish to find the dwarf.'

'Let us stay here no longer than need be.'

Branches rustled behind them. A couple emerged from the bushes, ad-justing their clothes. Carmine from the woman's lips smeared her cheek. She laughed as the man smacked her rump, and they disappeared into the crowd. Fields grunted disapprovingly after them.

The next stage had a family of fish-people, a merman and a mermaid, and their many merchildren. The showman, his robes billowing behind him extravagantly, emerged from inside the circle of stages, through the canvas doorway, to begin his tale of their rescuing.

Harry and Fields worked their way through the crowd until it became ragged, thinning out to people sitting on the ground, some with fires lit, most drinking and smoking.

The banner on the next stage showed a man contorted into an im-possible position, every joint bent or twisted abnormally. So extreme was the angle of his neck, his head seemed in danger of detaching from his body.

Behind them, the showman told the tale of how a fisherman had caught the mermaid in his net, and how it came to be her entire family joined her, and ended up with the Exhibition. As his voice grew more dis-tant, and quieter, the place became darker; the lights by these stages had not yet been lit. Harry picked up the last lit lantern, wrapping his hand in the sleeve of his coat to protect it from the hot metal handle.

They stared at the paintings at each tent. One promised a giantess. Another, a boy without arms, but able to write and shuffle cards.

Harry went between them, venturing into the circle made by the tents.

'I do not think you should go there, Harry,' Fields said. 'Those inside may take against you.'

His words soon proved prescient. A low, guttural growl came from the darkness behind them. Harry turned towards it. The lantern showed only open ground, uneven and tussocky.

Fields pulled at his sleeve. 'We should return to the mermaid.'

'Let's see the next stage. Then we'll be on the opposite side, as quick to continue as go back.'

The same growling sound came again, but this time from behind the giantess's tent; from inside the secret space of the Exhibition, where the monstrosities waited.

And again, but from over to their right, from the side of the butte they had not yet explored.

As well as his unease from the growls around them, Harry had an odd sensation, as if his stomach was lighter. Something was amiss. He knew he had left something behind, without being able to say what it was. Dismissing the thought, he continued around to the next tent, Fields staying close by. The lantern revealed a painting of a man owning skin too large for his body, falling from him like a pale blanket.

Again, the noise. Fiercer, more urgent. It seemed to be right next to them, but Harry, swinging the lantern around, could see nothing.

Although a growl, Harry knew it to be human. Each time it came from another direction, it was subtly different. Different people making the same sound.

Both men gripped the other's arm, as if to let go of each other would throw them into a fathomless abyss.

Here, it was Harry and Fields who were the aberrations. They had chosen to leave the crowd and the lights. They had ignored the show's careful timing.

They walked sideways, crablike, next to each other, as the twins had presented themselves, both looking in different directions into the darkness beyond the lantern. The trees of the Jardin du Roy showed against the lighter sky, but otherwise a flat, impassive blackness surrounded them.

Then, a sudden glow of orange, perceived in the same second as a man wearing nothing but a loincloth. The glow was the colour of his cheeks. He spat a burning coal at them, then disappeared as quickly as they had seen him. The hot coal landed on Harry's coat, and worked its way under the collar. Harry quickly put down the lantern and brushed off the coal, burning his fingers. It dropped onto the thick grass, which charred and sparked.

Fields patted at Harry's smouldering shirt.

'What best to do, Colonel? Advance, or retreat?'

'Go forwards. There are only two more stages, I think, and then we are back to the road.'

The next stage, the last but one, had a large and complicated frame with ropes hanging from it. Juggling equipment was piled up, waiting for the people to make their way there, as they worked through the merpeople, the contortionist, the giantess, the armless boy, and the man with too much skin.

The canvas behind had a wide narrow painting across it.

Dwarves, climbing and tumbling, juggling and sword fighting, on board a ship.

The growl.

An enormous woman advanced through the doorway. She strode through the apparatus and jumped down from the stage. Easily seven feet tall, she came towards them, from an angle, making it plain she wanted them to move on, to continue around the butte. Behind her came the boy with no arms, with a hairy man whose face showed no skin at all apart from his eyelids. The man whose skin was too large flapped towards them, his shirtless body undulating and billowing. The contortionist advanced on all fours, stomach to the sky, his head turned backwards over his shoulder to stare at them.

In among them, taking two strides to every one of the giantess's, ran the dwarves: about ten of them, one back-flipping towards them.

Harry reached for his pistol, but felt only the empty holster.

The growling sound, now continuous, enveloped him. It came from the ground, from the air, from anywhere, from everywhere. All the monstrosities were baring their teeth as they made their unsettling noise.

Another hot coal came at Harry, just missing his forehead. He could see the lamps hanging by the entrance to the Exhibition, and the crowd of people come to see the monstrosities, unaware that most of them were in the darkness, chasing off Harry and Fields.

Fields's broad back was already out on the road, jogging away, away from the noise of the growling.

Harry ran, too, dropping the stolen lantern.

As he got to the lights, the conjoined girls stood by the entrance. Both stared at him as he went past. Their identical faces were the last thing he saw as he left the butte.

The last thing he heard was them laughing.

CHAPTER THIRTY-TWO

THE

MAGICKING AWAY

HARRY WAITED BY THE PONT MARIE. This far from the Exhibition, he was sure, Fields would have stopped to wait for him. Yet he was nowhere to be found, even with all the bright lamps hanging along the quay. Harry had seen him running beside the Jardin du Roy towards the Seine. He must have turned off somewhere to rest. By the shipyard perhaps. Or else along the Rue du Faubourg, on the other side of the abbey.

Harry waited for an hour. Parisians noticed him, regarding him suspiciously. One even questioned him. *'J'attends pour mon amour,'* Harry answered. The man nodded, squeezed his shoulder sympathetically, and took him to be Dutch.

On his eventual, reluctant return to the Hôtel de Bouillon, Mercier seemed amused at the two men's separation. 'He bought a woman. Plenty to be had by the Butte des Copeaux.'

'No, no.' Harry almost smiled at the thought. 'The Colonel's a God-fearing man. A moral man. I can't understand how I lost him.'

It was as if Fields had been magicked away. Harry went to bed, but slept only fitfully, half his mind listening for his friend's return.

IN THE MORNING, he knocked at Fields's bedroom door, then let himself through. There was no sign of the Colonel's return.

Worry gnawing at his chest, Harry left the Hôtel de Bouillon and returned to the Butte des Copeaux.

Back at L'Exhibition de Monstruosités, all the tents were securely fastened. Harry did not disturb those who slept inside. Only if the Colonel stayed missing would he brave them again. And besides, why would Fields turn back on himself?

In the early morning light, the tents looked worn and grubby, even with the dew glittering on their canvas. The banners, so garish by lantern light, looked faded and poorly done. They seemed ridiculous, especially compared to the reality, the monstrosities on the little wooden stages, or growling from the darkness.

Only the painting of the two girls resembled its subject. The same green eyes, from the same blank expressions, stared steadily at him from the canvas.

He passed the Jardin du Roy, walking down towards the Seine. Few people were about, so he chose a moment to climb unobserved up and over the wall. Wiping dew from his hands, he found himself among plants laid out in orderly rows. Being closed, no one was in the Jardin to study the plants, and no sign yet of any gardeners.

The place was entirely empty. Harry was sure Fields had not come in, stumbled, hurt himself, and been unable to rise. If attacked, he had not been left there to die, at least.

He came up against a sturdy gate, with an equally sturdy lock. Again, he climbed the wall, landing on a riverbank of one of the stinking tributaries flowing into the Seine. He put his hand over his nose to keep the stench from it. He remembered Mercier telling them if they found themselves at the Bièvre, then they had gone too far.

The mud was a repellent greyish-brown colour, with seams of scarlet and fat. Waste from the tanneries, and the dyes from the Gobelins manufactory, stained the water. The boggy ground soaked his boots. The mud pulled at them, sucking noises following him as he went.

Trees lined the bank. He checked behind each of them, wondering if Fields had tripped over roots, or collapsed and sat himself down against one to die. He felt a keen pain in his chest at the thought his friend might have died alone, on a chilly night in a foreign land, his death caused by being chased away from the Exhibition. He should have taken more care of the old Colonel, who was only there because Harry had wanted him to come. All Fields had wanted was to stay in Half Moon Alley with Mrs. Hannam, yet he had agreed to accompany Harry to Paris on a fruitless quest to find a dwarf.

The smell from the tributary was nauseating. Perhaps Fields had fallen in, or, worse, been attacked and pitched in by a robber. Harry had no chance of finding him under its opaque surface.

At the tributary's mouth, the stained water rolled and folded into the clearer water of the Seine.

Harry decided to go back to the Hôtel de Bouillon.

Perhaps Fields would be there, and would tell him cheerfully of his nighttime adventure, and why he was unable to return earlier to the Duchesse's home.

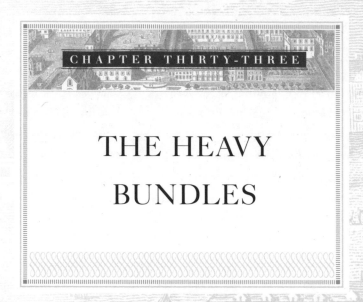

CHAPTER THIRTY-THREE

THE HEAVY BUNDLES

OVER LONDON, THE SKY WAS A piercing blue. Clouds stretched across it, looking like strands of fat pulled from meat. At the rear of Somerset House, the Thames lapped against the floodwall, splashing against the bricks, spray wetting the river stairs.

Two skiffs tied together, the one behind pushed deep into the water by the bundles inside it, were moored tight in behind the *Folly*, a barge once the conveyance of royalty, but now a floating coffeehouse.

Two men hefted equipment from the laden skiff onto the little quay.

The man with a sharp chin and one uninterrupted eyebrow across his forehead supervised them. He spoke constantly, giving detailed instructions for the unloading of each bundle, and how they should be set down. Some bundles were so heavy it took all three men to lift them. Thick canvas hid their contents. Muffled metallic noises sounded as the men strained with their weight.

The three men carried the bundles, journey after journey, through the garden.

Scaffolding covered the south wall of Somerset House, its roof being repaired, retiled, and releaded. Made soft and black by the sulphurous fumes from the burning of sea coal, the old stone was being replaced by new, carved on site. Rotten window frames were being pulled out and replaced.

Nodding to the Queen's guards in the guard chamber, the men made their way inside. The guards were quite used to builders; after the first couple of times, they had not even acknowledged them as they passed. If they had bothered to look, the guards would only have seen what appeared to be yet more scaffolding, and angular shapes stretching the canvas-covered bundles.

In the house, dust filled the air and clung to every surface, working its way under the sheets protecting the furniture. The men could taste it when they ran their tongues over their lips to lick away their sweat. It lay in their eyebrows, along their eyelids, and clogged the creases of their faces.

The other builders acknowledged them with waves, which were returned cheerfully, or with a pretend exasperation at the work they were ordered to do. And looks which said, we're too busy to talk. Men worked on the windows, some replaced ceilings, some repainted panelling. A team of carpenters worked to rehang the immense doors leading into the Great Room, their new hinges as long as a forearm.

The man directing the works was there: a grey-faced man with a hunched back, whose hair was tied back with a ribbon. His silver eyes passed over them as they went past, but he was too preoccupied to think further on their presence.

Past the Queen's apartments at the back of Somerset House, overlooking its gardens.

Higher in the house, the dust sheets stopped. Despite Parliament's great sale of Charles I's goods, on every table stood an object, and on every wall hung a gilded-framed picture or mirror.

Negotiating the stairway's narrow turn. All three men lifting together, each sweating freely.

'*Continuez jusque sous les toits.*' The sharp-chinned man instructed.

Continue to the attic.

CHAPTER THIRTY-FOUR

THE IMPROVISED CODE

BY THE AFTERNOON, HARRY WAS CONVINCED his friend must be dead. Marie-Anne, returned from her visit, listened to his story with growing concern. She instructed Mercier to go with a couple of the footmen and search for the Colonel, sending them back to the Faubourg Saint-Victor. They were to ask at the abbey. Perhaps he had become confused, suffering an apoplexy, and been taken in by the monks. They were also to ask at Notre-Dame-de-Pitié, the hospital for beggars, the elderly, prostitutes, and their children. Marie-Anne shot Mercier a steely look at his moue of distaste; he hunched his shoulders dutifully.

Harry wanted to go with them, but Marie-Anne told him, as imperiously as she had treated Mercier, it would be her men, with their knowledge of the place and easier relationship with those they would question, who would find Fields, and more quickly than he ever could.

If Fields was to be found.

So, Harry retired to his bedroom. He tried lying on his bed, but his limbs would not stay still. Instead, he wandered in the garden, but its high hedges made him feel confined. His imagination became ever more darkened by thoughts of old Michael Fields suffering, lying mangled in an alley, stabbed for his purse. Perhaps killed by the same man who had stolen his pistol.

He felt useless, and guilty he did nothing, but knew Marie-Anne was right: he stood little chance of finding the Colonel. Instead, as evening fell, he left the Hôtel de Bouillon and walked the short distance beside the Seine back to the Collège des Quatre-Nations. The lamplighters were out, climbing their ladders, the drizzle in the air a soft globe of light as each lamp was ignited.

The Bibliothèque Mazarine was the one place in Paris Harry had felt close to the man posing as Hudson, especially after the debacle of the Butte des Copeaux.

La Poterie was not there. Another librarian, more junior, read Harry's letter from Marie-Anne, and shrivelled at the sight of the Bouillon seal. He motioned to Harry expansively, to say the library was all his.

The ladder still leaned against the shelving. After La Poterie had pushed it aside, they had moved it back to see if it would serve for a dwarf taking the book from its usual place.

On his last visit, the librarian said the Bibliothèque had two first editions of *Advis pour dresser une bibliothèque*. One of which had gone missing.

Yet looking now, there were no gaps between the books.

Side by side, there they were, like the twins at the Exhibition. There was no way of telling which copy had been missing, as they were bound in identical leather. Harry took them over to a reading table. The lamp hanging above it flickered, a breeze blowing across the room, some door being opened elsewhere in the building.

He opened the books, inspecting each for differences. Each was only 150 pages long, but doubled it was quite a task. One he accepted gladly, for it helped keep the matter of the missing Colonel from his mind. Marie-Anne knew where Harry was; she would send someone for him if Fields returned to the Hôtel de Bouillon.

He turned the books at an angle, to see if the light caught any impression in the paper, or any difference in the ink. He looked at the letters, wondering if any had been modified. Slowly, he worked his way through each page, and through the chapters on why one ought to be curious on libraries, on what we are to know concerning a library's building, the requisite number of books and the quality and condition they should be, how they should be procured, the place they should be kept, the order in which they should be kept, the ornament and decoration to be observed, and what the scope of any library should be.

There were no physical differences he could observe: the two books were as similar as paper manufacture, and the vagaries of printing ink onto paper, and that leather derives from individual animals, allowed. Neither book contained marginalia or underlining. Harry felt sure there had been no additions to either copy since the day they were made.

A clock behind the librarian's desk struck the time. Harry saw he had been left undisturbed for nearly four hours. It was now late in the evening, yet he had not been asked to leave. No one else was in the library, unless you counted the authors of all these books. He was dimly aware a door had been opened earlier; later he had thought he heard footsteps, but could not remember precisely when. The footsteps had coincided with Naudé's discourse on how more books could be procured if you did not spend unwisely on their binding, as only the ignorant esteem a book for its cover.

Harry realized his French was improving. He had hardly referred to his copy of John Evelyn's translation as he studied each book, yet from his memorising of *Instructions Concerning Erecting of a Library* he was able to follow Naudé's argument.

If the books were used to convey messages, it must be by way of where letters or words were positioned on the page. A message would be impossible to decode unless you possessed the same edition.

As the second book had been returned, the false Hudson no longer needed to communicate with whomever else employed the code. Or, he would return to the Bibliothèque to use it again.

There still being no one else in the reading room, Harry went to the librarian's desk and found paper and a pen. He began to write, using a system where the page of *Advis pour dresser une bibliothèque* was given, and then the number of lines down, and the number of letters across, excluding punctuation and the spaces between words.

Perhaps Hudson's impersonator would communicate with him. Or, recognising the code was broken, he would change his method of communication. Unless someone else took the book. But Harry thought that unlikely enough to dismiss, especially as the library was not yet open to the public.

Harry copied his code onto a second piece of the Bibliothèque's paper. He put one in each book, and replaced them.

He walked out from the reading room. The place was entirely silent, but he had the prickling sensation he was watched.

CHAPTER THIRTY-FIVE

THE DANGEROUS BOOKS

HARRY WOKE EARLY FROM A DREAM of the twins spitting hot coals.

He left his bed and watched the dawn, his window facing north across the Seine. Impasto strokes of colour brushed the sky. The light from the rising sun clambered over the Palais des Tuileries, Quinze-Vingts, and the Louvre. It lit up the Palais-Royal, making it shimmer. He watched the shadows change as they bent over a rooftop or dropped down a wall.

On the horizon was a high hill. Chauve-Mont, Mercier had called it, when showing him his view. Its poor soil left it bare of grass. At its highest point was the old Gibbet of Montfaucon. Its stone pillars and beams, black lines against the pink sky, resembled a ruined house where time and weather had taken its roof. The gibbet could hang three rows of criminals at a time in its bleak glassless windows, one row suspended above another.

It had not been used—officially—for half a century, but it was allowed to stand: a memento mori for the people of Paris.

Fields had still not returned by the time Harry had gone to bed. Nor during the night, for surely the Colonel would have woken him. Nevertheless, leaving his room, Harry knocked at Fields's door.

On hearing the noise, Mercier appeared on the staircase. 'We spoke to all in Saint-Victor,' he said. For the first time, the butler had none of the superciliousness Harry associated with him. He looked genuinely sorry they had not found the Colonel. Seeing Harry's sallow face, and his eyes sunk into their sockets from worry and tiredness, Mercier bowed solemnly.

'Do not grieve yet, monsieur. There are many places in Paris he can be. The fact he is not here does not mean he is dead.'

'I know it's unphilosophical to presume his death, but it most easily explains his disappearance.'

At breakfast, Marie-Anne watched Harry pick at his poached fish, exposing the backbone, separating its ribs, delicate as pins, from the pale flesh. Anatomising it, rather than eating it.

'I will send Mercier to search again,' she assured him. 'You should go to the Châtelet to inform the Lieutenant Général. La Reynie may have news of the Colonel.'

'I shall, this morning,' Harry replied half-heartedly, staring at his fish. He felt sure that to visit La Reynie would be to hear of Fields's death. He had put it off last evening, going instead to the Bibliothèque Mazarine.

First, though, he wanted to return to the library, to see if his coded message still lodged inside the books. As much to stave off the news as to see if he had at last found Hudson's impersonator.

Sure enough, the steps of the Collège des Quatre-Nations proved irresistible. Entering the library, he saw a few people at the tables: three men, each on their own, and a boy. All had their backs to Harry. Harry wondered if the boy, who wore a simple hemispherical cap, like a Jew's yarmulke, waited for a librarian. His father perhaps. One of the sublibrarians placed books at the library's far end. This time, Monsieur La Poterie was present, writing at his desk, using the same pen Harry had borrowed the night before.

The bibliothécaire placed his empty hand vertically in the air, as if swearing an oath. 'You will be disappointed. The Naudé has not been returned.'

'But it has, monsieur. I saw it here last night.'

La Poterie gave an emphatic shake of his head. 'I looked again this morning, not a half hour ago. I could not help myself. Its stealing troubles me.'

Harry walked to the place on the shelves, the ladder still leaning next to it. La Poterie came out from behind the little desk and followed him, puffing out his cheeks at the stupidity.

On the shelf, one copy only of *Advis pour dresser une bibliothèque*.

Harry pulled at his spectacles, as if they were at fault. 'But, two were here.'

The old librarian stared disbelievingly at him.

Harry took down the single copy. 'I assure you, monsieur. I read each of them, all through.'

His code, numbers showing page numbers, lines and the positions of letters, was still pressed between the pages. He showed it to La Poterie. 'I left this in both.'

'Who are you? *En fait?*' He called to his assistant, the man placing books in the shelves. 'Sarazen!'

Harry tried to placate him by putting his hand on the librarian's shoulder. La Poterie, wide-eyed, pulled away from the touch.

Sarazen, a tall and thin youth, stepped over the pile of books by his feet, knocking them down as he paced towards them.

'*Messieurs!*' La Poterie called to the men at the reading tables. '*Voici un malfaiteur! Voulez-vous m'aider?*' Here is a criminal! Would you assist me?

Harry could not believe how the librarian was reacting. It was quickly explained.

'Lieutenant Général La Reynie asked me to watch you! Now I understand why!'

The three men still at the tables rose, reluctantly, eyeing Harry to gauge the threat he posed. They were men of words, not action, disinclined to be involved.

The boy had moved halfway between the group of tables and the reading room's large doors.

But he was not a boy. He was a dwarf. A man in his mid-fifties, perhaps, his face lined, suntanned, and leathery. His beard, invisible before when his back had been turned, was flecked with white. Pale blue eyes looked at Harry fixedly. No part of the man's body was disproportionate, apart from a slightly overlarge head, giving rise to the easy assumption, when observed from behind, that he was a child.

The man held the second copy of *Advis pour dresser une bibliothèque*, a pen, and some paper.

Behind him, Harry could hear the assistant, Sarazen, his feet slipping on the polished floor.

Not knowing the man's real name, Harry called out, 'Captain Hudson!'

Long arms wrapped around him from behind. For a librarian, Sarazen had unexpected strength.

Harry struggled to free himself. 'I'm no danger!'

La Poterie was not to be swayed from his conviction Harry was a villain. The Lieutenant Général's instruction and the suspicious code proved it to be so. He beckoned to the readers to hurry up and help them. He pointed to the meekest looking of them. *'Allez chercher la police!'*

Pale-faced, with a wig too low on his forehead, the man sidled from the room, relieved to be away from the trouble.

'Captain Hudson!' Harry shouted again, trying to slide his way down and under the sublibrarian's hold. 'Sir Jonas Moore has sent me!'

The man backed away towards the doors. *'Assassin!'* he cried.

'No, no,' Harry assured him, pushing against Sarazen, who was sweating and grunting to keep his grip. 'I've only come to find you.'

'You have found me. But you will not kill me.' The man had a strong voice, and a deep one. Surprisingly so, Harry thought, from so short a pipe to produce it.

Sarazen's arms slipped upwards, the sweat on his hands making them slide from around Harry's chest to his throat.

Harry could not breathe, or swallow.

He kicked backwards, as hard as he could. With a howl of pain Sarazen let go, clutching at his shin.

Able to breathe again, Harry saw La Poterie had retreated behind his desk, and wielded the knife he used to cut the pages of the library's books.

One of the remaining readers, a kind-looking man with thick-lensed glasses, took a book, imperial octavo size, from a shelf and held it before him like a little shield—a *bouclier*—and advanced towards Harry behind its protection.

Harry heard a roar behind him.

Sarazen had recovered from his damaged shin, enough to be back in the fray.

Harry broke into a run, both to get away from the enraged Sarazen and to catch up with the dwarf, who headed towards the doors to make his escape from the library.

'I mean you no harm!'

The imperial octavo suddenly appeared in Harry's vision, smashed into his face by the reader.

Harry went down, clutching his cheek. His spectacles fell to the floor, one of the lenses breaking. His vision—all the shelves with all their books, and the lights hanging down over the tables—broke into a mosaic of colours. He struggled to his feet, but another book came at him, this one thrown by the second reader, emboldened by the actions of the first. Its corner caught Harry painfully on the ear. Two yowls of anguish could be heard; one, he discerned, was his own, sensed dimly as if from far away. The other came from the librarian, La Poterie.

'*Non, non. Pas les livres!*' No, no. Not the books!

The first reader ignored him and threw another book. Harry sensed it coming, moving to the side just in time. It crashed against a marble bust. Groggily, he managed to pick up his damaged spectacles, then reach one of the tables. He tipped it over on its side. Another book smacked the tabletop.

The second reader reached up and pulled hard at one of the ceiling lamps. Its thin chain snapped, and he wielded the light as a weapon.

La Poterie shouted at his assistant. '*Sarazen, verrouillez les portes!*' Sarazen, lock the doors!

Sarazen circled Harry warily to get to the doors. Harry was momentarily bewildered by the timorous reaction to him, until he understood that all the men in this library thought him an assassin. He had no obvious weapon, it was true, but in their eyes, he was still dangerous: a man able to snap a neck with his hands.

The false Hudson was at the doors.

Sarazen placed himself firmly in front of him, blocking his exit. '*Non!*'

'*Je ne suis pas un criminel!*' the man replied. I am not a criminal!

'*Mais, vous êtes un témoin. Vous devez parler à la police.*' But you are a witness. You must talk to the police. Sarazen locked the doors and removed the key, placing it in his pocket with exaggerated care. '*C'est vous qu'il est venu assassiner.*' It is you he came to murder.

'Captain Hudson!' Harry called, still sheltering behind his table. His cheekbone felt as though it might be broken, a white-hot sensation searing through it. The pain made it difficult to speak. 'I call you Hudson, for I know no other name for you. The real Captain Hudson has been found. He was killed. I've no reason to believe you involved in his murder, I spoke to your housekeeper, Mrs. Leach. She thinks you a good man.'

With Harry still taking refuge from the threat of further books being hurled at him, the other men in the room stayed still, listening to the conversation being called across the distance between the upturned table and the library doors.

'Danby wishes me dead,' the little man said.

'I'm sent by Sir Jonas Moore. He's not asked me to kill you.'

'Ask your questions, then, but remain where you are.'

Harry risked raising his head. The second reader rattled his light to discourage him from moving further.

Harry stayed behind the table. 'Well, then, what do you know of Hudson's murder?'

'I know nothing of it. I only knew him gone.'

'Nothing?'

'Nothing at all. Priscilla spoke of him, but did not know his end.'

'Priscilla? Mrs. Leach?'

The man nodded.

'She knew you were not him,' Harry said.

'Straightaway. I believe she preferred me to the original.'

'How did you come to be him?'

'I was captured by Barbary pirates, who insisted I was him. My size, you see, being similar. When I told them I was not, they did not believe me.' He grimaced. 'Thinking I was Hudson, they treated me better, and so I let them think it. Also, it helped me when the King offered to pay for his release. I had suffered a cruel captivity for twenty years. On returning, I conferred my history onto that of Jeffrey Hudson, making us one man.'

'What do you know of the diamond?'

The man looked bewildered by Harry's question.

'The Sancy diamond.' Harry's voice cracked with his urgency. 'Hudson took it from Cardinal Mazarin.'

'I assure you, sir, I have no knowledge of any diamond, nor of Hudson's murder.'

The doors to the reading room shuddered, from being kicked from the other side.

'*Police! Ouvrez ces portes!*' Police! Open the doors!

Sarazen triumphantly produced his key. He, the readers, and La Poterie all brightened, cheered by thoughts of survival. They had supposed they would be killed, maimed, or at best witness the murder of this dwarf by an English assassin.

Four of La Reynie's men, all large, squat, and muscular, strutted into the library. Three had their swords drawn, and one, a capitaine, held a pistol.

The dwarf started to move. He climbed one of the ladders leaning up against a bookshelf, so quickly he almost ran up it, and then jumped to the balcony above the first tier of books.

The policeman with the pistol took aim at him.

'*Non!*' La Poterie cried, and pointed to Harry behind the upturned table. '*L'assassin est là!*'

Confused, the man lowered his weapon.

The dwarf climbed up the second tier, from shelf to shelf, up to the reading room's high ceiling. Finding his way blocked by a railing across it, he jumped the window gap between balconies, grabbing the rail to save himself from the dizzying drop to the ground, and made his way along and up more shelves, until he reached a little hatchway in the ceiling. His skill came from years at sea, in the high rigging.

Obviously, he knew he could escape this way, for he showed no hesitation. When he pushed at the hatch, it opened smoothly, and he was gone, up into the roof space. His feet disappeared, and the hatch closed behind him.

La Poterie was the first man in the room to speak, as they each pulled their astonished gazes from the ceiling back to Harry. The librarian pointed again, for the benefit of the Paris police.

'*L'assassin!*'

CHAPTER THIRTY-SIX

THE
MONTFAUCON
GIBBET

CROSSING THE PONT SAINT-MICHEL TO THE Île de la Cité, and then the
Pont au Change, the Grand Châtelet was reached quickly. Harry's wrists
were securely tied with rope. From time to time the capitaine kicked at him
with the point of his toe into the back of his knee, always finding the same
spot, to keep him moving along.

Onlookers wondered what Harry had done, his progress was so vigorously encouraged. The *policiers* had been severe with him, obviously, for
his cheek was swollen and bleeding. Perhaps the bone was broken. A lens
of his spectacles was smashed. He had the look of a foreigner about him:

the cut of his clothes, the paleness of his skin. His leather coat was not a Parisian design.

'Take me to the Lieutenant Général. He knows who I am, and that I'm no threat.'

The men laughed at Harry when he pleaded in English, then at his accent when he tried it in French.

'*Il vous interrogera quand il sera prêt.*' He will question you when he is ready.

The policiers pushed Harry through the vast gate studded with nails, and along the same passage that had taken him and Fields to La Reynie's office, when the Lieutenant Général had pretended to be one of his officers. Instead of going up the stairs though, this time Harry was taken down them, descending to a less hospitable part of the Châtelet. The smell of damp and misery swirled around him like fog. Vertical slit windows and a few weak lamps provided little illumination.

Another set of dark stairs. Descending on stone worn from centuries of unhappy prisoners and their guards. The treads seemed to sag, exhausted, in the middle. Harry was taken to a cell, its door standing open. The capitaine shoved him in.

'*Combien de temps devrai-je attendre?*' Harry asked. How long will I wait?

'*Une heure, un jour, ou une semaine.*' An hour, a day, or a week.

The rope was untied. Harry winced at the prickling sensation as the blood returned to his hands. The door to his cell slammed shut. A geôlier had arrived. This man locked the door, then smirked through the narrow hatch, beating it with his stick when he was done. His and the policiers' footsteps, sibilant on the stone, grew quiet as they left Harry in the silence of his cell.

Its walls were dull grey plaster, their dampness smelling sour, gaps revealing old brick. The brick was broken where the door's handle regularly hit the wall. Graffiti had been scratched into the plaster: words, doodles, patterns. Prisoners whiling away hours.

Shivering, Harry crossed to the window. Another slit, this time horizontal, high up by the ceiling. There were no bars, for it was too narrow for a person to squeeze through. He had to climb on the bed to see which slice of Paris it allowed him.

Doing so gave him a worm's-eye view of a quiet courtyard's cobbles laid out before him. He could see the church of Saint-Jacques-de-la-Boucherie, its pale tower ornately decorated. Behind it loomed the church of Saint-Merri. Beyond, overlooking all the rooftops of the Marais, stood the medieval fortress built by the Knights Templar, simply known as Le Temple.

On the horizon, exactly in the middle of his window, rose the Chauve-Mont. And at its top, the Montfaucon Gibbet.

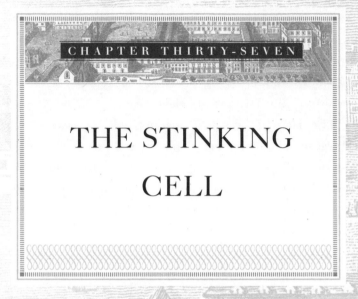

CHAPTER THIRTY-SEVEN

THE STINKING CELL

HARRY PACED AROUND HIS CELL, CHANGING direction, varying the route. At the end of each journey, he returned to the high window to take a breath of outside air, to clear the stink from his lungs.

Rotted through, a wooden bucket leaked in the corner. At first, Harry had resisted using it, thinking La Reynie might call for him at any minute. As the day went on, he had no other choice but to squat over it. With nothing to wipe himself, he used his hand, scraping his fingers afterwards on the cobbles outside his window. From the ground's slope, he knew the first rain would bring it all back in. Stains down the wall showed the repetition of this routine by previous occupants.

La Reynie would surely be quick to release him: an assassin in the Bibliothèque Mazarine would be reported to him immediately, and he knew Harry was no assassin.

But the morning became afternoon. Afternoon became evening. The clouds brooded on the hills, shrinking the world to the Marais and the Faubourg du Temple, beyond where the walls had once protected Paris. Only policiers walked past his window.

He had not been fed, nor offered any water.

Sometime in the evening, rain began to fall. The sound of it, as each drop deflected at different angles depending on the shape of the cobble it hit, diverted Harry for a while, as he tried to gauge the direction of a raindrop's bounce from the nature of sound it made. He considered trying to drink it, but the colour of it oozing down the wall discouraged him.

A rat scuttled across the narrow window's rim, pausing halfway as if wanting to join him, but thinking better of it.

A door up towards the guardhouse clanged open. From along the corridor, Harry heard footsteps. He jumped across his cell to look through the hatch in his door. He shouted through it, but there was no reply. Two bright lanterns drew near, but he could not make out who walked behind them until they were level with his door: the old *geôlier* with two policemen, holding up another prisoner limping between them, his head slumped down on his chest. As the lanterns went by, the geôlier beat at Harry's cell door with his stick. Harry flinched away from it, but caught a glimpse of the prisoner as he went by.

It was the Duchesse de Bouillon's butler. Mercier's face was battered, dried blood from his broken nose crusting his lips. Usually so fastidiously neat, his hair was tangled, and clotted with more blood.

'Mercier!'

The geôlier returned to beat at his door again. '*Silence!*'

The four men went on, further down the passageway, until another door slammed shut.

'Mercier!' Harry shouted again, but there was no reply.

There must have been another way around, back to the guardhouse, for the geôlier and policiers did not return.

Was Mercier the reason Harry was being held? Had the butler lied about him to the police, willingly or unwillingly? He had obviously faced rough questioning. Perhaps from La Reynie himself.

Evening became night. There was not even starlight or moonlight, for the clouds obscured it. No lamps were lit in this part of the Châtelet. No soft candlelight flickered from a window.

In complete darkness, Harry settled himself onto the bed, which was just planks covered by canvas, slimy to the touch.

What information had been forced from Mercier to turn the Lieutenant Général against him? That seemed the only explanation for Harry's still being confined in this stinking, coal-black cell.

Harry curled up on the slippery canvas and lay on his side, facing the window. He put his head down gingerly, his cheekbone feeling as if it had shifted across his face. He pushed at it, to see if it was broken, but was almost sick with the pain of it. After that, he left it alone.

Despite the bed's planks being roughly sawn and knotted, the canvas not cushioning them at all, eventually he drifted off to sleep.

Again, the twins visited him in his dreams.

CHAPTER THIRTY-EIGHT

THE RUE QUINCAMPOIX

COLONEL MICHAEL FIELDS KNEW THIS PART of Paris well. Little had changed since the Wars.

He thought of his younger self, who had climbed the Pont Marie's steep ramp with barely a thought of the effort it demanded. Now he had to rest before it, and rest again after. His lungs felt as if they wanted to break his old ribs. His run two nights ago, after the show of aberrant creatures, had almost done for him.

Breathing hard, he walked to Saint Josse, where the road became the Rue Quincampoix. Its gradual rise had to be taken in short bursts of exertion, his thighs begging for respite. The street was ancient and narrow, crumbling stone showing the age of the houses. Its cobbles were deeply rutted, grooved by countless cart journeys. His way was difficult to see, and he

stumbled often. Only a few solitary lamps hung here: each one became a
waystop, a rest to catch his breath, before continuing on to the next.

He could see the house everyone tiptoed past. No one wanted to disturb
the man who lurked inside like a malevolent toad.

There was the sign, polished and bright: *Monsieur Gabriel Nicolas de
La Reynie, Lieutenant Général de Police.* A high wall with a large arch, big
enough for a grand carriage and its horses, showed a more substantial house
than its neighbours.

No sign of frailty in the Colonel's booming knock.

The Lieutenant Général himself answered, holding a candle and
dressed for the night in his nightshirt and a silk Persian gown. Without his
yellow wig, he looked older, and far less threatening than in his office with
its sinister owl.

Once inside, in a room lined with books, and sitting by a fire dying
down for the night, La Reynie showed Fields the letter of introduction
from the Board of Ordnance. The sword Fields had given up lay across a
low table.

'Why?' La Reynie asked. 'Why present this letter to me, inside this
sword's scabbard? I remember the way you tapped it, and so I looked inside.'

By way of answer, Fields produced Harry's pistol.

'Four shots, successively,' Fields said.

La Reynie felt the weapon's cumbersome weightiness. It was heavier
even than it looked.

'Hunt took a care to withhold his true mission for the Board of Ordnance from you,' Fields said. 'He is an assassin. He has killed before. With
the weapon you hold in your hand.'

La Reynie inspected the pistol's extra barrels. 'That is why he went to
the Butte de Copeaux?'

'Ah, your *mouches*. He hoped to find the dwarf there.'

'But to kill him?'

'He had the weapon with him. Even after you forbade him to carry one,
anywhere inside Paris.'

La Reynie placed it down gingerly, as if the pistol owned murderous intent rather than the man who used it. 'Sir Jonas, I know, of course. He is a man to be wary of. His spies are often to be found in Paris.' He stroked his nose, deep in thought. 'The people of L'Exhibition de Monstruosités resented your being there, and chased you both away.'

'They sought to protect their own.'

'But hundreds go to the display. Every year it comes, to the Butte des Copeaux. Why should they take against you? I wondered upon it, when informed of the emprise.'

'We searched the place, away from the crowd, so made ourselves unwelcome.'

'Perhaps Monsieur Hunt is not so clever, after all.'

'Oh, he is clever. After your prohibiting us from asking of the dwarf's whereabouts, he thought to bring the dwarf out into the open.'

'He failed to do so. The man calling himself Hudson was not part of the show. Instead, Hunt found how he communicates, using a book describing the workings of a library.'

Fields nodded. 'Written by Cardinal Mazarin's librarian. I forget his name.'

'Gabriel Naudé. Hunt thinks he uses a code based on where the letters and words lie in the book. Hunt found his quarry at the Bibliothèque Mazarine. My men arrested him before he could carry out his assassination.'

'The dwarf was fortunate.'

'Does Hunt know with whom he communicates?'

'By nature, he is a secretive man. Which is why Sir Jonas employed him, of course. And for his skills learned at the Royal Society. His rare knowledge of poisons is why the Duchesse de Mazarin recommended him to her sister, the Duchesse de Bouillon.'

'I already know this. Her butler gave us the information readily enough.' La Reynie paused to consider the old Colonel in front of him. 'Tell me, as you did not tell me before: Why did you deliver to me the letter from the Ordnance? And why do you now bring me this pistol?'

Fields looked into his hands rather than at the Lieutenant Général, and sighed. *'Je me retrouve dans une situation difficile. Je cherche le meilleur pour chacun. C'est ma solution.'* I find myself placed in a difficulty. I seek the best for everyone. This is my solution.

'*Si vous êtes comme la plupart des hommes, vous souhaitez quelque chose en retour.'* If you are as most men are, then you wish for something in return.

'*Je suis comme la plupart des hommes, je trouve. J'ai passé ma vie à me mentir, me croyant meilleur que le troupeau.'* I am as most men are, I find. I have lived a life of self-deception, thinking myself better than the flock.

Fields stood, and straightened his coat, ready to leave. '*Ma maison et la tranquillité, c'est tout ce que je désire.'* Home and quietness is all I desire.

After showing Fields to his door, and watching him head back slowly towards the Seine, instead of going to bed La Reynie went back to his room with the fire and all the books. He lit an extra candle, and went to one of the shelves.

He took down his own first-edition copy of *Advis pour dresser une bibliothèque.* Then, he produced the notes Harry had left inside the copies at the Bibliotèque Mazarine.

CHAPTER THIRTY-NINE

THE ROUGH QUESTIONING

HARRY WAS AWOKEN BY A KEY'S scrape in the lock. The cell door swung open forcefully, its handle chipping more brick from the wall. In the doorway stood the capitaine who had arrested him at the library. With him, picking his nose and chewing tobacco, was the adjudant who had fetched La Reynie when Harry and Fields first reported to the Châtelet.

In his sleep, Harry had got so cold his spine would not bend. He had to roll sideways off his bed, able to stand only by pushing himself up from it.

The two men watched him blankly, seeing nothing they had not seen before.

The capitaine advanced into the cell and produced some large and heavy manacles. He secured Harry's hands in front of him. 'Le Lieutenant

Général veut vous interroger maintenant.' The Lieutenant Général wishes to question you now.

The manacles were overtight and dug into Harry's flesh.

The adjudant looked disappointed. Was this prisoner really the assassin spoken of throughout the Châtelet, a man sent by the English to kill one of their own? But when Harry flexed his shoulders, trying to encourage some life into his muscles, the man flinched, and stepped backwards.

The capitaine sneered at his colleague and dragged Harry from the cell.

They led him up the stairway, through the Châtelet, towards their Lieutenant Général's office.

One foot on his chair, elbows leaning on his raised thigh, La Reynie waited behind his desk, an elegant china cup full of coffee held before him. Its aroma filled the room.

Harry had gone without food or drink since the previous morning, when he breakfasted on fish with Marie-Anne. It seemed more like a week ago; a hazy memory of civility. Although a pot steamed on his desk, La Reynie did not offer him any of the coffee. Instead, he frowned, and pursed his lips, as if Harry were a puzzle of some kind. An interesting theoretical conundrum.

On the desk was an object Harry had not noticed there before: a wooden baton, painted white.

Pushed into place by the capitaine in front of La Reynie's desk, Harry stood uncomfortably close to the fire. His broken spectacles were smeared, but with his hands manacled he could not wipe them clean. Strangely, it was this that troubled him most of all. He was desperate to see La Reynie more clearly.

The Lieutenant Général waved the cup at him, and let out a long, slow breath. 'What do you know of poisons, Monsieur Hunt?'

Harry knew plenty of poisons. He had answered La Reynie before, at their first meeting, when he had asked the same question.

He swallowed, made difficult by his parched throat. 'I know of plants, and airs, and strong waters, which must be used with care. I don't know why you again ask the question.'

'Yes, you do,' La Reynie said quietly.

Harry ran his tongue around his mouth. It stuck to his gums, and his lips were cracked and sore. 'I know all of Paris is made anxious with poisonings. I know you're charged with finding those who undertake them.'

'You know, also, the Duchesse de Bouillon plots against her husband.'

'That's false testimony, maliciously given against her.'

La Reynie snorted. 'You *have* become her friend. The Mazarin nieces. Bewitching, aren't they?' He caught Harry's look, one mixing distaste with apprehension. 'You mistake me, for I do not believe in witchcraft. Anyways, it is by the by. Your name was given to me. With an accusation of accepting employment from the Duchesse, who desired your knowledge of natural philosophy and the chymical arts.'

'It's not true!'

'You deny it?'

'I do deny it. Who makes such an accusation?'

'It explains your presence in her house, and in Paris,' La Reynie said, ignoring Harry's question. 'A more believable story than you being here to find a dwarf. And, more ridiculous still, to question him on the murder of another dwarf.' La Reynie tapped his temple derisively. 'When you first came here, to the Châtelet, you told me the Board of Ordnance had sent you. You provided no proof. So why should I not believe the person who willingly, for no profit to himself, offered this information?'

'Because it's a lie.' Harry's tongue felt like an old piece of leather. La Reynie, he grasped, had deliberately left him in the cell for a day and a night with no food or water, to ready him for this interrogation.

'You say that. I cannot know it.'

'I assure you, Lieutenant Général, I'm here on the orders of Sir Jonas

Moore. Also, as you found out, of Lord Danby. Both desire me to find the man calling himself Captain Jeffrey Hudson. Lord Danby said he was named by Titus Oates as a plotter against our King. I thought the second Hudson might know who killed the original. He does not. It's the one thing I've established to my satisfaction since arriving here in Paris.'

'Why come all the way to Paris to question a man about a killing, one amid many, from your Civil Wars? It was a lifetime ago.'

'Sir Jonas ordered me. Then, so did Lord Danby. He's not a man to be refused.'

'No, another reason,' La Reynie said. 'Why, really, have you come here?'

'In truth, monsieur.' The manacles' weight was suddenly unbearable, and Harry's forehead dripped with sweat from the heat from the fire. The sweat ran into his eyes, making him blink. 'I came to Paris to find the dwarf. Firstly, I thought to question the captain of *Incassable*, the ship in which Hudson made his last journey to England.'

'Capitaine Eugène de Beauchene.' La Reynie placed his cup onto the desk. 'He has stood exactly where you do now. Another reason.'

'There's no other reason.'

'You expect me to believe you?'

'Yes.'

'No.' La Reynie said this sadly, as if he had expected something great from his prisoner, but found his hopes dashed.

Harry's proximity to the fire was unbearable. The backs of his legs were roasting. The pain from his cheek, damaged by the book thrown in the Bibliothèque Mazarine, made his eyes stream.

La Reynie saw his distress. 'Would you like some water?'

Without needing Harry's reply, he motioned to his capitaine to fetch some.

Harry wanted nothing more than to drink water, but de Beauchene's story of being forced to drink more than he could bear made him retch from fear. Strands of spittle hung from his lips. He could hardly stand. His legs were shaking, from fear of rough questioning, from the fire's heat, and from the lack of food and water.

The capitaine returned with a glass and a large pitcher.

'Drink. Please,' La Reynie said pleasantly, as if offering his best Bordeaux.

The capitaine poured some water, warm and cloudy, from the pitcher, and held out the glass. Harry stretched his neck forwards, to sip from the rim. Some water spilled from his uncontrollable shaking. Apart from the water escaping down his chin and soaking his shirt, he swallowed the contents of the glass.

'Would you like another?' La Reynie's eyebrows were arched in polite enquiry.

Harry stepped back, as far from the Lieutenant Général as he could, almost into the fire, away from the capitaine's arm stretching towards him with a second glass of water in his hand. The capitaine grabbed him with his other hand and jerked him back into position.

Until Harry had forced himself to drink the second glass of water, La Reynie said nothing. The capitaine filled another one.

With sick rising in his mouth, Harry began to drink it.

From inside a cherrywood box on his desk, La Reynie produced a piece of paper. He crossed the distance between them, took the glass from Harry, and held the paper close to Harry's face, aware that he was struggling to see.

Recognising the letter at last through his smeared and broken spectacles, with the Board of Ordnance's seal on it, Harry almost collapsed with relief. The letter of introduction he had lost. How had it come into the Lieutenant Général's possession? He did not know: it was of no matter. Grateful tears pricked his eyes. He would soon be free of this room, and of La Reynie, who maliciously toyed with him, trying to get information by frightening him, when all along he had known Harry was Sir Jonas's man.

'I have another letter, too,' La Reynie said, reaching again into his box. 'This letter is interesting. It tells me of your proficiency in natural philosophy. And that you proved yourself before as an investigator.'

'Thank you,' Harry said fatuously. He lifted his forearms to the two men in the office for the manacles be removed.

'It is from Lord Danby, in answer to mine.' La Reynie began to walk around Harry, his capitaine moving smartly out of his way. 'Let me read what Danby writes of you: *Mr. Hunt could not keep his position within the Royal Society, for all he demonstrated there was his own incompetence. Luckily for him, he found alternative employment with the Board of Ordnance, with Sir Jonas Moore, a man well known to you. I know not the fullness of Moore's design, but cannot think it anything but mischievous. I doubt it is to the good of our two nations, or relations between us.*'

Harry had gone from joy to despair again. 'Why would he write such a thing?'

'Because you came to kill the dwarf, not to question him, by order of the Board of Ordnance.'

'No, no . . .' Harry protested. A thought struck him. 'Who gave you the Board's letter?'

It must have been Mercier, Marie-Anne's butler. He had found it in the Hôtel de Bouillon. The letter, and the lies of poisoning had been forced from him by torture.

La Reynie replaced both letters inside the box, and softly closed its lid. 'Your companion. Colonel Michael Fields. He also confirmed your assistance to the Duchesse.'

Harry stared at him wildly, and felt his knees buckle. 'I don't believe you!'

'The Colonel gave me the letter from the Board wrapped around his sword blade, when he handed it to me here. Also, he told me of your promise to kill the Duchesse's husband. That you would deliver the fatal dose yourself, and that even the most skilled physician would think he had died only from an apoplexy.'

'Colonel Fields is the most honest man I know—to his own detriment. Why should he lie? I have nothing to do with any poisoning, of anyone.'

The capitaine made a move to strike Harry for his insolence, but La Reynie raised his hand to stop him.

'He came to my home. He gave me your pistol.'

Harry's face was still incredulous. La Reynie produced Harry's pistol from a desk drawer and held it high in front of him, balanced on the flat of his palm.

Harry felt as if all the strength had left his bones. He could not believe the Colonel would have done such a thing. He had not been dead at all, but instead had visited—and lied to—the Lieutenant Général.

His betrayal made no sense.

'You do not deny it is your weapon?'

He could deny it, but as well as the Colonel's word against him, Marie-Anne had seen it, and so had her man, Mercier. Everyone at Marie-Anne's salon had seen it. Fields, Harry recognized, had been careful to ensure it.

'It's mine,' Harry admitted. 'I brought it to Paris for my own protection.'

'An impressive weapon. As well as poisons, you are proficient with pistols, too. You worked upon it yourself, I understand, to improve it.'

'It fires four times before it needs to be reloaded,' Harry said dully. 'I replaced the original barrel with four, and redesigned the mechanism.'

'Remarkable. An assassin's weapon.'

'I'm no assassin.'

La Reynie lowered the pistol. 'Here are the accusations against you. Firstly, you helped the Duchesse de Bouillon prepare poisons to murder her husband, the Duc. Secondly, you came to Paris to kill the man who uses the name Hudson, on the Board of Ordnance's orders. Fortunately for both men, your plans were discovered. Sir Jonas Moore should not have taken one of the Royal Society's discards. You are not really competent for the role he started you upon.'

'Neither of your accusations are true! You could fill me with water to overflow, to break me under such duress, and I would plead to you my guilt. It would still all be falsehood.'

'Sadly for you, the Duchesse's man, Mercier, aligns himself with everything the Colonel told me.'

'You've broken him.'

'Persuaded him. To tell the truth.'

From the same drawer he had kept the pistol, La Reynie took out another letter. On it was the royal seal of King Louis XIV.

'A *lettre de cachet*, signed by our Sovereign himself.' La Reynie then picked up the white baton from his desk. Harry cringed away from it, raising his hands to protect his face. The capitaine grinned, but the Lieutenant Général looked grave.

Instead of hitting him, he lightly tapped Harry on the shoulder with it.

'Mr. Henry Hunt, in the name of *Le Roi* Louis Quatorze, you are to be confined in the Bastille, until we have finished our investigations, and have readied ourselves for your trial.'

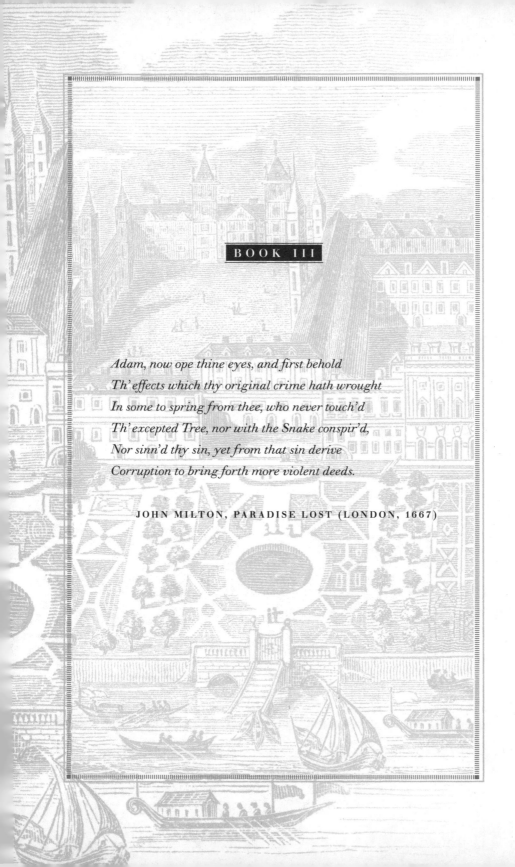

BOOK III

Adam, now ope thine eyes, and first behold
Th' effects which thy original crime hath wrought
In some to spring from thee, who never touch'd
Th' excepted Tree, nor with the Snake conspir'd,
Nor sinn'd thy sin, yet from that sin derive
Corruption to bring forth more violent deeds.

JOHN MILTON, PARADISE LOST (LONDON, 1667)

CHAPTER FORTY

THE USEFUL
TOOL

LORD DANBY SAT IN HIS OFFICE, eating a luncheon of lamprey pie. He had worked through a bottle of wine. Now he wondered if he should embark upon another. He decided against it. He wanted his wits sharp for this afternoon, ready to question Titus Oates on new allegations against five Jesuits: Thomas Whitbread, William Barrow, John Caldwell, John Gavan, and Anthony Turner. All had attended a Consult of Jesuits at the White Horse tavern in the Strand. So had Titus Oates, who overheard them plotting brazenly to kill the King. William Ireland and John Grove, also there, had already been executed, but evidence was lacking against the others.

Since then, damning letters had been found.

Danby wiped at his moustache with a corner of his napkin. These men should be put to death as soon as possible, to dissuade other Catholics from harming the King's person. The King, he knew, had little faith in Titus Oates. Israel Tonge, too, he discounted. His Majesty's insistence on scrutinizing their testimonies too closely threatened his own well-being. The King was distracted by details, such as when Oates and Tonge contradicted themselves on some matter or other. He did not seem cognizant of the danger of the threats against him. He still played the ridiculous game of going out and about London in disguise, as William Jackson!

Luckily, the King had Danby to look after his interests—which, after all, were the interests of them all.

He took another bite of pie.

The thought of a Catholic insurrection horrified him. Not only would they lose their King, and their religion, and their liberties, and be ruled by a Pope—with all the fanatical superstition that would bring—but he himself would lose everything. He had aligned himself with Oates, against the Catholics. They would never forgive him. They would burn him, as was their vicious inclination.

Hundreds of others, too, would be killed. It would be like Mary's reign, come again.

These were desperate times, needing men of strength to guide the kingdom.

From outside his office, he heard Merritt's characteristic stride. The ponderance of his man's walk hid a quick but contradictory mind, one intelligent yet unthinking. Merritt was usefully shallow, with a gratifying willingness to follow his master even on his most exuberant schemes.

Merritt claimed to be a philosophical agnostic: not in the sense of neither believing nor disbelieving in God for philosophical reasons, but in professing himself interested in all the various philosophies, but not accepting any of them. He could discuss if he existed, or if he did not, and bring forth reasons for and against. Or if there existed a world external to himself, or else it was entirely imaginary. He could quote philosophers at length; their arguments one way or another. But to decide which notion was true, or even the most likely, sparked no interest in him at all.

Yet Merritt could predict other people's behaviour with an uncanny accuracy. It was as if he could see directly all their motivations, and their inner complications, with the various influences acting upon them. This was a feat of calculation rather than imagination, it seemed to Danby. Merritt was the fastest man to determine the outcomes of a loan at a percentage over a time that he had ever come across. Yet if Danby were to press him for a decision on the matter of free will, Merritt would just shrug, and smile his bovine smile.

Whether Merritt was for the Protestants, working against the Catholics, or for the Catholics against the Protestants, all would be the same. He was careful to avoid recusancy, of course, from self-interest. Danby had thought, before he met the man, that he could never trust anyone without religion, but Merritt had proved himself utterly dependable.

Like Oates and Tonge, Merritt was a useful tool to further his plans.

Here he came, in the same way he entered every time. The knock. The pause. The door's gradual opening. The sheepish look around the stile.

Danby saw an excuse to open the second bottle. 'Some wine, Merritt?'

'Very kind, my Lord.' Merritt saw the empty bottle, and went to its partner. 'Shall I?' He expertly removed the cork with the screw, speaking as he poured the wine. 'We've intercepted a letter, which will be of interest to you.'

Of course it would. Danby trusted his judgment. He looked at the letter Merritt held out to him. From the Paris police. La Reynie's own seal.

'For Sir Jonas Moore?' He untucked his napkin from his shirt front, and placed it across his meal, leaving nearly half the pie. 'Care of the French ambassador.'

'Who receives most of his post late,' Merritt observed wryly.

Danby stood and walked to the window to read. 'Henry Hunt now languishes in the Bastille. Far enough away, I think.' He tilted his head from side to side, weighing up the information. 'La Reynie informs Sir Jonas of Hunt's arrest for his spying on the Board of Ordnance's behalf, and of his own suspicion of orders to kill the dwarf. La Reynie takes against Sir Jonas's having sent Hunt to Paris. My letter to him would have helped with that. And—here is a welcome addition—Hunt is held for his attempted poisoning of the Duc de Bouillon. Apparently, he helped the Duc's wife to prepare inheritance powders.' Danby smiled lugubriously. 'Hunt is embroiled in all these Paris poisonings. King Louis has placed him in the Bastille. He has done our work for us, then, as far as Hunt is concerned. We do not want him in London, at least not before the Queen's Catholic Consult. He is too dangerous a man. Remember how he thwarted Lord Shaftesbury.'

'No need, surely, for the Lieutenant Général to receive a reply from Sir Jonas,' Merritt suggested.

'No need at all.' Danby passed the letter back to Merritt. 'Burn it.'

He was pleased with his assistant. He would invite him to finish off the lamprey pie.

'How goes the work at Somerset House? The Consult is almost upon us.'

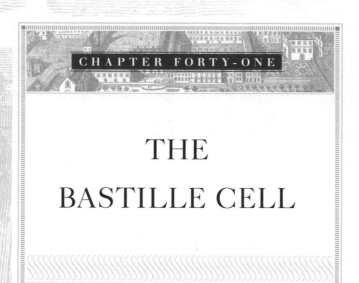

CHAPTER FORTY-ONE

THE

BASTILLE CELL

ON WAKING, HARRY REMEMBERED WHERE HE was, and groaned. His wrists were raw from the iron bands chafing them. Chains attached them to the wall, long enough so he could cross to the window and make a semicircle around the room.

When he did, there was poor reward for his labour. The window's bars were an inch in diameter. Horizontal and vertical, forming squares about four inches across. Three of these grids, each offset to obscure the view through the others, made the room dim, and he had been given no candles.

This cell, unlike the one in the Châtelet, was at the top of a tower. A rough octagon, none of the walls matched exactly. Its high ceiling disappeared into darkness.

He had rejoiced to see a proper mattress, until he found it alive with maggots and lice. He had dragged it against the wall and slept on the bed's wooden planks. The only other furniture was a table, with a pitcher and a pewter cup. A chair, too, kept cruelly out of reach by the chains, left there by a geôlier made happy by this simple act of malice.

There was no fireplace, just a slab of stone by the wall. Every day, a geôlier brought logs—poor wood and moist, which filled the cell with stinging smoke—but after the fuss to get it going, all its heat disappeared into the roof.

His arrest now seemed an indistinct dream populated by phantoms: watching the dwarf disappear up the Bibliothèque Mazarine's shelving, and make his escape through the ceiling. There was one sure sign it had happened: his cheek, still tender, injured by the book flung at him. He rubbed at it, feeling his beard, growing since he had arrived at the Bastille. He was not allowed a razor.

He was still in the same clothes he had worn at the time of his arrest. There was no privy, not even a bucket. He used a corner of the room, as far as his chains could reach from his bed, using the infested mattress to divide the area off.

Harry was convinced the cell's foul air would kill him, but to go to the window was to breathe in the pestilent air from outside, where the fosses carried away the Bastille's filth. He had developed a cough which hurt his ribs, and a habit of gagging, his throat continually spasming. After days of this retching, he had almost stopped noticing it.

By the sun's path, he knew he was to the east side of the Bastille. He was in a tower which must project from the prison's wall, for through the tiny gaps left between the bars he could also see south, towards the Seine. Trees lined each side of the Rue des Fossés-Saint-Antoine. He could see over the Petit Arsenal's rooftops, and also the Grand Arsenal, where Marie-Anne had been questioned by the Chambre Ardente. Across the Seine, he recognized the Bièvre river, and the Jardin du Roy, with its plants laid out and orderly. At the top of the Jardin was the Butte des Copeaux. The Exhibition's tents and stages were gone.

As well as all this forlorn looking over Paris, Harry marked out time by following the movement of the grates' shadows cast over the wall, and listening to the noises from around the Bastille and the Porte Saint-Antoine, and from the Seine's busy traffic. Otherwise, he walked the arc afforded him by his chains, backwards and forwards. Each time he reached the wall terminating his journey, he pressed his forehead against its dank stone, breathed deeply, then returned. In the nights, kept awake by the iron bands chafing him, he found comfort in watching the movement of the stars engraving their curves across the sky.

Inside the prison, he could hear the geôliers climbing the stairs and pacing the floors, accompanied by the mournful clatter of bolts. As well as a lock turned by a key, every cell door had a long bolt, sliding shut on the outside. From the sounds changing, he could imagine the geôliers' movements, and their different trajectories. He tried to gauge how many other prisoners suffered here, but he had not been allowed out from his cell for exercise, and had seen no one brought past his door.

Lacking a timepiece, for his watch had disappeared on the first night, having stupidly left it on the table as he slept, he resorted to counting out how long it took for the geôliers to cross from one tower to his, their footfalls going along the roof above his cell. There must be a bridge, he thought, connecting the walls over the middle of the building. He listened out for them on the lower floors, and for the creaks on floorboards that might speak of other prisoners below him. Their movements seemed to be regular.

Once, an alarm had sounded, a bell being rung and a man shouting, but the geôliers' pace had been no quicker, and there was not enough sound to piece together what had happened. Perhaps an attempt at escape. Perhaps an attempt to shorten King Louis's arbitrary sentence.

The waymarkers of each dreary day were breakfast, dinner, and supper. The first was about seven in the morning, thin gruel brought in a wooden bowl with no spoon: no chance for a prisoner to slice himself in his despair, or fashion a weapon. Harry sipped the gruel reluctantly, swallowing in the knowledge he would see it again. Dinner, before midday, was a more extravagant affair, usually sparrow or pigeon, and perhaps with vegetables and fruit. Then, the long wait until evening, around six o'clock, when the plates from his earlier meals were taken away and he was presented with day-old bread. A couple of times he had cheese, and once, the dinner again, served cold.

With his sickness, he kept little of it down. He was getting weaker and thinner. Without his belt, taken away when he had first arrived, his breeches were loose: he had to bunch them with his hand as he moved around the cell. The bones of his wrists protruded, banging ever more painfully on his irons.

When the geôliers came with his food, he had tried to question them on what they might have heard about La Reynie's investigation into his supposed crimes, and if they had heard of a forthcoming trial. There were always two men together, and sometimes a surveillant behind them.

Saying nothing, they looked at him as if he were entirely mad.

In the seven days he had been here, he had heard no word at all of the world outside the prison. Only one change to this pattern had occurred. On the fifth day Harry had asked again. The surveillant, a bull-necked man with a hard face, and scars showing he had once had his nose snipped, had cuffed him on the ear, but given an answer, of sorts. Harry understood his French well enough: 'You are here at the King's whim. He has no need for proof, so there is no need for a trial. So, no need to rush.'

Harry had been taken out of the world. He wondered if anyone even knew he was in the Bastille. Had La Reynie informed Marie-Anne of his incarceration, or about her man Mercier? Did Sir Jonas Moore or Lord Danby know of it? It suited Danby to have him imprisoned, it seemed. Otherwise, he would not have written such a letter. Harry pondered more on why that should be, again trying to connect Richard Merritt, Danby, and the revivified assassin with the strangely shaped forehead.

Harry had heard nothing from Sir Jonas since the morning he had left for France. No letter or word to ask of his progress throughout the time Harry had sought Hudson's impersonator in Paris. Nothing to show he might be engaged on getting Harry released from the Bastille.

And what of Colonel Fields, who had lied to ensure his imprisonment?

His old friend's betrayal was almost impossible to believe, but the more Harry held his actions up to the light, the easier his disappearance after the Butte des Copeaux was explained. It explained, also, the Colonel's recent moodiness, his uncharacteristic silences.

Harry had suspected Marie-Anne's butler of stealing the Board of Ordnance's letter of introduction. Mercier, he had thought, was not to be trusted, but he had been prejudiced by his dislike of the man. Had Fields given false testimony against Mercier, too? Had Mercier been brought to the Bastille? Perhaps he had been tortured further.

Harry did not know if he could withstand such pain. Would he say anything to save himself, even if it meant putting others through the same? He thought of La Voisin. Marie-Anne had told him she kept herself alive by incriminating others.

At the thought of torture, Harry put his head in his hands and sobbed.

He sobbed not only for himself but also for the man who had been like a father to him, who had trained him in the New Philosophy, and who had given him a home. And how had he repaid Mr. Hooke? Harry had left the Royal Society merely for money, and for the petty reason of his pride hurting after the failed experiment at Gresham. He sobbed, too, for Grace, and his poor treatment of her. Caused by his callow desire to impress the Duchesse, Hortense Mancini. In fact, by his desire to impress all those grander than himself. He had shown a contemptible disrespect to the woman he loved.

Robert Hooke and Grace were in London, going about their lives without him. He was inside the Bastille. As he sobbed in his cell, he could scarcely believe his own actions. How could he have behaved so atrociously? It was as if an imposter had acted in his place, like the man who posed as Captain Hudson.

With such questions, Harry tortured himself far more effectively than La Reynie ever could. He knew they were all, each one of them and a thousand more besides, unanswerable while he was locked inside this cell.

Trying to stave off despair, he forced himself to consider matters other than his own torment. Mechanics. Instrument making. Horology. Mapping the world. Mathematics, running through his knowledge of Euclid and Descartes. Architecture, and flight, and ways of making lamps. He thought about navigation at sea, the properties of the air, attempts to forecast the weather, and the landscape changing over time. Shells, and all the sorts of fossil in the Royal Society's Repository. He thought of the stars, and the motions of the planets. Gravitational attraction. Electricity being emitted from the pressing of bone.

Robert Hooke's interests had become his own. He was merely a poor copy. He wondered what he could claim for himself.

Harry had no paper to write out his thoughts. If he had, then perhaps they would not have revolved around and around inside his own self-pity. He could have recorded them, then put them aside. If this were to be the last place he resided in, if this were the cell from which he was taken to be executed—for a crime he was innocent of—he would have liked to write down his wishes.

And his regrets.

The seventh day crept slowly towards afternoon, exactly as all the other days had passed, each hour dragging by. Dinner: mashed swede with fatty ham, and hardly a word said by the geôliers. Afterwards, Harry lay on his bed, on its uncomfortable boards, staring up blankly at the dark ceiling, not awake nor quite asleep, seeing phantasmal limbs emerging from the shadows.

The sound of movement by his door roused him.

In a second, he sat up, listening intently.

Footsteps, of five—or was it six?—people.

One of them La Reynie at last, he thought, to tell him of his release.

The lock was turned. The door was unbolted. A man, looking more fit for Versailles than a prison, entered Harry's cell. The two geôliers and their surveillant came with him, all careful to impress with their efficiency, for he was the Bastille's Capitaine-Gouverneur, François de Montlezun.

He looked Harry over, studying his thin, pale face and patchy beard. How small and frail this English assassin was. Such an insignificant specimen.

He returned to the door, and went through it, leaving Harry wondering why this man had bothered to inspect him, and what his visit might mean.

Then, someone else entered his cell. When Harry saw who it was, the room began to rotate, and tilt, and stretch. The last thing he knew before he lost consciousness was the burning sensation in his throat, as the swede and ham resurfaced.

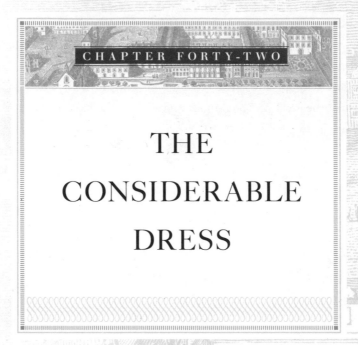

CHAPTER FORTY-TWO

THE CONSIDERABLE DRESS

LITTLE DROPS OF RAIN FALL ON his face. He is in a forest, lying on his back. A glade among the trees. A secret place, hidden from the world. Talking softly with Grace. Jagged stripes of sunlight, reaching through the gaps between the branches, warm their faces. Grace smiles at something he says. Her face is close to his, and full of love. He can feel her breath's caress against his ear. He can smell her, and the wet dark earth beneath them, and feel, growing lushly from it, the wet grass.

Despite the sunshine, the rain again. It must be running from Grace's hair, onto his face, onto his damaged cheek. One drop landing in his eye, making him blink it away . . .

'*Haarrry! Haarrry!*'

The glade shimmered, and collapsed, shrinking to a glimmer of light at the far reach of his memory. Grace left him, too, leaving only her fragrance, freshly soaped, as if just stepped out of her bath.

The cup's rim was pushed gently between his lips, and brackish water poured over his gums. He could feel a hand stroking his forehead.

He opened his eyes, forcing them wide.

It was Hortense Mancini, Duchesse de Mazarin, whose hand and whose breath he could feel. Her fragrance he could smell.

She looked radiantly unconcerned by her surroundings. Would she disappear, as Grace had disappeared? Was she as imaginary, brought forth by his dreams?

Reading his mind, she put her hand back into the pitcher set on the floor beside her, and flicked more water at his face. 'Haarrry, you fainted quite away. You thought you were with Grace. I heard you speak with her. But you are here, with me.'

'In the Bastille prison,' Harry said, with the lurch of despair that came with knowing it.

'You must come to your senses quickly. I have bargained for only ten minutes with you.'

Instead of the mannish clothes she usually favoured, Hortense wore the clothes of a lady. One whose concerns centred wholly—to a deranged degree—on the display of wealth. She was draped in jewellery: necklaces and earrings, rings on every finger, as extreme a vision of aristocratic femininity as could be. It looked as if she were too indolent to decide which pieces to wear, and so wore everything. Her petticoat was white, heavily inlaid with gold thread. A patterned silk manteau, deep purples and greens, with bows and ribbons fussing from it, contrasted with a startling lemon-yellow stomacher. The manteau flowed over an enormous farthingale, years out of fashion. Her hair was arranged over a wire palisade, with more ribbons and lace holding it all together.

The Capitaine-Gouverneur put his head back through the door. Hortense waved at him dismissively. Unable to contain a look of surprise at his superior, the surveillant with the snipped nose stepped forwards to lock the door. They all moved away, the Capitaine-Gouverneur, the surveillant, and two other geôliers. Harry could hear their footsteps descending the tower's stairs.

'You would not believe the price of this audience with you,' Hortense said, smiling despite the cell's stink and Harry's miserable condition. 'Not only money. The Capitaine-Gouverneur values some things more highly than I do, I think.'

'I did nothing of these crimes I'm accused of! Nothing! I've had no orders to kill the dwarf! I've not helped your sister kill her husband. I did no such thing!'

'I know, I know,' Hortense soothed him. Harry was babbling, sounding frantic. 'Marie-Anne has no interest in poisoning her husband. She can bleed him dry far better alive than dead, as most of his estate would then be shared with his family. No, La Reynie believes what he wants to believe. He himself visited Marie-Anne, to inform her of her butler's imprisonment. He is still held at the Châtelet. La Reynie told her Mercier had testified freely against you. Of course, we did not believe it.'

'I saw him. It looked like he withstood a great deal, before he broke.'

'Many tell La Reynie what he wishes to hear, to avoid their courage being tested.'

'Have you heard word of the Colonel? La Reynie says Fields told him I was an assassin, sent to kill the man who calls himself Captain Hudson. And that I helped your sister against her husband.'

'We have seen or heard nothing of him. I am sorry, for I know how much he means to you. It is hard when one you love betrays you.' Hortense squeezed his hand between her two hands, the rings on her fingers pressing them painfully, but he did not pull away. This human contact felt miraculous to him.

'I have a further surprise for you.'

Harry shifted, to push himself from the bed. 'You work towards my release?'

Hortense looked uncomfortable. 'Only two men can influence your release. Louis Quatorze and La Reynie. Marie-Anne has gone to Versailles to petition the King. Did you know he once loved our sister, Marie? He wanted to marry her. Imagine! She turned him down. We must hope he has forgiven her enough to listen to Marie-Anne.'

'What's the surprise? Please tell me. I'm desperate for news.'

'Are you well again?'

'My strength. The food.' Harry heard his own impatience at her solicitousness, but then reflected on how he must appear. Like a wild creature, not a man.

She stepped over Harry's chains and went to the door, walking awkwardly within the huge circumference of her dress, to check no geôliers loitered outside. From being the glamorous and carefree Hortense, she had become nervous. More like her sister, Marie-Anne, Harry thought, as he sat on the edge of his bed, wondering what she had to tell him.

Walking slowly towards him, she seemed to notice her dress dragging along the dirty oak floor. She lifted its hem. Perhaps it had snagged on a splinter. The floor was rough in places, especially outside the chain's orbit. But she continued to lift the dress, at the front. Harry froze. What was she doing? This, surely, could not be why she had come to see him. He could see her knees! He tried to read her expression, but she only looked nervous. As the dress continued to ascend, he saw her thighs. Her legs were muscular, and lean. She placed one foot firmly, then stepped with the other to one side, spacing her feet wide apart. She had not looked at him, concentrating on gathering the material in her arms.

Inside the dress, trailing behind her, was another piece of material. It moved, seemingly by itself, rising up as her dress had risen up.

From beneath the farthingale's frame, emerging between her legs, came a head, and then a body: it was the dwarf Harry had seen at the Bibliothèque Mazarine.

He crawled out from his hiding place, then stood and bowed to Harry.

Hortense introduced them. 'Mr. Henry Hunt, Mr. Bartholomew Slough. Mr. Bartholomew Slough, Mr. Henry Hunt.'

'Mr Slough.'

'Mr. Hunt.'

The two men nodded formally to one another. Neither mentioned the eccentric means of Slough's conveyance, thinking it indelicate to do so. Hortense rearranged her dress from around her waist.

'Pleased to make your acquaintance, sir,' Slough said.

'Likewise, sir.'

'Providence being a mischievous creature, unusual circumstances bring us together. Good may come of them.'

'Little hope of good in here,' Harry said dejectedly. 'There's little we can do for one another.'

'Oh hush, Harry,' Hortense admonished him, as if his confinement in the Bastille Saint-Antoine was a minor irritant. 'You are part of a wider game. Mr. Slough has told me.'

'And you have no notion of its rules,' Slough said cheerfully.

Harry gaped in disbelief. The subterfuge they had resorted to—and the troubles Hortense had taken to get them into his cell—only to tell him he was a plaything. He already knew, full well. He had been pushed this way and that since starting his unwise search for a dwarf pretending to be another dwarf. Well, now he had found him. His name, apparently, was Bartholomew Slough. Found, through no agency of his own, and little joy did it bring him.

'You must take cheer from Mr. Slough's news,' Hortense said. 'Your captivity has led you to dark thoughts.'

He had allowed himself to become gloomy again. He had not even thought to thank her for her willingness to pay whatever price the Capitaine-Gouverneur demanded.

He looked more closely at Slough, whose face was lined with experience. His skin had a dark hue, permanently stained by his years at sea. Even in the darkness of Harry's cell, his eyes were narrowed, as if he were the ship's lookout squinting in strong sun. His beard, flecked with white, was combed forwards to a point. It was the same style worn by some of the crew of the chebec in King's Lynn. Slough's exotic appearance was heightened by a small black tattoo on his cheek, by his right eye: a hand, palm forwards, an exhortation to stop. A hamsa hand, a Hand of Fatima. Despite this tattoo, around his neck Slough wore a gold crucifix hanging from a chain. He looked tough, strong enough to fight anyone twice his height. He had no wig or coat, having foreseen the heat of being smuggled into the Bastille under Hortense's dress.

'How do you come to be here with the Duchesse?' Harry asked, his voice transparently suspicious.

'After you were missed, her sister's searching took her to the Bibliotèque Mazarine,' Slough answered. 'I see your doubt—yes, she went there herself, for you. I overheard her asking La Poterie if he had seen you there. He told her of your arrest. Her protestations of your innocence drew me to her, and to you, revising my first thoughts of you. Listening, I thought her a possible ally, and so she has proved to be. I introduced and explained myself to her, and she took me to the Hôtel de Bouillon.'

'And I had just arrived,' Hortense filled in.

Slough nodded at her, with a consequent shake of his beard. 'And so we met.'

'I was never sent to kill you, Mr. Slough,' Harry said, starting to feel easier. Slough's manner, like his words, was direct, unhesitating, and seemed entirely straightforward.

'As I have been assured, by two Duchesses.'

'Will you tell me everything? For all to me is currently confusion.'

Slough promptly dropped to the floor, sitting cross-legged. Harry motioned to Hortense to sit on the bed, but she declined. The difficulty of sitting in such a dress had not occurred to him, until she gestured at it to clarify. Instead, she moved closer to the door, able to see out through the hatch. Harry chose to stay standing, too, the chain clanking as he paced about.

'Firstly, I know nothing of the diamond you both seek,' Slough began. 'I never met with Jeffrey Hudson, so could not have murdered him. I admit, I took advantage of the space left at his home, where I resided after my enforced service with the corsairs. Over ten years ago now. It was a risk, but if my pretence was seen through, I reckoned to have enough wits to escape punishment. At Oakham, the gods be praised, I found Priscilla Leach, allowed to live there by Hudson's family, for she had been a loyal servant to the man. They had no need for his house, and, also, they still hoped for his return. Priscilla and I immediately became friends. It was as if we had known each other since childhood, we found our company together so easy.'

'As she had known the real Jeffrey Hudson,' Harry said. 'From childhood.'

Slough looked away a little guiltily, and shifted his position on the floor. 'She knew I was not him. I had little need for duplicity, except with a few neighbours. As for his family, Hudson had not seen them since the age of nine. Although I was taller, I explained this away by the food I had eaten in my captivity, especially the quantity of fish. Those who loved the original wanted to believe he had survived, and saw what they wanted to see. They became caught up in the story of it. Word spread about: Hudson had returned, and though I stayed reclusive, I became an object of celebration. And speculation. So it was that before long I was approached by His Majesty's Intelligence. At first, I worked for those answering to Sir Joseph Williamson, who had paid for my release by Government Scheme. Then I worked under Sir Jonas Moore and the Board of Ordnance. As do you. Eventually, the Lord High Treasurer Danby used me, too, through his man Merritt.'

'The King's security is ensured by men who have no trust for one another,' Hortense observed.

Slough raised his shoulders. 'One gets in the way of another's ambition. It was ever so, I am sure.'

'I've met them all,' Harry said. 'Sir Joseph Williamson's now President of the Royal Society. Sir Jonas is its Vice President. I met Danby at Whitehall, taken to him by his man. Merritt, then, is the tall man Mrs. Leach spoke of, who came to you at Oakham?'

Slough nodded. 'Such is his distrust of sending letters, Danby often sent Merritt in person, if instructions were to be given.'

'What did you do for them, Mr. Slough?'

'I worked as an intelligencer, as so many do. Sir Jonas wanted me for my knowledge of France, where I had lived before my captivity. France was preferable, I found, to living through the Wars in England. Danby, though, was more interested in Catholics. He was keen I listen out for sedition in Rutland, and Norfolk, too. He thought it a return on the investment made in getting me released from the corsairs. Jeffrey Hudson was a Catholic. I had to pretend to be so, to be his copy.'

'You learned the Catholic rites, to pass as Catholic amid Catholics?' Hortense asked.

Slough nodded. 'In my childhood, I was brought up a Seeker. In Africa, I became exposed to the religion of the Berbers, who venerate the land, the rocks, and the life all around us. They have many gods. Anzar, god of rain. Gurzil, the god of war. Ifru, the goddess after whom Africa is named. When mingling with the Catholics in Norfolk, I found a respect for their way of worship. I kept back much of what I heard, as it was merely tittle-tattle, but I fed Danby enough to not risk him putting a stop to my pension. As I never heard anything against the King's life, it did not overly trouble my conscience. An easy existence, there, with Mrs. Leach, sending my reports every month. They were seldom questioned.'

'How did you hear of the real Hudson being found?' Harry asked.

'Merritt came to see me. Sir Jonas Moore had used a courier to inform the King, but the man provided intelligence to Danby. Would you desist with the walking, Mr. Hunt, as your chains are dragging?'

Harry returned to the bed, thinking of what Slough had told him. 'You knew you would no longer be able to live as Hudson, so you decided to escape back to France.'

'No, I was ordered to leave by Danby, through Merritt.'

'But why France? Why Paris?'

Slough looked at him in surprise. 'Why, Mr. Hunt, I thought you knew. You had the book. You guessed at the code. I read your message to me, using *Advis pour dresser une bibliothèque*. Yours was not the same system we used, but I quickly unpicked it.'

'You had left it out, in the window of your library. That is why it came to my attention.'

Slough tutted, castigating his carelessness. 'They were rushed, my final moments there. I hardly had time to say my goodbyes to Priscilla.' His voice thickened at the memory of leaving her behind, and he wiped at his eye, the one over the little Hand of Fatima. 'I came to Paris for the one friend I have here. A friend, I say, and a man I have served since I became Jeffrey Hudson. You found me out. This convinced me you must be an assassin.'

'Who's your friend in Paris?'

'The Paris police's Lieutenant Général, Gabriel Nicolas de La Reynie.'

Harry stared at him in confusion. 'It was La Reynie you communicated with, using Naudé's book?'

'The numbers were always part of a message, made to look innocent by being disguised as quantities of things seen, or required. La Reynie found a hiding place for me, in the attic rooms of the Bibliothèque Mazarine.'

'It was you I heard, when otherwise alone in the library. That's why you thought you were to be killed? I knew only you'd impersonated Jeffrey Hudson, and worked for the King's security. But you helped the French.'

'Not the French,' Slough corrected him firmly. 'La Reynie. You must think them separate, Mr. Hunt, for a man's conscience cannot always be in concord with his country. Danby wanted to feed him false information, and so, often, I did, but I placed the true message within the false, using the code I had devised with La Reynie.'

Harry stared with revulsion at the man sitting so calmly on the floor of his cell. 'You serve La Reynie rather than our King?'

'I do not work against the King's interests. I work against those who plan to commit murder. Murders, I should say. I have told La Reynie of Danby's plan. The Lieutenant Général now seeks to stop it.'

'Danby's plan is what, do you say?'

'There is to be a Catholic Consult, at Somerset House, the home of our Queen, Catherine of Braganza.'

'I know. Mr. Hooke oversaw the work there, before I left England.' To Harry, this seemed a very long time ago. Days of travel, of looking for the dwarf, and of being imprisoned, all merged together to become an age of being away from everything that he knew.

'Her Consult is provocative,' Slough said. 'Titus Oates's evidence has the Protestants stirred up. Now, he has been joined by others, also claiming knowledge of Catholic plots against the King. Prance, Dugdale, Bedloe . . . Danby promotes them all, and encourages them. Nevertheless, the King allows the Consult, just as he allows his wife to keep friars in her home. He seeks to calm her, I think, after she was named by Oates as one who would harm him. She has invited Catholics from all over Europe to attend it. They are to discuss how best to reassure the people that they pose no danger to them, their religion, or to their monarch. The timing of it would be ill-judged, anyways, to my mind. The King does not know his own Lord High Treasurer plans to take advantage of their all being together, in this one place.'

'Take advantage of it?'

'Danby wishes them dead.'

Harry scoffed incredulously, which led him to more of his choking spasms. When he had calmed, he saw Slough, still sitting cross-legged on the floor, looking steadily at him.

'I said before, I had a peaceful life, in Oakham. Until Merritt, Danby's man, instructed me to shelter three Frenchmen.'

'Mrs. Leach told me of them,' Harry said. 'Verdier, Boilot, and Chasse.'

'Yes. Chasse was their leader. Strange looking. I can talk, can't I? He was, my vanity compels me to say, even more peculiar. More a beast than a man.'

'How so?' Harry prompted, remembering the three men with Merritt at Billingsgate, one an assassin he knew as Lefèvre.

'Well, he has an intimate relationship with his razor, to keep his chin in check. His eyebrows meet, and his hair grows low on his forehead. He has strange teeth, too, none touching its neighbour. It is not so much his appearance that disturbed me. I wish to accept people as God made them. It was more his way of looking, as if I was of no consequence to him at all. He has the habit of not blinking. Once I noticed it, it became unsettling.'

'I've seen this Sisyphus,' Harry muttered. 'I took him to be dead.'

'Oh, he is very much alive. He took over my house. Priscilla and I were happy when they left. I had no time to enjoy the peace again, though, for it was then I received news from Merritt of Jeffrey Hudson, found dead at the Denver Sluice.'

'But why did the Frenchmen come to you?'

'They had a machine, which Merritt instructed me to help them store.'

'Do they mean to use this . . . *machine* . . . to kill all the Catholics at the Queen's Consult?'

'I cannot say *all* of them. But, certainly, as many as they can. Danby employs them to do so.'

'What more can you tell us of it, then?' Harry still looked openly doubting.

'I saw bundles, all covered over with canvas,' Slough replied, refusing to take offence. 'When they had locked it away, they watched it constantly, and even kept a hold of my key, so I never knew what it was they had brought with them.'

'What is it their machine, as you call it, is built to do?'

'*Machine* is the word I heard them use,' Slough replied patiently. 'Pronounced in the French way, obviously. As I say, I could not inspect it. It seemed to consist of many pipes, and large metal sheets.'

'Can you recall anything else about it?'

'I saw Chasse with a large key.'

'For a door?'

'No, more like a key to wind a clock. Symmetrical.' He made a twisting movement with his hand, as if holding a T-shaped key, its imaginary stem protruding between his fingers.

Hortense looked worriedly from the hatch. 'Mr. Slough, our time is nearly up. The Capitaine-Gouverneur will return.'

Slough stood, an easy movement upwards from his cross-legged position on the floor. 'My conscience does not let me stand by to allow these murders, even if it means seeking help from the French. No one in England would believe me, as I have been found to be not the man I claimed to be. La Reynie, too, would be seen as untrustworthy. He is a French Catholic. Who at all in the King of England's government would believe him? Who among them would not rather believe he seeks to make mischief? Especially as Danby would deny all. Danby is unassailable, secure against any accusations La Reynie could make.'

'The Queen would believe him,' Harry said.

'Would she?' Slough asked. 'His intelligence comes from a discredited dwarf. La Reynie has no word other than mine concerning these three French assassins.'

Harry turned to Hortense. 'She would wish to ensure the safety of the Catholics under her roof. You must get word to her. She must order a search for this equipment. Bulky as it is, it will not be hard to find.'

Hortense began to gather the material of her dress. 'She thinks me too close to her husband, so does not like me, but I will tell her.'

'She must employ more guards to keep any strangers from the Consult,' Harry replied.

'Let us hope she does,' Slough said. 'Otherwise, I fear, all Catholics at the Consult will be killed. Goodbye, Mr. Hunt.'

'Goodbye, Mr. Slough.'

From the corridor, they could hear the thumps of footsteps. Hortense lifted the front of her dress for Slough to return inside. Although the Duchesse had not asked him to, Harry turned away.

After Slough was hidden again, Harry helped straighten Hortense's dress. 'When is this Consult to be?' he asked her.

'In seven days' time,' she told him.

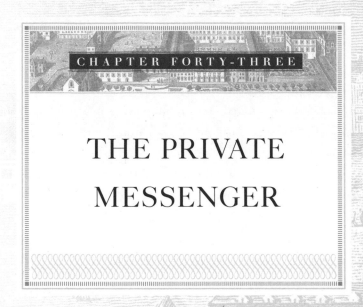

CHAPTER FORTY-THREE

THE PRIVATE MESSENGER

LA REYNIE DESIRED TO KNOW THE truth.

Seeking the comfort of his books, he sat alone in his library at his home on the Rue Quincampoix. A single candle flickered in its holder, lodged on a shelf beside him. A servant had prepared a fire, then been given instructions he was not to be disturbed. On the low table next to his reading chair, La Reynie had placed Harry's pistol.

He had left the Grand Châtelet earlier that afternoon, blaming such an extraordinary absence from his work on a headache. In fact, he had received a letter, and, after reading it, he craved solitude: some time away from the pressing affairs of Paris, with everything urgent, everyone desperate. For matters only came to him if his underlings considered their Lieutenant Général should be bothered with them.

He wished to consider what to do about Henry Hunt. Now, darkness had fallen, and still he did not know the role the young Englishman played—or was about to.

The letter was delivered by a private messenger. The man, in a tricorne hat and overly neat in his appearance, had assured him he had carried it from London himself: it had never left his person. He had taken it from its author's hand, and insisted on giving it only to La Reynie.

This letter was a reply to his own, also sent by private messenger. To use the Post Office and even the embassy post was to risk his message being seen by Sir Joseph Williamson, or by Lord Danby. More than a risk: nearer a certainty. Therefore, he had composed a letter for Danby's eyes, hoping he would see it. Although addressed to Sir Jonas Moore, it told Danby what La Reynie knew he most wanted to hear. La Reynie had received no reply from the Board of Ordnance yet. Perhaps Sir Jonas had not yet seen the letter at all, it having been diverted.

It must suit Danby to keep Harry in Paris, La Reynie thought. Otherwise, why word his letter so damningly? *I know not the fullness of Moore's design*, Danby had written, *but cannot think it anything but mischievous. I doubt that it is to the good of our two nations, or relations between us.*

La Reynie knew the Lord High Treasurer, for they had traded feints and blows before. His damning of Hunt seemed too straightforward a strategy. But this, in turn, might be so signalled to deceive him. A double bluff.

He sighed, a long, low sound, the air from his lungs making the candle's flame dance.

He had no wish to do Danby's work for him. He had sent Robert Hooke a plea for a fuller description of his one-time apprentice.

He had thought his friend, Bartholomew Slough, overwrought after his identity was undone, after the actual Hudson's body was discovered. Everything Slough valued, the tranquillity of living in Rutland, in the little town of Oakham, where he had settled with Priscilla Leach—a marriage in all but name—was turned topside-turvy. Slough's claims of three Frenchmen with mysterious equipment had at first seemed unbelievable. La Reynie had never heard of Verdier, Boilot, and Chasse. The man calling himself

Chasse sounded familiar, though. The hairiness of his face, the rodent-like features. No, it could not be. He was dead, killed in London. He had tried to kill the English King, some of La Reynie's intelligencers said, but that was more hearsay than proof.

Danby had ordered Hunt to Paris, supposedly to find Slough. Sir Jonas Moore, too, had instructed Hunt to find him. Colonel Fields said, to kill him. La Reynie was sure there was more to it. Hunt kept something back, he knew. But why else would he be there, if, as he claimed, he was not an assassin? Perhaps his suspicion of the Duchesse de Bouillon misled him, and he had strayed along a wrong path. Even so, for Hunt to have her help and hospitality seemed too fortuitous. Hunt was an assistant at the Royal Society, recently moved to the Board of Ordnance. She was a *Mazarinette*. And now, he knew, her sister Hortense, the Duchesse de Mazarin, was in Paris.

La Reynie stood and placed another log onto his fire. He spent some time watching the sparks rise, the flames take a hold of the wood, the first charring, the orange glow. This spring was a cold one, he thought, warming his hands, the tips of his fingers insensible from the chill.

He needed to turn this puzzle around, to look at it from the other side. His current thoughts took him nowhere new.

What if he were to assume that Henry Hunt told him the truth? What if he were not an assassin, despite Fields's testimony? Despite the modified weapon he brought with him to Paris, concealed upon his person? Hunt had admitted the improvements were his handiwork, but put the weapon aside. A man who claimed to be an experimentalist, brought up in the methods of the New Philosophy, taught by its most proficient Fellow, the famous Robert Hooke, was unlikely to have such a murderous pistol in his possession. But, put all that aside.

If Hunt had no mission to kill Slough, that meant Fields had lied to him. But why?

La Reynie had asked Fields, when he had come to him at the Rue Quincampoix, why he testified against Hunt. His reply had been an odd one. The Colonel said all he wanted was peace. Home and quietness. *C'est ma solution*, Fields had said. The man had looked full of emotion—mainly, La

Reynie judged, one of sadness. La Reynie looked at the chair opposite him where Fields had sat. The cushion still bore the imprint of his weight.

And what was he to make of Colonel Fields keeping back his fluent French, until he visited La Reynie alone? Had he kept it back from Hunt? Why should he wish to do that if he had accompanied him to Paris, supposedly to help him?

Perhaps it suited Fields, then, as it suited Danby, to have Hunt in Paris. Assume, then, neither man wanted Hunt in London. Perhaps Danby paid the old soldier to ensure Hunt stayed in Paris, and so Fields lied for his employer.

Assume Slough was correct that the English Queen's Catholic Consult was to be attacked by these three Frenchmen.

La Reynie felt himself shrink back from all these assumings. Too many for comfort. But to see things afresh, he must do so. He had no wish to see an innocent man condemned unnecessarily. Of course, he had no qualms if it were *necessary*—but that was another decision facing him.

He rubbed the top of his nose, and squeezed his eyes tight shut. Now he really did have the beginnings of a headache.

He wanted evidence. Proof beyond doubt.

Again, he looked at the letter he held, from the Royal Society's Curator, and acting Secretary, Mr. Robert Hooke.

Who had nothing but praise for Henry Hunt. Hooke's account of Hunt's leaving the Royal Society was full of regret, completely overturning the version supplied by Danby. Hooke only praised the man, for his mechanical abilities, his quickness, his exemplary character. He told him of the bloodless boys, and his saving of the English King.

What if Hunt were the one honest man among the lot of them?

If La Reynie wished to release him from the Bastille, he would need to approach King Louis. His change of heart would vex him; Le Roi would see it as indecision, and he would be vexed too at being asked to negate his *lettre de cachet* so soon. La Reynie would have to put aside at least a day for the journey to Versailles and back again. A longer time than that, perhaps: sometimes the King kept his ministers, and his Lieutenant Général, waiting for hours—days, even, if they were out of favour—before he granted an audience. A reminder to them of his power.

La Reynie became aware he was holding his breath. He let his lungs empty, slowly, exhaling stale air through his nose. He would sleep. See if his dreaming mind made the decision. In the meantime, he would relax the regime for his prisoner, and inform the Capitaine-Gouverneur that Henry Hunt was no longer a prisoner of state. His chains would be removed. He would be allowed exercise. He would no longer be restricted to the Bastille ration, so his pocket, with his money, would be returned. Then Hunt could send out for food, clothes, and even for furniture, to make his stay more comfortable.

La Reynie called for his servant to deliver the message to the Bastille.

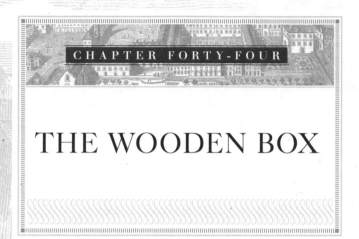

CHAPTER FORTY-FOUR

THE WOODEN BOX

THE GEÔLIER REMOVED THE SHACKLES, AND gathered the length of chain that joined them.

Harry's arms felt suddenly light. A blissful relief overwhelmed him, so intense he saw stars. He had to sit, and close his eyes. When he opened them again, his vision was blurred through his tears. The man looked at him with sympathy until he saw the sharp expression on his colleague's face.

The other man, the surveillant with the snipped nose, handed Harry a wooden box. *'Vous avez des amis, l'Anglais.'* You have friends, Englishman. He sounded resentful that anyone should have friends. *'De plus vous allez avoir un nouveau lit. Il arrivera bientôt. Un cadeau de votre amie la Duchesse.'* Also, you're going to have a new bed. It will soon be delivered. A present from your friend the Duchesse.

He also sounded upset by the Duchesse de Mazarin's influence, however she had brought it to bear upon the Capitaine-Gouverneur.

When they had gone, also leaving more ham, some hard winter cabbage, and the door locked firmly behind them, Harry inspected his wrists. Deep grooves in the flesh were agonisingly sore; the flesh was weeping a sickly yellow colour. He cleaned each wrist with the murky water from the pitcher, grimacing from the pain, but at the same time rejoicing that the shackles had at last come off.

Having washed as gently as he could around the wounds, using the hem of his shirt to wipe them, he looked at the box the turnkey had delivered.

It was heavy, and rattled as he moved it. It had a hinged lid with a simple clasp. After a moment of pause, wondering what sadistic game this might be, he opened the lid cautiously, half expecting something to spring suddenly from it.

Only paper, pens with glass tips, a little pot of ink, and some sand to dry it.

Why had La Reynie ordered him to be treated more leniently? He must want to see how Harry would use these pens, or who he wished to contact. Anything Harry wrote would be studied: a letter might never reach its intended recipient. Even so, the sudden allowance of writing materials felt gloriously luxurious, no matter what the reason for its being given might be.

Harry took a piece of paper, opened the bottle of ink, dipped in the pen, and began to write:

Mr. Isaack Newton,
Ses chambres à Trinity College, Cambridge.
Angleterre

CHAPTER FORTY-FIVE

THE OUTSIDE AIR

THE MORE HUMANE OF THE GEÔLIERS walked just behind him. He had told Harry he would need his coat, for they headed outside, onto the Bastille's roof. Smelling of the ripe cheese enjoyed at lunch, the surveillant walked in front. His deliberate pace frustrated Harry, for at the corridor's end was a flight of stairs illuminated by the light of a Paris afternoon. Almost panting, Harry was desperate to run towards it, to feel the sun's warmth on his skin.

The surveillant's broad back lumbered slowly before him. Behind them, a man was being shown into Harry's cell, carrying the components of a new bed: long poles, struts, and sheets. Harry was benefitting further from La Reynie's instruction to relax his regime, and from the sultry effect Hortense had exerted upon the Capitaine-Gouverneur.

As they went past the other doors, entrances to grim cells like his own, he saw no movement through their viewing hatches. No other prisoners went by, none being exercised as he was, so Harry had no clue how many other souls languished there with him. For all he knew, the Bastille devoted itself only to him.

After an eternity of trudging, they reached the top step, a short length of passageway, then the roof. At once, the sensation of being outside made Harry stumble. The breath of air on his skin and riffling through his hair, his scalp prickling at its movement, the taste of it, its coldness on his eyeballs, all overwhelmed him. He had to cling to the wall to steady himself. The sudden sight of Paris rooftops and the walls and fosses surrounding the fortress, and a squad of soldiers marching past the Capitaine-Gouverneur's house below, moving like the little machines La Reynie spoke of, made him spin.

Harry had the sensation of performing a somersault, although he stood utterly still. His breaths were shallow, fast, irregular, and all the colour had left his face. His eyes were distant, unfocused.

The surveillant looked at him with surprise, this English assassin hugging the wall like a slapped girl. The kinder man squatted in front of Harry. '*Calmez-vous, calmez-vous,*' he said softly, as if to a nervous horse. He took deep, regular breaths, showing how Harry should breathe. Harry knew well how he should breathe, but his lungs betrayed him. He tried to swallow, but could not. Fear lodged in his throat as if someone forced their fist down it, making him panic more. Pulling him up, the geôlier stood Harry upright, still enacting deep, heavy breaths.

Harry pushed his broken spectacles more securely onto his nose, and opened his eyes wide. He saw the surveillant's face with a contemptuous twist to his mouth, and behind him half the length of the Bastille. The towers of Notre-Dame in the distance, high above the other buildings on the Île de la Cité, framed the surveillant's head like the devil's horns.

'*Êtes-vous calmé maintenant?*' Are you calm, now?

'*Oui, oui, merci,*' Harry mumbled, his mouth tasting bitter.

'*Alors. Votre promenade.*' So. Your walk. The men started walking, and their business-like manner took Harry with them. His legs started to obey the instructions of his brain. He followed them, not daring to look down to the triangular bastion surrounding the Capitaine-Gouverneur's house, at his gardens laid out neatly in rows—a small version of the Jardins du Roy, where Harry had searched for the Colonel.

They walked over the Trésor tower's flat roof, Harry's cell directly below them. Here, they were about a third of the prison's length away from the Comté tower, which stood at the Bastille's southeast corner. Harry scanned the building, and at the castellated battlements surrounding it. The parapets allowed movement of the garrison between its eight towers. Each tower had a bell-shaped structure projecting from its roof, little taller than a man, with a door leading onto the parapet. Extending from the Bastille's east parapet to its west, a bridge crossed the great drop below, as Harry had realized when listening to the geôliers' movements. Nervously, he estimated the fall was easily as far as from the White Tower's battlements in the Tower of London. A hundred feet or so.

To the east, he could see the woodyards by the Rue de la Planchette, their stacks looking set to topple. Just behind stood the Hôtel des Mousquetaires Noirs, the home of the regiment which once belonged to the Cardinal Mazarin, until brought under orders of the King. Scarlet uniforms under blue cloaks strode across its yard. Further off, the Faubourg Saint-Antoine spread before him, and faded into the distance. Running beside the ditch leading to the Seine, the Rue de la Contrescarpe was quiet. Boats clustered around the Île Louvier, swaying with the water's movement, looking like piglets suckling at their mother.

Harry's normal way of breathing had returned, the colour come back to his cheeks. He nodded at the geôlier, grateful to him. The surveillant snorted derisively, and gestured to hurry Harry along, at the same moment as from behind them the sun momentarily dimmed. So quickly did it happen, that none of the three men saw quite what *had* happened, until it was too late. Something leapt, with a curious fluttering sound, out of the same doorway from which they had emerged onto the roof.

As it ran towards them, the guards threw their hands up to fend off this fearsome creature.

The creature stared wild-eyed at Harry, at the same time swooping around, knocking the surveillant onto his back with a long wing, the arcing movement sending him dangerously close to the walkway's edge. He only just stopped himself from going over, clutching at the parapet's low wall.

The creature had a human head, with blond hair flowing behind it. He dropped a bundle of equipment at Harry's feet, long rods and taffeta.

It was the man he thought was delivering his bed.

'Monsieur Besnier!'

Jacob Besnier grunted a quick greeting, then set to with seeing off the second guard, a stabbing action of a wing forcing the man backwards, towards the battlements, and the long drop beyond them.

A shout came for reinforcements from the other side of the bridge. Figures began to appear from the little bell-shaped towers, emerging one at a time through the narrow doorways. Harry saw two men kneel and take aim from the Bertaudière tower on the opposite side of the prison, but neither man fired, nervously indecisive, unwilling to risk a hit to their colleagues.

Hurriedly, Harry picked up the first wing, unwrapping it, separating its fabric and poles, and strapped it to his arm. He tried to recall Besnier's demonstration in Marie-Anne's garden, but the great difference between the salon's serenity and the Bastille's busy roof was that it had just dawned on him what Besnier intended him to do.

The wing had simple leather belts and buckles, with a handgrip, but it was far more difficult to place his foot into the other end of the apparatus, shaped like a stirrup with another strap to tighten its hold around his foot. Harry had to laboriously remove his forearm from the belts, and place his foot in first, and then retie the belt around his arm. As he shook violently, this was challenging. He winced as a leather strap scraped his wrist, snicking the wound made by his manacles.

More difficult still was fitting the second wing, as one arm was encumbered by the rigidity of the first, and especially as the surveillant had returned to his feet and was doing his best to stop him. The man grabbed the end of a pole running the length of the wing. Harry threatened the same scooping manoeuvre Besnier had downed him with. The surveillant let go and moved back warily, deciding instead to wait for reinforcements.

More uniformed figures approached. The other geôlier stood by the outside wall's edge, trying to gauge if he should attack Besnier or stay exactly where he was on the edge of oblivion, or else flee along the castellated parapet. Besnier moved towards him, his wings both pointing forwards at him, menacing to force him off.

'No, no!' Harry shouted. 'He's a kind man. *Un homme gentil.*'

He managed to pull on the second wing, but it was difficult to fix the belt around his arm. Besnier came to him, clanking stiffly in his own flying apparatus. He must have separated himself far enough away from the turnkeys that one of the garrison risked a shot. The ball smacked into the wall next to Harry, sending chips of stone fizzing into the air. One caught his face, lodging into the side of his chin.

'*Vite, vite, vite!*' Quickly, quickly, quickly! Besnier intoned to himself as he pulled at Harry's straps and fastened the buckles, jerking them painfully tight.

Another shot ricocheted off the walkway. The two geôliers edged away in opposite directions, allowing a clearer aim.

Besnier gave a last pull. '*On y va!*' Let's go!

He began to run, not looking back at Harry, his flying equipment making his movements unnatural, an automaton striding towards the Comté tower. Harry followed him, wondering why they did not just drop from the Bastille roof where they were, down towards the Faubourg Saint-Antoine.

'More quickly!' Besnier shouted, still looking forwards, focusing only at the point of wall he intended to leap from. 'As quickly as you can!'

More shots. Harry ducked, but kept running. They had almost reached the Comté tower. Harry could see the Seine snaking through Paris.

'You remember? I showed you!' Besnier called, as he reached the south battlement. Without pause, he leapt up onto the wall, then pushed himself far from the parapet, out into the air.

Another shot, its impact blowing a chunk of Bastille stone from next to Harry's ear. If he had had enough time to think about the insanity of Besnier's action, his leap of faith from the wall, Harry would have slowed, and reconsidered the foolishness of following. But the bullet made him accelerate almost before he had heard it or thought about it.

He was up on the parapet wall. The garrison soldiers ran towards him from all corners of the prison, from every tower of the Bastille. Some knelt, to steady their weapons. Another shot was fired.

Before he could launch himself away from the wall, the wind took him sideways. He stumbled, his feet dragging along the stone, the taffeta panels stretched and bulging, full of air. He felt his feet lift, and then he was over the edge, dropping, dropping, the acceleration making his stomach seem to revolve.

The ground rushed up towards him.

CHAPTER FORTY-SIX

THE BASTILLE FLIGHT

HE FELL FEET FIRST, DROPPING PAST the windows of the Comté tower, the prison's rough stone wall a blur. His instinct was to flail his limbs wildly, but because they were strapped into Besnier's flying apparatus there came an enforced cohesion to his movements, soon bringing a more horizontal inclination. The memory of Marie-Anne's salon asserted itself, and he reached out, pointing his arms frantically at the Seine. Once the air caught him under his taffeta wings, it brought him to an abrupt halt. His shoulder sockets felt as if they would tear. One wing threatened to twist beneath his body, nearly causing a disastrous spin, but he managed to stretch it out sideways as far as he could, straining to keep it level.

A gust of wind took him, filling the little wings.

A second pushed him away from the Bastille's wall, but sent him into a sharp turn. He adjusted to it, now able to lie level on his stomach, arms and legs outstretched, the wings gaining as much air as he could give them. He felt the lift under them, turning them so he was no longer falling, but instead gliding, banking, floating on the swirls of air around the prison.

From the battlement, a shot whistled past him. He dodged his head. The movement sent him pitching steeply downwards again, diving into the invisible cushion holding him. He managed a glance back at the parapet, now with men between its castellations.

All aimed at him.

More shots.

One heated the air beside him, passing so close he thought he had been hit. He wondered what would happen if a ball pierced one of his wings. Would the material start to shred from the point of weakness? Would only one rip develop, or many? And would it hold enough to support him, at least to ensure a landing not so hard as to break him?

Harry was now further away from the wall. The turnkeys and the soldiers of the garrison, with their angry faces—for the consequences of allowing a King's prisoner to escape his most secure prison would be formidable—could no longer be differentiated from each other.

Besnier swooped some distance to his left and ahead of him, following the Fosse de l'Arsenal, the stinking ditch to the Seine. Harry had left the roof more sideways, so he found himself over the Palais de Saint-Paul's orchards, heading towards the Couvent des Célestins. Its high towers fast approaching, he searched desperately for any air to hoist him upwards, for eddies whipped up between the buildings. With a sudden twist of his body, which made him drop alarmingly, he flew between them, almost scraping his feet on the ridge of its roof.

As he cleared the rooftop, he hit air coming in fresh from the Seine. He soared upwards, but felt he would surely stall, to drop straight back down, feet first, or even go over backwards, the rapid vertical rise threatening a final somersault impossible to escape. He stretched forwards, feeling the poles and straps and buckles strain, needing as much of the fabric's surface to keep him aloft as possible. The muscles of his back groaned from the effort, each rib stretched from its neighbour. He hovered, Besnier's flying apparatus seeming to consider quite what to do with him, until another push of air sent him onwards.

Now he flew over the Seine, close enough to see its waves releasing little splashes of white. Past the Pont de Grammont spanning between the Quai des Célestins and the Île Louvier, on over the boats clustered at the Port Saint-Paul, and towards the Pont Marie.

Despite his eyes streaming from the cold, he could see the streets were almost deserted. It must be a Sunday, he reasoned. In the Bastille, time had ceased to flow in any way he was used to. Days and nights in a dark and stinking cell had merged inextricably. Even when Hortense had visited, bringing with her Bartholomew Slough, he had been incurious enough not to ask what day it was.

Ahead of him, the riverbank opened up as a muddy beach, with boats pulled onto it. By the Hôtel de Ville, its back to the Seine, he could see a dark feather on the skyline. Smoke. As the wind changed direction, he thought he could hear cheering, but it was too far away to be certain.

The river's surface came closer. If he landed in water, could he release himself from the flying apparatus before being drowned by its weight? There was no way of loosening the straps as he flew. He had to find firm ground for his last descent and landing, but that risked a breaking of bones. The wind would not bring him back over the bank.

The few people who were on the Quai Saint-Paul began to notice him. Some pointed, and stared. Others ran, terrified by this apparition from the sky.

The river turned. Harry was no longer over water, but over land. It would have to be here. He brought the wings to his side, turning them edgeways so the air was expelled from under their fabric.

He dropped rapidly.

Thirty feet above the ground became twenty.

Ten feet.

Five feet.

His drop seemed to double in speed, until he hit the road, hard. Unable to land on his feet, stretched forwards as he was, the first impact was an elbow, the second his side, the third his head. The friction between the road and his body at last brought him to a halt.

CHAPTER FORTY-SEVEN

THE FLYING MAN

CAUTIOUSLY, HARRY MOVED HIS LIMBS, EACH one in turn. Deciding none were broken, although his elbow throbbed with pain, he rolled from his side onto his back, then slowly began unbuckling and unstrapping himself from the wings, both crumpled from the landing.

Undoing the last buckle, he released himself from the wing, and scrambled clear from the apparatus. He brought himself upright and stood shakily before the gathering crowd, exploring with his fingers the split in his forehead where it had smacked the road. He saw his spectacles glinting on the ground and bent to retrieve them. Miraculously they had not been damaged other than their one already broken lens. Blood trickled into his eye, and he blinked it away to survey the people around him, to see if they were friend or foe.

In their nervousness, no one had yet approached close to him, their faces pictures of caution. Curiosity battled their fear, desiring to see if this was man or beast who had descended from the sky. Or a devil. Or an angel.

What they saw was a grimy, thin youth with a patchy beard and damaged spectacles, bleeding from his head and his shoulder, in a battered leather coat, its sleeve ripped where it had slid along the ground.

Although exhorted not to by his wife, a man in the crowd came nearer. Another looked around, eager for a figure of authority to take control. More people started to arrive from the nearby buildings, and from the Île Saint-Louis, crossing the Pont Marie. Others arrived from the Place Moneils, the Place Aux Veaux, and the tenements of the Rue de la Mortellerie. All had seen at least the bumpy conclusion of Harry's flight from the Bastille. From having been almost deserted before his landing, the road filled quickly with people.

The man nearest, fleshy and wearing a red woollen cap, still ignoring the pleas of his wife, tentatively touched the material of Besnier's flying apparatus, as for all he knew it might be hot from the flight. Having felt it only to be taffeta, he lifted one of its poles. Seeing the wing's shape revealed, he gave a low whistle, marvelling at Harry's pluck to risk flying in such a construction, and on such a small area of fabric. He turned to the people behind him, who gestured disbelievingly, as if what they could see was all the more bizarre because of its simplicity. Just a contraption made from wood, taffeta, and leather, and some bits of brass and steel.

The man who had flown it, however, was something else. Extraordinary. Incredible. Heroic.

The fleshy man laughed loudly, short staccato bursts of sound, then turned to address them all in a loud voice, sounding like the bald man at the Exhibition. He took off the red cap, to wave it as he spoke.

'*Regardez! Un simple mortel. Un homme, juste comme nous.*' Look! A mere mortal. A man, just like us.

Others stepped forwards to inspect the broken apparatus, but also to inspect Harry, and even to touch him. They pulled at his coat, some at the skin of his face to prove to themselves he was not the stuff of angels. One old woman gripped his hand, thinking his touch might cure her ailments, until she was pushed away by another.

'*Je l'ai vu! Il a volé depuis la prison de la Bastille.*' A squirrelish man with a ginger wig had elbowed his way to the front of the crowd. I saw it! He flew from the Bastille prison. The man had a high, agitated voice. '*Il s'est échappé!*' He has escaped!

The fleshy man turned to Harry. '*C'est vrai? Vous étiez un prisonnier du Roi?*' Is it true? You were a prisoner of the King?

Harry felt his chest tighten, and he involuntarily clenched his fists. What best to do? What would he do to keep his freedom? Was he prepared to fight for it? Fight these people? They had no clue of who he was or why he had been held; what crime he was supposed by the King—and La Reynie— to have committed.

The first man who approached him, having set himself up as ring-leader, stared at Harry's face, into his eyes, as if to do so was to ascertain the truth. Harry looked back at him, and then past him, at the circle of people around him, who all regarded him curiously. He sighed, and hung his head, seeing the cobbles they stood on. Perhaps one was loose: he could pull it up, bash some heads. Or he could use a strut of the flying apparatus, be as assertive as Besnier with the geôliers up on the Bastille roof. He sighed again. Of course, he couldn't. Too many people, who did not deserve him trying to do them harm. What did they know of La Reynie's machinations?

'*Oui, c'est vrai, monsieur.*' He held his open palms up, to show he would not try to hurt him.

The man started at his accent, and narrowed his eyes. '*Vous n'êtes pas de Paris. Vous n'êtes pas de France!*' You are not from Paris. You are not from France!

'*Je me nomme Henry Hunt. Je suis anglais. De Londres. Je n'ai commis aucun crime.*' My name is Henry Hunt. I am English. From London. I have committed no crime.

The man nodded sternly and motioned to a couple of his friends in the crowd, a pair who had been with him when Harry first landed. They, too, wore red caps.

The ginger-wigged man pointed a trembling finger at the fleshy man. *'Vous parlez contre le roi, si vous cherchez à le protéger.'* You speak against the King, if you seek to protect him.

'Nous allons l'emmener au Châtelet.' We shall take him to the Châtelet. *'La Reynie décidera.'* La Reynie will decide. The fleshy man bowed, and the other man touched his ginger wig in acknowledgement, puffing importantly, pleased with himself, for he had performed a subject's duty.

The three men led Harry through the crowd, people parting to let them through. The ginger-wigged man made to follow them, but was dissuaded by a snarl from the leader. Harry swallowed. The men who escorted him looked tough, and their leader had a hard demeanour. No one else seemed willing to follow them. The fleshy man was obviously one to be wary of.

The three men did not hold him, having no need, as Harry offered no resistance. He walked, head bowed, blood obscuring his vision, feeling utterly defeated. Hortense, Marie-Anne, and Jacob Besnier had tried their utmost to help him escape the Bastille. They had risked being arrested—Besnier had risked his life.

For nothing.

Despairingly, he looked back at Besnier's flying apparatus, broken in a heap on the road, surrounded by curious onlookers. A couple of youths picked it over, one trying to fasten himself into a wing, the other studying it, trying to understand the system of belts and buckles, and how it could have taken a man, even one as slight and insignificant as this English stranger, all the way from the Bastille prison's ramparts to the quayside of the Seine.

●

INSTEAD OF CONTINUING along the Rue de la Mortellerie, the three men led him across the Pont Marie, between the high houses either side of the bridge, and onto the Île Saint-Louis.

After a time considering why they veered from the straightforward route, Harry asked them.

'You do not know, Englishman?' The leader answered in heavily accented English. 'There is an execution at the Place de Grève. The poisoner, La Voisin, burns today. It would take forever to get you through the crowd.'

Harry remembered the plume of smoke he had seen from the air, by the Hôtel de Ville. The streets were not quiet because it was a Sunday at all, but because most of Paris had gone to see Catherine Montvoisin die. He wondered about the three men with him. Why had they not gone, too, as the crowd who had gathered around him at his landing place had not?

The Rue des Deux-Ponts was perfectly straight. As it crossed the Rue Saint-Louis, the two roads dividing the island neatly into quarters, Harry saw that the Île Saint-Louis was laid out following a geometrical scheme. The buildings were made of slate and stone, all recently built, and all resistant to fire. Like Robert Hooke's scheme for London.

He was thankful Mr. Hooke could not see him now: dishevelled, miserable, and being led back to prison.

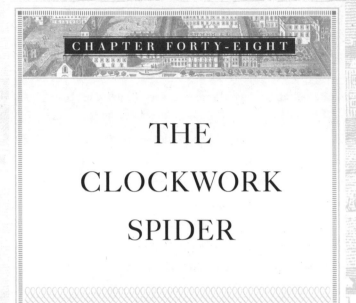

CHAPTER FORTY-EIGHT

THE CLOCKWORK SPIDER

HIGH IN THE ATTIC OF SOMERSET House, in the roof's apex, Boilot's back pressed against the beams. With no space above him to hang his lantern, he was in his own light, working by feel, checking the join was airtight by moving the lantern up and down the edge, looking for light seeping through. He tightened the last bolt, leaning all his weight on his spanner. The bolts along each seam made a constant row of protruding heads. Sweating from the monotonous effort of tightening all these bolts, and aching from the strain of maintaining his contorted position, he looked again down the seam between the two metal sheets. No light came through, no gap between them, no deformation of the brackets.

Satisfied, he climbed down the ladder, his muscles stiff from the work.

The three Frenchmen looked over what they had built. Six square metal sheets forming a large cube, six feet or so in each direction. The poles and struts supporting it looked strong, and were joined securely to the roof's frame with more of the bolted brackets.

The man Harry knew as Lefèvre, and who Bartholomew Slough and Priscilla Leach knew as Chasse, grunted. A noise which seemed to indicate satisfaction, for the other two bent down to continue. Long pipes lay along the floor, most copper, some lead, lined up together amid the broken and dusty furniture of a long-disused schoolroom. Verdier lifted one to Boilot, who methodically fixed it against the wall. Another went up the slope of the ceiling to join it, turning towards a stopcock mounted on the metal tank's side. One end was opened with a cone-shaped block hammered into it, then lead flux was used to seal the join between the two pipes. More pipes were placed, and joined, leading down the wall from the tank.

Working quickly, expertly, with no pause, Lefèvre did the more delicate work. The other two left it for him, knowing what he expected of himself, and what they should do.

Hardly talking, the men and their work went on, hours going by in the stuffy attic schoolroom. From elsewhere in Somerset House, they could hear the bangs and thumps from the frenetic making-ready. The Queen's return from Newmarket was expected at any moment. The builders had been offered generous sums to finish. The work was slapdash, crudely done, but to an untrained eye looked perfect, the surfaces shiny and smooth. Closer inspection would have shown edges missed, fixings omitted, plaster poorly mixed.

But in the attic schoolroom, the work was completed exactingly. When the three men had finished, pipes ran to the tank from every side, rows of stopcocks clustering around its base.

The whole thing looked like a giant mechanical spider.

Lefèvre—for surely it was him, even by lantern light the similarity was remarkable—checked each stopcock in turn, working around the spider. Then, going to the dwindling pile of equipment on the floor, he took out a box. From it, he removed what looked like a metal cage a bird might be held in, but which instead contained an elaborate clockwork mechanism: cogs and gears and springs. He positioned it onto the tank. More bolts to be fastened.

Having climbed to the very top of the ladder, he leaned in close to the mechanism. Angled precariously forwards, the upper part of his body pressed across the tank, he wound the clockwork. Short, violent twists, the shaft hard to turn. Both his feet on the last rung, one hand gripped the highest beam across the roof space.

Finally, the spring was coiled as tight as it would go. He shook out the ache in his hands. After a close inspection of the clockwork—all its springs and ratchets, wheels and pinions—another adjustment of the suspension spring, and a superstitious polish of the bob, he set off the pendulum.

The clock awoke, starting into its motion, wheels clicking smoothly. The minute hand started its progress around the face, dragging the more reluctant hour hand behind it.

Hardly blinking, Lefèvre watched for a full minute, before he could bring himself to leave it. Slowly, he backed down the ladder. He joined Verdier and Boilot, and all three men looked up to inspect their machine, its heart now beating, with all its legs and antennae, the tubes running from it on every side spreading over the attic walls, and with all its stopcocks connected to the intricate workings of the mechanism.

And the platform suspended from its base, large enough to hold a man.

Then, they began their work to conceal the machine.

CHAPTER FORTY-NINE

THE RED CAPS

THEY DID NOT GO OVER THE Pont de la Tournelle, on the opposite side of the island. Instead, they turned sharply right, following the quay.

'Do you not take me to the Châtelet?' Harry asked them, suddenly fearful, bewildered by the mazy course of events.

'Settle yourself, flying man,' the fleshy red-capped Parisian said. He laughed, bursts of sound that hurt Harry's ears. 'We have no sympathy for La Reynie, and no liking for the Bastille. The King uses it to keep us cowering, supplicant to his wishes.' He looked around him, then leaned in towards Harry conspiratorially. 'I am Guillaume Theriot.'

'I'm Henry Hunt, as I said before. Harry, more usually.'

'We are out of sight of those who may disagree, back in the crowd there.

The little *rouquin*, the ginger man, for instance. If you escaped the Bastille, then La Reynie's policiers, and its garrison, will be after you. Perhaps, by now, also the Mousquetaires Noirs.'

One of the other two with him, shorter, harder-looking, with an imperturbable manner that made Harry think he must have been a soldier, cleared his throat. '*Nous retournons. Nous restons. Nous continuons.*' We go back. We stay. We go on. He listed their options in a low, urgent voice, a thick finger uncurling for each.

The Frenchmen conferred among themselves, Harry learning the taciturn man was Gauthier, and the other, younger and more slight, was Dragaud.

'Where will you go?' Theriot asked Harry, after their discussion.

Harry thought for a moment. 'I can't return to where I stayed before my arrest. It would be dangerous for the people there, who are my friends.'

'We will send them a message. They may not even know of your ever being held in the Bastille.'

'They know. They came to visit me.'

Theriot looked amazed. 'You are lucky. Others languish inside, no news of them for years. You could ask the King to his face, and he would not say if your father, or your sister, or your son was held there. In this way, our security is preserved. By royal *caprice*, only.'

What if this were a trap laid by La Reynie? Harry thought. Perhaps Theriot was one of his *mouches*, a spy for the police. Looking at the Frenchman's flushed face, though, especially at his eyes, glazed with zeal, Harry could not believe it.

'Will you send a message to them? At the Hôtel de Bouillon. On the Quai Malaquai.'

Gauthier shifted uncomfortably. '*La Voisin est morte aujourd'hui.*' La Voisin died today.

Theriot shrugged. '*Je sais. La duchesse est suspectée, aussi.*' I know. The Duchesse is also suspected. He rolled the inside of his cheek between his teeth thoughtfully, then returned his attention to Harry. '*Société intéressante* you have.'

'That's why I was held in the Bastille. She's innocent, as am I, of anything to do with poisoning.'

Theriot looked at his partners. *'Dragaud, tu vas chez la Duchesse.'* Dragaud, you go to the Duchesse. 'Then, Monsieur Hunt, I think we have done enough to help you.'

Harry clasped his hand. 'Thank you, Monsieur Theriot. *Merci.'* He pulled Theriot to him in the French way. 'I find I cannot thank you enough.'

Theriot laughed again, but more strained this time, for fewer bursts. Dragaud left them, continuing across the river over the new Pont de la Tournelle. Harry, Theriot, and Gauthier watched him as he walked alongside the Seine, losing him behind the houses by the École de Médecine.

Apprehensively, they awaited his return, walking up and down the length of the Île Saint-Louis to lessen suspicion. Three men standing would draw more notice. Shivering in the cold, Harry held the bundle of his ripped leather coat, rubbing at his arms. Theriot had told Harry to take it off, saying it would immediately identify him as he had worn it when arrested, and when he had leapt from the Bastille wall. He gave Harry his red cap to improve the disguise.

Growing restless for their friend's return, the two Frenchmen became nervous of him. When Harry tried to start conversation, they were quick to rebuff him. Gauthier smoked continually, repetitively refilling his pipe. His front teeth had worn to shape themselves around it.

Over an hour passed before Dragoud returned, appearing in the Bouillon coach. They heard its four horses clopping loudly, turning from the bridge onto the quayside's cobbles. Dragoud waved at them, leaning through its window. All three men broke into a jog to reach the coach.

Dragoud jumped down and held the door open.

Harry thanked them all for their friendship.

'Goodbye, flying man,' Theriot said. 'I shall tell my children of this day.'

Harry embraced him again, and then Dragoud and Gauthier, and hoisted himself up into the coach.

Inside the Duchesse's coach sat Bartholomew Slough. And with him, Denis Papin.

CHAPTER FIFTY

THE PARIS ESCAPE

THEY COULD NOT RETURN TO THE Hôtel de Bouillon, as La Reynie's men had already been there to search the house for Harry. The police informed Marie-Anne her sister had been apprehended. La Reynie wished to question Hortense. She was not under arrest, apparently, but would be if she resisted. As far as they knew—Slough and Papin sharing the story between them—she had been taken to the Grand Châtelet. Mustapha was there now, with provisions to make her stay more pleasant.

'The Duchesse de Bouillon sends her farewells to you,' Slough said. 'And godspeed.'

'What of her man, Mercier?' Harry asked. 'Has he been released?'

'They broke his shoulders,' Slough said grimly. 'He is back with the Duchesse.'

Anticipating the police would think they would choose to go west, they decided to head north, towards Dunkirk.

Harry's cheek still ached from the impact of the book, and his chin was sore from the splinter of Bastille stone raised by a bullet fired across its roof. His wrist, from the manacles, was weeping, and his shoulder and elbow, after the landing on the Quai Saint-Paul, were tender, the skin raw from the road. Remembering he still wore Theriot's cap, he used it to wipe the blood congealed in his hair.

The blood made him think of Jacob Besnier. He wondered where Besnier had landed, and hoped he had enjoyed a gentler reunion with the ground than his own. He must thank him for his assistance, and the courage he had shown to rescue him.

Approaching the Les Halles marketplace, the driver reversed the coach away from a crowd of men, unsure if they were traders protecting their stalls from revellers after La Voisin's execution, or police.

Their heads rocking with the coach's motion, Harry looked at Denis Papin sitting opposite. Papin's hair and his clothes, all tidy, made him feel ashamed, for he looked like one of the poor souls reduced to begging who shivered in Paris doorways.

Harry felt a muddle of emotions, making it difficult to speak.

Papin had been his competitor for the position of Curator, and was a rival for the affections of Grace Hooke. He was taller than Harry, broader, and—so Grace had told him—owned a more likeable face. Now, Harry learned, Papin had come to Paris, as Mr. Hooke had asked, to help extricate him from French justice. At no little risk to himself, being a Huguenot.

Papin leaned forwards, and clasped Harry's knee in a tight squeeze. 'Really good to see you, 'Arry,' he said. His accent always meant he dropped the H of Harry's name. Before their friendship clouded, they had found it comical that neither friend could quite pronounce the name of the other.

Harry searched for something to say. 'Mr. Hooke knew of my incarceration?'

Papin shook his head vehemently. 'He received a letter from La Reynie, and knew you were in trouble. Lord Danby maligned you, did he not, to the

Lieutenant Général? It seems La Reynie does not trust him. He wanted a different account. I saw him yesterday, when I delivered personally Mr. Hooke's reply.'

'You came to help me, even though I was in the Bastille.' Harry felt ashamed of his previous jealousy.

'I never knew of that, until told by the Duchesse de Bouillon.' Papin smirked playfully at Harry. 'I like to think I would have come, had I known, but who knows? Perhaps I would not.'

Harry gave him an exhausted smile. 'I think you would, Denis. I think you would.'

Slough moved a cushion to set it beside Harry. Harry looked at him gratefully, taking it and pushing it under his back, rocking to settle it into shape.

'How far do you come with us, Mr. Slough?' he asked.

'Well, firstly, to Dunkirk,' Slough replied. 'There I shall help to find a boat. We need a trustworthy man to take us across.'

'Us? Will you not return to Paris?'

'That is not my intention. I would come with you, to help you.'

Harry sat forwards, away from the seat and the comfort of the cushion. 'You seem to know more than I do of my future self. Help me with what, Mr. Slough?'

A little jerk of his pointed beard signalled Slough's disappointment. 'Why, what we spoke of in the Bastille. The attack on the Catholic Consult. In only five days' time. We must stop it from happening. I believe, all of us being together, we may do so.'

CHAPTER FIFTY-ONE

THE HARD RIDE

FROM PARIS TO DUNKIRK BY COACH, some 180 miles, would take them at least five days, depending on the weather and the availability of horses. Too long. Having made good time along the Roman road through the forest of Chantilly, they left Marie-Anne's coach at the mailpost in Thiers-sur-Thève, and said their goodbyes to her driver.

They rested with a family in the town, buying their way in. Their cottage stood by the ruins of the old château. The couple could not do enough for them, for their hospitality was paid for with more money than they had seen in a year. A solemn-looking son regarded the visitors—especially Bartholomew Slough, a nut-brown dwarf with a Hand of Fatima tattooed on his cheek—as if they had descended from Jupiter.

The husband went to the local inn, saying that there he would find horses, taking more of their money to do so. He came back with three fine-looking animals; the three men slept soundly, happy to have evaded the police for at least a day, and that next day's transport was assured.

After breakfast, the horses saddled, they bade farewell to the little family. The wife pressed a package of food into Papin's hand, almost moving to kiss him, until her husband stepped between them. Harry shook hands with the boy as if he were fully grown, making him laugh for the first time since their meeting. Slough pulled a coin from the boy's ear, making him laugh for the second.

●

ACCORDING TO SLOUGH, they had taken too big a risk resting rather than travelling on through the night. They should not have stopped until the early morning, he grumbled, and they should have camped in the woods. It had allowed La Reynie's men time to spread the word, and engage more men to find them. They were still only thirty miles from Paris. Perhaps all along, La Reynie had guessed that north was the direction they would take. The post could carry a letter over a hundred miles a day, using mailposts and fresh horses. The police could match that, for they would commandeer the horses from the mail.

If they could reach Péronne, a town on the Somme river, Slough would be happier. That was the halfway point; two more days would find them at the port of Dunkirk. It meant no breaks, for them or the horses.

Mile after mile went under the hooves, tedious riding along sun-dappled roads taking them through the forest of Ermenonville, one mile indistinguishable from another. Harry suffered from the food scoffed at the cottage, too rich after the poor stuff of the Bastille. By noon the cramps in his stomach were almost too much too bear, continuing even after he had retched up his supper, his breakfast, and the quick meal of smoked meats they ate on the road, shared between them on horseback.

To keep his mind from his ailments, he mulled on the Colonel's inexplicable betrayal, and on Danby's letter to La Reynie, and of his failure to make any progress at all towards finding the Sancy diamond in Paris.

Papin steered his horse next to Harry's, so close their knees were touching. 'La Reynie's men could be anywhere. We cannot stop.'

Harry stared back at him vacantly, feeling nothing but exhaustion and pain. 'I can stay with you.'

'We would not leave you.'

'No,' said Slough, over his shoulder, riding a little ahead. 'We would tie you to your horse, to keep you with us.' He slowed, moved to Harry's other side, and looked matter-of-factly at him. 'I have witnessed men seemingly broken achieve great feats. I have seen men take in sail in a storm, when so ill they could hardly stand. How could they do this? I shall tell you,' he said, not waiting for an answer. 'Because they had no choice.'

'Mr. Slough, I promise you, I can do it.'

'You know why they had no choice, Mr. Hunt?' Slough continued, oblivious to Harry's assurance. 'The lives of others depended upon them. It was for a cause greater than themselves.'

'For their ship, and for the crew,' Harry replied. 'You refer to the Catholics.'

'We must warn the Queen and convince her of the plot against her life, and against those of all her guests. She trusts Danby as one who looks out for her. She sees him as a friend, when in fact he is her mortal enemy.'

'I doubt I can change her mind, to set her against Danby.'

'You can persuade her, surely, to search for the machine.' He sensed Harry's doubt. 'No one would take my word. An impostor, who has pretended to be a man now found murdered over thirty years ago. You, though, have the trust of Mr. Hooke, and the continued employ of Sir Jonas Moore.'

Harry nodded, trying to sit straight in his saddle, and to keep his eyes open, and to keep the scant contents of his stomach in rather than out.

'We cannot rest if we are to reach London in time,' Slough urged. 'You must do it, Mr. Hunt. You must find it within yourself.'

'As you managed with your flight,' Papin said. 'How afraid that must have made you feel.'

Harry jerked his head. He had never mentioned to Papin his fear of heights.

'Grace told me,' Papin said, seeing his friend's reaction. 'Yet you jumped from the Bastille's roof. You made that leap, Harry.'

'There were bullets flying,' Harry replied. 'I had little alternative.'

'You flew to the bank of the Seine.'

Seeing Papin's and Slough's encouraging expressions, Harry remembered the houses far below him, the drop and then regaining control of Besnier's flying apparatus, the near miss over the roof of one the buildings—a convent, possibly—and the effort to ensure he did not land in the river. He had not felt a shred of fear. He had thought only of self-preservation, of performing the actions necessary to land alive. The height had not worried him at all—he had simply no time to take account of it.

'In truth, we've no time for all this talking,' he told them. 'Let's press on.'

THE SECOND NIGHT saw them at Péronne, at an inn where they changed their horses. Papin did the talking, but the owner did not take to him, regarding him with suspicion. They wondered if he had received word of an Englishman's escape, for he asked each of them their names, and grew irate when Papin answered for them. Papin furnished them with French names, which the man openly disbelieved, but he accepted their overpayment readily enough.

In the morning, they found new clothes for Harry at a tailor's in the town. Papin persuaded him to buy shirts fashionably festooned with ribbons. They found new boots, too. But, to Papin's disgust, Harry refused to replace his coat. Despite its scars, he was fond of it.

Wearing new clothes and being astride a fresh horse lifted Harry's spirits, and encouraged him to make the day's journey. They would not reach Dunkirk by evening, but they hoped for Lille, once stronghold of the Burgundians, only recently taken from Spain.

The lack of police made them more nervous rather than less, so as time went on they became jumpy and tense. They did not speak, but concentrated on the road ahead, each man settling into a fugue state brought on by the incessant drumroll of hooves on the road, and the fatigue brought on by gripping the saddle. They had left the forests behind, now crossing flat open ground, the fields dark earth like the Norfolk Fens. The wind was relentless, the horses having to lean into it, each rider bending close to his animal's neck for shelter.

Each approaching animal or coach, or even rough cart, made them worry that it carried men sent to recapture Harry, and arrest any accomplices he might have.

All passed by, travellers nodding as befits the fellowship of the road, and by dusk they made Lille. The intricate shapes of Vauban's new citadel, built on the swampy marshland to the city's west to make attack more difficult, reminded Harry of Hooke's engravings in his *Micrographia* of snowflakes, geometric and angular. From their slight elevation, he could see into it: concentric pentagons, made complicated by the addition of hornworks and lunettes, each protecting the next, one inside another, getting ever smaller, until in the fortress's centre there was just an open piece of ground, as if the whole edifice protected nothing at all.

The city, too, was protected by more walls and bastions, but the men faced no questioning at the gate, no squadrons waiting there to arrest them, no demands to see documents of travel. They ventured inside, and were directed to another inn with horses.

They were only fifty miles or so from Dunkirk, an easier ride for them the next day, but there they would have to find a ship. Slough was desperate for them to sail overnight. For enough payment such nocturnal transport could be found, with no questions asked.

The Catholic Consult was in three days.

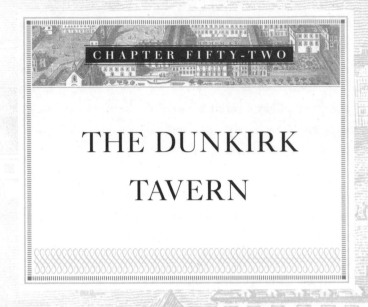

CHAPTER FIFTY-TWO

THE DUNKIRK TAVERN

ORIGINALLY A SMALL PORT FOR HERRING boats, Dunkirk had become a harbour for privateers, who, with their King's backing, attacked anyone with booty to be taken. In 1658, it was taken from the Spanish by French and English troops fighting together. Mazarin honoured his agreement with Cromwell, giving the port to the Commonwealth. Charles II, after his restoration, then sold it back to France, for the sum of half a million pounds. He still awaited the money from his cousin.

Like at Lille, Vauban had designed its fortifications. The whole port looked as if it had rained triangles. Another citadel protected the harbour entrance. Two jetties, over half a mile long and running parallel, created a sheltered lane for the ships to enter and exit the harbour. Declared a free port by Louis Quatorze, all merchants made exempt from duties to be paid, it was a vastly busy place. Work still continued to deepen the harbour, excavating it and the channel between the jetties to accommodate ever-larger ships, and the French Navy.

As Harry, Papin, and Slough rode further north, the wind had grown stronger still. By the time they entered Dunkirk, it banged the shutters of the houses, and signs swung wildly from the walls. Rain fell, cold and inquisitive, searching into their coats, finding its way down their collars. The port's streets, despite the weather, thronged with people jogging through the rain, splashes raised behind them.

Slough knew the place well, having often called in when with the corsairs, who regularly traded there, sometimes to sell goods forcibly taken from ships just left. They should not risk the harbour itself, he said, as the traffic between the jetties was too liable to being controlled, the authorities numerous and vigilant, duty exempt or not. A large garrison was stationed at the citadel, and the port had its own police force, modelled on La Reynie's. They could be sure that La Reynie himself would have agents there: a message would have been sent to alert them. Sea captains would already have been warned about suspicious travellers seeking the shores of England.

Slough—his shortness and appearance not even meriting a second glance, the denizens of Dunkirk being comfortable with strangeness—led them to a tavern south of the great market, by the citadel's bridge. By now, the rain had turned to hail, cold pellets vicious on their skin.

As they stepped in, heat blasted their faces, raising a sweat as soon as they shut the door behind them. One wall was taken up by a great oven, a devilish iron creature seeming to breathe as the hot air passed out of it. The smell of pork roasting made Harry nauseous again, and he stopped to steady himself.

He thought of La Voisin in her last minutes, the flesh melting from her.

Recovering, he followed closely behind Slough, Papin in train behind them. They had to dislodge people to get near the serving table. No one turned in complaint, being used to the nature of the place. It was full of merchants, sailors, garrison men, engineers, builders, and men who recognized no authority and no flag. The tavern was full of chatter, in different languages, as cosmopolitan a place as Harry had ever seen; everyone there seemed different from each other, with hardly any to be matched as a pair.

Confidant he could find a ship with a captain prepared to take them, Slough left to enquire around the room.

Before long, Papin managed to get them served, asking for weakened beer, taking an extra pot for Slough, then they insinuated themselves through to an imaginary clearing between the drinkers. They stood together, sweating in the extraordinary temperature.

'We could both roast in here, Harry,' Papin observed, his cheeks flushed, wiping moisture from his nose. 'Like the poor pig on the oven.'

'I'm half done already,' Harry said, trying not to look at the pig. His new clothes were too warm for the room, the cotton of his beribboned shirt too thick. He held his coat. Everyone in the room, no matter what they wore, perspired freely. He looked for someone leaving their seat, desperate to sit down himself. His thighs and his back ached from the constant riding. He would have liked a bed, but Slough demanded they get a ship tonight.

No, it dawned on him, it was not Slough, but himself. He had to get to England, to London, to warn the Queen. Mr. Hooke had overseen the recent work at her home, Somerset House, and was known to her. With him, Harry could meet with her, to tell her of Slough's story.

He felt an elbow in his back, and he shifted to let the customer go past him. Pressed up against Papin, they had to hold their drinks to the side to avoid spilling them. The man behind was clumsy, for Harry felt his elbow again.

'I'm sorry, Denis. I don't believe I've seen a place so crowded.'

Papin looked at him from a distance of about six inches, with an expression on his face that Harry could not read. He must be exhausted, too, Harry thought, for he had travelled from London to Paris, then turned around again, staying only one night at the Hôtel de Bouillon.

He felt the elbow once more. Every other customer behaved with courtesy to their fellows, a necessity when pressed up to them, one against another.

He turned, his cheeks reddened not so much by the heat from the oven, but from annoyance.

A man, much taller than himself, looked down at him.

'I have found you,' said Mustapha. 'And also, I have found a ship.'

CHAPTER FIFTY-THREE

THE NARROW SEA

TRAVELLING ON HIS OWN FROM PARIS, Mustapha had beaten them to Dunkirk, arriving there earlier that afternoon. He had negotiated with a fishing boat's captain to take them from the port of Gravelines, ten miles or so along the coast. They were to meet with him at midnight.

Mustapha had spotted their arrival, but with the weather, and everybody rushing to keep out of it, they were almost impossible to follow. He had searched the streets and tried other taverns before this one, until at last he spotted Harry, recognising him by the brown leather coat bundled in his hand.

Quickly, he appraised them of what had happened back in Paris. His mistress, Hortense, convinced by Slough's story, had been on the point of leaving for England. But La Reynie had stopped her, and questioned her.

Whatever she had said, he must have been convinced, for he had released her from the Châtelet.

La Reynie had also promised her he would not stand in Harry's way. Harry was free to leave France. They had not met with any police, for there were none after them.

'You cannot trust La Reynie,' Mustapha told Harry, before he became too cheered by the news. 'He still wants evidence against the Duchesse de Bouillon.'

'Remember, also, what he did to Mercier,' Papin said darkly. 'He may well have men here, in Dunkirk, or even in Gravelines.'

Slough rejoined them, overhearing the last of their conversation. 'His *mouches* do not only infest Paris.'

Leaving the tavern's warmth, hiring more horses, by half past ten o'clock they were in Gravelines, by the mouth of its canal. Another heavily fortified port, Gravelines was a toy passed between England, France, and Spain: now French again, but for who knew how long?

Slough spoke Spanish to the people along the quay: late-night fishermen expertly taking the trout that jumped from the sea. He asked for Peras, the trawlerman.

They were directed to a small trawler, around thirty feet in length. Rigged fore-and-aft, looking well-used and stained, its main sail was an almost-square. Her name, painted on the archboard, was *Luz de la Luna*.

Peras, it transpired, was worried about the weather. Despite Slough speaking with him urgently, and despite the bulk of Mustapha standing before him, he was resolute. He would not take them unless they met his new demand: three times the amount agreed. Slough insisted the sum was already enough, even in a storm. He had been incredulous when Mustapha told him the price.

Harry, comprehending that Slough haggled with the man, shook him by his arm.

'Pay him whatever he wants. We must leave now, if we're to get to London before the Consult.'

Slough stepped back from his confrontation with the man. 'Of course,' he said to Harry, then handed over more money to the captain from the bag given to him by Marie-Anne. '*Mis disculpas, Señor Peras.*'

As they edged their way out to sea, the wind buffeted *Luz de la Luna* with hard blasts, making the ship lurch and stop. The rigging rattled and shook, and the masts groaned from the strain put upon them.

Harry began to shiver violently. He longed for the heat of the tavern. The only shelter on the deck was a low cabin full of bails of wool. Peras would fish once the wool was delivered, and he would rather his wool stayed dry than his passengers.

The storm turning against them in earnest, sleet whipped around in the air, lacerating them with icy points of pain. The sea rolled sickeningly. Mustapha looked the most affected: his black skin was grey, and he leaned over the side, bidding farewell to the contents of his stomach.

When climbing a wave, held by the wind at its crest, *Luz de la Luna* paused as if to consider her best route of descent into the trough, then dropped violently, her bow disappearing into the thrashing sea, before racing up the face of the next seemingly vertical wave.

Peras, young to have his own ship, black hair worn long down his back and tied with a ribbon, looked far from concerned. His worry had been more for his purse, Harry thought, seeing the sky suddenly as they went up another wall of water. Peras, and the three men with him who served as his crew, grinned as they watched their passengers rolling about the deck.

Slough, though, they recognized as a sailor. He stood almost perfectly still, nonchalantly chewing tobacco, one arm resting on a line, anticipating even the most sudden of gusts. Of them all, he was the only one who did not mind the soaking. As the storm worsened, Peras set him to work climbing the lines, helping his men as he concentrated on steering the ship. Slough assisted them willingly, bringing in the sails, leaving as much as they dared without them being ripped off by the squall. While he was busy with the crew, the other passengers grabbed anything they could to stop themselves being flung into the Channel. The wind seemed to change direction at will.

'How long will it take us, in this weather?' Harry yelled at Slough when he passed.

'We are being taken across nicely,' Slough answered, looking happier than Harry had yet seen him. 'Generally towards the English coast, which is helpful. We will be there by morning.'

Harry spat out some saltwater. 'By daybreak?'

Slough looked up at the sky, then at the boiling sea beneath them. He turned the corners of his mouth downwards in a doubtful grimace. 'A little later.' He winked at Harry. 'You concentrate on holding on, Mr. Hunt. It would be difficult to fish you out in this tempest.'

The waves washed over the deck, making it slippery. As he had seen Slough do, Harry wound a line around his forearm. He crouched down by the side, pressing into the little shelter it gave him, thinking of Grace Hooke, presumably safe and warm at her uncle's lodgings at Gresham. Or else she was out on the town. Perhaps with an admirer.

He had not yet quizzed Denis Papin yet. On a trawler, in the middle of an angry sea, was not the place to do so.

About three hours into the journey, the wind became even louder, which Harry had not thought possible. Now one constant noise, it filled every recess of his mind, taking any thoughts he had of home away with its howl. Before either Slough or the crew could reach it, the mainsail was torn away, the gaff spar spinning around the mast, splintering it in two with a shriek. The pieces hung lopsidedly, hanging from their lines, swinging with the motion of the ship.

Slough took out a knife from his belt and cut the lines, bringing down the spar. He passed an end to Mustapha, who was still grey-faced from the sea's motion. Together, they placed it down on the deck, where it would not hit them on the head.

Peras scratched his chin. They would have to rely on her lateen, and risk more sail on the jibs. The tides would be little help: the flood tide would take them more north, the ebb tide would bring them more south, so they would be sent in an arc, if they could get any forwards motion going at all.

The storm was now so ferocious no one could hear anything of what they shouted to one another. Peras directed Harry and Papin by gesture, frantically signalling that the ship lay low in the water. The sea was leaking through the hull, *Luz de la Luna* battered by the waves, her planking forced apart as she twisted. He opened the hatch, and sent Harry and Papin down into the hull, giving them his lantern. Rough wooden buckets rolled around on the hull's floor—to call it an orlop would be too grand. The inside still stank, even though Peras had scrubbed it after his last trawl. Harry stared after him resentfully as he left them. They could have been down here, with the rest of his wool, but Peras had kept them up in the weather. The water coming through the ship's caulking trickled ominously between the planks, every so often spurting through as *Luz de la Luna* was assaulted by another wave. The sea roared against the hull, the thin barrier holding them apart from oblivion.

The ship having no pump, the two men used the buckets to lift water out through the hatch, throwing it onto the deck. They took it in turns to be the man at the hatch, or the man below scooping water into his bucket and hefting it full back up to his partner. They made little headway against the water pouring in. Harry, bailing below, saw another spray of water come through the hull. He shouted to Papin to fetch Mustapha.

Mustapha eased his way through the narrow hatch, his face sullen, eyes a dull yellow, especially in the light from the swinging lantern. He set to work, taking another bucket, staggering with the ship's rocking over the waves, hitting the sides with his shoulders and falling against the stacks of wool, trying to keep the bucket level. Whereas Harry and Papin had each passed their bucket up to his partner, Mustapha simply lifted his straight out onto the deck, where it ran away over the sides, and back into the sea.

The rest of the night passed this way, frantically bailing, until daylight hazed the sky: a milky-grey colour advancing over the horizon and seeping into the clouds racing above them. For another four hours of daylight, they continued. Mustapha worked like an engine, pausing only to vomit copiously around the hull. Harry thought with some satisfaction of Peras when he saw the state of his wool. Working together, Harry and Papin kept up with Mustapha's rate of clearing the water from inside the hull. They were so involved in the work they ignored another crashing and splintering of wood outside in the storm. A jib sail had been torn away, taking its ropes and the bowsprit with it, all blown clean out to sea.

So intent were they, it took them a while to notice their rocking was no longer so violent, the level of noise not so great.

The twisting of the hull had diminished, too. The three men slowed their work as the water's ingress slowed. Then, they tried to climb from the hatchway. Their limbs were so tired, Slough had to pull them up, gripping them with his iron-strong hands. He had been busy, too, he assured them, helping the crew fight with *Luz de la Luna* to keep her from spinning like a hamstrung horse. The deck was a mess of trailing lines and broken lengths of mast rolling across it, no time to have stowed them properly.

As the ship's movement was still strong, Harry had to grip a line to keep himself from falling, but their rise and fall was now more regular, like riding on a great beast's back. In the distance, he could see a pale stripe smudged into the sky, barely discernible. He thought he could see a light shining at them, as if beckoning them home.

It was England.

CHAPTER FIFTY-FOUR

THE

ENGLISH RAIN

LUZ DE LA LUNA LIMPED INTO the shelter afforded by the cliffs. The wind was still strong, but had eased enough that the remaining sail filled nicely, taking them along the coast as they tried to find a port.

Uncertain where he was, Peras kept repeating '*Canal de la Mancha*,' as if cursing it. He knew the storm had blown him too far north. It was Slough who first recognized the outline of the Isle of Thanet, its low chalk cliffs meandering around the shore of Broadstairs and St. Peter's, the sands sloping gently from the sea at Ramsgate.

On a promontory of high cliff, which Slough told them was called the North Foreland, they could see a house. Looking unwieldy on its perch, mostly built of timber, it had a large glass lamp built onto its roof, to keep ships clear of the Goodwin Sands. It was this light Harry had seen.

Either they could land at Broadstairs and ride to London, or they could ask Peras to round the headland and continue on to the Thames. Slough asked the question, although he knew what the man's answer would be: his vessel was too broken to sail on, and it was almost evening. Peras would take *Luz de la Luna* into the small port at Broadstairs.

It was the obvious place to put up for repairs. A ship being built, in the shipyard west of the town, was the tallest structure apart from the church. Steering by only his lateen, Peras brought his little trawler to the pier. It bumped the wood, the waves still lively. Slough helped with the hawser.

Harry jumped from *Luz de la Luna*, and walked along the flimsy jetty, which vibrated with the wind. Rain still fell, now a fine, cold drizzle. Papin, Mustapha, and finally Slough, who saluted Peras as one seaman to another, followed him along the jetty and onto the shore. Harry had not said goodbye to the trawlerman. Putting aside his resentment at their being kept on deck rather than down with the wool, and his suspicion Peras had made his passengers bail to save the effort of his men, Harry turned and waved. Peras had brought them home. He gave only a curt wave back.

At last, Harry stood on firm ground. Turning to look at the others with him, who had rescued him from Paris, he knelt, then raised his face to the sky. Papin, laughing, joined him, and clasped Harry's head between his hands.

'You are home!'

'English rain,' Harry answered, smiling at the notion's absurdity. He stood, and shouted in exultation, until the wind took his breath away, making him gasp. He laughed back at Papin, and jumped around him in sideways steps, a madman's dance. Papin jumped, too. They were two little boys, playing by the sea.

Mustapha, feeling better on the land, watched them, a smile playing on his face. Slough, though, drawing up with them, looked stern. Faced with his disapproval, both men stopped their antics.

'You think of your own good fortune,' Slough said. 'I blame you not. But now you must think of those people we go to save. It is a long ride to London.'

They climbed the steps cut into the cliff, making their way to the town. At the sign of a farrier, who was still working, they asked where they might get horses. He directed them to the manor house, where they bought three horses for nothing above the usual rate, even though their desperation was apparent.

Again Harry found himself in a saddle.

Eighty miles to London. An evening and a night of hard riding, and hoping the horses would last.

The Catholic Consult was the next day.

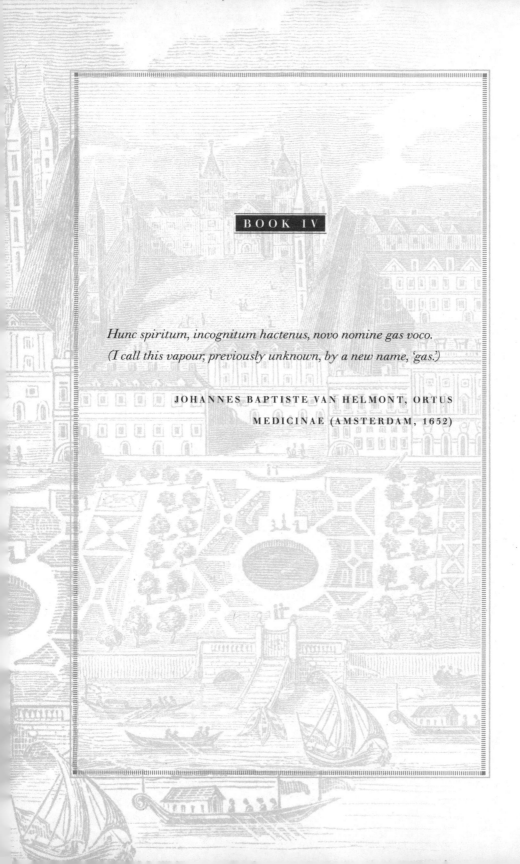

BOOK IV

Hunc spiritum, incognitum hactenus, novo nomine gas voco.
(I call this vapour, previously unknown, by a new name, 'gas.')

JOHANNES BAPTISTE VAN HELMONT, ORTUS
MEDICINAE (AMSTERDAM, 1652)

CHAPTER FIFTY-FIVE

THE GRACIOUS

PARDON

THEY GATHERED EARLY TO BE NEAR the Tyburn Tree. As near as they could, for five men were to be executed today. Hanged, then butchered: disembowelled, quartered, heads cut from their bodies. By the time the condemned appeared—more malicious Catholics found out by Titus Oates, the Saviour of the Nation—their cart's driver had to force the spectators aside.

Nooses already around their necks, hands bound, the five stood unbowed—despite being all at fault, for none had admitted their guilt.

Listening to their final speeches, the men's preparations before God, some in the crowd jeered, but most craned forwards, wanting to hear what the malefactors said for themselves.

The last man finished his talking. The ropes were tied to the gallow's beams, a horizontal triangle held up by stout posts. As the executioner opened his mouth to instruct his man holding the cart, there came a shrill bellow.

'A pardon!'

A horse and its rider moved through the crowd.

The people made way. A few started to worry the execution would not happen. Others felt entertained, for this was unusual. Some were secretly thankful, through reasons of shared religion, or a certainty the five were innocent.

A captain-lieutenant of the King's Life Guards, ridden from Whitehall Palace, agitatedly waved a piece of paper. 'A King's pardon!'

The executioner, hood covering his face, knife in his hand, snatched it from him and read it through.

The cart's quintet watched him closely, wondering on their fates.

'You, all of you, are offered a pardon,' the captain-lieutenant gasped. 'From the gracious King.'

The executioner held the paper before him, checking it again. His words were carefully chosen, but his face betrayed his displeasure. 'The King is merciful. He asks you only to admit your guilt, and tell everything you know of the plot against him.'

Each man, Thomas Whitbread, William Barrow, John Caldwell, John Gavan, and Anthony Turner, smiled bleakly at Fate's capriciousness. By looks only, they wordlessly conferred on what they should do. It did not take long. They seemed to come to an agreement, for the crowd saw them nodding, and standing straight again.

The executioner turned to the crowd, silencing them with his raised hand.

Thomas Whitbread spoke for them, his voice powerful and deep. 'We cannot tell a lie before God. We cannot, then, save our lives, for what comparison is there between our physical bodies and our immortal souls? You must kill us, executioner, though we be innocent of wishing harm against His Majesty. We—none of us—know of any plot.'

All five had the same expression: one of serenity. The executioner was a little unnerved. Rarely had he known men go so calmly to their deaths.

He signalled to the man to take the cart forwards.

CHAPTER FIFTY-SIX

THE STRETCHED FRIENDSHIP

AS SHE LED HIM UP THE stairs, Grace did not utter a word. Not even to enquire why Harry had hammered on the door so urgently.

She wore breeches and a man's shirt. Apart from her hair, flowing loosely, and the bright cleanliness of her shirt, dazzling as she went to the window seat, she looked just as she had on their return from King's Lynn. Harry had last seen her, wearing Papin's tricorne hat and disappearing through the crowd at Cornhill, just before he was taken to Whitehall by Danby's man.

Robert Hooke sat at his dining table writing in his diary, catching up, for he had neglected it for almost a week. Feeling awkward, Harry stood facing him, the table solidly between them.

Hooke's metal-grey eyes were as unwelcoming as Grace. Despite asking

Papin to go to Paris to help Harry, now he seemed unfriendly. Rather than rise to greet him, he waited for Harry to explain himself.

'Mr. Hooke.' After the voyage from France and the nighttime ride from Broadstairs, Harry's voice sounded strangled; his head was full of phlegm, making it hard to breathe or swallow.

'Mr. Hunt,' Hooke replied, his tone as chilly as his stare.

'Denis Papin found me, and helped to bring me home. Thank you for all you've done. I wish I had time enough to share the tale of my days in France, but I don't. I need your help again.'

'You have stretched our friendship, I feel.' Hooke shut his diary, the pages closing with a crump of air. 'Further than it can bear, perhaps.'

Harry swayed on his feet in his exhaustion. Relenting a little, Hooke motioned for him to sit. Harry dragged a chair from under the table, then fell down onto it.

'You stink to highest Heaven,' Hooke observed.

'I rode all night from the Isle of Thanet.' Harry pushed his chair a little further back. 'I've learned of a plan against the Queen's life. But I lack the influence to persuade her of it.'

As if she had put Harry up to this idiocy, Hooke looked incredulously across at Grace. He had still not forgiven her for travelling with Harry to the Fens. Her adoption of mannish clothes ever since continued to offend him. Who should wish for a match with such a creature, dressing between the sexes?

'Paris made you fearful, as all of London seems to be, finding plots where none exist,' Hooke said. 'I have heard of the poisonings, an obsession with the French.'

'The Queen's threatened at her Consult. I've learned of equipment to be used against her, a machine, taken into Somerset House,' Harry said.

'I thought you owned a keener mind.'

'I'm persuaded by the man I was ordered to seek.'

'Who poses as Captain Hudson?' Grace asked, the first thing she had said since Harry's arrival.

'Bartholomew Slough's his name.' Harry risked a smile, but it failed, ending as a weary grimace. 'He described the machine kept at Hudson's house. You remember his servant informed us of it.'

'I do. It was me she told,' Grace replied, coolly.

Harry scraped his chair back, about to go to her, but smelling himself thought better of it. 'Mrs. Leach would never have informed me, nor Colonel Fields, without your being there, I know.'

'Grace told me of your taking her to all the corners of Norfolk.' Hooke spoke as if it were the unmapped territory of *Terra Australis*. 'And of your being shown the remains of Captain Hudson. A surprise to find him there, undoubtedly, for no one knew he was dead.'

'I found his replacement in Paris. Mr. Slough helped me to escape from France.'

'You had need to escape?' Hooke's eyebrows were near the top of his head. 'You found yourself in trouble, I know. I received a letter from the Paris police's Lieutenant Général, wishing to know of your character.'

Harry answered to Grace, rather than Hooke. 'The Colonel lied to the police, saying I was sent to kill Mr. Slough. And that I assisted with a poisoning. A betrayal I don't yet pretend to understand.'

'You are mistaken!' Grace turned her head away, dismissing the idea.

'It's true, Grace. I was imprisoned because of his story. It's of no consequence now. For Mr. Slough told me more of the three Frenchmen. They were sent to his house by Lord Danby.'

'Danby?' Hooke spluttered. 'Frenchmen? To what end?'

'To kill the Queen, as I say. What the machine's for, Slough doesn't know. He saw sheets of metal, and pipes.'

'His brain is as fevered as yours, to give this story credence. Listen to yourself! Danby does not plot against the Queen! He is loyal to the King, zealously so. He would never murder his wife.'

'Queen Catherine is Catholic,' Grace said. 'Perhaps Danby would, in thinking he served the nation.' Harry shot her a grateful look, which she pretended not to see.

Hooke was stern. 'Grace, I beseech you, take a care. You risk descending into the same lunatical madness as Harry.' He stood suddenly, to bring the conversation to a close. 'What you need, Harry, above all things, is rest. Your nerves are pulled taut. You have become frenzied. Look at you. You do not suit the role Sir Jonas pushes at you. Working here at Gresham kept you happier, I think.'

'Mr. Hooke, I beg you to listen. I wouldn't ask you if I didn't think it true, and if I didn't think you could persuade the Queen to at least search her house. I believe she's in danger—but what I believe's no matter, is it? If *you* believe me, or not, is no matter. Mr. Slough's story might be the fictions of his cracked brain, so I, therefore, am a fool for trusting him. I ask you only to speak to the Queen. If Mr. Slough's wrong, then there's been no damage, has there? Apart from to my reputation, which already lies tattered. We'll only have inconvenienced her, and the men she orders to put in place the search. If, however, there is a machine, then we'll have saved the lives of people who would otherwise have been murdered.'

Hooke pushed his chair slowly under the table, adjusting it until it was perfectly straight in relationship to the table's edge. 'My relationship, rather, is with the King. Having met her on only a few occasions, I do not know Queen Catherine well.'

'You've overseen the repairs to Somerset House.'

'A Queen does not discuss how best to paint a wainscot. I have hardly spoken to her, other than to exchange pleasantries.'

'The King is at Newmarket, Uncle,' Grace said. 'You cannot speak with him.'

Hooke turned to her sharply, but she continued, undeterred. 'I saw it in the *Gazette*. He is gone there at Lord Danby's behest, supposedly for his safety.'

Hooke made an exasperated noise at her. 'He seeks to keep the King secure from harm. As you would expect. Harry, if you wish to search Somerset House, you should approach the new Justice of Peace, Sir John Reresby.'

'We can't trust him,' Harry replied. 'Nor anyone in the judiciary, for they look to incriminate Catholics.'

'We?' Hooke looked deeply unhappy, swaying his weight from one foot to another. 'Presumption, Harry. You have not yet persuaded me.'

Grace moved from the window to stand by her uncle. 'There is no harm, surely, in asking to speak with the Queen?' Harry managed a smile this time, which she ignored with a flick of her head. 'You may distance yourself from Harry if nothing is found, with fulsome apologies for wasting her time, and no harm done to your name.'

Hooke blew his nose loudly.

'Or,' Grace continued, 'could you not go simply as the work's overseer? Tell her you must check the house finally, before the people arrive for the Consult this evening.'

'Saying I cannot be comfortable with my conscience unless I survey it once more?' Hooke asked, looking at them both in turn.

They both nodded.

'Lie to the Queen?'

They nodded again. Hooke turned away from them in disgust. 'Where would my conscience be then?'

'Where would it be if she were killed, and her guests killed, too?' Harry asked.

'Word has got about of the Consult,' Hooke replied. 'People plan to protest against the Catholics being there. It will be heavily guarded by the Queen's own men.'

'They will look outwards, rather than in.'

Hooke raised his eyes to Heaven, then slumped his shoulders. 'I will go with you to Somerset House.'

Harry felt choked with emotion, and stood to shake Hooke's hand, but Hooke waved him away.

'Firstly, however, you must have a bath. You cannot meet the Queen reeking as you do. Mary shall heat the water.'

'Also, I need new glasses. I would go home—I need to speak with Mrs. Hannam—but there's no time.'

'There are lenses in the workshop.'

'Might Sir Jonas help you, too?' Grace asked. 'His would be a useful voice to convince the Queen.'

'Could you get a message to him?' Harry asked her. 'Perhaps he'll agree. Although his view of Slough must be a dim one.'

'I shall go to the Tower myself,' she replied. 'I can state your case better than any messenger.'

Hooke harrumphed at his niece, then saw she was not to be dissuaded. A strange look, of jealousy perhaps, flashed across his face. 'A package has arrived for you,' he informed Harry. He sniffed, and pointed down at the mess of things on his table. Buried in it all was a box wrapped in brown paper. A cube around six inches along each edge. 'From Cambridge.'

Harry picked it up, feeling its weight. It was heavy. 'From the Lucasian Professor, Mr. Isaac Newton.' He placed it back down and dismissed it with a wave. 'In truth, I have no time now for that.'

CHAPTER FIFTY-SEVEN

THE QUEEN'S HOUSE

GRACE HAVING FORBIDDEN HIM FROM WEARING his brown leather coat in front of the Queen, Harry had only a waistcoat over a shirt, and breeches, all borrowed from Hooke. He still wore his new French boots, despite their being wet through from their soaking on *Luz de la Luna*.

Harry and Hooke disembarked from their wherry at the river stairs and made their way through the gardens to the rear of Somerset House. The hedges cast deep shadows, and the sunlight threw stripes of sallow green across the neatly mown lawns. The gardens were nature trammelled and confined, their bushes and trees geometrically topiaried.

The house's exterior shone from being repaired and repainted. The last of the scaffolding was being carried back to the river.

When the guard patrolling soon perceived the urgency as they explained breathlessly why they must see the Queen.

He led them inside and past the guardroom at the house's rear, then continued towards the front, a long journey of corridors and several flights of stairs, gradually gaining height, the house following the land's rise from the river. The building work, overseen by Hooke, was now complete. An army of workmen had been replaced by an army of cleaners, sweeping and dusting busily. The smells of waxes and oils pervaded the air, as all the wood had been polished to a glassy shine. Rugs, put away during the works, had been beaten in the gardens and were now being smoothed out over the vast floors.

The guard instructed them to stay in a reception room with windows overlooking the Strand. It was nearly as grand as Marie-Anne's parlour with her harpsichord and its disgraceful picture inside.

Both men fidgeted as they waited.

Harry and Hooke could smell meats roasting, and rich sauces and gravies. The clanging of pans and the voices of men under pressure reached them through the wall. Guards in different uniforms passed, including those worn by the King's own Foot Guards, going through the gallery. Some eyed the pair suspiciously.

At last, the Master of the Queen's Household appeared. Walking self-importantly towards them, as upright as he could, he appeared to hang from an invisible string. He stood before them, but said nothing, pursing his lips as if to utter words was beneath him.

Hooke rose to bow, gesturing to Harry that he should do the same. Harry did so, although he could not see why such a man required such deference. He was a servant; Harry saw him as just such, and no more.

'We must put in place a search,' Hooke explained to the Master, who replied by flicking his eyes to the bustling scene around them, managing to signal both his esteem for Hooke and his belief that a search could not possibly be necessary.

'The Queen's life has been threatened.'

The Master looked suitably grave.

'And those of the people meeting here this evening.'

The Master presented a beneficent smile, as if he forgave them all their sins.

'We may be wasting our time. We shall endeavour not to waste yours. Will you let us peruse the house?'

The Master gave the faintest hint of a bow, a subtle shrinking of his neck so his head dipped almost imperceptibly. Hooke, who was used to him, turned to Harry. 'Excellent! Many thank-yous. Come, Harry. You have your wish. Now we must get to work.'

The Master spread his fingers at the gallery, opening up the way to them.

They looked at each other. No need to see the Queen, then. Easier than either man had expected. But neither man had thought ahead: where should they start?

'Let's begin where the people will gather,' Harry said, after considering.

'The Great Room,' Hooke replied, already walking towards it.

The Great Room: the room in which kings and queens and Oliver Cromwell had lain in state, conferences were held, masques played out, and where Captain Jeffrey Hudson was, when a boy, presented to Queen Henrietta Maria in a pie.

Its brooding oak floor seemed imbued with the importance of those who had walked over it. High above them, the ceiling was ornate, its panels intricately detailed. Two parallel lines of circular pillars across the full length of the room supported balconies along both sides. These pillars were decorated with carved woodland creatures, running along branches that coiled around them. The animals looked dumbly at Harry and Hooke, their mouths hanging open.

On opposite sides of the room, cavernous fireplaces had been built up with kindling, and logs were piled to feed them, ready for the evening.

Various doors opened into it: the huge double doors on the ground floor they had come through, and higher, smaller doors for the balconies overlooking them.

The main doors, kept open by long brass stays, were being adjusted by two workmen. A third man worked on replacing the lock.

The room was set out for a banquet, with long rows of tables. The Queen's table was raised on a dais, her chair a gilded mini throne. Servants with rulers set up the places for each guest, stepping back to check each plate and glass and piece of cutlery was lined up exactly with its neighbour. At least four hundred guests must be invited, Harry estimated. Despite all the tables to accommodate such a number, there was still a large area of floor left empty. They walked across it to the tables, Harry's damp boots squeaking on the polish.

Heavy tablecloths of cream-coloured linen hung almost to the floor. Harry motioned at them to Hooke. Together, they went to the nearest table, and lifted the hem, to check under the line of tables.

'You!' A servant challenged them, trotting towards them. Another man, waving angrily, joined him from a different side of the room.

'We have consent,' Hooke reassured them. 'From the Master.' It was clear neither man recognized him, nor believed him. 'I am Robert Hooke, of the Royal Society for the Improving of Natural Knowledge. I have been in charge of the works here, to improve the house.'

Both servants were undecided. 'Why should such a man inspect our dinner tables?' one of them asked.

Still kneeling where he had been looking along the underside of all the tables, Harry spoke up. 'We've been told of a threat to the guests.'

The servants glanced at each other in alarm.

'Some sort of machine,' Harry continued, aware he sounded unconvincing, even to himself. 'We don't know what it looks like, or even what it does. It may be false information. But we can't afford to take chances.' He stood, and looked at both men squarely in the eye. 'Have you seen anything unusual? Anything at all?'

His voice had changed. Noticing it, Hooke studied him with a renewed interest. The boy he had known was being left behind. It seemed Harry's experiences in France had altered him. He sounded more confident, more sure of himself, more at ease speaking with such men.

'Unusual?' the second man answered. 'Truth be told, only you two.'

Harry smiled at him as if sharing and enjoying a joke, although the man looked in earnest.

'Nothing is here that should not be here,' the same man insisted.

'Then, where can it be?' Hooke asked Harry. 'This, surely, is the place where the guests are most at risk.'

'The Queen's place, there, must be the target, if what Mr. Slough told me is true.'

Harry and Hooke walked to the head table. The two servants followed at a distance. Unsure what to do about these two interlopers, they settled on watching them suspiciously, as Harry and Hooke inspected where the Queen was due to sit.

Again, it was Harry who squatted to study the underside of the table. He pushed a couple of chairs back, to see along their seats, but the servants decided they had tolerated enough. They had measured the precise distances between the chairs; to see their work undone was too much to bear. Both men stood threateningly over him, but Harry ignored them, continuing his search. When all their looming failed to stop him, one servant sent his colleague to fetch help.

Hooke looked greatly uncomfortable, worrying that word would reach the Queen of the upset to her household, and of their interfering with the preparations for her Consult. It would be incommodious to her. Harry blithely continued to search under her table, crawling right under it. He could see nothing out of place: certainly nothing that could be described as a *machine*—definitely the word Bartholomew Slough had used. He came back out, brushing his knees, although the floor had been polished until its surface was lens-smooth.

He stared up at the ceiling above him. It was difficult to see, as it was so far away, but he could not discern anything suspicious. The chandeliers, hanging at regular intervals, had rickety-looking pairs of stepladders under them, tall and precarious. They reminded him of the lamplighters of Paris, and also of the ladders leaning against the high shelving in the Bibliothèque Mazarine. He went to the nearest. A man stood at its top fitting new candles, and another steadied the ladder, an arrangement Harry would not have entrusted his life to.

'We're charged with ensuring the Queen's safety,' he told them. 'Have you seen anything, anything at all, which has struck you as odd?'

The man peered down at him, at least ten candles dangling from his hand. 'I've seen nothing, sir, apart from this great business of the preparations.' His colleague bobbed enthusiastically, to show he agreed.

'Come, Harry,' Hooke said. 'There is nothing anomalous here. And nothing, I suspect, in the whole of the house.'

'But we must check the whole of the house.'

Hooke smiled ruefully. 'Of course,' he said.

Passing a fireplace, Harry stepped onto its hearth, and peered up into the chimney, careful not to dislodge the logs waiting to be lit. Inside it, he saw only unsettling blackness.

Shaking his head, he rejoined Hooke, who motioned that they should leave. They walked towards the doors, Harry still looking along the walls. Among all the fittings and furniture, and all the fine panelling, and all the decorated pillars, he could see nothing untoward. Reaching the doors, the three men who worked on them having gone, Harry turned to scan the room again, and reversed into another servant.

'Mr. Hooke. Mr. Hunt. Her Majesty wishes to speak with you.'

The servant obviously had some sort of rank, for his uniform was wildly ornate, and his hat magnificently shiny. He led them from the Great Room, through several connecting rooms, and down a flight of stairs. Waiting at their foot was the man who had silently communicated with them in the gallery, and given permission to search. The Master merged smoothly with them, none pausing in their progress. They reached a lower court, where he produced a key, letting them into a suite of rooms built on a smaller, more human scale. Keeping his silence, he motioned them into a room whose windows overlooked the garden and the grand bend of the Thames.

To their right lurked the huge mass of Westminster Abbey, and to their left Harry could see as far as London Bridge, distant and grey.

'Mr. Hooke! Mr. Hunt! Good day to you, sirs.' It was said with the richly

Lancastrian vowels of Sir Jonas Moore. He was rising from a sofa at the far end of the room, looking worried. He shook both men by the hand, then waited expectantly for Harry to tell him all.

'You asked me to find the man going about as Captain Hudson. I did so, in Paris. He's persuaded me of a plot against this evening's gathering.'

'And so, against the Queen. Miss Hooke informed me of it,' Sir Jonas said. 'Even though the man is deceitful, he has your ear. Grace told me also that you suspect Lord High Treasurer Danby's involvement.'

'I think it his scheme, and that his man, Merritt, does his bidding.'

Sir Jonas did not look surprised, or shocked. 'I remember Danby spoke with you. You told me of it before you left for France.' He glanced at Hooke. 'We have suspected Danby of much, but this would be his wildest plan.'

'I have no proof,' Harry said.

'I would not expect it. Danby is careful.'

'We must look for the machine.'

'We must,' Sir Jonas agreed. 'Thereon, I shall decide what to do about the dwarf.'

'Make no mention of Lord Danby to the Queen,' Hooke said, putting his hand on Harry's wrist. 'She will likely not believe it, and may refuse to let us continue our search.'

Instead of merely letting the time pass as they waited, the three men took the opportunity to search the room they were in. Harry wondered aloud if this might be the site of an attack: the Queen's own private apartment. Again they searched along the walls, under the furniture, in the fireplace, checking the windows, the floorboards; again they could find nothing that appeared to be a threat.

'Mr. Hooke. Sir Jonas. It is good to see you once more.'

Startled, the men turned quickly, Harry from inspecting one of the candle branches that clung to the walls, Sir Jonas from looking under the same sofa he had sat on, and Hooke from playing with a window's mechanism, twanging at its sash cord.

At the door stood a small and slender dark-haired woman, with an officer of the Foot Guards behind her.

She was Catarina Henriqueta de Bragança, the King's wife.

More usually, Queen Catherine.

Her face carried a hurt expression, to Harry's mind, as if, despite her riches, she found life disappointing. Her eyes were black and serious: Harry saw from them straightaway she was not to be underestimated.

In exchange for providing military assistance to Portugal against Spain, Charles II had received Tangier, the Seven Islands of Bombay, free trade with the East Indies, two million Portuguese crowns, and Catherine.

When first travelling to England from Lisbon, the storm she endured on the voyage to Portsmouth, and her husband's absence when she arrived, established the pattern of their marriage. Even though she had failed to deliver to the nation an heir to its throne, and even though he openly kept mistresses and had various children by them, the couple had grown fond of each other. Part of the marriage's settlement included her liberty of worship, which Charles insisted on extending to her, ignoring his advisors' outrage and even the evidence from Titus Oates.

Hence, the King's permission to hold her Catholic Consult, even at the height of the Popish Plot.

Hooke and Sir Jonas bowed deeply, and Harry did the same, a little after.

She stepped into the withdrawing room, regarding them warily.

'Your Majesty,' Sir Jonas said. 'There is news of a menace against your Consult.'

'The people already gather outside. It is not welcome.' Her accent was thick, so Harry struggled to understand her.

'Inside, Your Majesty,' Sir Jonas replied. 'Inside.'

'We have heard of harm intended towards your person,' Hooke told her.

'We?' She looked pointedly at Harry.

Sir Jonas bowed again, in apology. Hooke's normally grey face blushed pink from embarrassment. 'Your Majesty, I apologize. May I introduce Mr. Henry Hunt? Formerly my apprentice at the Royal Society, he now serves Sir Jonas at the Board of Ordnance.'

'He does,' Sir Jonas said. 'It was Mr. Hunt who learned this intelligence, hearing of three Frenchmen plotting against your Consult.'

'Your Majesty,' Harry said, 'you must order a search. I've heard of a machine to be used against you. It's hidden somewhere inside Somerset House. We cannot search alone'—he indicated the three of them addressing her—'for there's not enough time. There are too many rooms.'

The Queen went to the window, to look plaintively out across the Thames. 'Am I not safe, even here in my house? Since Titus Oates accused me of wishing to poison my husband—and he was believed over me—I feel I am not. This is why I have already ordered a search of the house. Which we have done, have we not, Captain MacWilliam?'

The officer at the doorway, ginger-haired and pale-skinned, bowed his affirmation.

She motioned them to sit. 'Tell me what you know of these Frenchmen.' She summoned a servant to bring tea. 'Where did you hear of this plot against me, Mr. Hunt? I should warn you, I have no time for tales of Titus Oates, who sees plots where there are none. I am disbelieving by nature. Even more so now.'

'In Paris, Your Majesty,' Harry replied. 'From a man named Bartholomew Slough. He fled there for his safety, thinking himself endangered for what he knew of it. He is friendly with its Lieutenant Général of police, Monsieur La Reynie.'

'La Reynie? He thinks one half of Paris tries to murder the other. You, too, I see, have succumbed to the French infatuation with the *Affaire des Poisons*. How did this Slough come to overhear such men?'

'He lived at Oakham, in Rutland, and heard them planning against you when they stayed there.'

The Queen, still standing, had her arms folded. Perceiving she was unswayed by his story, Harry spoke more urgently. 'Mr. Slough even saw the machine they had with them. Although, it wasn't yet assembled, and its parts were concealed, so he has no notion of its function.'

'So he has not really seen it at all! Also, why take such trouble? Why not shoot me in my garden, for example, when I take the air? Or stab me through the heart in St. James's Park, when I am riding?'

'Not only your life is threatened, but those of all your guests. The plotters know the house will be searched. I think the machine's designed not to be found. That's why we must look, and look again.'

Tea arrived, on a silver tray loaded with a pot, fine bone china, sugar, spoons, and macaroons. Catherine sat down on a sofa and poured the tea herself, fussing over the ceremony of it. She presented each man with his cup as if it were a relic: bone rather than bone china. Hooke refused a macaroon, feeling self-conscious at the thought of eating in front of Her Majesty. Harry tried one, but found he could not swallow it, still affected by the Bastille diet.

The Queen sipped at her tea, staring hard at Harry, although she addressed Hooke. 'I hold you in high regard, as does my husband, for you are a man of sense. Yet you bring *this* man to me. This is all fantasy, surely?'

Hooke made no reply, for so long the Queen was about to prompt him. Sir Jonas did not seem slighted by his omission from the Queen's high regard, but leaned in to hear his friend's answer. Harry found his own breaths had become loud to his ears. He could feel his blood pulsing insistently in his neck.

'Your Majesty,' Hooke said eventually, 'I believe Mr. Hunt to be convinced of its truth.' He paused to think again. The Queen's face became completely unimpressed after this weak affirmation of Harry and his warning.

Then a most unusual thing happened: Hooke gave a broad smile, even showing his teeth, an extravagance of expression Harry had hardly ever seen.

'You misunderstand me,' Hooke continued. 'I have absolute faith in what Mr. Hunt tells you. He will have considered punctiliously the information he has heard, and the nature of the man who told him of this machine. He has, I know, had time to reflect upon this intelligence. He has also, I know, suffered much to return to London with it. I would be astounded if what he says is not true. That is all as may be, and is all by the by. We *must* search your house, for not to do so is unthinkable. What if, somewhere in this place, the machinery lurks, designed to kill you all, and we did not even look for it?'

CHAPTER FIFTY-EIGHT

THE SOLDIERS' SEARCH

HARRY DIRECTED THE DOZEN KING'S FOOT GUARDS he had been allowed, men provided by the King especially for the Consult, to search the cellar rooms below the Great Room. He was still convinced that was the room where the attack on the Catholics would take place, for it was there that the guests would be most concentrated. It must happen either from above, or below; he was sure the machine was not concealed in the Great Room itself.

The soldiers felt their way around the cellars' rough walls, looking for loose stones, pulling at the floor slabs. They prodded their lanterns into dark corners, and pried under covers. Wherever they looked, the men grumbled. Their uniforms became shabby, their eyes filled with dust. But the Queen had instructed them to assist this odd-looking pair, placing them senior to Sir Jonas: the older man with the twist to his back, and the younger one, looking like an urchin who had not eaten for a month—a gentle push would take him down.

The soldiers were unsure what they were being asked to find. The pair directing them made vague noises about machinery. The dissatisfaction in the soldiers' eyes was clear. Harry, aware their efforts became half-hearted, asked them to keep searching for their Queen's sake. Some still looked unimpressed, until he reminded them of their regiment, and that she was the King's wife. He wished he knew more, Harry told them, but he only knew what he knew, and that was enough. He saw them looking at one another, but they busied themselves around the cellars with renewed vigour, tipping over barrels, pulling out screens, peering into the spaces revealed.

After an hour or so of searching, the soldiers emerged from the cellars, faces streaked where they had wiped their hands across them. They fretted for their uniforms so soon before the Consult, when their colonel would demand they looked their best.

They entered the kitchen, opening every cupboard and pulling out every pan. Surly cooks watched them, clutching their knives. Some ancient plumbing was mistakenly stripped out from the washhouse, old elm pipes that had not carried water for more than fifty years. Sir Jonas led a search of the house's upper court, even the guardroom, which had always contained soldiers. Then, the waiting room beside it, the privy chambers, and the Queen's presence chamber. Harry took some men to search the outbuildings along Duchy Lane, the coach house and stables, and the various other storehouses to the west side of the house. Hooke's party searched the east side, and the Queen's chapel, much to the chaplain's consternation as he prayed there, seeking calm before the Consult.

All the men came together on the first floor, to begin the tricky business of searching the bedrooms, many occupied by guests from all over the kingdom; some had even travelled from abroad. Soon the corridors thronged with guests waiting for the soldiers to finish lifting up beds, turning aside wardrobes, and opening chests.

The number of rooms, and the requirement to search each and every one of them, led to a brevity in the soldiers' manner. Arguments ensued, but the soldiers were adamant. The search would not be stopped. Inexorably, they worked their way through the house, knocking the walls, kicking the skirtings, testing the wainscotting, even finding a secret door none had known was there, leading to rooms long neglected.

The household was now in uproar. The soldiers had offended the guests, as well as the servants trying to clean. Several of the Queen's household found themselves in tears: grown men, even. The Consult was only a matter of hours away, and their weeks of planning and preparation had been swept aside in an afternoon. The chief butler suspected Captain MacWilliam of enjoying the upheaval, and accused him of disregard for the Queen's household's rules. He and his underbutlers formed a line against them, but the soldiers snarled at them to stand down.

'If we do not search, there may be no household,' MacWilliam told the butler. 'And no Queen.'

The Queen herself was called upon—by the angry butler—but she referred him to Mr. Henry Hunt. Harry found himself temporarily the ruler of Somerset House's arcane and intricate society: a ruler with strong feeling against him, despised for the revolution he had brought, but backed by the Foot Guards' might. His voice became firmer, his decision-making more swift, the succession of his commands ever more rapid.

Once all the rooms on the first floor had been searched, he gathered the men together and assigned them roles to mollify the guests and the staff. Harry required them to return all the furniture displaced, refill drawers emptied, and straighten all furnishings disturbed. All the ornaments, and the pictures on the walls, must be realigned. By now he had nearly forty men obeying his commands, all much more at home with the business of doing rather than guarding, which better suited their restless natures.

He took a small number of men, including Captain MacWilliam, up to the attic rooms. Some were servants' quarters, so there were more protests again. Most were used simply as storerooms. Each one had to be checked.

One was an old schoolroom. A couple of child-scale desks faced a teacher's table. There were slates and chalks, paper and pens, and little pots of ink, and shelves with histories and atlases, and a long-broken abacus. A large map of the world hung on the wall, tinged brown with age.

The schoolroom was directly above the Great Room. There were marks from the movement of people over the floorboards, and handprints in the dust. Obviously, it had been searched before. Also, it had been improved in the recent works, for its walls were freshly plastered and its ceiling newly painted. Again, they searched for the mysterious machine of Bartholomew Slough's report, but found nothing.

With no more rooms to search, Harry looked at MacWilliam, who had scraped paint against his coat sleeve, in defeat. He directed the various attic room doors to be locked, then descended the servants' stairway.

He would have to inform the Queen that all their searching, and all their disruption of her Consult's preparations, authorized solely after his insistence on the truth of Bartholomew Slough's intelligence, had revealed precisely nothing.

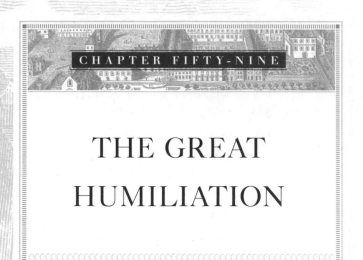

CHAPTER FIFTY-NINE

THE GREAT HUMILIATION

ROBERT HOOKE AND SIR JONAS WENT with him to see Queen Catherine. Noting Harry's mortification, she was understanding and kind, although from a certain stiffness around her mouth Harry knew she wanted him out of her house. Her guests had to be pacified, as the rumours among them grew ever wilder of an assassination threat—unavoidable, as they had watched their rooms being overturned—and that the guards looked for some kind of *machine*. To do what? Nobody knew, but everyone was ready to guess. Talk went about of it being built to pull the house apart stone by stone, or to shoot fire over the guests at their tables, to roast them as they ate.

The guests themselves felt accused, thinking the soldiers sought anything to incriminate them in a Jesuitical plot.

Oddly, Harry did not feel so abjectly humiliated as after his failure at Gresham in front of the Fellows. Perhaps the scale of his mistake numbed him, keeping him from feeling the shame of it. Or else, it was a sign the last weeks had changed him.

The King would hear about it, of course. He would ensure Harry had no place in the Board of Ordnance, or perhaps even in London. Sir Jonas could not meet his eye, preferring to look out at London instead. Doubtless, he would agree with the King, wanting to dissociate himself from the debacle, especially with his own embarrassment after one of his intelligencers proved to be an imposter. Harry hoped Mr. Hooke would not suffer from their association, and his support of Harry's search for the fictitious machine.

Even these thoughts, as the three men crossed the gardens back to the river stairs, did not completely depress him. Harry still considered he had done the right thing. He had forseen the consequences of Slough being mistaken, but had taken the action necessary to save the Queen and her guests.

It did not really matter what others thought.

He even felt a kind of contentment. Rocking in their wherry on the Thames, a smile played around his mouth as he contemplated the enormity of what he had done. Hooke regarded him with concern, thinking he had descended into a state of shock: the grip on his mind loosened by hardships in France and an exhausting return to London, followed by his nearly destroying the Queen's preparations for her Consult.

'Return home with me, Harry. Mary shall prepare dinner. We shall light a good fire and drink my best brandywine. Grace shall be there. I am sure the both of you have much to discuss.'

'Thank you, Mr. Hooke. I'll gladly come with you.'

They left the wherry, Sir Jonas bidding them a curt goodbye before he continued on his way to the Tower. Up Fish Street Hill, past the Monument to the Fire, on up where the road became Grace Church Street, then Bishopsgate Street, taking them towards Gresham College. Harry was reminded of all the times he had made this same journey with Hooke as his apprentice, as a Royal Society Operator, and then, proudly, as its Observator. He had left the man who had made him, who showed him so much of the world and its secrets, merely for the lure of money. He felt a sting at the thought, but knew he was being hard on himself.

He had gone for other reasons, too. For adventure. For independence. To prove something to himself: that he could make his way in the world without Hooke to guide his steps. Also, to show Grace he could stand up for himself. When in the Fens with Colonel Fields, she had accused him of being too anxious to impress those above him. Grace would understand how he had acted from the best of intentions, and that those same intentions had led him into error. Grace would not hold his mistakes against him. Grace would see them as stemming from a noble sentim—

He blew out his cheeks. Grace would do no such thing. She would dismiss him as a fool.

Hooke had read his mind. 'Come, Harry,' he coaxed him. 'You seem atrabilious. After sleep and nourishment, and in a week or so, you shall have regained your former constitution, and your equilibrium.'

Entering the quadrangle, Harry saw Hooke's front door was wide open as if to welcome him back: a prodigal son, one who must show penitence, but who would be returned to the comfort and safety of his friendship with Robert Hooke.

Mary Robinson stood outside, talking animatedly with Walter Pope, Gresham Professor of Astronomy, who resided in the College's opposite corner. Her chubby face was red, her skin shining—Harry guessed from cooking in Hooke's kitchen.

Her expression though, was fearful. Her eyes were wide, and she held her hands out oddly, as if she had no inkling what to do with them.

'Grace is gone,' she told them, her voice quivering. 'She has been taken.'

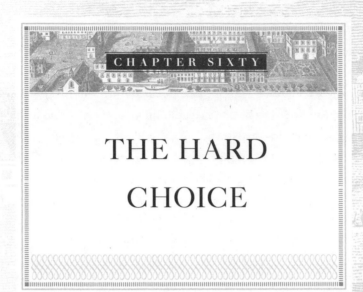

CHAPTER SIXTY

THE HARD CHOICE

MARY HAD CAUGHT SIGHT OF STRANGERS loitering in different corners of
the quadrangle. Three men, she said. Pope had seen them, too. The most
striking of the trio, he said, was a Mephistopheles, with long and pointed
teeth. The other two were less demonical, more nondescript: one larger than
the other, one darker in complexion.

These three had pounced when Grace came out from Hooke's lodgings
not five minutes ago. As one engaged her in conversation, seemingly
friendly, the others grabbed her from behind.

'Did you overhear them speaking French?' Harry asked, to the Professor's puzzlement.

'I cannot say I caught anything they said. The most alarming was definitely foreign, for I have never seen a fellow like him.'

Certain straightaway who these men were, Harry ignored Pope's imperfect logic.

'One would be easy to recognize again,' Mary said, her voice still shaking. 'For Grace fought with him, and scratched his face.' She slid her finger down her own face, from temple to chin. 'She drew blood.' Her voice dropped. 'Yet he did not flinch.'

'Was this the bestial-looking one?' Harry asked her.

She shook her head. 'One of the others with him. The bigger of the two.'

'Which way did they take her?' Hooke asked, his voice cracking.

Mary pointed to the passageway beside Hooke's lodgings, leading to the College's Reading Hall and the porter's rooms. 'I followed them. Out through the courtyard, into Bishopsgate Street, pulled her into their carriage, and off towards the river.'

'What did *you* do, as they took Grace?' Harry asked Pope accusingly.

Pope was shamefaced. 'I protested, Harry. They were three. I was one.' His voice became indignant. 'I could do no more.'

Harry swallowed his reply. He was being unfair; Pope was elderly, older than Hooke. An astronomer could never be expected to fight off villainous Frenchmen.

'It took them no time at all,' Mary said. 'We chased after, but had hardly reached their carriage before they turned its horses in the road. Then they were gone.' She could hardly believe it as she said it.

The carriage must have passed them as they walked up Bishopsgate Street, Harry thought. As he had concentrated self-pityingly on his own sentiments after the disaster at Somerset House. It had not registered in his mind at all.

He turned to Hooke, who had the little colour of his face all drained away. 'These are the men Mr. Slough says intend to kill the Queen. I've seen them before. They chased me at the quayside, when I left for France.'

'But how do they know of Grace?'

'Danby's man must have told them. He was with them, at Billingsgate. Danby knows of her. I remember he forbade me from taking her to France, if she had wanted to go.'

'Did they wait in hope of her appearance, or did they expect her to emerge? Mary, had Grace arranged to meet with anyone?'

'I know not,' Mary answered. 'She is secretive, nowadays.'

'The Queen's life must still be in danger,' Harry said. 'Otherwise, why would these men take Grace?'

'They mean to keep us from them as they work towards their plan. They have taken my niece to do so.' Hooke was trembling. 'We missed their machine. It's there, at Somerset House.'

'They're forcing us to choose,' Harry replied heavily. 'Either Grace's life, or the Queen's.'

'And those of all her guests.' Hooke lowered himself to sit on the colonnade's low wall, beside the quadrangle.

'What best to do, Mr. Hooke?' Harry asked him. 'Grace is your niece. She's your flesh and blood.'

Hooke looked haunted. 'She is but one life. We must return to Somerset House. We must endeavour to put a stop to this plan.'

CHAPTER SIXTY-ONE

THE DISPARATE FRIENDS

AT DUSK, THE THAMES LOOKED FATHOMS deep. From his wherry, Harry observed the moon's reflection as it zigzagged over the ever-changing shape of the water's surface. Every so often a fish swam by, bubbles from its gills looking like balls of glass.

Swaying and dipping on the water, he had the sudden sensation he was still, and it was London rolling and tipping around him. London was as fragile and unstable as this wherry on the waves.

It was not the feeling of vertigo he had become used to, but felt more a more profound connection with the city he called home. And somewhere in this city, he was sure, was Grace Hooke. He thought of Mrs. Hannam, and her insistence she could sense Colonel Fields even from miles away, a curious mental action at a distance.

Grace's taking confirmed that the attempt on the Queen was real.

There had been no other message. No instruction. Harry had no notion where to look for her. And there was no time. Not if he were to return to Somerset House.

Night, clear and cold, had fully descended by the time he disembarked at the Hungerford Stairs; he deemed it less likely that any of Danby's spies would spot him there than if he used the busier Whitehall Stairs. The hazy band of the Milky Way arced overhead.

Harry thanked the waterman, who was reassuringly solid. He paced through the deserted market, then cut through Scotland Yard. To Charing Cross, then Pall Mall, the people walking with lanterns. No street lighting here, unlike in Paris. He reached the old Tudor buildings of St. James's Palace, and, almost next to it, Hortense Mancini's townhouse, loaned to her by the King.

At his knock, Mustapha opened the door, and ushered Harry in.

Hortense waited in the hallway, expecting him after messengers had been sent across London between them. She knew of his failure to find the machine, and gave him a consoling squeeze of his arm.

Even though she had been held in the Grand Châtelet, then had ridden even harder than Harry to return for the Consult—admittedly, her sea journey was easier—Hortense looked impeccable. Her olive skin, left unwhitened, was flawless. Her eyes looked even darker than he remembered them. She wore a dress of deep turquoise. Her wig was tall and white, with ribbons tied into it, the same colour as the dress.

'We have a suit, Harry. Mustapha went out for one this afternoon. It should fit well enough, though you are narrower even than when I last saw you.'

'As are you, since there's no need to conceal Mr. Slough,' he answered.

'He is here, and readies himself.'

'I do not, for I have!' There was the sound of loud treading down the stairs. Resplendent in silks and satins, all purples and mauves, Bartholomew Slough appeared. His nut-brown face, with its Hand of Fatima a darker silhouette on his skin, stood out starkly under his powdered wig.

Hortense stepped back as Harry, Mustapha, and Slough all grasped one another, happy being together again after their hazardous voyage from France. She made a pretence of jealousy at being left out, until she offered her cheeks to them all to be kissed, having to stoop low for Slough.

'Oh, I nearly forgot,' Hortense said to Harry, after they had all released each other. 'La Reynie gave me this, to give to you.' She went to a cabinet, and found a package wrapped in paper. Tearing it open, Harry saw it was a book, *Discours de la méthode pour bien conduire sa raison, et chercher la vérité dans les sciences*, written by René Descartes.

'A gift, or a message?' Hortense asked.

'Both, I think.' He put the book down without opening it. 'I must tell you of Grace. She's been taken.'

Slough guessed at why. 'Lord Danby?'

'To stop me from going to the Consult, I'm sure. This afternoon, I searched the whole of Somerset House with Mr. Hooke. We found nothing.' He looked hopefully at them, as if they could tell him anything he had not already run through in his mind a hundred times.

'If nothing is there, why, then, have they taken Grace?' Hortense voiced the question they had all arrived at.

'They still mean to kill the Queen,' Slough said.

'And wish Harry to steer clear,' Mustapha added.

Harry nodded despondently. 'But what of Grace?'

They all looked at one another, saying nothing.

Harry cleared his throat. 'If I go to Somerset House, I fear Grace will be killed by these men who plan to kill the Queen.'

'And all her guests,' Slough said.

Hortense reached out for Harry's hand. 'Grace is one life threatened, against the lives of many others.'

'As Mr. Hooke said, despite his pain at the thought of losing her.'

'You must sacrifice your happiness, too, as well as her life,' Slough said grimly. 'It does not equate to all those at the Consult.'

Mustapha poured Harry some wine, and insisted he took it. 'You cannot know they will kill her. They only wish to keep you away.'

Harry shared none of his apparent certainty. He had to force himself to turn his thoughts to the matter of the Consult. 'Tell me again, Mr. Slough. What's the machine you saw?'

'As I have said, I have no notion of its operation. Large metal sheets, square in shape. And pipes. Other shapes hidden beneath canvas.'

'I've been thinking on the squares. You said the sides were the length of a man.'

Hortense looked at the men with her, her lips involuntarily twitching. Before her, she had a perfect spread of heights: her servant Mustapha, towering over them all; Harry, the most average of heights; and Bartholomew Slough, reaching no higher than her waist.

Knowing exactly what she was thinking, Slough raised a sly eyebrow at her. 'A tall man. Six feet or so.'

'I wondered if they're made to be fixed together, to form a cube.' Harry said. 'The pipes, then, might lead from this cube.'

'Equally,' Hortense said, 'they could be made to sit side by side, and remain flat.'

Harry conceded her point with a shrug.

'But if they do come together,' Slough said, allowing the idea, 'to form a box of some kind, then what could it hold? Its purpose, remember, is to kill the guests.'

'A poison, then?' Hortense suggested.

'If it's to be filled with a liquid,' Harry said, 'its weight would be prodigious. A cubic foot of water weighs over sixty pounds.' He did a swift mental calculation. 'A cube six feet each way, full of water, would be about six tons. There was nothing nearly so heavy at your house in Oakham. How would they ever transport it?'

'Perhaps they filled it later,' Hortense said. 'In London, perhaps.'

'I considered the same.'

'Or it does not contain liquid. It could contain a powder.' Hortense rubbed her fingers together, to signify fine grains.

'Still heavy.'

'Or a noxious air,' Slough said.

'How could we miss such a cube in our search?'

'Harry, you cannot blame yourself,' Hortense said.

'It is there. I am certain,' Slough said. 'And we must stop it.'

'We shall disguise you,' Hortense told him. 'They will never know you.'

'Until we have stopped them,' Mustapha said.

Hortense's clock in the hall told them it was seven o'clock. The Consult would start in an hour.

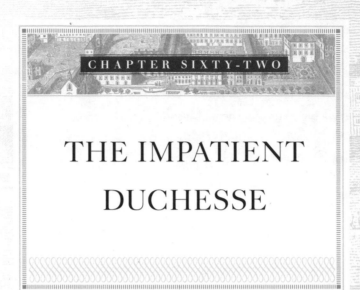

CHAPTER SIXTY-TWO

THE IMPATIENT DUCHESSE

ALONG THE STRAND, THE NUMBER OF carriages heading the same way was apparent. By the time they passed the narrowing of the road at the Exeter Exchange, their progress was all stop and start. Waiting to get through the protestors by Somerset House, the carriages were backed up east towards Temple Bar, and west towards Charing Cross, and as far north as Covent Garden.

But it would have been unthinkable for Hortense Mancini and her entourage to arrive by foot.

To help clear the way, more soldiers of the King's Regiment of Foot Guards had been sent for from the Savoy Hospital, now turned into a barracks. More of these men passed them as they waited.

Sitting inside Hortense's carriage, Harry could not get used to his breeches. The way they slid over his skin was unnatural. The suit she had found was so comfortable, it was like a new state of being. Until he had worn silk, he had never perceived the scratchy discomfort of his own clothes.

His borrowed breeches and coat were chocolate brown. His waistcoat was a bright silver. His shirt was silk, too, a creamy white, worn with a red cravat. His new shoes, too tight, with enormous square buckles, shone like polished jet. His face was powdered and pale. Hortense had painted a black heart on his cheek: to further his disguise, she said, although he was unhappy about it. It seemed out of keeping with the nature of the Consult, a meeting to discuss how the Catholics should respond to the legislation to limit them, and Titus Oates's assertions against them. She had waved away his protests. She was equally unhappy about his spectacles, for their frames were plain, but they had no others suitable for the occasion. And without them, Harry could hardly see five yards away.

Hortense exhaled. A long, impatient breath. It was obvious she had something to say, and was ruminating on the right way to say it. Her right hand was clenched, and she knocked it against her thigh as if knocking on a door.

'What of the Sancy diamond?' she asked finally, as they inched forwards again, travelling a whole wheel revolution before the driver had to stop. She huffed at Harry, perplexed by his seeming surprised at her question. 'My sister said you showed little interest in its whereabouts. You made no search for it in Paris.'

'I thought finding Captain Hudson's replacement would lead me to the diamond. It did not.'

'Surely, you have not forgotten my offer?'

'I've hardly had time to consider it.'

'If you find it, I will make you a rich man.'

'In Paris, I searched for Mr. Slough. For the past few days, the Consult's been to the forefront of my mind. Now, I'm also preoccupied by the Frenchmen taking Grace.'

Hortense sat silently, chewing the inside of her cheek. All three men with her could tell she still thought of the Sancy.

Eventually, Slough spoke up, breaking the silence that had begun to feel oppressive. 'We must make sure these Frenchmen do not succeed.'

'Yes. We can speak of the diamond later,' Harry said, looking out through the window, the glass pane rattling in its frame.

Hortense frowned crossly. 'You will not discuss it, even now, while we wait?'

'I will not.'

'For a natural philosopher, you seem strangely incurious.'

For the first time in their journey, Harry smiled.

CHAPTER SIXTY-THREE

THE CATHOLIC
CONSULT

FOOT GUARDS STOOD ON EACH SIDE of the road, stationed between their coach and the protestors shouting from the pavements. Having only the view directly to either side, Harry found it difficult to make sense of the movements going past them, of soldiers and of Protestants decrying the Catholic religion, offended by the Queen's Consult. Some in the crowd called out against Catherine—'Popish bawd! Mother of abominations!'— but they were quickly dealt with: dragged away, or musket-butted to keep them quiet.

From the protestors, there were shouts for the soldiers to join them. One man took a run at Hortense's coach—shouting, 'Mazarin, Romish slut!'—to be pushed aside by a soldier.

Harry was sure he heard Israel Tonge, his high voice rising above the crowd's din. 'Papists lusting for Protestant blood! Apprehend their Baalish bigotry! Espy the Whore of Babylon!' He looked for the old preacher, but could not see him. Nor did he spot Titus Oates, but where one went, the other usually followed.

The window next to Harry suddenly shattered, a stone sending glass over him. Standing up to remove it from his suit, Hortense helped him brush the splinters to the floor.

As they turned in through its gates, the front of Somerset House came into view. Light spilt from every window. Over the entrance, it had a great central arch, with four more archways to either side, making a colonnaded walkway across its width. The house had once been symmetrical, but with James I's Queen, Anne, lavishing money on the place, and the requirements of being Parliament's headquarters during the Civil Wars, and after a fire or two, it was now a motley assortment of wings, pillars, pediments, poking towers, extensions, and outhouses. All its various roofs turned messily in different directions.

Carriages lined up in the courtyard, their drivers' disgruntled faces lit up by their lamps. The Queen's footmen directed them clockwise around the courtyard for an easier flow. Each move was the length of a coach with its horses, after the coach at the head of the line had disgorged its passengers. The disembarking guests were assisted by more footmen, made panicky by the protest outside and the earlier search of Somerset House. They inspected the guests for signs they might mean harm.

When their own coach reached the front of the line, Mustapha, a vision also in silk—a long dark-red coat and an extravagant cravat—exited first, to help Hortense. Then Slough hopped down, looking about him, up at all the windows, and the roofs, and the excrescences from the walls, as if working out how best to scale them. Behind him, Harry eased himself out, brushing away more pieces of glass.

The enormous front doors stood open, but the same captain, MacWilliam, who had searched the house with Harry and Hooke, guarded the way. About twenty of his men stood with him, beneath the arches. In their black tricorne hats and red coats, blue-grey stockings and breeches, they presented a forbidding barrier. All were armed: Harry saw swords, and pistols, and muskets with bayonets fitted.

Those arriving not yet aware of the rumoured threat against them were quickly appraised of the reasons for heightened security. Some stood fearfully in the courtyard, uncertain whether to venture inside. Unsettled by the protest and the grim-looking soldiers, others decided to climb hurriedly back into their carriages, and exit back to the Strand.

All visitors had to submit to the soldiers' scrutiny. Guests were asked to surrender their weapons. A selection of swords and daggers, and even pistols, had been placed in a large chest lying open on a table by the wall. Anyone who complained was taken aside and spoken to sharply by MacWilliam, who showed little deference to those even of highest social rank.

People stood shivering in their finery, watching with approbation the busy routine ahead of them. There was no choice if they wished to attend. The soldiers explained they followed instructions given by the Queen herself.

After passing the inspection, MacWilliam ushered Harry's group in, failing to recognize him under his silks and powder, and with the heart painted on his cheek. Just inside stood the Master of the Queen's Household. An assistant held a list out to him: he was too important to sully his fingertips by holding such a list himself.

Harry looked down at the fine silk of his breeches, the high polish of his shoes, and the fussy ornamentation of his coat.

Hortense touched his hand. 'You are unrecognisable,' she reassured him. 'Nephew.' She smiled at him, and then the expression was killed, her face assuming a masklike stillness. 'Leave the talking to me.'

He swallowed, and puffed out his thin chest, hoping for an impression of ease.

The list was consulted ostentatiously, even though the Master recognized her immediately—for she was Hortense Mancini, Duchesse de Mazarin. He knew full well the Queen's feelings, but Catherine had invited her, one Catholic to another, ignoring Hortense's previous relationship with her husband.

The Master subjected Harry to a disapproving scrutiny. Offended by the painted design on his face, Harry assumed, blushing under his whitener. Slough affected to ignore the Master, looking over and beyond him, as if it gave him equal stature to do so.

'My servants, Mustapha and Bartholomew,' Hortense drawled. 'My nephew, Sébastien 'Espinasse.' Where she had got the name from, Harry had no idea, but she said it smoothly. There it was, like a hat to be worn: he was to be Sébastien for the evening. 'My nephew,' she replied to the Master's questioning eyebrow, 'visits London from Paris.'

'Vous êtes les bienvenus à la maison de la reine, Monsieur 'Espinasse.' You are most welcome to the Queen's home.

For a moment, Harry froze, as much surprised by the Master speaking as by his use of French, then blurted, *'Je suis arrivé récemment à Londres. En fait, aujourd'hui. Merci. Merci.'* I arrived in London recently. Indeed, today. Thank you. Thank you.

The Master frowned, unsure of his accent.

'He tours, all over Europe,' Hortense explained. 'Spending the last of your father's money, eh, Sébastien!' The Master's frown deepened further, the creases meeting together in a point at the centre of his forehead. Harry hoped he was not aware of the intricacies of the Mancini family tree.

'You find London in a state of heightened excitement, monsieur. I trust you do not think too poorly of our city.'

Harry looked at him cluelessly, as if he did not understand.

'Il dit, Londres est dans un état de grande excitation,' Hortense translated for her nephew. *'Il espère que vous ne pensez pas trop mal de lui.'*

The Master of the Queen's Household glanced at his assistant, who gave the smallest of shrugs. There was room: some guests had turned back, he had seen them from the doorway. Those behind waited impatiently.

The Master nodded, allowing them through.

Hortense led the way.

ONCE INSIDE THE grand entrance hall, servants took their coats and cloaks. Silver trays laden with hors d'oeuvres and drink floated through the crowd, carried by more servants. Everything was served in the finest of china and the most fragile of glass. The guests promenaded slowly towards the Great Room, its huge double doors visible at the hall's far end. Musicians played unobtrusive chamber music. Louder was the people's chatter. The conversation sounded brittle: the guests were tense, gathering despite the threats against them, not to socialize or celebrate, but to discuss strategy.

How were they to withstand the attacks from those in thrall to Titus Oates, and his ever-growing band of accomplices, willing to perjure themselves to incriminate Catholics? How could they hope to appease the authorities who used him as an instrument to repress them? What was the word on the threat to them tonight? Another search, they knew, had been carried out that afternoon. Nothing found, but still their worries persisted. The guests arriving by coach that evening had all witnessed the protestors' anger. Those who arrived early, before the crowds had gathered, could hear the splenetic cries from the Strand.

A harried-looking waiter, summoned by a flick of Hortense's wig, offered glasses of wine. Slough spotted a tray piled artfully with little countess cakes. He had to pull at the waiter's leg to get his attention. The man looked tactfully away when Slough took three. As Harry watched him eat, it occurred to him the food might be poisoned, but everyone around him munching and drinking still stood, and it was machinery Slough had seen.

Slough stared around him busily as he chewed: Harry discerned that Slough suspected he was not completely believed, even though they had willingly gone there with him.

He put his hand on Slough's shoulder, but then took it away, sensitive that a man so small might think him condescending. 'I believe you,' he said. 'It's here, somewhere.'

'I know it,' Slough said, giving no flicker that he appreciated Harry's solicitude. 'We must find it, or everyone we see might be dead by morning.'

They entered the Great Room amid the other guests funnelling through its enormous doors. Harry thought of an hourglass: the people coming through these doors being the grains of sand dropping through its aperture, as the time approached, ever nearer, the killing of them all.

No way of knowing when the killing would start, or how. Harry felt it would be later, when all the guests had arrived. Perhaps while they sat eating at these tables. Whatever this machine was, to have taken the trouble to bring it into London, and to build it and hide it from view somewhere inside Somerset House, suggested an urge for complete annihilation.

As many dead as possible.

The room currently held around two hundred people, Harry guessed. About half as many as the number of places set at the tables. The guests' general movement was to the far end of the room, where Queen Catherine, surrounded by people, sat facing them.

CHAPTER SIXTY-FOUR

THE PRESSING DARKNESS

DARKNESS PRESSED AGAINST HER. GRACE FELT it crawling slowly over her, seeping in, invading her. It filled her ears and nose, and flowed thickly under her eyelids like oil. With it came a cold movement of air, a gentle swirling over her skin, and a silence so intense her ears played tricks on her. She thought she could hear the air itself, fluttering against her eardrums.

Her body was numb. It felt as if to move would break it. When she tried to, the exertion made her dizzy, giving her the sensation of spinning slowly on a wheel: her head the central point of her turn, her heels on its rim. Whatever it was she lay on moved with her, spinning, too. She tried to reach out to either side of her, to see if her hands met anything solid, but her arms felt so weighty she could not lift them.

She had thought the man wanted her silence, pressing his hand over her mouth, but ever since she had felt this heaviness. His hand, hot and re- pellent, had tasted strange, bitter, smelling like Uncle's tinctures of opium.

Able only to move her fingers, she pushed their tips into the ground's rough texture. Stone, covered with silt. Exhausted from the effort, she re- laxed her hands.

A tear ran slowly over the curves of her cheek, across the furrows of her ear, tickling the skin.

In the carriage with her, two men had held her down, until life drained from her muscles and she was powerless against them. She had scratched one of them. An icy satisfaction rose inside her, worming through the fear, at the memory of his blood.

The second hardly looked like a man at all. Like a rodent. A bat, more precisely.

A third man, she reasoned, must have driven the carriage.

Had there been a fourth man, too? She could not be sure, as her memory was not of seeing one, but more of sensing one.

Her fear of the darkness beginning to grip more tightly than the fear of her kidnap by violent men, she shuddered. She had no intimation of what lay in wait for her. Her foreseeable future was just this slow spinning in darkness, and the tiredness freezing her limbs.

As well as the smell from the man's fingers—she could not be certain if the odour was still present, or a memory—there were other smells. Damp- ness. And an unhealthy, musty smell. The smell of sickness.

She tried to push away the thought.

But the thought would not be deterred: it was the smell of death.

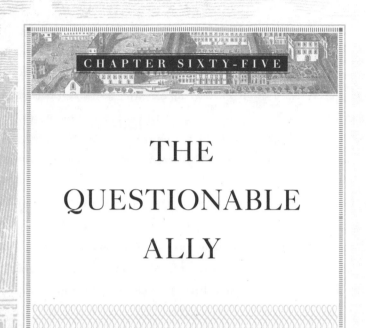

CHAPTER SIXTY-FIVE

THE QUESTIONABLE ALLY

QUEEN CATHERINE SHOWED NO TRACE OF worry. Perhaps a little paler, Harry thought, than in the afternoon, despite the room's heat from the two great fires. Perhaps the bright light made her look blanched: all the candles in the chandeliers, put up laboriously by the men he had questioned, with their rickety ladders.

Guests clustered around her, waiting for her assistants to bring them to her notice. He caught her expression change when she spied Hortense Mancini: a fleeting darkening of her face, gone as quickly as it appeared, replaced by an overly bright smile and a look of spellbound concentration on the person addressing her.

More Foot Guards stood behind her. Harry recognized some from the search. Their uniforms were as clean as could be, the ribbons tied above their knees given out new, their brass as bright as when first issued. Most men carried muskets, with bayonets fitted. A couple had flintlocks. Surely, more for show, he thought, conscious of the mayhem if they started shooting through the crowd. A sergeant wearing a scarlet sash stood with a halberd, its vicious point stabbing towards the ceiling. The regiment's colonel was present, too, standing just behind the Queen. An enormous wig tumbled over his shoulders, a feather in his hat and yellow silk stockings setting him apart from his men.

Despite the rich adornment of all the guests, their clothes and jewels agonized over for the Queen's Consult, Hortense's party still drew attention. Harry felt awkwardly self-conscious as he walked with them: the flamboyant Duchesse with her African servant, Mustapha, along with a nut-brown dwarf whose rolling gait gave him a swaggering, haughty air. Harry's painted heart made his face more suited to a masque or a ball. His clothes had begun to feel alien to his skin, making it irritable, as if it rejected the finery loaned to him.

They joined the movement of people towards the Queen. Harry was sure Catherine looked at them again, with another disapproving tightening of her mouth.

Behind him, he felt a presence; a shadow cast over him. Turning, he was confronted by the tall and cadaverous figure of Richard Merritt.

His heart lurched. Already, they had been found out.

●

'I MUST SPEAK with you.' Merritt said urgently, clasping Harry's arm. He was covered by a sheen of sweat, the neck of his shirt visibly damp, yet he still wore his long purple cloak.

Harry pretended to be puzzled.

'Sébastien?' Hortense stared at the stranger, immediately sensing his presence meant trouble.

'*Pardonnez-moi, monsieur,*' Harry said. '*Je ne parle pas anglais.*' I do not speak English.

'You've forgotten, then. When you left these shores for France, perhaps,' Merritt said. 'Come, Mr. Hunt, for we are grown men.'

Harry looked past him, towards the Queen, wondering how far Merritt was prepared to disrupt the Consult. He looked to see if Danby's man had others with him, perhaps even the three Frenchmen, to eject them from the house. The Foot Guards all seemed oblivious of him, concentrating on other guests entering the room. If any looks came their way, they were towards Hortense and Slough. If Merritt did not have the soldiers, or Lefèvre and his men, then who else was here with him? Danby himself would not be here. The Lord High Treasurer would stay distant from his own plan's execution.

'Mr. Merritt,' Harry said coldly.

'I know you know of what goes on here,' Merritt said into his ear. The man's breath smelled of disease. All the sweat made him look sick, rather than just warm from the heat of the fires. Harry tried to back away, but Merritt still gripped him. 'The plot against the Consult. For you've found Mr. Slough.'

'He's told me all,' Harry replied. 'I wonder what you know of it.'

Merritt signalled towards one of the pillars, which gave a semblance of privacy. Slough went with them. Hortense and Mustapha stayed with the people awaiting the Queen, thinking it would draw too much attention if their whole party went.

Standing by the pillar, a carved-wood weasel looking about to jump onto his back, Merritt's eyes scanned the room. Ever more people streamed through the doors. 'Danby's mad!' He looked to each side of him; ears were likely to hear when you denounced the Lord High Treasurer's name. 'We must stop him. Will you help me? He uses Frenchmen.'

'The men I saw you with at Billingsgate?' Harry asked. 'And who stayed with Mr. Slough?'

Merritt nodded agitatedly, his eyes bulging.

'One is named Lefèvre,' Harry said. 'A man I saw killed.'

'He is Lefèvre. He shows no signs of being dead.' Merritt gave a sheepish grin. 'The dead do not rise again, except by God's command.'

'He means to use a machine,' Slough said.

'Danby employs him to kill as many Catholics here as possible. All of them, if he can. Using a gas.' Merritt fussed with his cloak, clutching the material, the knuckles of his hand pale from the tension in his fingers.

Confirmation, then: the man was Lefèvre—but how could this be? And the cube of Harry's surmise was to hold a lethal gas.

'Where is Grace Hooke?' Harry demanded.

'I heard Danby speak of her with Lefèvre. I'm truly sorry, I know nothing of her whereabouts.'

'Was them taking her meant to keep me from this house?'

'Lord Danby risks all. He seeks to protect his plan by any means possible. That's why he tried to keep you in Paris.'

Harry studied him dubiously. 'Do you not seek, also, to kill these people?'

'I've worked for Danby for years. I've helped him in much—some of it would doubtless meet your disapproval—but I can't support him in this. Nor can I act against him on my own.'

'Where is it? This machine?'

'*That*, I did not overhear.'

'You really have no notion?'

Merritt raised his open hands and grimaced, a picture of contrition.

'Why should Danby wish to murder the Queen?' Harry asked.

'As a way of better controlling the King.'

'Why all the people here, also?'

'They threaten all that Danby holds dear. The Protestant way of worship, and independence from France. The King relies on his French cousin for money, as he's denied it by Parliament. In return, Louis influences the way we're ruled.' Merritt wiped his brow with a slender hand. 'If we're to defeat Danby, then we must find the machine, and break it before it can do its work.'

'We, you say? In truth, I don't trust you, Mr. Merritt.'

'Why should you? I've assisted with this treasonous plan, and ensured Lefèvre's being here, in London, to carry out Lord Danby's wishes. Lefèvre's an expert in poisons, so is the perfect man for the scheme. He advised La Voisin herself.'

'I saw her die, when I made my way from the Bastille.' Harry murmured it almost to himself, remembering the plume of smoke. 'Why do Lefèvre and his men hate Catholics so, that they would murder this many?'

'You expect me to tell you they're Huguenots, do you not? That they seek their revenge for repression. They're not. They're Catholics. If offered enough money, most men can put aside their religion. I've never before suffered such scruples. But, as you must see, I've come to my senses. I hold no ill-feeling towards Queen Catherine. I've no wish to see these people dead. My eternal self would be sentenced to Hell! Besides, it's not only the Queen and her guests you've so far seen. The King's brother, James, is due. Danby means to kill him, too.'

'Why tell us, Mr. Merritt?' asked Slough. 'Why not walk over to the Queen there, and tell her?'

'For the same reason you don't,' Merritt replied. 'She would not believe it. It's too great a scheme. You could never convince them—especially as you, Mr. Hunt, have searched Somerset House already. The soldiers wouldn't believe it. And men with muskets are little use against poison.' Merritt smiled dolefully; an odd expression, as if he felt sorry for Harry.

Harry and Slough shared a glance. Merritt looked almost crazed with his story of poisoning all at the Consult. They did not doubt, though, what Merritt said, as far as no one ever believing him. Even if his story were wholly true.

Harry heard a loudening of conversation in the room, but kept his eyes on Merritt, still unsure of him. What best to do? Should he join forces with Merritt against Danby, or take him to be a liar?

'Is Lefèvre here, at Somerset House? Are his men?'

'Why, Mr. Hunt, that's the beauty of his plan—or, rather, I should say, its iniquity. They've no need to be. The gas will release on its own. That is the function of the machine.'

The rise in volume from the guests had become a commotion. Harry turned to look behind him, across the rest of the Great Room.

The King's brother, James, Duke of York, had arrived.

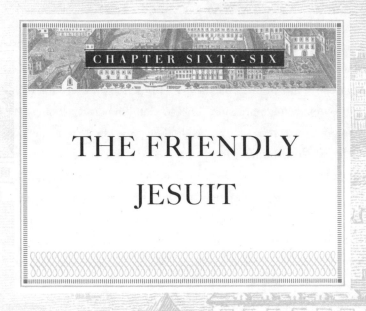

CHAPTER SIXTY-SIX

THE FRIENDLY
JESUIT

THE DUKE OF YORK'S ENTOURAGE MADE its way towards Queen Catherine, the guests moving aside to let them through. He had at least ten people
in his retinue, including two astonishingly burly men who could only be
there to protect him. He had heard of the threat, as by now everybody in
Somerset House had heard, and he went to his sister-in-law with his arms
outstretched in concern.

James was not as lean as his brother, and had a ruddier complexion.
After his bravery in fighting London's Great Conflagration, the people were
admiring of him. Their affection quickly waned, though, when as Lord
High Admiral he was required to submit to the Test Act: to denounce as
superstition the notion of transubstantiation in the sacrament of the Lord's
Supper. This, he had refused to do. Thus, his Catholicism became known.

His Catholic wife, Mary of Modena, walked with him. His second wife, less than half his age, she looked startlingly young. In London, she was known as the 'Pope's daughter'. She had an easy, coltish grace. Hortense, Harry could see, looked approving.

Catherine stood to receive them, welcoming them to her Consult. The soldiers tensed with so much movement going on around her. One man with the Duke and Duchess was a Jesuit, attired in the cassock and biretta of his kind, in darkest black.

To Harry's amazement, when the man turned, he saw it was Denis Papin.

Slough spotted him, too, and turned to give Harry an extravagant wink. Soon the guests would be called to their places, and the meal would begin. With Papin by the Queen, in among the Duke's group, that must mean Hooke had asked him to join them, to help protect them.

He must get to Papin, Harry decided, to tell him of Merritt's story of the gas.

Harry turned to Merritt. 'We must search the house again.'

'If you'll let me, I'll help you.'

'What have you heard of the gas? Is it, for example, lighter, or heavier, than air?'

'Does it fall, or does it rise? I see why you'd wish to know . . . I'm sorry, Mr. Hunt, I would help you further if I could.'

Harry tilted his head in thought. 'The gas may be lighter than air, in which case it'll rise up through these boards.' The oak floor did not appear to have gaps between them, but perhaps a gas could work its way through. 'Or else, the poison's heavier than air, in which case it'll fall. Either's more likely than from the walls, which would need a way of taking the gas sideways. Apart from the draft through those doors, there's little motion of the air in here.'

Slough perceived Harry's reasoning as indecision. 'We should search the cellars again.'

They returned to Hortense and Mustapha. Hortense readily agreed that Mustapha should join them to search for the machine. She would remain in the Great Room, waiting for signs the poisoning had begun, to try to direct people away if it did. They would only believe it if it started to happen.

Harry, Slough, Mustapha, and Merritt made their way back to the big double doors.

There, Denis Papin caught up with them. He wore a ferraiolo cape, and carried a long staff with him, to better guide his flock. Looking severe under his black hat, he bowed to them, as if only being courteous to guests happening to be by the doors at the same time.

'It's good you're here, Denis,' Harry muttered. 'But you expose yourself to danger. They plan to use a gas.'

'I have seen nothing suspicious.' He pressed his hands together. 'I shall stay with the Duke and the Queen, to help them if I can.' Harry, Slough, and Mustapha all bowed respectfully to the Jesuitical soldier of God. He made the sign of the cross to them, then returned to the Duke of York.

As they left the Great Room, and all the guests inside it, a servant chased after them, to enquire if they needed help. Did they know the house had flushing lavatories, based upon the French *angrez*? Harry thanked him, then they moved on, further into the heart of the house.

THE DOOR TO the cellars was by the servants' stairs, which, Harry remembered from the afternoon, meant going past the kitchen. Its doors were open, and it was busy with red-faced boys running to the commands of red-faced cooks, and loud with the incessant din of pans clanging and sharp knives chopping. Cooks bustled and swerved around each other. Others leaned over benches, plucking, slicing, mincing and mixing, wielding skillets and spoons, graters and blades. A turnspit dog rotated roasting venison.

As the four men passed the doorway, a cook with a piglet dangling from his hands shouted after them. Ignoring him, they made their way along the corridor, its floor slippery with juices and fat.

They reached the door leading down to the cellars. Harry tried it, but it was firmly locked against him.

'Is there no other way down to the cellars?' Slough asked him.

Harry thought back to the afternoon, when stumbling around in the cellars with Hooke, and Captain MacWilliam and his men. 'There must be. Some daylight came in, from a low window.' Like the window in his cell at the Châtelet, he remembered, little more than a slot along the ground. 'It must be on the house's western side.' He understood what Slough suggested. 'You could get through, if you break the pane.'

'We can break this door,' Mustapha said.

'We'd gain the attention of half the house,' Harry said. 'The Queen made me promise not to return. The captain of the Foot Guards knows me, and would eject me.'

Slough disappeared, looking for a way out without having to go back through the front doors, past all the guards and the Master of the Queen's Household.

'Why do I not search upstairs, as you wait for Mr. Slough?' Mustapha suggested. 'There is no point in both of us being here.'

'I'd prefer to stay together, in case Lefèvre and his men are in wait.'

'I'm sure they're not here,' Merritt assured him.

Harry regarded him doubtfully.

'You don't yet trust me. I understand why.' Merritt sat himself down on the stairway, quiet since all the servants were busy with the guests.

'We'll wait here, for Mr. Slough,' Harry told him.

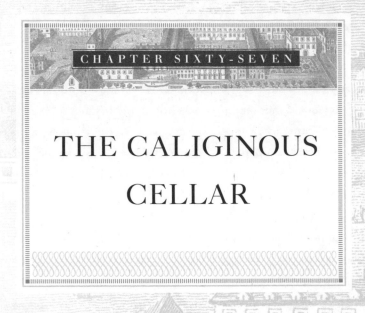

CHAPTER SIXTY-SEVEN

THE CALIGINOUS CELLAR

BUT SLOUGH DID NOT REAPPEAR. HARRY tried the cellar door again, lifting it by its handle. It refused to move on its hinges at all, let alone by enough to ease it from its bolt. He peered through the keyhole, trying to make out the intricacies of the lock's tumblers.

'Mustapha, would you return to the kitchen? I need a rod, or a wire, or perhaps a thin blade.' At Mustapha's look of reservation, Harry prompted him. 'Say you're lost, or that you search for the Duchesse.'

'I do not think the cooks will want me in their kitchen.' Mustapha registered Harry's determined look. 'I will try.'

Left with Richard Merritt, who still sat on the stairs, Harry could smell the man's sweat, which was pungent, especially so in the confines of the space they were in.

'Why not take off your cloak?' Harry asked him.

'I've kept my sword, for my own protection, which I don't wish the soldiers to see. You've seen Lefèvre. You know how dangerous a man he is. Indeed, you believe him returned from the dead.'

'A few moments ago, you were sure he's not here.'

Harry longed for the comfort of a weapon. But if he were to come up against Lefèvre and his men, he doubted he could hold them at bay with a knife or a sword, and a pistol would not keep three assassins from him. He wished he still had his, able to fire repeatedly. He assumed it remained in Paris with Lieutenant Général La Reynie.

If he were arrested by soldiers, being armed would make them suspicious of him. They would take him to be the plotter they sought, as all guests had been told to leave their weapons at the door.

'How did you get it past the Foot Guards?' he asked Merritt. 'They searched everyone, as we came in.'

'As I came with Lord Danby, they perceive me as someone of authority. He was here earlier this evening, under the guise of wishing the Queen well with her Consult.'

A soft tapping from the cellar door's other side interrupted him.

'Mr. Slough?' Harry hissed through the wood.

'Well, I am in,' came the muffled reply. 'I can find no way of opening this door, apart from breaking it.'

'Mustapha's in search of a tool to unlock it,' Harry told him.

'Other doors down here are locked, too.'

'The soldiers shut them up, in case of attack upon the Queen. With your fresh eyes, you may find something we missed. Remember, a cube, with each of its sides as long as a . . . tall man.'

'Don't dillydally about the subject, Mr. Hunt. I am used to the fact that I am small.'

Despite their situation, and the threat against the Queen, Harry could not help but smile. 'Yes, Mr. Slough, you're small. I've become used to it, too.'

'I am hampered by having no light.'

'Then we must find one, and open this door.'

Merritt pulled at Harry's arm. 'Your African hasn't reappeared.'

Harry looked back along the short length of corridor towards the kitchen.

'He's not *my* African, Mr. Merritt. Stay here, if you please. I shall see what's happened to Mustapha.'

CHAPTER SIXTY-EIGHT

THE SUSPICIOUS COOKS

RETURNING DOWN THE CORRIDOR, HARRY DISCERNED that all the preparations in the kitchen seemed to have stopped; its metallic noises had been replaced by voices, raised and argumentative.

He reached the kitchen doorway. There was Mustapha, surrounded by cooks. Although they shouted at him, and slowly advanced on him, he tried to reason with them. As no one had put their implements down, Mustapha was being pointed at by a collection of sharp knives, as well as stirring spoons, birch whisks, and pans.

A thickset, austere-looking man, who from the cowering way the others responded to him must have been the head cook, directed a kitchen boy to inform soldiers of their discovery: that of a plotter. As the boy rushed by, Harry had to move aside.

Entering the kitchen, Mustapha saw him and pointed at him for all the excitable cooks, who all turned at the same time, their heat-reddened faces angry and accusing.

'Mustapha!' Harry said crossly, aiming at highborn diction. 'Your mistress wonders where it is you have got to.'

'Please, sir, tell these fellows I am the Duchesse's servant. Not a one of them believes me.'

'It is true,' Harry announced to the dubious faces. 'He is the Duchesse de Mazarin's manservant.'

'Then he should not be in our kitchen,' the head cook told him. 'You tell us why he is, for his story fails to convince.'

Whatever he told them would have to tally with Mustapha's account. Harry looked at his beleaguered friend for help.

'I told them of the Duchesse's dog, gone missing,' Mustapha said.

'You have not yet found Poodle?' Harry looked apologetically at the cooks. 'We have sought him everywhere.'

'It did not seem like he looked for an animal.' The head cook folded his arms belligerently. 'He searched along our tables.' Although grizzled, the man was still impressively built. When his forearms squeezed together, they looked alarmingly large. The other cooks consulted one another, all sounding doubtful.

'You must be alert, no doubt of it,' Harry said agreeably. 'The Foot Guards warned us of strangers who look to do us harm. But, with all the searching of the guests, and the great number of soldiers, I am sure it will all come to nothing.'

'Here, in the kitchen, we've heard only rumours,' another of the cooks said, receiving a lambasting glare from the head cook.

'The soldiers searched the whole house this afternoon, with Mr. Robert Hooke,' another said.

No mention of his assistant, Mr. Henry Hunt. 'Mr. Robert Hooke, of the Royal Society?' Harry enquired.

Various of the cooks nodded. 'A man of high repute. He'll have found anything, if there's anything to be found.'

'There were no explosives, nor signs of anyone hiding,' another cook offered.

'Then the Queen and her guests are safe, I am sure.' Harry stopped himself, wondering if the men of the kitchen might have seen anything suspicious. 'Do any of you have reason to think otherwise?'

'This African in our kitchen is untoward.' The head cook unrolled his arms, and took a firm hold of Mustapha by his shoulder. 'Otherwise, only gossip. I believe not a word of it.' He spoke into Mustapha's ear. 'Begone, and let us go about our business.' Mistaking him for a gentleman, he was more deferential to Harry. 'Take him with you, sir, please, and return to the other guests.' He gestured to two of his men. 'Make sure they find their way.'

The two cooks walked closely behind, as Harry and Mustapha returned along the corridor towards the Great Room. Harry glanced around at the entrance to the cellars, where presumably Slough still waited behind the door.

No sign of Richard Merritt on the stairs.

As they rejoined the other guests, Mustapha gave Harry a nudge. After making sure the cooks had left them, he revealed the keys he had stolen from the kitchen.

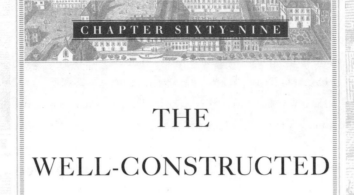

THE
WELL-CONSTRUCTED
SERGEANT

THEY WEAVED THROUGH THE CROWD TO get back to Hortense, who stood alone by a pillar.

'You've lost your dog,' Harry informed her.

'Sad news,' she replied. 'For I was fond of it.'

'Mustapha was stopped by the cooks in the kitchen, who thought him poisoning our dinner.'

'So, you told them you looked for my dog.'

'Mr. Slough found his way to the cellars, but we couldn't follow.'

'You have lost him, too?'

'He'll be searching down there now, I'm sure.'

'He will find his way back,' Mustapha said. 'He is resourceful.' Smirking, he showed Hortense the large bunch of keys he had purloined from the kitchen. Surely one of these keys would allow them into the cellars.

'Put them away!' Hortense moved close to her servant, masking him from the view of two Foot Guards approaching them briskly with a cook.

Leading was the sergeant holding a halberd, a tall and well-constructed man.

'Your manservant made his way to the kitchen.' he said. 'Please keep him with you.'

Hortense bridled at the way he addressed her. 'He went on an errand for me.'

'This gentleman, too.' He indicated Harry.

'My nephew went to find my manservant. Neither are to blame.' She ran her tongue along her teeth. 'If you are cross with anyone, it should be me.'

He bowed to the Duchesse, rapidly remembering his manners. 'I apologize. I am made abrupt by the stories of harm against this Consult.'

'He aroused our misgivings,' the cook said, implacable.

The sergeant frowned at him, then turned back to the Duchesse. 'You have vouched for him, so I am sure we have nothing to fear.'

'This is my nephew,' Hortense said. 'My sister's boy. Monsieur 'Espinasse.' She seemed quite taken with the sergeant, by the way he filled his uniform, his regained civility, and obvious good breeding.

Harry wondered why he was not an officer, and if he had been demoted through some transgression or other. Perhaps his family had fallen on hard times, so he was unable to buy a commission.

'He visits London,' Hortense continued. 'He grew up in France, in a little place called Veauce. He has travelled all over Europe, as far west as Madrid, as far south as Athens, as far east as the Carpathian mountains, and as far north as Laponia.'

'A well-travelled man.' The sergeant grinned wolfishly at her.

Harry wished Hortense did not have the habit of letting her mouth run away with her.

'He's never French,' the cook declared. 'I heard him in the kitchen.'

Harry's mouth dried. He had not attempted to sound French in the kitchen. He had not thought the two worlds, that of the cooks and that of the guests, would ever collide.

'His English is excellent, as you would expect from his education, and his travels.' Hortense tossed her head, making her wig sway. 'Why do I explain this to you?'

The sergeant put his hand on the cook's arm. 'Let us leave them. I have warned them to stay away from the kitchen.'

He bowed again, and pulled the cook, who still stared at them pugnaciously, away.

Harry, Hortense, and Mustapha watched the sergeant and the cook work their way through the guests, who either entered the Great Room or waited to be introduced to the Queen. A feeling of panic rose in Harry's chest—the sergeant had not returned to his previous spot by the Queen. Instead, he spoke to his colonel, then exited through the vast double doors.

'The man is doubting,' Mustapha observed. 'I think they will return.'

Harry nodded, sure they had been found out.

'Oh no,' Hortense said. 'Now the Queen calls for us.'

CHAPTER SEVENTY

THE QUEEN'S SUMMONS

THE CONVERSATION WAS OPENLY SPECULATIVE. SOMETHING excep-
tional had happened. The Queen had not only stood from her golden chair,
but she had stepped from the dais. She had sent the colonel of Foot towards
the Duchesse de Mazarin. The people parted before him, creating an ave-
nue for him. Already heightened by the reports of plotting, the guests'
senses became even more alert.

They watched as the colonel reached the Duchesse's party, and motioned them to the dais.

They had to make their way through the inquisitive crowd. The Queen
settled herself down again, and stared coldly at Hortense, her husband's
sometimes lover, and once the woman he wanted to marry. The Duke of
York and his wife stared, too.

'Hortense, welcome.' Catherine sounded brittle.

Hortense curtsied submissively, her head almost touching her knees.

'I cannot help but wonder,' Catherine said, Hortense still prostrate before her, 'why you cause such consternation in my household?'

'A thousand apologies, Your Majesty,' Hortense replied, when she had risen again. 'Your cooks found my man in the kitchen. They thought him a plotter. I have reassured them.'

Catherine's eyes narrowed. Her dislike of Hortense was apparent, even to those standing at the back of their audience. 'Why should he go to my kitchen?'

Hortense glanced uneasily at Harry and Mustapha. 'He looked for my dog.'

'You brought a dog?'

Hortense stared at the floor, presenting a facsimile of utter embarrassment.

The colonel coughed into his handkerchief. 'Your Majesty, may I?'

'Of course, Colonel Sackville.'

Sackville stepped forwards, being careful not to step in front of the Queen, and addressed Mustapha, speaking very slowly. 'You know we guard against people with a design upon the Queen's life? That is why my men are in here, and also outside on the road, wanting to protect her from harm.'

'Yes, yes, I know this,' Mustapha said, as meekly as he could.

'Yet, *you* wandered off, away from the other guests.' Sackville's voice was hectoring. 'You went into the Queen's kitchen. Surely you knew you would arouse suspicion?'

'I should have thought of it.'

'You should, boy!' Sackville said triumphantly, as if winning a great debate. He inclined his head to Hortense. 'This is the difficulty, keeping those of his race. Useful for work, but they need constant guidance.' His voice adopted a more reasonable tone. 'Like children, Africans cannot be trusted to think for themselves.'

Hortense made a curious snakelike motion of her neck, and closed the gap between her and Sackville, until they were closer than he found comfortable. Taller than him, she looked down into his eyes. Her own eyes had gone completely black, and her cheeks were flushed with anger.

Mustapha stepped forwards, and to the Queen's and Sackville's great surprise, and that of everyone else close enough to see, he slid his fingers gently into hers. She whipped her hand away from his touch, but stepped back, to regain a more conventional distance from the Foot Guards' commander.

'Please forgive my foolishness,' Mustapha said.

Catherine looked sharply at Sackville. She wished she had not let him speak. He seemed a smug man, and unthinking. Even though she disliked the Duchesse intensely, she saw no need to insult her, or her servant.

'Did you find your mistress's dog?' she asked Mustapha.

'Your Majesty, I did not.'

Trying to remain unnoticed, Harry had stayed back from this exchange, painfully aware he stood in silver silk and with a heart painted on his face. Behind the Queen, and the pompous Sackville, he could discern the spike of the sergeant's halberd coming back into the room, along with its carrier, and along with Captain MacWilliam.

His heart sank.

They would not argue themselves out of this one.

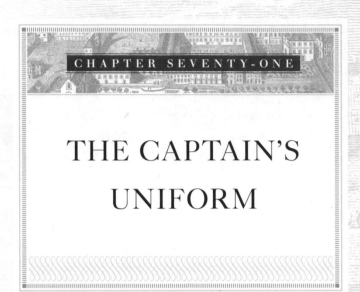

CHAPTER SEVENTY-ONE

THE CAPTAIN'S UNIFORM

MACWILLIAM BOWED TO THE QUEEN, BUT made no such show of deference to Hortense Mancini. 'My sergeant tells me you sent your man to the *kitchen*.' He said it as if she had required Mustapha to swim to Svalbard.

'Alright, MacWilliam,' Colonel Sackville said. 'We have straightened the matter.'

MacWilliam's bow to his commanding officer was perfunctory. 'But who is he?' He pointed at Harry.

'I have explained,' Hortense said hotly. 'My nephew. Monsieur Sébastien 'Espinasse.'

MacWilliam cocked his head back sceptically. 'Is he English? Is he French? Which one, we cannot fathom. I have spoken with the Master. The Duchesse told him her nephew is French. When questioned in French, he answered in French. When spoken to in English, he could make no reply.

Yet when in the kitchen, supposedly to retrieve the Duchesse's man, he spoke English.' He looked directly at the Queen. 'With no Frenchness in his way of speaking.'

'Who is he, Hortense?' By now, Catherine had completely put aside any pretence of formality.

'Your Majesty . . .' Hortense said miserably. 'I cannot lie to you, as I have lied to your men. We seek to protect you, too.'

Harry bowed his deepest bow. 'Your Majesty, I am Henry Hunt. This afternoon, I came with Mr. Hooke, and we searched your house. With you, Captain MacWilliam.'

'God's blood!' MacWilliam stared at Harry's painted face. 'I never would have—' He paled, realising he had sworn in front of the Queen.

Catherine waved off his ashen apology. She took a long look at Harry, only vaguely able to put the two men together: Hooke's malnourished assistant, searching her home for misfeasance, and this man, passing amid them all as a Catholic gentleman.

'You wasted my time this afternoon, with your insistence on machinery,' she admonished him. 'You had the whole household looking for it, distracting us from our making ready. Your search disquieted my visitors, and left them sorely inconvenienced. This evening, you lied to make your way in, arriving in disguise. Captain, escort these people away. Then I can at last concentrate on the Consult. Hortense, we have shared little in the way of friendship. What little there was, is gone.'

Catherine turned her back to them. Two ladies-in-waiting, in colourful Portuguese dress, moved across her, to block anyone from saying anything to try to change her mind.

'The Strand is too busy with protestors,' MacWilliam said. 'We shall take them through the gardens, to the river.' He looked at Colonel Sackville less for confirmation of his plan than daring him to countermand it.

'All very well, Captain,' Sackville said. 'Carry out the Queen's wishes as expeditiously as you are able.'

MacWilliam led the shamefaced group, and his sergeant followed behind them. Crowded around the dais to catch as much of the talk as possible, the other guests made way. Harry, Hortense, and Mustapha had to suffer their looks, unanimously hostile despite most having no clue what the confrontation was about. Word spread from those in earshot. By the time the news reached all the way around the room, most were convinced that these were the plotters of rumour. Surely not the Duchesse de Mazarin? Their incredulity came at the same time as their relief.

They were safe.

The conspirators had been discovered, and were being escorted out.

As they went through the Great Room's doors, Denis Papin made the sign of the cross towards them.

Somewhere, perhaps down in the cellars, Bartholomew Slough was still in Somerset House. Papin and Slough could continue the search, and find Lefèvre's machine.

Following MacWilliam, Harry noticed he wore a different uniform from the afternoon, its coat a darker red. The one he had on earlier must have become shabby in the search.

Harry closed his eyes. He made a fist, and hit himself—hard—on the forehead. He could not believe his own stupidity. He remembered seeing MacWilliam's sleeve smeared with paint. Paint from a wall in the very last room they had searched, an old schoolroom up in the roof. He had been too tired; he had missed it. When so many shortcuts had been made to complete the work for the Consult, why paint a room the visitors would never see? The plastering, also, had been done, and too perfectly. Unlike most of the work, which was rushed.

'Captain MacWilliam,' he said. 'The machine's in the attic. In that schoolroom.'

MacWilliam hardly slowed. 'Enough from you, Henry Hunt. We have heard enough.'

The captain and the sergeant, joined by more Guards coming with them, escorted them out of the rear of the house, through the gardens, down to the river stairs, and saw them all off on board a wherry.

The waterman took them out to the middle of the Thames, where the current was stronger, speeding them east.

CHAPTER SEVENTY-TWO

THE

SHIFTING WALL

ON WAKING, STIFF FROM THE COLD, Grace realized she had rolled over in her sleep. Movement had returned. Her face was pressed into the ground. The damp surface she lay on was covered with tiny stones and shale, the points prickling her skin.

She was able to stretch her back, the sensation as the muscles eased making her cry out. Gradually, by an utmost effort of will, she rolled back over. After a few minutes resting, she managed to sit herself up. It made her sick to do so. She gasped, her lungs filling with the malodorous, foul air.

The smell made her stomach churn.

She listened into the darkness. Although she heard nothing, she was sure there was a presence. Some extra sense could feel another human nearby. Whoever it was—either in the darkness with her or on the other side of a wall, somewhere—did not help her. They just waited.

But for what?

She shuddered at the memory of the man with the single eyebrow and the pointed teeth. His breath had smelled of rusted iron. He had a curious way of looking: unblinkingly, as if to see straight through a person. To expose and to study their innermost thoughts and feelings. Grace wondered if he waited nearby. It would not surprise her if such eyes preferred the darkness, able to see her perfectly well. He did not seem quite human.

What little remained in her stomach rose in her throat. She spat out the bitter liquid, and it splashed over the floor.

She had no sense of the size of place she was in. There was no sign where there was a door—no strip of light around one—or even if there *was* a door. Or, if there was, if it was locked or unlocked.

Although she could see nothing, she decided she had to explore.

Unsure if she could summon the strength to stand, she reached above her, but was suddenly fearful of touching a roof of some kind, suffering panic at the thought. Her hands felt nothing but the clammy air.

Tentatively, she slithered across the earth, still sitting, pulling herself forwards by digging her heels into the ground, then bending her knees. She fought the effects of whatever substance the men had pressed across her mouth. She felt above her head again, waving her arms in the darkness. Touching nothing, she pulled herself up, shakily, to a standing position. She could not quite do it; she had to squat down again, a hand on the ground to steady herself.

She staggered forwards like this, little shuffling steps, one hand extended before her, one on the ground, until she felt a wall in front of her.

When she pushed her hand against it, its surface shifted slightly. She pushed harder, and felt it shift again. She could hear the sound of something sliding against something else. She ran her hand gently down the wall's surface. She touched something rounded. Its texture was rough, and bumpy. Like the floor, it was damp and slimy from being inside this space.

It was one among others. She could feel them, and was able to move more of them.

Other than the sliding sound, still she heard nothing. Her movements had not alerted the presence she felt. Or, at least, it made no response. She pulled at more of the curious objects. One lifted, coming away slightly. It was long. Longer than her forearm. Able to get her fingers behind it, she traced its outline. She pulled at it again, and brought it clear from the wall.

She felt its weight.

She pictured the object she held in her mind. She had seen such things before, shown them by her uncle.

It was a human thighbone.

CHAPTER SEVENTY-THREE

THE INEXPLICABLE SHUDDER

MOONLIGHT ILLUMINATED ST. PAUL'S CATHEDRAL, STILL being built. The Monument to the Fire and all the spires of all the churches were lines of silver jagging a sky full of stars. London Bridge stretched over the river, looking like a giant's cloak thrown across it.

Their wherry rocked over the water's ingress from the Fleet.

Hortense pulled at Harry's shoulder. 'We must try again,' she said.

'But how could we ever get inside?'

'We will find a way. We cannot leave them to their fate, if they are all to be poisoned.' She shivered, not having been reunited with her cloak. Harry was without his coat, and goosebumps rubbed against the silk of his shirt. Only Mustapha still wore his red coat, having never taken it off.

With the hem of her dress, Hortense rubbed vigorously at Harry's face.

The heart on his cheek smudged, and gradually softened away, the powder coming away, too.

'Waterman,' she said, using her most imperious voice. 'The Fleet Bridge.'

Taking the turn into the Fleet Canal was like falling into a hole, it was so dark. Hardly anyone was about, its new quayside almost completely deserted. Only a couple of lanterns carried by lone walkers, perhaps returning home from an Alsatia tavern, could be seen.

The man had to work harder now, taking them against the flow of the canal. Past Bridewell Prison, over a thousand people inside, then Green's Rents, and on until they reached the stairs by the Fleet Bridge. They said their thanks to the waterman, paid him, and walked through the darkness up to Fleet Street.

By St. Bride's, back in use but still lacking a spire, Harry felt a shudder of dread. It skittered up and down his spine, as if Death himself had tapped him on the shoulder. Their proximity to the churchyard, he thought, although he was not usually nervous around such places, even at night.

'Are you well, Harry?' Hortense asked.

Harry stopped to steady himself. The church's black windows seemed endlessly deep, pulling him in.

'I'm tired, is all,' he said to her. Mustapha and Hortense did not believe him, but together they pressed on along Fleet Street, and through the new Temple Bar marking the City's western limit. Despite the threat to London from Jesuit plotters, its posterns were unmanned. All the soldiers were further west, protecting the Consult.

When they arrived at Somerset House, its gates were closed. They could see Foot Guards through the bars, holding muskets with bayonets fitted. The line of soldiers along its front had been swelled by men who previously had patrolled on the street. All the coaches had gone. A small crowd of protestors remained, their clamour more desultory now no guests arrived. Rubbish, and stones unpicked from the pavement, lay strewn on the ground.

'We cannot go in through the front,' Mustapha said, as they walked on past the gates.

'We cannot,' Hortense agreed. 'We are too recognisable. But Harry can. Mustapha, give him your coat.'

Harry swapped his waistcoat for Mustapha's coat, even though it was far too large. It changed his appearance considerably, the bright silver of his waistcoat replaced by dark red.

'MacWilliam might be there,' Harry said, folding back the coat's cuffs. 'He'd know me at once. There's a way in from Duchy Lane. We searched the stores and stables this afternoon. I saw a low wall.'

'The same wall the King scaled for his trysts with the Duchess of Richmond,' Hortense said. 'Be careful of soldiers once you have climbed it.'

The place, when they found it, was obvious. Although not much lower than the rest of the wall surrounding the house, its worn bricks served as easy holds.

'You will need these,' Mustapha said, as Harry prepared to climb. He held out the keys from the kitchen. Having no pocket in his borrowed coat, Harry tied them to his belt, ripping a ribbon from his shirt sleeve to do so. When Harry had mounted the wall, checking over its top for prowling Foot Guards, he waved a farewell to Hortense and Mustapha.

●

FOR THE THIRD time that day, Harry was in the grounds of Somerset House. He would look for the way between the stable blocks and the stores, which he remembered from the earlier search, but it appeared very different in the darkness. He must find Bartholomew Slough, and then Denis Papin, to go with them to the attic. He was positive, now, that the threat was at the top of the house.

He could hear the horses in the stables, made nervous by his movement past them, kicking the partitions between their stalls. He hoped they would not rouse the soldiers' attention, or any of the Queen's household staff.

He reached the end of the stable block and ran to the chapel. Finding a murky shadow where the lights from the house did not intrude, he sat on his haunches, looking across the gardens.

Every one of his muscles begged for rest. It would be easy just to sit here, and sleep. He had tried enough. Just stay . . . hope Bartholomew Slough was wrong . . .

He had almost gone. He stretched open his mouth, moved his jaw from side to side, took a deep breath, and opened his eyes as wide as they could go.

The sound of conversation reached him from across the garden. People obscured by a high hedge. Guests taking the air.

Had the first courses been served? Harry tried to think how much time had elapsed since their ejection from Somerset House. He found it difficult to do so. He had no watch, as his had been taken at the Bastille.

The guests were still alive. Still time enough, then, to find Lefèvre's machine.

CHAPTER SEVENTY-FOUR

THE RETURN

INSIDE

SLOUGH HAD FOUND HIS WAY INTO the cellars from near the kitchen. To reach the same place, Harry had to cross the gardens. He hoped Slough had managed to get himself back out, assuming he had completed his search and found nothing. Of course, like him and Mustapha, Slough may have been seen, thought to be suspicious, and marched from the house. Or, more likely, arrested as another who planned to kill the Queen and her guests.

Looking past the chapel from behind the low wall, Harry perceived the vast scale of the building in front of him. Even if Slough continued to search for the machine, or for Lefèvre and his men to stop them, they might pass each other by in the multitude of corridors and rooms inside.

There was also Denis Papin, though, dressed as a Jesuit. Harry had badly misjudged him; Papin had proved a loyal and dependable ally. What help could he be, though, in a house full of soldiers?

And what of Richard Merritt? Harry had not seen him since before rescuing Mustapha from the suspicious cooks. Was he still inside Somerset House, trying, as he had said, to thwart Danby's plan?

Harry did not like the man, but was that reason enough not to trust him? Perhaps Merritt spoke at least half the truth, self serving as most men's accounts of themselves usually were.

At the top of the stairs leading to the house, two of the King's Foot Guards had been posted outside the doors. Harry would have to get himself past the guardroom, too, where the Queen's Guards were stationed.

The lights from inside striped the lawns. Brightness and darkness, like the bars of a prison window. Harry left the chapel's safety, and followed a dark line, stooping as he walked, hoping the soldiers at the doors would not notice the movement. He reached the house's side wall, where gravel had been laid. Even walking as softly as he could, the crunching of the stones was loud in his ears. He could not believe every guest, and every soldier, would miss it.

He stopped and waited again, expecting to hear heavy boots along the gravel at any moment. When none came, cautiously he moved on, searching for the long low window, the one Slough had used to enter the cellars. The size of the house made it difficult to visualize its interior from the exterior, even after an afternoon of searching it. Harry imagined the walk from the Great Room to the kitchen, and the door to the cellars. It could not be far along.

Something brushed his face, and he let out a reflex cry. It was a mulberry's branch, scratching his forehead. He pushed his way through it, moving aside the branches. There, right down at ground level, was the line of windows he looked for. One had been relieved of its glass, the pane angled against the wall.

Bending down to look into the cellars, he could see a soft light. It moved around slowly as he watched it. He could make out the shape of a man.

'Mr. Slough!' Harry hissed through the opening.

The light moved towards him. Slough had found a lantern in the cellars. His illuminated face, with the Hand of Fatima on his cheek, appeared from the darkness, as he climbed up on a table below the window.

'I have searched these cellars thoroughly,' Slough said. 'I am certain nothing is here.'

'The machine's in the attic, I'm sure,' Harry answered. 'A room up there was repaired, and repainted. Stupidly, I didn't think it strange. I thought you would be gone.'

'Wine is kept down here, and more was needed. I had to hide. What happened to you? You have been an age.'

'We were dismissed from the house by the Queen. I've left Mustapha and Hortense in the lane.'

'You have changed your coat,' Slough observed approvingly.

'And I have keys, one of which, presumably, will fit the cellar door.' Harry jangled them, hanging from his belt. 'Then we may get back inside the house.'

'They have missed their keys. I heard them complaining. We would come out too near the kitchen. You risk recognition by the cooks.'

'The only other way, then, is through the back doors, with the other guests.'

'Mingle in amid them?' Bartholomew asked, thoughtfully. 'No one suspects me, I am sure, for I have kept out of sight.'

'The Master of the Household would remember you being with the Duchesse. We must steer well clear of him.' Harry reached into the cellar's gloom. Slough grabbed his hand, from politeness, and swung himself nimbly back up through the glassless window.

'Let's replace this window,' Harry said. 'In case a soldier finds it.'

Having done so, they returned along the wall until they reached the corner of the house. A group of guests returned from the gardens. They watched them ascend the stairs and go back inside, the soldiers at the doors scrutinizing them but letting them through. Harry and Slough nodded their understanding at one another.

They saw their moment, and left their place of hiding. They waved merrily to a couple walking back across the grass, whose dress pointed to their station as the middling sort, the husband a merchant, perhaps. The couple were with an earnest young man in a long black wig, who held forth upon the calumny of Titus Oates, and expressed his outrage that Parliament saw fit to overlook the glaring inconsistencies of Oates's evidence.

Harry joined them, with Slough following closely behind.

'Oates lied that the Justice, Sir Edmund Bury Godfrey, was taken from here after he was killed,' Harry said loudly, gesturing at the house, 'then placed in a ditch by Primrose Hill.'

The three guests looked at the newcomer in the long red coat who had joined them out of the darkness. Oddly, he had a dwarf with him, holding a lantern.

The young man looked delightedly at them, for they seemed as willing as he to inflate conspiracies. 'Three were hanged for it, and the Queen's chaplain disgraced!'

'I know it to be untrue,' Harry said. 'For I saw him dead under London Bridge, on the Morice waterworks there.'

'That was Sir Edmund?' The merchant's wife looked shocked. 'I have never heard it said.'

'Believe me,' Harry replied ominously, his voice dropped an octave as they reached the steps leading to the back doors. Slough assented with vigorous shakes of his head. 'I was there,' Harry continued, 'and saw his face clearly, before they covered him up.'

The merchant looked aghast. 'They were secretive.'

'As you have it, sir,' Slough agreed. 'It suits Parliament to withhold such information.'

'Keeping it back counts against the Catholics,' the young man added.

The couple looked relieved as the man moved around them, to fixate instead on Harry and Slough, finding them a readier audience. As they stepped through the doors—nodding to the soldiers guarding them, the wife blessing them for their protection—the young man was in full flow, promising Harry that the future would reveal Oates as a pernicious deceiver, and his soul would be eternally damned for his perjuries. Harry and Slough concentrated fully upon him, their eyes never leaving the man's fervent face, as they walked past the guardroom.

Harry knew they must keep out of sight of Captain MacWilliam. Hortense had wiped his face clean, and so the black heart, an obvious marker, had gone. MacWilliam, though, knew him from the afternoon, when he had worn no such covering. The Queen, too, would recognize him. He thought of her stiff anger, convinced he was mistaken about Lefèvre's machine.

He must find Denis Papin. The three of them would try again. They must get to the attic rooms, upstairs, above the Great Room. If poison was to be used, it was meant to descend upon the guests.

CHAPTER SEVENTY-FIVE

THE MACHINE REVEALED

THE LIGHT FROM HIS LANTERN FELL onto smooth plaster. They had finished it perfectly. No one would ever think the boarding concealed machinery. No trace, either, of the pipes descending inside the walls from the tank, through the floor and into the room below.

Richard Merritt cursed. He had moved the teacher's table, but when standing on it, the ceiling was still out of reach, even when jabbing at it with his sword. He swung again, trying to break though, but the sword's tip was at a least six inches short. He looked for anything he could see to close the gap. He shone his light into the attic room's dark corners.

He spied old, musty books: he would pile them up.

He grabbed them, and placed them on the table, to make a precarious tower.

Sweating with effort, although he had taken off his cloak, he climbed back up on the table. He placed his foot on the books, checking if they were likely to slip from under him.

He placed his weight onto the pile; one foot, then the other, and slowly brought the sword up to rest against the ceiling. Convinced he would fall, he was unsteady, but by pushing up against the ceiling through the length of his sword he was able to keep his balance. He pushed more. The point went through the board under the ceiling's apex. He withdrew it, and re-placed it a little further along, stabbing again, making another hole. Each time he made a hole, a finger of moonlight poked through from a skylight the board had concealed.

He had been with Henry Hunt until the younger man told him— arrogantly, he had thought—to wait by the cellar door. Hunt had then returned to the kitchen. Merritt had watched him come out with the black man and a couple of angry cooks. He had followed them to the Great Room, where they spoke with the Queen. He smiled at the mem-ory of the Duchesse de Mazarin being led ignominiously from the Con-sult, her African and Hunt with her. A Jesuit had blessed them as they went, pitying their disgrace.

With the exit of Henry Hunt, it was left to Merritt to set off the poison.

He succeeded in making a series of holes through the ceiling, but needed something to break a larger hole. Then he must raise himself up to the machine, a good twelve feet above the floor. He climbed off his pile of books on the table, and studied the way the beams spanned across the roof. His light flickered across the largest beam stretching over the room's width, the new boarding butting up to it.

He heard applause, muted through the floorboards. Down in the Great Room, a speaker had finished addressing the guests—Merritt could not make out who it was. A male voice, he knew. Perhaps the Queen's new chap-lain, or one of the many Catholic dignitaries invited.

He did not really care. All would soon be dead, if only he could get up to the machine.

That child's desk, looking tiny compared to the table he had stood on, might do to break open a larger hole. He picked it up; it felt absurdly light in his hands. He placed it on the table and stood again on the books. Picking up the little desk, he threw it at the ceiling, up above his head. It crashed into the board, making it reverberate, but not breaking it. He caught it before it fell to the floor. He could not let those below hear him now. He was so close to the end.

Sweat now poured from his face. When he raised the desk above his head again, it was slippery in his hands. He flung it at the ceiling, and this time the desk made a gouge through the board. He did it again. The position was awkward. Although the desk weighed little, his muscles quickly burned with the work. His neck ached from staring upwards, trying to make the desk break down the rest of the board.

Finally, the last piece came down. The machine was fully revealed. Squatting under the roof's apex, fixed to newly installed beams, its tubes spread from it like tree roots. Inside a strong-looking cage, its clock ticked loudly.

But the machine was well above his reach. He rubbed at his slick forehead with his sleeve. Could he pull his bulk up onto the beam? First things first. Find some furniture. Another table, to make a stack he could climb up. Other attic rooms, used as servants' quarters, were along the corridor. Some, like the classroom, had been out of use for years.

Merritt peered out along the corridor. Beyond his lantern's light, all was dark and silent. The soldiers preferred to make a defensive ring around the Queen rather than venture to the remoter parts of the house. He tried the next room along, but its door was locked. The key Lefèvre had given him for the schoolroom did not fit. He tried the next room, becoming impatient, giving its door a harder rattle. Locked, too. He would try one more, then he would start breaking down doors. Henry Hunt must have ordered them all to be locked, after the soldiers had searched the attic rooms.

The next door was at the passageway's end. It was shorter than the others, to fit under the ceiling's slope. He could hear the rumble of another speech downstairs, and he waited until its intonation sounded like it came to a close. These Catholics did like the sound of their own voices. The man, whoever it was, droned on for an age.

At last, a burst of clapping. Using the noise to cover him, he took a couple of steps back, then ran at the door, almost falling through it as it gave way under his weight.

The room smelled dank from water getting in through the roof. Perfect: there was a wardrobe, a simply built thing appropriate for a servant. He dragged it out, the wood scraping along the floorboards. He wondered if anyone would hear. Even if they did, by the time they found their way up here, he would have already released the poison.

He should not be doing this. Danby had assured him. Nevertheless, thinking their plan too intricate, he had been cautious, and remained inside Somerset House. Lefèvre thought Hunt would find the machine. Instead, he had been dismissed from the house.

The wardrobe was tall enough, with the child's desk on top of it, to be able to reach the beam. He placed it beside the teacher's table under the machine.

He thought he heard something. He could not be found out now, not right at the moment of their success. He listened again. Footsteps, definitely, coming up the stairs. More than one man.

Merritt paced to the door. No doubt about it. Three men climbed the stairs. It must be soldiers. He locked the schoolroom door. They might try all the other doors before they got to this one. They would see the broken door as they reached the landing; perhaps that would distract them.

He clambered up on the table, and then, his lungs rasping, managed to climb on top of the wardrobe. Hoisting himself up onto the little desk, he hooked his arm around the beam, and then his foot, his makeshift tower swaying precariously. Pulling his leg over it, he managed to straddle the beam, then shuffled his way along it. Up here, up by the machine, felt far higher than just twice the height of a man. It would make a painful fall, perhaps a bone-breaking one. He shuffled along the beam. He could almost touch the machine. The clock's loud ticking seemed to fill his head.

Someone tried the schoolroom door. Then, after a moment, the door breaking before them, a Jesuit and a soldier rushed in. No: it was not a soldier, as Merritt had first thought, it was Henry Hunt in a red coat, with the Jesuit he had seen downstairs. Behind them, the dwarf joined them, carrying a lantern. Bartholomew Slough.

Merritt frowned, trying to work out how it was that Hunt and Slough came to be together with a Jesuit. 'Mr. Hunt!' he shouted. 'You must help me. I've found the machine.'

Harry looked confusedly up at him, his breath coming in deep gasps after his run up the stairs.

'Is it stopped, Mr. Merritt?'

'I've only just uncovered it. I've no notion as to how it works. It has a clock.'

The clock showed five minutes to ten.

Papin stared at its face. 'Surely, a clock means there is a time set for the poison to be released.'

'Lefèvre said ten, I'm sure of it,' Merritt told them.

'In truth?' Harry asked. 'You didn't say that before.'

'Seeing the clock has returned it back to my mind.'

Papin looked at Merritt distrustfully. 'It may not be set to release the poison exactly on the hour.'

'If you climb up, we may inspect it together,' Merritt said.

'Why did you lock the door, Mr. Merritt?' Harry asked him.

'I thought I heard soldiers. I saw them escort you from the house. I thought they'd stop me.'

'Taking you to be a plotter?' Slough said, stroking the point of his beard.

'We'd take you to be a plotter, too,' Harry said.

'Please, join me,' Merritt replied. 'You're a mechanician, clever in the ways of such appliances. More able than I to save all the Catholics below us.'

'I don't believe you, Mr. Merritt. I think you're here to kill the Catholics. You're here to start the machine.' Harry turned to Papin, who unscrewed the end from his staff, then pointed it at Merritt.

'Come down from there,' Harry said. 'Otherwise, you'll be shot.'

Up on his perch, Merritt sighed. 'You make a great mistake. It's of no matter. You or I must stop this machine. If you don't believe me, then you must do it.' Merritt looked at Papin, almost smiling. 'What's that you hold, which you threaten me with?'

A hole appeared in the beam just above his head, fired silently from Papin's air-gun.

'I was wrong to doubt the weapon,' Merritt said. 'I'll come down.'

Merritt shuffled along his beam, backing away from the machine above them.

'Quickly, if you please,' Slough barked. If the poison was set to release on the hour, they only had four minutes to work out how to disable the machine. 'Harry, I can get up there in a trice. Do you wish me to be your hands, as you instruct me what to do?'

'I'm more used to the motions of clocks, I think. I can get up there.'

Merritt completed the climb down from the wardrobe to the table, and then to the floor. As he brushed plaster dust from his clothes, he looked slyly at them, as if merely caught preparing a mischievous prank.

'Well, Mr. Hunt,' he said. 'You've elected yourself for the role. Now, you must save the Consult.'

CHAPTER SEVENTY-SIX

THE TICKING CLOCK

HARRY CLIMBED FROM THE TABLE ONTO the wardrobe, then on the child's desk, and pulled himself up to the beam. The clock's minute hand moved forwards to three minutes to ten. From behind the clock, a long, narrow pipe led towards the cubic tank and disappeared into a jumble of other pipes. A narrow platform hung next to the tank, giving a place to stand to adjust a row of stopcocks. It hung from two springs, which was curious. While the clock ticked on, there was no time to wonder at that.

Once on the beam, he was unable to sit upright as it was so close to the roof. The moon shone through the skylight, frosting the machine with metallic light. Harry could observe clearly all the tubes running out from the tank, and the way they disappeared into the walls.

Of course, he should have questioned before why the attic rooms had been repaired, as no visitors would go there, but most of the house had been worked on. By the afternoon's end, he was so tired he had too willingly finished the search. If only Hooke had been with him. He would have known immediately that unauthorized work had taken place, high in the roof of Somerset House.

He looked down at Merritt being held at air-gunpoint by Papin. If Merritt was part of Danby's plan, why had he broken down the ceiling? If he had known the machine required its clock to trigger the mechanism, he could simply have left it to release the poison at whatever time it was set.

If that time was ten o'clock, Harry thought, then he must act quickly.

The clock's mechanism was placed inside a metal cage. There was no room between its bars to insert a tool to break it or block it. He looked as far behind the cage as possible, asking Slough to move his lantern so he could see. There was not enough room to access behind it with his fingers, to pull it from the tank it was bolted to. A pipe ran from beneath the clock mechanism to the panel with the stopcocks. He attempted to twist it, but it held fast. He would break it, and run the risk of poisonous gas being released: there was more chance, he decided, to stop the machine if he did than if he didn't.

Now he had just two minutes.

He kicked hard at the pipe. It did not budge. He angled himself across the beam for more force behind his next kick. He tried again, but still the pipe stayed fixed.

Beneath him, the schoolroom's door swung open. Two muskets advanced into the room, one pointing at Slough and the other at Papin. The second musket quickly veered upwards, as the man behind it saw Harry lodged on the beam.

Three Foot Guards had arrived: the two musket bearers, and, behind them, Captain MacWilliam.

MacWilliam surveyed the room, trying to make out what went on there. A Jesuit pointed a stick at Danby's man. The Duchesse's dwarf stood on a table. And Henry Hunt balanced up on a roof beam, near a contraption that mostly resembled a giant metal spider, its legs descending into the walls.

'So, there *is* a machine,' MacWilliam said.

'You found it, Harry,' another man said, entering after the Foot Guards.

'Concealed behind boarding and plaster, Mr. Hooke,' Harry replied, relieved to see who accompanied the Captain and his men. Otherwise, MacWilliam, it could be trusted, would misinterpret his being up there. 'How did you find us?'

'Guests reported noises above them,' Hooke answered. 'The Queen asked me to investigate.'

'You've been here all evening?'

'After our search this afternoon, Her Majesty invited me back. In case of anything unseemly.'

Harry spread his hands at the machine in front of him. 'I would say, that case has arisen.'

Hooke smiled dourly, his grey eyes skating over the tank, and all the pipes, and the clock. 'Have you ascertained the operation of those stopcocks?'

'Not yet.' Harry gave the pipe behind the clock another hard kick.

'Denis points his gun.'

'Mr. Merritt is Danby's man. I think he tried to start this machine, to release poison on those below us.' He pulled at the pipe, trying to uncover how the clock connected to the tank.

Merritt, standing by the map on the wall, Papin's air-gun aimed steadily at his chest, shrugged meekly. 'It was me who told Mr. Hunt of Lord Danby's plan. I told him of the machine, and of its use to poison the Consult.'

At these mentions of poison, the two Foot Guards stepped backwards, both looking fearful. To steady them, MacWilliam snarled at them. 'Stand fast!'

'Don't trust Merritt,' Harry said.

'I shall not,' Hooke said. 'We may consider his role later. Forthwith, we must disable this machine.'

The clock ticked steadily. Thirty seconds to go, before it reached ten o'clock.

'If the clock's mechanism releases the poison,' Hooke said, moving towards the table, 'then I shall join you up there. For my knowledge of clocks, I do submit, is greater than yours.'

'There's no time, if this releases at ten. As Mr. Merritt says it does.'

Harry kicked at the pipe again. This time it groaned, and the metal gave a little. Ten seconds to go. He moved across the old beam, shuffling closer, and tried stamping on the pipe, with as much strength as he could muster.

To everyone in the room, all transfixed to its implacable movement, the clock's second hand appeared to slow as they watched it. Five seconds. Tick, tick, tick, and the sound of Harry frantically kicking at the pipe.

The minute hand moved into place, over the XII.

They waited, all holding their breaths.

Nothing happened.

No clicks or whirrs from the machine. No movement of gears or levers. No release of poisonous gas. Harry's last kick had bent the pipe enough that one more would release it from its mount. He kicked it again, and it clattered to the floor, landing by Denis Papin.

Merritt smiled his slow, ovine smile. 'Lefèvre said ten, I assure you.'

With the pipe gone, Harry could not see how the clock mechanism was joined to the tank. It had no rods or levers hanging from it.

'Is there no connection, then, between the clockwork and the rest of this machine?' Hooke asked Harry, peering up at him.

'None.'

'Curious.'

'Perhaps they had no time to complete it, needing to conceal their work before the Consult.'

'We are saved.' Captain MacWilliam, sweat on his pale skin, looked relieved. 'The machine does not work.'

Hooke was bemused. 'The pipe was fixed securely. We all saw how hard Harry worked to release it. They had time enough for that.'

'Why fix it so well, if there is no purpose to it?' Slough asked.

Harry and Hooke looked at each other, across the height between them, both with raised eyebrows. Why indeed?

'Harry, check the stopcocks, and see what is in the tank,' Hooke directed. 'Perhaps, as there was no reason for the clock, there is no poison, neither.'

Harry inched along the beam, until he had reached far enough that he could swing his legs onto the platform suspended from the tank. Before dropping to it, he looked across the tank's cover. He banged on the metal, which reverberated like a cracked bell. It was thick; hitting it with the side of his fist did not dent it. The top was obviously not a lid that would lift. There were no hinges, or sign of a handle. A neat line of bolts fixed it down, along each edge, as each side had been fixed.

'I can't tell if anything's inside, or no.'

From the Great Room, muffled by the floor, came another round of applause. The speeches continued. More Foot Guards would arrive soon, Harry thought, for MacWilliam had been absent some time.

He pushed himself from the beam and landed on the metal platform. It swayed, the two springs it hung from stretching to accommodate his weight. He leaned to inspect the row of stopcocks, to see if anything controlled them. He reached out to try one, wondering if these, too, were only for show.

As his hand gripped it, a rumble started from inside the tank. He felt the stopcock's handle vibrate, then start to turn. Despite his hold, it continued to turn, and did not stop even as he tried to twist it the other way.

The rumbling noise grew louder. The pipes began to rock against their mounts. Something was releasing through them, dropping down inside them from the tank.

His mouth hanging open foolishly, Harry turned to Hooke. His limbs refused to obey his brain's command to climb up from the platform.

'Harry!' Hooke cried. 'The platform. Its springs—you have released the poison!'

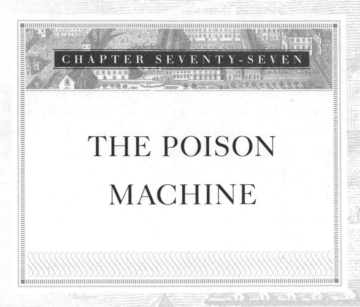

CHAPTER SEVENTY-SEVEN

THE POISON MACHINE

'WHAT BEST TO DO?'

'You must close the stopcocks.' Hooke was not simply telling Harry the brazenly obvious, but, rather, was trying to order his own thoughts. He stood staring up at the machine, fretting with his hands as if washing them.

Frenziedly, Harry tried to twist the stopcocks, but none of them would turn. Having tried them all, he inspected behind them. They were housed in a sturdy metal casing. If he attacked it, it may well release the poison into this room.

The platform swayed as he edged along it. He felt sick and light-headed, but not from its movement or from his fear of heights. It was from the knowledge that his weight on the platform had set off the machine. He steadied himself against the tank, which vibrated as whatever was inside dropped into all the pipes, down through the walls. He put his ear against the metal. Would gas not be silent? If under pressure, there might be a hissing noise. Instead, it was more a rushing, and a rumbling noise.

What happened now, below them, in the Great Room? He listened for shouts, or screaming, but only heard the noise of people talking. They could not yet be aware of what was in motion above their heads.

The machine was operating, and he could do nothing about it. Merritt had known all the while how the machine operated, and had tried to get to the platform to start it himself, after seeing Harry ejected from the house.

No—it could not be. He began to choke.

'Harry, are you unwell?' Hooke shouted, looking desperate. The tank must be leaking.

The two Foot Guards began to retreat, backing towards the door and away from the machine. MacWilliam stopped them, his hand resting on the handle of his sword. He ordered one to find Colonel Sackville and warn all downstairs of the poison. The soldier remaining swallowed and swore under his breath.

'Mr. Merritt,' Harry said, his understanding catching in his throat. 'Was the platform built for me?'

Merritt's expression was bland. 'You were a thread of the tapestry. To think more would be conceited. Lefèvre designed the platform to be set off by a weight. He hoped you would be the one to stand upon it, but it was no necessity. Danby warned against it, thinking his plan too elaborate. I thought you'd start it off—I should have gambled upon it. Your obstinate nature makes you predictable. I'd begun to doubt myself, but here you are. The plan worked well, after a hitch or two.'

'I remember Lefèvre's face, at Billingsgate. He seemed to hold a personal animosity.'

'Do not be too downhearted. He dislikes everybody.'

Harry started to climb from the platform. 'Leave with the soldiers,' he urged Hooke. 'Warn the house. Get everyone out. Mr. Slough, you go with them.' Hooke looked stubborn, and about to protest.

'Go, Mr. Hooke! I'll try to break the machine. There's no need for anyone else to stay.' Harry had nearly reached the beam's end, and he lowered his leg to make the step to the top of the wardrobe.

'Harry!' Hooke's face was nearly white. 'There must be another way. We must think . . . if all the guests evacuate the Great Room, the poison can be left to drop. Let me try the machine. You may have missed something.'

Joining them on the floor, Harry, looking at Hooke, seemed to reconsider. He put out his hand to shake Hooke's. Hooke's hand automatically raised, too. Harry pushed him violently towards MacWilliam.

'Come, Mr. Hooke,' MacWilliam said, catching him and stopping him from falling. 'We must get the guests from harm's way.'

Harry looked at Merritt. 'Lefèvre planned for that, didn't he?'

Merritt smiled sheepishly. 'Of course. There's no leaving the Great Room, now the machine has started.'

CHAPTER SEVENTY-EIGHT

THE LOCKED DOORS

'GOD BE WITH YOU, HARRY,' HOOKE said. 'We treated you badly at the Bell, which I regret.'

'No time for that, Mr. Hooke. And besides, I've forgotten it.'

Slough took his leave, too. 'Good luck to you.'

'Thank you, Mr. Slough,' Harry said. 'You've shown yourself a true friend to me, these last days.'

Hooke and Slough left them, both running along the attic corridor.

'Captain MacWilliam, have you heard enough?' Harry nodded towards Merritt, who observed them all as if for interesting and unusual behaviour.

'I have. He will be hanged for his assistance to these Frenchmen.'

'He carries out the Lord High Treasurer's orders.'

MacWilliam looked discomfited. 'I know nothing of that. Danby may be too powerful a man to answer for this.'

'He should stay here,' Papin said, his air-gun still levelled at Merritt. 'He knows more of this machine than he lets on.'

'I'll say nothing,' Merritt told them. 'I care not whether I'm here, or there. Death awaits us all.'

MacWilliam and his man followed Hooke and Slough, leaving Harry, Papin, and Merritt with the machine.

'Denis,' Harry said. 'You would be more help downstairs, to get everyone from the Great Room.'

'No, the soldiers can do that. I shall stay.' Papin's face was determined. 'Together, we may break this machine.'

'You know the gas will kill us, the moment we inhale?' Merritt enquired politely.

'I do not know it,' Harry answered firmly. 'I'm sure of nothing. Except, I must try to stop it.'

Harry took Merritt's sword and clambered back on the table and up on the wardrobe, onto the child's desk, and back along the beam. Harry could hear the machine's pipes shuddering with movement through them. He banged on the tank again. The metal was too thick to pierce through, he was sure. If Papin used his air-gun against it, then poison might escape through the hole, but would kill them before they could disable it further. He aimed the sword. 'I will try the pipes.'

'If you break one, will you not succumb to the poison?' Papin asked. 'Before you can break the others?'

Harry groaned with desperation.

'We should break a pipe each,' Papin suggested. 'That must slow the poison, at least. If it does not act upon us straightaway, then we may break another.'

Harry gazed feverishly at the new beams placed across the old, with bricks laid upon them, rapidly mortared together to support the tank.

He looked up at the little window in the roof. It was almost directly above the tank. He remembered the scaffolding he had seen being taken to the river stairs, when arriving with Mr. Hooke that afternoon. The house's exterior had been restored, stone repaired or replaced, stucco patched and painted, and much of the roof was new.

The assassins had filled the tank from the roof.

He tried to remember the faces of the men carrying scaffolding, but could not bring them to mind. Perhaps he had walked right past them: the men who had installed this tank, and its pipes.

He had not seen Lefèvre, he was sure, for that man was instantly recognizable.

Harry looked again at the metal cube, studying the way it was fixed. Perhaps if they dislodged the tank from its place, and let it fall to the floor, they could stop its release of poison into the Great Room.

'Can you make your way up, Denis?'

Papin passed the air-gun and the lantern up to Harry. They discounted any danger from Merritt, as he was without a weapon. It no longer mattered to them if he stayed or left the attic. It looked as if he was interested to see how this would all play out, for he leaned against the old map, watching them.

Once Papin had reached him on the beam, Harry stepped back onto the platform. He swayed as the springs adjusted to take his weight. He walked along it, then climbed onto the beam at its end.

'If we kick at these bricks, we may get the tank to fall. If we can tip it, it should drop between these beams.'

Papin looked at the distances between the beams, and the size of the tank. 'I am not sure it will go through, at any angle.'

'I see no other way of stopping it.'

The mortar was not quite dry. A few hefty kicks at the bricks had them loose. They were able to pull them aside, each working on opposite sides of the tank. Iron brackets were bolted into the beams, but with the tank's weight the bolts sheared. Harry's side fell first, the cube tipping. He stepped smartly aside as it descended past him. Papin completed his work on the other side. The cube's corners dropped into the space between the two beams and stuck fast. Papin had been right: it would not pass between them. They pushed at it, but its weight was too great for them. It would not be shifted.

They tried to rock it, getting a rhythm going between them, but it was immune to their efforts.

'Will you help us?' Harry asked Merritt. 'If you do, perhaps you wouldn't be tried so harshly.'

'I would hang, whatever action I choose,' Merritt said.

'Then do the right thing. Help us.'

Merritt seemed to seriously consider it, tapping his finger against his mouth, but then he made a dismissive noise. 'I will see this through to its end.'

From outside, the noise of boots. Someone running up the stairs and along the corridor.

In came the soldier Captain MacWilliam had sent to warn the guests, breathing heavily.

'They're all in the Great Room. The doors have closed, and can't be opened!'

'Who's locked them?' Harry asked him.

The man looked close to tears. 'Well, no one. They seemed to lock themselves. We tried to stop them, but we could not.'

'Who tried?'

'Me, and some dozen Guards. We could do nothing.'

Harry looked at the machine. Was there a connection between it and the doors? There could not be. How would it have been made, through the house's fabric? The doors themselves must have more machinery. He had seen the men working on them. He had been so close to them, but had not given them a second glance.

'Where's Mr. Hooke?' Harry's limbs felt frozen, although he was aware of them trembling. Not only had he started the machine, he had then sent Mr. Hooke to the Great Room. 'And Mr. Slough?'

'I saw Mr. Hooke go in, certainly,' the soldier answered. 'He must still be in there. And the Queen, and the Duke of York. And with them, some few hundred more.'

CHAPTER SEVENTY-NINE

THE FAMILIAR VOICE

THE WALL WAS MADE OF BONES. They felt mossy. Slimy. There were skulls: her fingers probed empty eye sockets. She lifted a jawbone, running her fingers over its teeth. Once, she thought, these bit into an apple, or were shown to a lover in a playful smile.

Grace continued along the wall, picking her way in the total blackness.

At last, the uncountable bones came to an end. She found the rough, more friendly texture of brick. She continued on around, turning a corner, following the wall, looking for a door. She stumbled on the uneven ground, which felt like packed earth rather than tiles, or slabs. Edging along, the palms of her hands sliding over the bricks, she met the first of a flight of stairs. They were stone, and steeply pitched. A short flight, ten steps or so. At the top, she found herself on a little landing, with a rail to either side. Her hand knocked against a doorjamb. She reached for a handle and scraped her knuckles against it.

She gave it a cautious rattle.

'So! You are awake,' said a familiar voice from the other side of the door.

CHAPTER EIGHTY

THE BESTIAL ASSASSIN

HARRY AND PAPIN REDOUBLED THEIR EFFORTS, pushing against the tank. Harry tried to enlist the soldier to help them, but he took a look at them, then at the tank, and backed away, favouring his chances downstairs. His musket caught the door, and it banged shut behind him.

Harry, cursing every god he could think of, set his back to the cube, pushing with his legs, straining to lift it, shift it, get it to drop between the beams. If it fell to the floor it might break open, and the poison would stop its deadly drop into the room below.

Merritt still remained. He stared beyond them, at the night sky through the skylight. It was difficult to tell if he was entertained or not, his face was so unreadable.

Harry had no time to ponder on how the man's mind worked. Merritt was not as other men he knew, who would flee, or panic. Or help, having changed their minds and comprehended the wickedness of murder on such a scale.

In fact, Merritt was not interested in the sky. He had seen the face of Lefèvre. The lantern in the attic room illuminated his peculiar features. The bestial Frenchman observed them through the glass: there was Henry Hunt on the platform, with a Jesuit, trying to break his machine.

Harry transferred his efforts to the beam supporting the tank, which had started to crack when the tank first dropped. He stood on it, and jumped on it as best he could, although the little space above him made it difficult. He did not see Lefèvre until Papin murmured to him, and pointed him out.

Harry pulled himself around the tank, so he could see up to the skylight. The assassin's face was pressed against the glass.

When he saw Harry looking back at him, Lefèvre opened his mouth, miming the action of biting. Harry could see his strangely pointed teeth, and the heavy brow, and Lefèvre's unblinking eyes, black in the lantern light.

Harry felt a shudder go through him.

Papin picked up the air-gun from where he had rested it, and pointed it to the skylight.

'No!' Harry shouted. 'He knows where Grace is.'

Papin lowered the gun.

Lefèvre took this as a signal to open the skylight. They heard the frame creak, and the hinges complaining. He lowered his head through the window, hanging upside down, then twisted his neck to look at them. His eyes settled on Merritt. His voice seemed to fill the room. Deep, with an accent difficult to place.

'Did Henry Hunt stand upon the platform?'

Merritt nodded vehemently, Lefèvre's presence seeming to animate him.

Lefèvre's eyes closed with pleasure. Then they snapped open, to gaze at Harry. 'You, then, have killed all those below. And, I will kill your woman.'

'Where is she?' Harry demanded. 'Where's Grace? She has no part in this.'

'I have given her a part. One she plays well. That of the innocent victim.'

He swivelled his black eyes to Papin and Harry in turn. Each man felt their own fear.

'You will die here, Henry Hunt. But your death alone is not worth the life of my brother.'

Jacques Lefèvre withdrew his head from the attic, and disappeared, across the roofs of Somerset House.

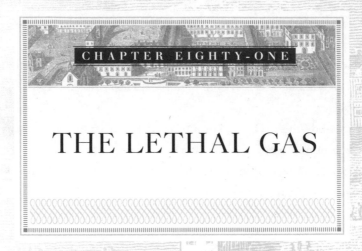

CHAPTER EIGHTY-ONE

THE LETHAL GAS

MERRITT HAD HIS SHEEPISH SMILE AGAIN.

'His twin?' Harry asked.

'Yes, his twin.'

'I thought them the same man.'

'Of course, for their appearance was identical. But in character, quite different. His brother made his way in the world by soldiering and assassination. The designer of this machine is more like you, Mr. Hunt. A natural philosopher. A more *theoretical* man.'

'An assassin, nevertheless.'

'Since his brother's death—for which he sees you as instrumental—he's turned his mind to murder.'

There was no time to think of Lefèvre, or even of Grace being held by his men. But although Harry tried to dismiss him from his mind, returning to his work to stop the poison's escape into the Great Room, his body could not let him forget. After hearing Lefèvre's voice, he shook. And after learning why Lefèvre had constructed the platform suspended from springs. And how he had anticipated Harry's movements: that it would be him who stood upon it, to set off the machine.

Merritt would not let him forget, either. 'Lefèvre has his revenge whether you live or die. If you survive, all these deaths together shall be on your conscience. He would consider that a fair price, too.'

Harry signalled to Papin, and they both kicked again at the beam, summoning as much strength as they could. The wood split, and splintered, and seemed to sag. Harry was sure the tank had tipped a little more.

There could be no doubt: the tank was tipping. The beam split more and began to fold, finally giving way with a shriek of the wood.

The metal cube shifted, then rolled, then started to drop.

A glimpse of Merritt looking up at them, his mouth open, trying to gauge how far he would have to move aside.

With a great smash, the tank landed on the old schoolroom's floor, its pipes pulling free from the wall. The plaster covering them came away, falling in broken shards and clouds of dust.

One of the cube's sides had split. An edge had buckled, and the bolts holding the sides together had given way.

From inside the tank, blue granules, the size of peas, spilled through the rent. As they met the air, each granule seemed to soften and blur, and a blue haze spread from them. More granules spilled from the pipes flailing from where they had been ripped from the tank. The haze soon hugged the floor, rolling across it in a wave, until it got to the walls, and the door, shut when the soldier had left them.

'So, heavier than air,' Harry was able to observe, even as he watched with horror as the blue gas spread across the room.

'The room will soon fill,' Papin said, his voice rasping.

Through the fog, they could see Merritt as he tried to stagger away from the gas. But the gas reached over him. His eyes bulged grotesquely.

His breaths were ragged, his lungs trying to pull for air, but he only dragged in more of the gas. He tried to get to the door, to open it, to escape from the poison, but could not.

He dropped to his knees, retching, his hands waving in front of his face, trying to keep the gas from his mouth.

Merritt knew it was futile, Harry was sure, but still he made the waving motion, an ineffectual flapping, as his breathing stopped.

He twisted, fell forwards, and lay sideways across the floor.

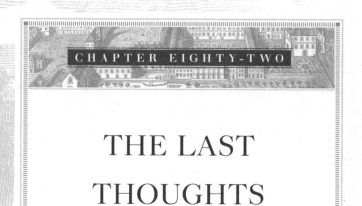

CHAPTER EIGHTY-TWO

THE LAST THOUGHTS

THE HAZE WAS RISING. IT COVERED the old teacher's table they had used to climb up onto the wardrobe, to get to Lefèvre's machine.

Aware these were his final moments, Harry thought of Grace. He had still hoped for a future for them—together—when he saw her at Gresham College. Even if only for a moment, she had warmed to him.

His head throbbed. The gas hung below them—was it affecting his mind already? He could not think what the poison was. He had never seen anything like it.

It had taken them too long to bring down the tank. The same gas must be coiling its way around the Consult's guests. How many of these blue granules had spilled into the Great Room?

How many had been killed already, and how many were still to die?

Harry thought, too, of Robert Hooke. When master and apprentice, their relationship quickly became more like father and son. Hooke would often surge ahead in his thoughts, thinking Harry had kept up. His patience redoubled when aware of his mistake, Hooke would return for him, and coax him along, showing him, explaining again. As Harry had learned what Hooke had to teach, and then to follow ideas of his own, he had detected jealousy in the older man. Harry felt a tender pull in his chest. Hooke was a complicated man, whose desire for Harry's well-being often showed as irascibility.

Harry had been an apprentice to England's greatest natural philosopher. Perhaps the greatest in Europe, for who else but Robert Hooke was so knowledgeable across so many disciplines?

Even at the moment of his death from poisoning, in the old attic schoolroom of Somerset House, Harry felt a swell of pride.

CHAPTER EIGHTY-THREE

THE
BOTTOMLESS PIT

'. . . I USED TO BE AGAINST GOD. Some I knew, especially in the Wars, even denied His existence. Seeing His work everywhere, I could never agree, but I thought Him flawed to allow such pain into the world.'

'What brought you back to Him, Michael?' Grace asked through the door. 'For you became a preacher.'

'Yes. An Anabaptist preacher, which this country's preferred way of religion looks down upon.' The old Colonel's voice was slow, and he kept having to catch his breath. 'Time was a balm, assuaging my bitterness. But I would say, most of all, it was fellowship among people. When with the Levellers, I found such care for one another I could put those darker thoughts aside. For God had created the connection between us. I suppose, besides, that when the peacetime came I was no longer confronted so constantly with suffering. In the Wars, I saw dreadful things. I did dreadful things, too, I cannot deny. They have scarred me as much as the injuries I suffered.'

Grace sat on the landing at the top of the stairs, in darkness except for pale strips of lantern light around the door. Fields had not unlocked it; she wondered if he was too ashamed to face her. She could not believe he had allied himself with the men who had taken her, who must be the same men Bartholomew Slough had sheltered at Oakham, in his previous life as Jeffrey Hudson.

Harry, at Gresham—no way of knowing how long ago, whether hours or days, for her sleep had been deep—had said there was a machine, and that the Queen's life was threatened.

Grace knew why she was taken: to try to make Harry bend to their will.

He would be trying his best to stop them, if he could, she was certain.

'There is a selfish reason I returned to God,' Fields continued. 'Not the least, I am ashamed to say. My loneliness. Being a preacher kept me busy, and kept me from thinking of the blackness that surrounded me. I was too far prone to wander into it. I risked falling into the bottomless pit. In the Wars, towards their end, I had loved a woman named Abigail Creed. Being too fond of the memory of her dead husband, she would never have me, but my love for her brought me back to Him. I thanked God for allowing me such strength of feeling. *Hatred stirreth up strifes: but love covereth all sins.* Ah, Abigail . . . I did not find anyone to take her place in my heart until I met Elizabeth Hannam. After so many years of being alone, I considered myself the luckiest man alive.'

At the end of the Colonel's speech, Grace found her throat was constricted, and tears prickled her eyes. 'That is why you do what you do. Why you went with Harry to the Fens, and then to France. Why you made sure he was imprisoned in Paris. And why you led the Frenchmen to me, to shut me inside this crypt.'

'I am sorry for it, Grace.'

'You betrayed your friends, Michael.'

'I did not lie, so much as guide the truth a little.'

Grace made a sceptical noise: a sharp exhalation through her nose.

'It was partly for Harry's sake I wanted him kept in France,' Fields continued. 'I knew he would seek to stop the plot against the Catholic Consult, and expose himself to danger. Mainly—a contemptible, despicable reason—I knew he would uncover the truth about me.'

'It is true, then, Michael, what I have suspected.'

Fields sounded as if she had hit him in the chest: a sudden escape of air. 'Do you think Harry knows, too?'

'I am sure he does.'

'You cannot tell Elizabeth, for her heart would surely break. Would you give to her a kinder version?'

Grace shifted her position on the cold stone landing. 'When Harry told you of his letter from Sir Jonas, you made sure to accompany him. You wanted to keep him from finding Captain Hudson's killer.'

'You are qualmish, Grace. You cannot bring yourself to say it.'

'I find I cannot.'

'When did you first think it?'

'We were in Cambridge.'

'Even then?'

'Do you remember your story of every town being the same? A river, a bridge going over it, and a church? You told us the Eastern Association was headquartered in the Bear Inn, by Sidney Sussex College. How could you know just where it was if you had never been? Straight after, you made a great show of being lost. I think you realized your slip. When you and Harry had left for Paris, I thought more on it. Of course, I could not know until I heard your voice on the other side of this door.'

'In Cambridge, I was given my orders. From the Earl of Manchester himself.'

'He told you of the Sancy diamond, and sent you after Captain Hudson. You found him, and you murdered him.'

'You speak dramatically, Grace. You forget, it was wartime.'

'Easy words, but this killing always troubled you, did it not? Otherwise, why would you have gone to Norfolk with Harry?'

'To help a friend, could be the reason.'

'That is not the reason. You were familiar with Cambridge. You also knew King's Lynn. The old sailor who directed us to the Kontor, whom we later found to be Japhia Bennett, recognized you, though he took you to be Royalist. Naturally enough, as he had seen you with the Queen's dwarf.'

'This does not constitute proof, even for the King's Bench.'

'You do not address the King's Bench. Here you speak with me.'

'Following my orders, I went to France, searching for Hudson. I discovered him in Paris and falsely befriended him. We returned together, on *Incassable*, as we made our way back to England.'

'You killed him with the cannonball.'

Fields laughed a sad, quiet laugh, sounding to Grace as if he were far away, not merely with the thickness of a door between them. 'Hudson refused to divulge the diamond's whereabouts. I had tried being friendly. I say this for him, the dwarf knew what he was about. He fought hard . . . I never expected such resistance from one so small. The cannonball was in his bag. He swung it at me. An effective way of self-protection, for it broke my arm, which never quite healed straight. I pulled him to the boat's bottom and brought the bag down on his head.' Fields suffered a fit of coughing, which took some time to die down. 'It was wartime. One soldier fighting another. One was defeated, and died. The other, victorious, lived. A tale often repeated.'

'If you truly believed that, you would not have worked so hard to keep from us the truth. Constantly, you doubted Harry's reasoning, seeking to cause him confusion. There must be another reason you kept back your killing of Hudson. You never found the diamond. For Parliament, or for yourself. Is this why your guilt follows you around, like a weight upon your soul? Did you wish for that diamond, avariciously? You did not fail the Earl of Manchester, but, rather, yourself.'

'Surmise, only, Grace. And what of it now, anyways, so long after? My desires as a young man are a historical curiosity only. Why continue to press the matter?'

'Your failure to find the Sancy was why you went with Harry to the

Fens. But why have you joined with these Frenchmen? To keep Harry from you?'

There was a long silence before Fields replied. 'You know, I have a question for you, Grace . . . Have you ever thought Harry to be an angel?'

Even in the dark crypt, Grace almost laughed at the thought. 'I have considered him many things, but never an angel.'

'A Samael. A dark angel . . . or God's instrument, perhaps. I could not believe it when he was to go to the Denver Sluice, the very place I had killed Hudson. Nor when he asked me to go with him. I thought myself already found out. I hoped, through Harry, God might offer me redemption, or at the least, vitiation, but that was not His will.'

'You could have told us at the Sluice you had killed Hudson. As you say, it was two soldiers in wartime. But you dared not admit to it. I think you feared losing what you value the most. Far more than any diamond. You feared losing Elizabeth Hannam.'

Fields coughed again, and loudly cleared his throat. 'In our travels across the Fens, I tried to keep Harry from the scent. I should have been more wary of you, I see. If I had thought of another way, I would have employed it . . . Everything I did, though, only made Harry more keen to find the dwarf's replacement. Even when the Lieutenant Général of the Paris police forbade him from continuing. He is a persistent fellow, angel or not . . .' The Colonel's breathing was becoming ever more difficult. 'A share in the Duchesse's reward for finding the diamond would have brought me comfort in my last days. It would have brought comfort, I hoped, for Mrs. Hannam too . . . No one deserves it more than her, in my eyes . . . It is no matter, anyways. We did not need it, for we had found one another. The thought of losing her, I resisted the most . . . You see, I have no proof, no piece of paper, to say I was ordered to look for the Sancy . . . I doubt, anyways, such a paper would keep me from the noose. The King's Bench would be eager, I think, to try the old Leveller who killed the Queen's dwarf . . . I killed Hudson in a rage, there in the jolly boat, when I discovered he did not have the diamond. I have forever since felt the guilt from it . . . Also, if I could have found a way of keeping the diamond for myself, without Parliament discovering the theft, I would have. The sin of avarice, Grace, is weighty upon the soul. I could declare self-defence, I suppose, as Mr. Hobbes would put it.' Fields started to laugh again, which turned into a furious bout of coughing. 'I have not read Hobbes, of course . . . Harry told me of it . . . Hudson swung at me first . . .'

Grace heard him grunt, with effort or with pain, his breaths rasping, and the sounds of him bringing himself up laboriously.

'*The Lord our God is merciful and forgiving . . . even though we have re-belled against him.* I never knew before . . . where the Sancy was. I never saw it . . . despite all my following Hudson back to England. I had no way of telling if he took it . . . or ever had it.'

Grace leaned forwards in the darkness, pressing her forehead against the door. 'Before? Meaning, you know now?'

'After watching Harry's investigation, I am as near to certain . . . as a man can be . . . when a man cannot be sure the sun will rise tomorrow.'

She heard his faltering footsteps going away from the other side of the door, and from her.

CHAPTER EIGHTY-FOUR

THE HIGH
SKYLIGHT

THE RECTANGLE OF NIGHT SKY FLOATED agonisingly out of their reach. Now the tank was down, there was no way of stretching from their beam to the skylight.

The blue fog lurked around the wardrobe, over half the distance up its sides, waiting for them if they ventured back down. The beams Lefèvre and his men placed under the tank had fallen into it. There was no way of retrieving them, to try to bridge the gap to the skylight.

'I can lift you,' Papin said. 'You could stand on my shoulders.'

'But, then, how shall you get through?'

'You would reach down for me.'

'We both know I couldn't reach you. I would fall back through. Equally, if you reached for me, then you would fall.'

'One of us, at least, can live.' Papin's eyes had grown wet. Harry could not decide if it was at the thought of leaving him behind, or staying to die, or if the haze affected him.

Harry was sure he could smell it, and there was a bitter taste in his mouth. 'I shall lift you, Denis,' he said firmly. 'Perhaps the gas will settle, and not continue to fill this room.'

'Both are doubtful. I will lift you. Then you must find Grace, before Lefèvre kills her.'

'It's you she likes, I think,' Harry said.

Papin looked at him, astonished. 'Me? No, no. You are completely wrong.'

'I'm not blind. I've seen you together.'

'She is my friend. Only my friend. I—' Papin broke off, and stared hard at Harry, but said nothing. Further tears appeared, and he wiped them away angrily.

Harry gaped at him. Enlightenment dawned. He thought of all the times Papin had reached out for him, touched him. He had dismissed it as his Frenchness. As foreign manners.

'Denis,' he said stiffly. 'Get onto my shoulders—'

Glass shattered above them, the noise sudden and shocking. Slivers dropped, spearing through the blue gas and smashing on the floor. Both men ducked, then looked back to the high window. The night sky was momentarily obscured, a silhouette, then the face of Bartholomew Slough appeared.

He gave them a crafty look, and dropped down from the skylight, landing easily on the beam.

'You get onto *his* shoulders, Mr. Hunt! And reach for Mustapha. Afterwards, Monsieur Papin, you may climb upon *my* shoulders.'

Long, strong arms reached down into the roof space.

Using the ceiling's slope to steady himself, Harry put his feet on Papin's shoulders, as Papin squatted down to take his weight.

'Are you on?'

Harry nodded. 'But how will you escape from this place, Mr. Slough?'

'You may watch me, from the safety of the roof.'

Papin stood, straining from the weight, and raised Harry up, his hands on the sloping ceiling's underside. Only the friction of his palms kept him from falling sideways into the fog below, now covering the top of the wardrobe.

Mustapha's hands gripped his, almost crushing them as he pulled him upwards. Harry's stomach lurched as he left Papin's shoulders and swung in the air, his legs dangling and kicking. Mustapha grunted under the effort as he backed away from the skylight, walking on the roof slates. Harry could hear his feet slip, a worrying scraping sound, but he stayed upright.

He was out in the open air, away from the poisonous gas, the sky full of stars. Mustapha pushed him unceremoniously aside as he went back to the skylight and stretched himself through.

Papin appeared, hoisted by Slough, held by Mustapha. He scrambled up onto the roof, looking pale.

'Sometimes, a dwarf is tall enough!' Slough shouted up at them. Harry kneeled down by the skylight, looking at Slough against the blue gas, so thick it looked more like a liquid, spreading languorously, seeming to use the walls to pull itself up towards them. Its roiling surface surrounded Slough's thighs.

'Quickly, Mr. Slough! Climb back up!'

Slough looked below him at his disappearing legs, then uncertainly around him. He gripped the angled roof beam running under the ceiling and eyed the distance to the skylight.

'I cannot do it.' He looked up at them, and shrugged, as if it were no great matter. The fog was as high as his belt. He gave each of them a shake of his beard, and a pretence of a salute.

'You must at least try, Mr. Slough!' Harry shouted.

'If I am to die here,' Slough answered, 'then let it be on first name terms.'

'Bartholomew, you can't just wait for death.'

Slough looked again at the beam. He gripped it, pushing his fingers into the grain, trying to find purchase. He pressed his hands to either side of the beam, and lifted his feet. They scrabbled on the wood. Flush against the ceiling, there was no gap to find a toehold. He looked at them despairingly, his face red and his eyes bulging from the effort to keep himself up on the beam.

'Mustapha, drop me through,' Harry demanded. Mustapha did not think twice about it. He lowered Harry through the skylight, and Harry slid down his arms, until he was held by Mustapha's strong hands. He dangled his legs into the space beneath him.

'Take my feet!'

'I cannot reach them. If I let go of this beam, I fall.'

'Mustapha!'

Mustapha managed a further stretch through the skylight, lowering Harry some more. Harry could not see behind or below him. He could not see Bartholomew.

'A little to the left,' Slough said.

Announced by a sudden weight that stretched Harry's spine and emptied his lungs, Slough launched himself from the beam and grabbed for Harry's ankles.

All three men, Slough, Mustapha, and Harry in between them, roared with the effort of keeping their chain together. Harry was swinging, and Slough hung from him. Slough managed to grip higher up his legs and lock his arms around them. Harry prayed his silk breeches would not give way, and that Slough could keep a hold.

Mustapha gave another roar, backing away from the skylight. Papin wrapped his arms around his waist and pulled him. Harry's head drew level with the roof, and again he was out in the night's cool air. Mustapha and Papin pulled Harry, with Slough still attached, out from the poison-filled room.

Sitting on the steep angle of the slates, Slough straightened his clothes and nodded to each of them.

'Thank you,' he said. 'Now, we must get to the Great Room, and open up those doors.'

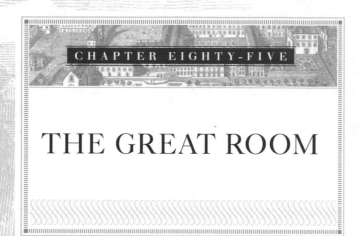

CHAPTER EIGHTY-FIVE

THE GREAT ROOM

FOLLOWING SLOUGH ACROSS THE ROOF, HARRY'S borrowed shoes offered precious little grip on the slates. Mustapha, at one perilous point, had to grab him by the elbow to steady him. Getting to the balustrade across the front of the house, after looking to check he had reached the right place, Slough sprang over it. Suspending himself nonchalantly by a hand from a gargoyle, he motioned for them to follow, and began the climb down. Less eagerly, the others went after him. Harry was sure the gargoyle, old and weathered, shifted in his grip. He forced himself to breathe naturally, instead of the quick ragged panting he wished to do.

Patiently showing them footholds in the stone, Slough pointed out their route. Harry dared not look at the drop to the courtyard, as he traversed a window ledge to reach a shutter, which allowed a swing across the void to projecting cornerstones. His wig was dislodged, and it fell to the ground. He had forgotten he still had it on.

'Like a ladder,' Slough assured him, as Harry prepared to descend the corner of the house. Slough was up and down and across, showing them where to go, urging more speed from them as they gingerly felt for footholds, or rammed their fingers into lines between the bricks.

After a careful walk across the last slope of roof, which served to keep the rain from the main entrance to Somerset House, they dropped to the welcomingly solid ground. Looking as grey as he had been aboard the *Luz de la Luna*, Mustapha looked most relieved of all.

Harry was gratified by the way his body had not let him down. Since his flight from the Bastille, it seemed, the limiting fear of heights had subsided, becoming a more commensurate respect.

No soldiers blocked their way. All must be inside, either trapped in the Great Room with the guests, or trying to break in to release them. Harry, Slough, Papin, and Mustapha all took weapons confiscated from the guests on their arrival from an iron chest by the door. They entered the house, running through the hall towards the Great Room, to be confronted by the sight of cooks hacking at the enormous doors with cleavers and knives. So far, the timber, although scarred, withstood their attack.

'Someone changed the lock,' one said, wonderingly.

'Where are all the soldiers?' he asked a cook, who had managed to break a handle from the door using a meat hammer, and now stood holding it, knowing his efforts had done nothing towards getting them in.

'Most are in there.' He pointed at the doors. 'Some are gone upstairs, to the balconies. Again, all the doors are locked.'

'There's been shouts of poison,' another cook told him. 'From inside.'

Harry did his best to listen for sounds from the Great Room, but it was difficult with all the banging of kitchen utensils. He could hear no sounds of screaming against the door, as people pushed to get themselves out. Was there a room full of corpses on the other side?

He had witnessed the speed of Richard Merritt's death.

He searched for the hinges, wondering if the doors could be lifted from them, but their knuckles were inside, the doors opening inwards.

The cooks spread their efforts over the doors, going at them across their surfaces, bashing and stabbing wherever they could reach through the crowd.

The head cook stood a little way back, holding a vicious-looking knife. He had given up using it against the door.

'Direct your men's efforts at one part, only, of the door,' Harry suggested to him. 'Around the lock.'

The head cook looked at him suspiciously—was something familiar about this newcomer?—but saw the sense in what he said. With a few words to his murderous-looking men, he ordered them to reorganize.

Soon, pale wood opened up from their more concentrated efforts. They all gouged at the new scar, and levered in their blades, until the wood began to separate. An old door, made of hardest teak, it put up stiff resistance, and as cooks fell back, exhausted, they were replaced by more behind. Asking them to step aside, Papin used the remainder of his ammunition, firing with his air-gun at the hole. As the scar became a split, turning into a hole, they all started kicking at the door. At last, it began to move, and shake in its frame. Encouraged, they redoubled their efforts. Finally, the wood splintered with a great cracking noise, and one of the doors swung open.

'Stay back!' Harry commanded. 'The room's full of poisonous gas!'

It crept towards them, out into the corridor: a blue, thick haze, menacing, spilling through the widening gap. A glimpse into the room told Harry nothing. All he could see was murk.

'Don't breathe it in. We saw a man die.' Harry, like all the other men, backed up along the corridor, keeping out of the deadly cloud's reach. It uncoiled itself at them, like a creature unrolling itself from sleep.

They continued to back away, Harry thinking it a mistake to release it into the rest of house. They retreated almost to the kitchen. But the level of the blue gas, at first the same height as the top of the doors, was definitely dropping. Its sluggish speed slowed further until, almost imperceptibly, it came to a stop.

'Open every door and window,' Harry said, to no one in particular. 'Go to the laundry. And the bedrooms. Fetch as many sheets as you can. And where are all the dustsheets, which covered the furniture during the works? We can disperse this cloud.'

Looking back down the corridor, he saw no one had yet emerged from the Great Room. No one staggered out, coughing from the poison. He urged the cooks on, but in his bones he knew it was fruitless. The gas had done its work and killed everyone inside. He choked down an involuntary sob. It stuck in his throat. All those lives, including the Queen—but it was Robert Hooke's whose death affected him most. Harry would miss him dreadfully.

Their efforts to break the machine, and to escape the attic schoolroom, had been for nothing.

The sounds of windows clattering open, and every external door, and then the sight of cooks wafting sheets, cheered him slightly. If they could save just one life, if only one person in there had survived because of their preventing the drop of more poison from the tank, then all their trouble was worthwhile. And, he reflected, he could have done nothing else: his actions to try to save the guests had been a moral requirement of him.

The cooks had tied cloths around their faces, wetting them from the kitchen taps. None knew if it was an effective stop to the poison, but it seemed the thing to do. The bravest ran at the cloud with their sheets. The blue gas was definitely thinning, although slowly, the draught from all the windows encouraging it across the floor and transporting it out to the gardens.

As men started coughing from the effects of the poison, they moved back into fresh air, to be replaced by more men from the kitchen. Some other servants had appeared, and the soldiers who had stayed outside the Great Room joined them, too. They had not managed to break through the doors onto the balconies. All were solidly bolted. Shooting at them had done nothing, nor slashing at them with swords. Even breaking furniture against them had yielded no success. So, they had gone back downstairs to help the cooks, to find them battling the fog with sheets.

More sheets were fetched. The blue haze started to clear. The movement of air through the house was sucking it from the Great Room, and men chased it along the corridor.

It cowered against the floor as it retreated.

At last, Harry could return to the doors, one now wide open. Inside, a faint blueness still hung, like a fine mist on an early morning, but he decided to risk going in. He, too, had placed a wet cloth across his mouth, with no real certainty it would protect him, but urgency propelled him forwards, into the room where the Queen had held her calamitous and tragic Consult.

None had died by the doors, crushed up against them in their panic to flee. The enormous floor, too, was empty of bodies. Across the room, chairs and tables were knocked over. Food and drink had been spilled.

Where were all the people? The room had been crowded full. Where was Mr. Hooke?

Tendrils of mist clung around the pillars. The carved animals all stared stupidly, oblivious to what they had witnessed: mice, weasels, ferrets, minks, and pine martens, balancing on the carved branches they climbed along.

Holes in the ceiling showed from where the poisonous blue granules had descended.

Behind him, he heard his friends Bartholomew Slough, Denis Papin, and Mustapha. Some cooks, servants and soldiers came in, too, their work clearing the haze all done. They looked around them, turning to see each part of the room. Looking to find the guests.

Where were they all?

As they reached the room's centre, treading cautiously, worried about the remaining mist, and ready to run back outside if they began to feel unwell, they heard the sound of clapping. Someone else starting to clap, too. And then, someone else.

More clapping. It came from above them, from the balconies. As they looked up, people started to stand, showing themselves over the rails.

Soon, they could see four hundred people or so, all standing and clapping them. The noise of cheering started, then became so loud it hurt their ears. The guests stamped their feet on the balcony floors, and thumped their hands on the rails, so the noise became thunderous.

Harry spun around, desperately searching the balconies to each side of him.

There, standing next to Queen Catherine, by the Duke of York and his wife Mary, clapping as hard as the rest of them, was Robert Hooke.

CHAPTER EIGHTY-SIX

THE HEARTFELT THANKS

ON REACHING THE GREAT ROOM, HOOKE had first looked for the ladders the men had used for lighting the chandeliers. To the guests' bemusement, he asked Foot Guards to carry them in. Some even thought they were to be entertained by an experimental trial.

From the tank's positioning up in the attic schoolroom, Hooke supposed that whatever the poison was, it was designed to drop upon them. He reasoned, therefore, it must be heavier than air, although he had not foreseen it was in the form of pellets, which reacted with the air to release gas.

As he came in with Captain MacWilliam, Bartholomew Slough having decided to try outside the house, the doors had slammed shut. No number of guests pulling at them could make them move.

Hooke had been right, though: the gas had stayed at ground level, as it had in the attic. It spread slowly, first covering the floor, then finding the walls, before it began to rise on itself.

When the pellets began to rain down upon them from the ceiling, the guests had started to panic. Hooke told the Queen what was happening. It was she who commanded the guests to begin an orderly climb to the balconies. At the foot of the ladders, though, in their fear, they had fought for position. MacWilliam and his men ensured a more orderly progression to escape the cloud forming at their feet.

'You saved them all, Mr. Hooke.'

'No, Harry. I did not. The poisonous gas almost reached the balconies. It billowed just below us. If you and Denis had not broken the tank when you did, the room would have filled entirely, killing us all.'

'Jacques Lefèvre was too meticulous. He judged how much poison he needed to fill the Great Room, without allowing for any to be lost.'

'Jacques Lefèvre? Not Pierre?'

'There's no time, Mr. Hooke.'

If he had let them, Harry would have been personally congratulated by every one of the Consult's guests. Queen Catherine began to apologize for doubting him, and to thank him, but he politely shut her off.

He had to find Lefèvre, for he still held Grace.

CHAPTER EIGHTY-SEVEN

THE SHIVERING
WOMEN

BACK OUTSIDE SOMERSET HOUSE, THE AIR was cold on his skin. Harry had spent most of the evening sweating, and now the night made him shiver. He stood in his silks and his silly shoes, which had caused blisters on his toes.

'What will you do now?' Slough asked. Papin and Mustapha were with him, too.

'Jacques Lefèvre came back. He wanted to know if his scheme had worked—that I'd set off the poison. If I had not, he would have done so him-self, I'm sure, from through the skylight. He will want to see, also, if the Queen's guests have been killed. He's not far away, I'm sure of it.'

'Grace could be anywhere in London,' Papin said.

'She's close. I know it.' Harry's words portrayed more confidence than he felt. He had *known* he would die in the attic schoolroom. He had *known* all the guests of the Consult were dead. But, thankfully, he was proved wrong. Was this a different sensation, then? Another quality of knowledge? He *knew* Grace was nearby. Was it not just hope that told him so?

Papin looked doubtfully at Slough, who turned away. Mustapha looked to be the only one who believed what Harry told them.

Harry began to walk, and his friends followed him. The moon was so strong, it brightly lit the courtyard. They could each see each other clearly. He turned back towards Somerset House, half expecting Lefèvre to still be up on the roof, perhaps next to a gargoyle. Was that the gargoyle he had gripped on? Harry could not remember the way they had come. Looking back at it, that they had managed the descent seemed impossible.

They left through the front gates, going out to the Strand. All the protestors had gone. The road was almost deserted, apart from an early coach arriving to return guests from the Consult, its driver unaware of what had occurred inside. None of the Queen's guests had yet left, still inside busy reliving their almost-deaths, and their seemingly miraculous rescue, recounting the events of the night in wondering tones, reinforcing its truth by the retelling.

On the opposite side of the road, a couple of women waited, shivering as Harry did. They looked as though they would do better up by Covent Garden.

Harry crossed to them. They eyed him shrewdly, wondering which of them he would ask for. Perhaps, being a gentleman, both of them together. This one had already made a night of it, his wig lost, his coat creased and dusty. He could do worse than finish it with them. Companions with him, too, although one was a dwarf, and one a Jesuit. And an African, who was admirable.

'Have you seen a man who looks peculiar?' Harry asked them, after pleasantries were exchanged. 'You would know what I meant if you had, for there's no mistaking him.'

'We've seen no one this past quarter hour,' said one of the women, a little older than her companion, although both were young. Between her patches, Harry thought, she was pretty. 'We await the end of the Consult.'

'Who was it you saw, a quarter hour ago?'

The other woman huffed at the waste of her time. Her friend though, looked at Harry more interestedly. He had no wish to use them, it was obvious, so no money to be had, but she liked the way he spoke to them. As his equals, with none of the usual airs of his class.

'The last person I saw was a lady. I recall her, for she waited on her own.'

'In a turquoise dress? And a big white wig?'

The girl was nodding. 'You know her?'

'I do,' Harry said. 'When she left, which way did she go?'

The women both gestured eastwards, towards the Temple Bar and Fleet Street.

Having thanked them, Harry recrossed the road.

What had made Hortense leave along Fleet Street? She lived in St. James's, so she had not gone for home.

'Hurry,' he said to the others. 'Let's follow on.'

Earlier that evening, after he was ejected from Somerset House with Hortense and Mustapha, he had returned from the wherry ride to the Fleet Canal. By St. Bride's church, he had felt an inexplicable dread. The sudden sensation had made him feel dizzy, it was so intense.

His pace increased.

'Where are we going?' Papin asked him, moving faster to keep up.

'It's difficult to explain—it's unphilosophical of me—but I'm certain Grace is nearby.'

CHAPTER EIGHTY-EIGHT

THE UNPHILOSOPHICAL FEELING

ST. BRIDE'S CHURCH ROSE ABOVE THEM, just behind the Bell tavern, where Harry, after his failed experiment, had drunk too much with the Fellows. They had mocked him. Even Mr. Hooke. Harry's pride had been so injured, he had resolved to leave the Royal Society for the Board of Ordnance. If they had not laughed at him, perhaps he would not be here to-night. Grace would be safe, and he would be with her. Perhaps, also, Harry thought, four hundred Catholics at the Queen's Consult would be dead. Who knew how events would have rolled on, one from another, like a ball hitting another on a billiards table, to send it on its way?

As they approached the church, Harry felt none of the dread he had experienced before, but only the conviction he was right. Robert Hooke had spent Harry's apprenticeship teaching against such sentiment. It was not the way of the New Philosophy to rely on intuition, but on the evidence of the senses. Knowledge of the world must be grounded on observation, not mystery. On that which can be measured, and counted, and witnessed by others. That was what the weekly demonstrations at Gresham College were all about.

Mr. Hooke, Harry knew, would seek to explain away his feeling. As something in his mind, something he had witnessed without realising, which led him to believe Grace was inside.

It was of no matter. Harry had to look somewhere: the sensation was as much of a guide as he had been given, wherever the source.

He heard a noise ahead of him, and put out his hand for the others to stop. He listened intently, hearing only his breaths and those of his friends with him.

'There was a sound, from by the door,' he whispered.

'I heard nothing at all,' Slough replied.

'Let us look,' Mustapha said.

'Mustapha?' A voice came at them from the darkness.

'Mistress,' Mustapha replied.

'I left the Great Room to look for you, after Mr. Hooke came in,' Hortense told them, appearing from the church doorway. She had taken off her wig, for it made her too visible. 'I saw a man descend from the roof of Somerset House. I followed him here. He disappeared. I have been around the church.' She looked at them. 'It was the strangest thing. I could see him clearly ahead of me. Then he was gone.'

'Inside the church, do you think?' Harry asked her. Hortense looked a little ashamed, Harry thought.

'I did not go in.' She reached for Harry's arm. 'He stared at me. He did not blink. He made me afraid.' She sounded amazed. She was unused to being afraid. 'The way he climbed down the wall of Somerset House was not natural.'

'You should have seen Mr. Slough,' Mustapha said.

'What of all the people there?' Hortense asked. 'Did you find the machine?'

'Yes, we found it.'

'Harry saved them all,' Papin told her.

'Mr. Hooke saved them all,' Harry said. 'And you did as much as me in that attic room, Denis.'

'You are modest,' Slough observed. 'I intend to tell everyone of my part in the saving.'

'We must find Grace,' Harry urged them. 'Lefèvre threatened to kill her. Come. Let's go inside.'

CHAPTER EIGHTY-NINE

THE BLINDING

LIGHT

SITTING ON THE STAIRS, GRACE HAD become colder still. The cold, though, had at last chased away her lethargy after her kidnapping.

How long would they keep her here, down with the bones of the dead? Surely, if they wanted her dead, they would have murdered her when they took her from Gresham?

If Harry had thwarted their plans to harm the Queen and her Consult, then what would they do with her?

She had heard nothing more from Michael Fields. Repeating her pleas to release her from the crypt brought no answer from him. She rattled the door, but again, he did not respond.

Back in her thoughts, unbidden, a picture of Harry arrived clearly in her mind. She felt her throat tighten. Would she ever see him again?

Grace knew Harry better than anyone. Even her parents kept themselves opaque. Conducting the duties of parenthood, their desires and feelings on the world were largely hidden from her. Her father, mayor of Newport in the Isle of Wight, had managed to conceal his melancholy until suspending himself from a rope. Her mother suspected the expense of being mayor had forced his choice, and he had incurred secret debt. Grace knew her uncle had loaned money to help him, but could not save him from himself. Uncle, too, was a private man. He wanted what was best for her, she knew, but his vision of her benefit was not the same as hers. He acted from duty to his family, insisting on making a suitable match for her. It was as if she was his property, to dispose of to the highest bidder.

Now she was imprisoned in a cold dark crypt by Frenchmen, with the help of Michael Fields, who she had supposed to be her friend. It was as if her body were never hers, used and bartered with by others. By men.

Harry was freer with his thoughts. Willing to share his own self with her, he also showed her the great respect of listening. It was astonishing how few men did. Denis Papin took pains to listen to her, but selfishly. Sooner or later, he always steered the topic back to himself. For he was anxious. Anxious for someone he could never have.

Someone she would never want him to have.

Harry cared about her thoughts, but not for the effect they had on him, as most men did. He did not need her to be a human mirror to reflect a satisfactory version of himself to himself. He seemed endlessly fascinated by her motivations and desires, and could be tireless with his inquisition. What were her responses to this sensation, or notion? He wanted to know how she experienced the world. It could feel suffocating, all his attention on her. Sometimes, it felt as if he studied her like a knickknack in the Royal Society's Repository, along with the fossils and the shells and the shrunken heads.

If she did ever see him again, she promised herself, she would let him study her as much as he wished. She was so very sorry they had argued. Harry's behaviour with the Duchesse had enraged her. Through fear of losing him, her rage had led her to cut out of her life the one thing she wanted the most.

Footsteps. If the Colonel had been gone, now he was back.

'Michael?' She said it through the door, her sudden doubt making her voice quiet.

The footsteps stopped, and then there was a scrape as feet turned on the tiled floor. More footsteps.

They approached right up to the door. And then they stopped again. She could hear conversation, but too quietly held for her to make out the words.

Grace inhaled sharply, then held her breath. She noticed her hands trembling.

'Who is there?' she demanded. 'Will you release me?'

The talking stopped, but there was no reply to her. The silence from behind the door became oppressive. As well as her hands, her arms and her legs now shook. Why should she feel so fearful? It was the doubt. The not knowing. She would be far calmer if she knew she was about to be killed.

A key was inserted into the lock, and she heard the noise of its turn. She backed away, her foot reaching for the first step.

The door opened, a rectangle of blinding light as a lantern swung into view.

As the pain from the brightness faded, and Grace's eyes adjusted, she could make out a man's silhouette. She saw it was one of the men who took her from Gresham and brought her here. The man who seemed to be their leader. The hairy one, with the heavy brow and the sharp chin.

He stepped onto the landing above the stairway leading down to the crypt.

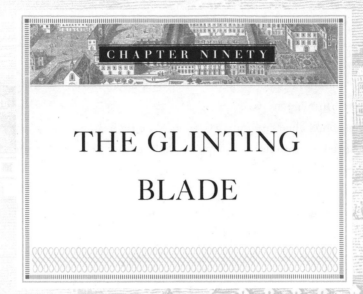

CHAPTER NINETY

THE GLINTING
BLADE

EVERY MUSCLE IN HER BODY QUAKED. She felt light-headed, as if she would fall.

Lantern light cast a sickly yellow over the bones: hundreds of skulls and thighbones, precisely stacked against the walls. To be resurrected at the End of Days, some remains must survive. Skulls and femurs, lasting longest, were the bones taken from graves, to be stored inside the crypt.

Not as big as Grace had thought, the room for all these bones. She could tell where she first bumped into them: the thighbone she had handled lay on the floor. Frantic for a way of escape, she looked for another doorway, but there was none. She would have to get past the man now descending the stairs. But up them were two more of his men, presumably, and also Michael Fields, who had aligned himself with them.

The lantern was so bright it made the man's face look like a shadow, but she caught sight of his strangely pointed teeth, none touching its neighbour.

She must control this shaking.

Although he was not tall, and not wide, the man looked muscular, and in the graceful way he moved, he exhibited an intimidating power.

He reached the bottom stair, then paused again. Perhaps he had not been here before, for he lifted the lantern to light the whole of the room. Or else he did it sadistically, to reveal to her all the bones.

Her vision blurred. She wiped the water from her eyes. She would not cry in front of this man.

He stepped forwards, coming directly towards her. When she had backed up to the wall, no further room to retreat, he placed his lantern down.

'Will you let me go?' Grace asked him, her voice shaking as she shook. She would not let him take her again without resisting him.

'Not possible,' Lefèvre replied. He reached to his waist and withdrew a knife from the sheath at his belt. One way, then the other, he turned it in the lantern light, to show her the blade. He moved towards her, the final step he needed to cross the gap between them. Grace pressed herself against the stack of bones, dislodging some, making them clatter to the floor.

She registered a last glint of the blade as he raised it high above him, holding it in both hands, then he thrust it down to her head.

Steel immediately hit bone, going into skull, and continuing through, the full length of the blade.

Holding it by the eye sockets, Grace nearly dropped the skull she had grabbed, but managed to keep a hold until his thrust was complete. Lefèvre grunted when she turned the skull aside, twisting the knife from his grasp. By the full extent of his strike, he was unbalanced. Grace reached again to the wall of bones and took another skull. She brought it down onto Lefèvre's head as hard as she could, hitting him so forcefully the old bone shattered. The skull flew from her grasp, stinging her hands.

Lefèvre, on his knees as if in prayer, looked up at her, his expression a dazed surprise.

Grace took a femur and swung it at his temple. He went down, forwards, his face smacking the hard floor. She heard the break of pointed teeth.

Keeping a firm grip of the bone, and picking up Lefèvre's lantern, she edged around his body. Expecting him to jump up. To attack her again.

But there was no movement at all, except of his blood seeping over the crypt's floor.

CHAPTER NINETY-ONE

THE BRIGHTEST ORANGE

LOOKING BEHIND HER TO CHECK LEFÈVRE did not stir, Grace climbed the stairs. Cautiously, she went through the door, passing into a little vestry under the church's eastern end, beneath its tower.

When she emerged from the vestry, she saw moonlight shining through the church's circular window, spilling silver over the galleries and columns. In the quietness, she was sure anyone would hear her on the tiles. She removed her shoes, so her footsteps fell as lightly as possible.

Staying to the safety of the shadows, she crept under the gallery along the west wall, past the steps twisting their way to the pulpit, and tried to keep out of sight from the nave. Not knowing the church, she had to guess where its doors were. They might be locked when she tried them. She could not bear the thought of being shut in again, with the bestial man still down in the crypt.

The rows of pews, simple oak benches, looked eerie with moonlight across them. Grace scanned along them, searching for any sign of the other men she had heard.

The outline of a shoulder appeared, belonging to someone in a pew across the aisle. The rest of him—from his size, she was sure it was a man— stayed in the shadows. She squeezed her eyes shut, then opened them again. The shoulder, which had been moonlight-silver, had disappeared. She stared at where it was until the cloud moved on.

Visible again. Then, the side of his face.

He must be able to see her from there, Grace knew, but he made no movement.

What best to do? She almost smiled, knowing she had caught the phrase from Harry.

If the man saw her, he could easily leave his pew to block her off. Could she run to get past him? She had a weapon with her: the thighbone from the crypt. She clutched it tightly, prepared to swing it once more.

The man made no movement at all.

She crossed the aisle and edged along the row of pews. The moonlight faded, then strengthened again, the light playing over the man's head. Over his ear, whose top was missing.

Looking sadly at him, she put out her hand to his face. The skin was cool to her touch. His eyes were wide open. She turned to see what his last view had been. Through the window, above the communion table and its raredo, she could see the moon; the cloud separated its light, so silver be- came all the different colours in a rainbow.

The orange, she thought, was brightest. She hoped the old Parliamen- tarian had seen it so.

She sat next to him, and clasped his hand.

In Fields's other hand was his *Book of Common Prayer,* given to him by

Elizabeth Hannam. It was now battered by his travels with it, and dog-
eared where he had folded corners back. His stout index finger separated the
pages, and she took it from him to see where he last read.

> *Dearly beloved brethren, the Scripture moveth us, in sundry places, to
> acknowledge and confess our manifold sins and wickedness, and that we
> should not dissemble nor cloke them before the face of Almighty God our
> heavenly Father, but confess them with an humble, lowly, penitent, and
> obedient heart, to the end that we may obtein forgiveness of the same, by
> his infinite goodness and mercy.*

Grace still sat with him when Harry, dressed oddly in a red coat far too
large, and her friend Denis Papin, dressed in Jesuit black, and the Duchesse
with her man Mustapha all arrived.

And someone else she had never seen before: a little man dressed in a
fine silk suit, who had a curious tattoo on his cheek. A palm of a hand, like
an exhortation to stop.

Even by moonlight, she thought, you could tell he had a pleasant face,
belonging to a good man.

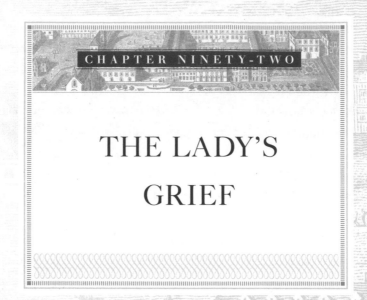

CHAPTER NINETY-TWO

THE LADY'S GRIEF

'I DON'T BELIEVE YOU,' ELIZABETH HANNAM said, tipping her head up and away from him. She sat opposite Harry in her withdrawing room. Her colour was high, and she was breathing heavily.

'I'm so sorry,' Harry replied. 'But it's true. He was found in the church of St. Bride's. As Godly a place as anyone could wish. Sitting on a pew, looking through its window. His age, I suppose, and his lungs.'

'Why did he not return straight home from France to me?'

'I still don't understand why he was there.' Harry reached out to touch her hand, but she snatched it away. 'I wish I'd never asked him to come with me, when I went to meet Sir Jonas. And I wish he'd never agreed to do so.'

Elizabeth's eyes shone wetly. Michael Fields would have been her husband. She had worried after his return from Norfolk, as his breathing and his cough had worsened, and she worried more when he left again for France. Again, in his kindness, he had put his own frailty aside, wanting to help Harry. His decision to go had killed him.

'The body we went to see proved to be a Captain Jeffrey Hudson,' Harry went on, 'a loyal servant of the last Queen, Henrietta Maria. Hudson was killed for a diamond he had stolen from France, during the Civil Wars. Michael helped me look for it, in the flooded ground by the Denver Sluice. I should never have allowed him to do so, for afterwards his health was badly affected. He was no longer the young man he used to be. He forgot that, I think, when we travelled together. When we went to France, he became ever more frail. I had to leave him behind in Paris when I came back, for there was some urgency to my return.'

Harry had shown little care, Elizabeth thought bitterly, using Michael as an instrument to help him do the Board of Ordnance's work. Perhaps, after a while, her anger towards him would soften, as her pain after Michael's death lessened. But that, she knew, would be a very long while indeed.

Leaning forwards, Harry went to squeeze her hand again. This time she stood from her chair, moving away to the fireplace, where the Colonel used to stand with his pipe.

Harry wondered what else to tell her. Grace had told him about her conversation in St. Bride's with Fields, just before he died. She told him of her suspicions in Cambridge, and Fields's confirmation he had killed Hudson.

Mrs. Hannam was saying something to him. Harry refocused his attention, and became aware she had started to cry.

'I thought myself so lucky,' she told him. 'He was so *noble*. I couldn't believe he would become fond of anyone like me.' She shook her head at the wonder of it. 'I could feel him, you know, even when he was away. I *knew* he was on the coach when I came to meet you at the Cornhill station. I *knew* he was in trouble, when the two of you were in Paris. Do you believe in such a connection between people, Harry? So strong they can feel each other, even though they're miles apart?' She looked at him, her nose red, her eyelids swollen, desperate for him to answer yes.

When shut away in the Bastille prison, Harry had thought of Grace, wanting her more than anything else in the world. He knew just how fervently Elizabeth had loved Michael Fields, for he felt that same fervour himself.

'You felt him, Mrs. Hannam. I'm sure of it.' He stood, too, and passed her his handkerchief for her to dry her eyes. 'I shall miss him. You're right, he was a noble man. No one ever would say otherwise.'

He glanced at her little clock on the wall, the brass lantern clock he had improved by adding a pendulum with a spring mechanism.

It was nearly six o'clock.

He had arranged to meet with the Fellows at Gresham College.

CHAPTER NINETY-THREE

THE CLOSE
SCRUTINY

ON REACHING ROBERT HOOKE'S ROOMS, THE first thing Harry did was kiss Grace.

The second was to remeasure the object Isaac Newton had sent to him from Cambridge, as he had done earlier that afternoon. As it was not completely regular, he turned it this way and that, studying it with a feeling of misgiving. Having finally decided on its measurements, and noted them scrupulously in his new notebook, a present from Grace, he dropped it into some water. A simple way to ascertain its volume, by observing the amount it displaced.

He chewed on his thumb, thinking. Then he weighed it again, as he had also done earlier, using a pair of Hooke's scales. Again, he noted the results.

He felt the soft leather of the notebook's cover. His decision to leave Grace when held by Lefèvre and his men, instead going to help those gathering for the Catholic Consult in Somerset House, must make her doubt him. If only he could have done both, rescuing her too like a hero from a fairy tale, but he could not.

He knew Colonel Fields had been hurt by his own choices. He had acted from love.

But Fields had led Grace into danger. For that, Harry could not yet find it in his heart to forgive him.

Captain Hudson had killed a man in a duel, and then the diamond went missing. Of course, Parliament would want the Sancy. Having it would bring a double benefit, for the King's side would be without it. Fields had been sent to get it. Fields must, then, have spoken French. Otherwise, he would not have been chosen for the mission. At Marie-Anne's salon, he had communicated with her guests easily, even though he made a show of needing an interpreter.

The old sailor in King's Lynn had remembered Fields as a Royalist, as he had pretended to be on board *Incassable* with Hudson. Its capitaine, his memory corroded by mercury, thought he remembered Fields from the port of Saint-Martin-de-Ré. Although Fields had claimed not to know of *Incassable*, or the size of its cannon, it was *Incassable* the capitaine knew him from.

Convinced Harry would discover the truth of Hudson's murder, and that his guilt, when found out, would put an end to his dream of being with Elizabeth Hannam, Fields had tried to mislead him.

Fields stole the Board of Ordnance's letter of introduction, presumably when Harry was asleep. When La Reynie allowed them to continue their investigation without it, Fields insisted Harry demonstrate the pistol at Marie-Anne's salon, hoping for witnesses to incriminate him. After La Reynie's prohibition of them continuing, Harry sought Hudson at the Exhibition de Monstruosités. Fields, becoming more fraught, used the pistol to paint Harry as an expert assassin. He also told La Reynie a story of Harry helping Marie-Anne poison her husband.

Reminded of his crime by Harry's investigation, ridden with guilt, and desperate to hold on to his vision of his last days, Fields was even prepared to help Jacques Lefèvre take Grace. He identified her for them at Gresham, still in the hope Harry would abandon his search.

Fields could not have known of their plan to kill all at the Consult, surely. Harry could not bring himself to believe so. Harry wondered if Fields had descended into madness, for the Colonel was always the most fair-minded of men. Perhaps his illness, his shortness of breath, had affected his mind. A lack of air to his brain.

Fields had forgotten himself.

Harry still sat at the table when Hooke arrived, smelling of the coffeehouse.

'Having been found with letters from King Louis Quatorze, Danby has been impeached,' Hooke announced. 'They show he secretly negotiated with the French, without the King's permission, trading England's friendship for money. The talk at Garraway's is all about it. He languishes in the Tower.' He had the gleam of triumph in his eyes. Danby had employed Lefèvre, who had captured Grace and threatened her life.

Grace had to fight her way past him.

'I wonder which letters were these,' Harry said.

'You know full well. Your friend, Monsieur de Paris, arranged it.'

'I've received a message from him, in his code using a book he gave me. He had help from the King of France. Louis wants Danby punished for his role in the attack on the Consult. And Sir Jonas ensured the letters were found.'

'Danby is also accused of incompetence, after failing to prevent the plot against the Queen.'

'In truth, he did not fail to prevent it. He commissioned it.'

'There will be no evidence of that. Danby's a careful man. His man Merritt's dead, and the three Frenchmen are gone. La Reynie has done as much as he could.'

When Sir Jonas's men of the Board of Ordnance had entered the crypt at St. Bride's, Lefèvre was no longer there. They only found a great amount of blood. His men must have arrived and spirited him away. By Grace's account, if he lived was doubtful. A search of London, every soldier utilized, had so far failed to find him or his men. Their only discovery was the body of an old watchman, pulled from the Thames near Limehouse, and it looked to be murder.

'Bartholomew Slough's attestation would not be enough against Danby,' Harry said. 'Even with Sir Jonas's support. He pretended to be Captain Hudson. Also, he communicated with La Reynie, sharing his intelligence against Catholics. He sought to do right, but the Bench would find him duplicitous.'

Hooke noticed an unusual bitterness in Harry's voice. He placed his hand on the younger man's shoulder. 'You cannot be surprised. As ever, the truth will be smoothed a little.'

'Broken up, more like, and reassembled in an entirely different way.'

'You have partaken in a little of that, in your story for Mrs. Hannam. You have seen her?' At Harry's nod, he continued. 'The King changes events to suit him best. He still punishes Danby, as does his cousin. Do not let your mood grow dark, Harry. You will always have the thanks of those you saved.'

Instead of answering, Harry picked up the object from Newton. Earlier, he had felt some elation at his forthcoming demonstration, but now he felt an enervated flatness. His body's exhaustion, perhaps, was pulling his mind towards melancholy.

Hooke looked across at his nighttime clock. 'Nearly seven. You have been very secretive. I wonder what your experiment will reveal.'

'Let's go down to the workshop, Mr. Hooke, and there you may observe.'

CHAPTER NINETY-FOUR

THE GRESHAM FURNACE

The Fellows waited in Gresham's metal workshop, one of the rooms beneath the Repository. The gathering included all the men who had mocked him at the Bell: Wren, Aubrey, Wylde, Colwall, Henshaw, Croone, Hill, and Hoskyns. Sir Jonas Moore was present, looking jovial. Denis Papin was also there, free of his Jesuit disguise. Harry waved, and both men grinned at each other, happy their friendship was intact.

It was not one of the regular meetings. Harry had asked for it to go unrecorded in *Philosophical Transactions*. All the Fellows were suitably intrigued, and had arrived in plenty of time.

Sir Christopher had even seen fit to invite the King, speaking with him at the Office of Works that morning, but His Majesty was due at Somerset House, having rediscovered his devotion to his wife.

Harry had invited the Duchesse de Mazarin to attend, and her manservant Mustapha, and a Mr. Bartholomew Slough, even though none were Fellows. The muttering against women at a Royal Society meeting, even an unofficial one, had soon gone quiet when Hortense arrived in riding clothes, her trousers cut tight to her legs. Next to her, also unsettling for the Fellows, sat Grace Hooke, who looked almost recovered just three days since her confinement under St. Bride's.

Everyone in the room had reddened faces, for a furnace blasted heat at them all. Its bellows were operated by a young boy of the College, looking much as Harry had looked when first apprenticed to Robert Hooke.

Harry carried just one object with him. He looked at them all, coughed to clear his throat, and proceeded to tell them a convoluted and unlikely seeming story about a dwarf named Jeffrey Hudson, so small that as a boy he was presented to the last Queen in a pie. By the time of the Civil Wars, he was a man. A soldier. He won a duel against a foe who badly underestimated him.

Duelling being forbidden in France, Hudson escaped to England, but was murdered on his return. He was suspected of having with him the largest diamond in Europe: the Sancy diamond, sold by the Queen to Hortense Mancini's uncle, the Cardinal Mazarin, to raise money for her husband's army. Hudson had been murdered by a man serving the Earl of Manchester, who wanted the diamond for Parliament.

Harry held up the object he had so carefully weighed and measured. At the last, he had doubted himself, as was his nature.

Now he was sure.

It was the cannonball found resting on Hudson's remains. Carried inside a canvas bag, it had been swung at his head, breaking his skull.

Why did Hudson have with him such a cannonball? During his time inside the Bastille, Harry had pondered the question. The way the scraps of canvas clung to the ball showed it had been inside Hudson's bag, not simply resting on it, as Harry had first thought. Grace confirmed his realization when she told him of her conversation with Michael Fields at St. Bride's. But why inside the bag? For use as a weapon, Harry had thought, for self-protection—until he remembered Michael Fields's words at the Denver Sluice: *I remember them as heavier.*

Harry ran his hands over the pitted, rusty iron. The ball was roughly made. Quickly made. Then, he placed it in a large, shallow crucible and passed it to the apprentice.

He nodded at the boy, who opened the furnace. Almost at the limit of his strength, struggling with the long, awkward tongs as well as the weight of the ball, the boy carefully positioned the crucible inside.

After Harry closed the furnace, everyone watching had to wait, and wait some more, Harry's instructions to the boy now back at the bellows maintaining the colour of the flame, until he judged enough time had elapsed.

Harry took the tongs to withdraw the crucible from the furnace. He lowered it to the workshop floor, feeling his eyebrows curl in the heat.

Most in the audience had guessed what he was about, Hortense first of all. They all moved forwards, leaving their chairs to gather around the crucible, Hortense closest of all.

In the crucible, the hot air shimmering around it, floating on an orange pool of molten iron, was the Sancy diamond.

THE POPISH PLOT AND THE AFFAIRE des Poisons were complicated, with many people involved. Contemporary and subsequent interpretations often conflict. I've therefore felt the need to simplify and omit. I've brought events closer in time than they were. I've even changed their order.

I've also made stuff up.

I've consulted various books when researching. For the history of the Sancy, Susan Ronald's *The Sancy Blood Diamond* is enjoyable and informative. Harry's misery inside the Bastille is indebted to Simon-Nicholas Henri Linguet's account *Mémoires sur la Bastille*. I must mention Anne Somerset's *The Affair of the Poisons*. It's subtitled *Murder, Infanticide, and Satanism at the Court of Louis XIV.* What more could you wish for? I used extracts from the last speeches of various Catholics condemned by the 'evidence' of Titus

Oates and his collaborators. For the Popish Plot, the clarity of J. P. Kenyon's *The Popish Plot* is exemplary.

When Captain Jeffrey Hudson was a boy, he *was* presented to Queen Henrietta Maria in a pie. He *did* kill a man in a duel. On his return from captivity with Barbary pirates, he *had* increased in height. (I shall leave you to research Hudson's own explanation for this.) That this taller Hudson was another man is my invention. For Hudson's biography, I recommend Nick Page's excellent *Lord Minimus*, which, pleasingly, is a very small book.

Harry Hunt's natural philosophy is sometimes in advance of the record. If it had succeeded, his bone-pressing experiment could have led to the far earlier discovery of the piezoelectric effect, which today allows all our touchscreen devices. This is generally credited to the Curie brothers, working in the 1880s. Harry's experiment, like so many of Robert Hooke's, seems to have been put aside and not returned to.

Jacques Lefèvre discovered hydrogen cyanide early, too. Later to be known infamously as an ingredient of Zyklon B, it was first prepared from Prussian blue pigment by Carl Wilhelm Scheele in 1782, although it was discovered by Pierre Macquer in 1752.

Experiments in flight *were* carried out at this time by the brave Parisian locksmith Jacob Besnier.

The new year at this time was usually celebrated in Britain on the 1st of January—a good example of this is Robert Hooke's diary—but the civil or legal year began on Lady Day (25 March). Dual dating was used to avoid confusion, hence Sir Jonas's Moore's letter showing the date as *15th March 1678/79.*

It's very difficult to find an accurate 'exchange rate' between late-seventeeth-century money and today's. We can use various measures, such as the average annual salary, or the price of a loaf of bread, or the average price of a house, but these have changed comparatively over the years. The Bank of England, at the time of writing, suggests that 1d—an old penny—was worth 94p in today's money. Professor Sir Roderick Floud suggests a far higher figure should be used, between £4 and £5.

ACKNOWLEDGEMENTS

ACKNOWLEDGEMENTS AND THANKS ARE DUE TO those who read versions of the manuscript, reacted, advised, and encouraged.

Rob Little, Sonia Little, and Kate Lloyd (my patient wife) all read and gave advice on early drafts. Rachel Gyte, Pascal Lelièvre, Gregory Moutry, and Anne Schiller helped me with French and with Paris. Barrie Upton of the Sealed Knot informed me about the First Foot Guards. Bill Gregory helped with matters metallurgical. Professor Sir Roderick Floud, economic historian and former Provost of Gresham College, advised me on the value of money during the Restoration period.

All at Melville House Books: Dennis Johnson, Valerie Merians, Carl Bromley, Michael Barson, Sammi Sontag, Emily Considine, Amelia Stymacks, Beste M. Doğan, and Peter Kranitz.

Sonia Land and Gaia Banks at Sheil Land Associates. Gaia has championed my writing with amazing energy and attention.

The first book in this series, *The Bloodless Boy*, benefitted from the generosity of other authors: Piers Alexander, Andrew Child, Lee Child, Catherine Cooper, Martin Edwards, Jemahl Evans, Joseph Finder, Christopher Fowler, A. J. Griffiths-Jones, Janice Hallett, Felicity Hayes-McCoy, Dan Mayland, Adrian McKinty, Leonora Nattrass, Cate Quinn, Andrew Taylor, A. J. West, and Julian Woodford. I also thank critics from various newspapers and online magazines, and the many and various book bloggers, who helped spread the word.